BIRD'S EYE VIEW

To Barb and Hugh – Enjoy
this glimpse into our
proud wartime history!

BIRD'S EYE VIEW

ELINOR FLORENCE

All the best,
Elinor Florence

DUNDURN
TORONTO

Editor: Jennifer McKnight
Design: Courtney Horner
Cover design by Harrison McKay/smoove.ca
Author photo by Kelsey Verboom
Printer: Webcom

Library and Archives Canada Cataloguing in Publication

Florence, Elinor, author
     Bird's eye view / Elinor Florence.

Issued in print and electronic formats.
ISBN 978-1-4597-2143-2

     I. Title.

PS8611.L66B57 2014   C813'.6   C2014-901010-9
                                                         C2014-901011-7

2   3   4   5   18   17   16   15   14

Conseil des Arts   Canada Council
du Canada   for the Arts

ONTARIO ARTS COUNCIL
CONSEIL DES ARTS DE L'ONTARIO
an Ontario government agency
un organisme du gouvernement de l'Ontario

We acknowledge the support of the **Canada Council for the Arts** and the **Ontario Arts Council** for our publishing program. We also acknowledge the financial support of the **Government of Canada** through the **Canada Book Fund** and **Livres Canada Books**, and the **Government of Ontario** through the **Ontario Book Publishing Tax Credit** and the **Ontario Media Development Corporation**.

Care has been taken to trace the ownership of copyright material used in this book. The author and the publisher welcome any information enabling them to rectify any references or credits in subsequent editions.

J. Kirk Howard, President

The publisher is not responsible for websites or their content unless they are owned by the publisher.

Photo of Danesfield House, formerly RAF Medmenham, courtesy of Danesfield House Hotel and Spa, *www.danesfieldhouse.co.uk.*

Photo of Pas-de-Calais, France © RCAHMS. Licensor RCAHMS, *ncap.org.uk.*

Printed and bound in Canada.

VISIT US AT
Dundurn.com
@dundurnpress
Facebook.com/dundurnpress
Pinterest.com/dundurnpress

Dundurn
3 Church Street, Suite 500
Toronto, Ontario, Canada
M5E 1M2

To my mother
June Light Florence
with love and gratitude

PROLOGUE
November 7, 1944

The control room was warm and cozy in the quiet hour before dawn.

To relieve the tension while waiting for the bombers to return from their raid on Berlin, two girls played chess and another read aloud society gossip from the *Tatler*. A teakettle simmered on the hot plate.

Rose looked up sharply from her knitting needles when the gentle rain against the windowpanes began to make a scrabbling sound. "It's changing to sleet," someone said in a low voice.

The first snow had fallen on Yorkshire's desolate moors that morning, and all personnel were ordered to shovel the runways and brush off the aircraft. The homesick Canadian boys had frolicked like overgrown children, throwing snowballs and washing each other's faces.

Although Rose longed to join the horseplay, it was against orders to fraternize with the aircrews because she outranked them. When nobody was watching, she lifted her face to the skies, opening her mouth to feel the cold kiss of snowflakes on her tongue.

But this icy sleet was something else altogether.

"Update on the weather, please." The control officer spoke to the meteorologist sitting at his wooden desk in the corner, surrounded by his maps and instruments.

"One moment, sir. I'll ring and see what's up." He picked up the black telephone handset on his desk and spoke briefly, then hung up with a grim expression.

"It's a ruddy ice storm, sir, blowing in from Norway."

Immediately the room was electrified. Everyone pushed back their chairs and hurried to the long bank of windows overlooking the runway.

An aircraft could ice up in minutes. Not only did this add tons of weight, but if even the very thinnest layer of ice distorted the upper curve of the wings, the aircraft's balance was affected and it became impossible for the pilot to control. Iced up, a thirty-ton bomber could tumble from the sky like a falling leaf.

The station's forty-eight bombers, now strung out over the cold, black sea, running short of fuel after ten hours in flight, some trying desperately to limp home with flak damage and wounded men, were just beginning their descent.

"What's the forecast?" asked the control officer.

All faces turned toward the meteorologist. "Not so good, sir. The temperature's dropping like a stone."

Nobody needed the official report to see that the sleet was rapidly worsening. A cloud of icy pellets rattled off the windows and a thick white blanket descended. The parallel rows of searchlights lining the runway were no brighter than flickering candles in the ghostly fog. Rose saw the dim shapes of ground crew running and sliding across the icy tarmac, the crash wagons moving into position.

The young clerk beside Rose made a small agonized sound in her throat. Rose knew she was secretly engaged to a rear gunner. The two girls clasped hands tightly as they stood at the window, straining their eyes into the whirling white darkness.

Then, over the sound of the storm, the first faint engine was heard.

BOOK ONE

September 1939–October 1941

I

I awoke to the familiar rustling of poplar leaves. My bedroom lacked the view of brilliant grain fields sweeping away to the southern horizon, but I didn't mind. In summer I preferred the coolness and the dim light, with the sound of the trees that backed up against the north side of the old farmhouse. They always seemed to be whispering secrets.

Outside my window, the breeze freshened and the whispering swelled as if a new piece of gossip had arrived. I opened my eyes and saw the brass pendulum clock on the wall.

Instantly I threw back the covers and sprang out of bed, already reaching for the skirt and blouse I had laid out on my chair the night before. Twenty minutes later I was pedalling my bicycle toward the town of Touchwood, four miles away.

It was a flawless autumn morning, but I didn't even glance at the vast cobalt sky above me, bigger than half the world, or the great swaths of golden grain lying in the fields. I was too busy composing a front-page headline for this week's newspaper.

"Canada Enters Conflict!" That was too long.

Perhaps "Canada Goes to War!"

Better yet, perhaps my editor would agree to a giant ninety-six-point banner: "WAR!"

Probably none of them. The man was not only lazy, but maddeningly unpatriotic. Still, there was always hope.

When I crested the east hill and saw a snowy pillar of steam rising from the morning train, I knew I was late. It was my job to open the office at eight sharp.

I stood on the pedals and coasted at frightening speed down the long slope toward town. The edges of the gravel road poured past me like twin grassy streams while I wondered how to convince him that here was real news at last.

Except that it wasn't exactly news. Britain had declared war a week ago, after months of anticipation. Then our federal government pretended to deliberate for an entire seven days, just to prove that we were no longer under the royal thumb.

After practically holding my breath all week, I wasn't even at work when the decision came. Our parliament had inexplicably chosen Sunday afternoon to proclaim war against the German Reich. I heard the news bulletin, along with the rest of the country, on CBC radio.

My bicycle whirled around the post office corner. Several seedy young men were sitting on the broad stone steps, wreathed in a cloud of cigarette smoke. One of them whistled as I tore past. I jumped off my bike while the wheels were still spinning in front of *The Touchwood Times*.

The newspaper's name appeared in faded gilt letters on a grimy plate-glass window that hadn't been cleaned in decades. When I pushed open the heavy front door, I heard the clatter of typewriter keys and saw the top of Jock MacTavish's scruffy head above the heaps of newspapers stacked on his desk.

"Well, those morons in Ottawa have done it now!" His voice was always pitched as if I were standing on the far side of the street. "They're going to deliver us up to the Limeys like lambs to the slaughter!"

"Sorry I'm late, Mr. MacTavish."

He didn't even glance up. "I'm writing an editorial, urging Mackenzie King to hold his ground! Nobody but the prime minister can stop the Brits from turning our boys into cannon fodder! Maybe, and it's a thumping big maybe, he can stand up to the muckety-mucks running the show over there!"

"And what about the front page?" I tried to sound casual as I hung my cardigan on the coat rack.

MacTavish's enormous tangled eyebrows bristled like cat's fur. "I suppose you want a big splash about Canada springing to the defence of the Mother Country and all that malarkey! Well, you can put that idea out of your little head!"

"Mr. MacTavish, please! Every newspaper in the country will have the war on the front page!"

"Not this one. And the last time I looked at the masthead, it was still my newspaper!"

He began typing again, hammering the keys as if pounding nails. "You can run it on page two. The news will be as old as last year's Christmas hat by Wednesday, anyway!"

While I poured water into the battered tin coffeepot, I wondered whether to try again, but immediately gave it up as a bad job. Jock MacTavish hadn't been fussy about fighting for the British when he left Touchwood back in 1914. Four years in the trenches had hardened his dislike into stony contempt.

He was convinced that British officers had saved their own skins by sending in the black troops — including Canadians and Australians — when the situation looked bleak. Now he was determined to warn our readers, through the power of his old printing press, against what he called "The Brutish Empire."

I handed over his coffee and went to my own desk. Dividing the room in half was a massive slab of glass-topped oak where customers stood to place an advertisement or purchase a subscription. Behind the counter, MacTavish hunched over his desk, partially hidden by his newspaper fortress, while I sat in the opposite corner, as far away from him as possible.

I had tidied my little nook and hung several photographs over the old rolltop, including one of King George and Queen Elizabeth taken during their recent train trip across Canada. I gazed up at the royal couple and mouthed a silent apology.

Although I couldn't quite bring myself to say the words aloud, I secretly agreed with the letter-writer who had called MacTavish a narrow-minded, contentious old bastard.

For a few minutes I dwelled on the vision of newsrooms across the country, their reporters galvanized by the greatest news since the Great War had ended twenty-one years ago — three years before I was even born.

And here I sat, restricted to a story on page two, forced to listen to MacTavish sucking his coffee through his teeth with revolting gusto.

I vowed once again to get the hell out of Touchwood.

2

After finishing high school at the top of my class, I made a humbling trip around town, report card in hand, looking for work as a secretary or sales clerk, even a waitress. But the depression had hit Saskatchewan hard and jobs were scarce.

I hadn't even considered applying at the *Times*. It was one of those mysterious male preserves that had passed from old man MacTavish to his son Jock when he was mustered home from France. Neither of them had ever hired a woman.

So I spent the long summer days pondering my uncertain future while I picked potato bugs in our vegetable garden, and my evenings curled up on the blue mohair chesterfield with our house cat Pansy — we had numerous barn cats, but only one was allowed in the house — reading my beloved Victorian novels.

My luck changed one afternoon when I was fetching a parcel from the train station and overheard Pete Anderson, the one and only reporter for *The Touchwood Times*, calling down a black curse on MacTavish's head as he booked a ticket for Toronto. Pete hadn't lasted long; the newspaper cast off reporters as often as MacTavish lost his temper.

After hastily combing my hair in the station restroom, I hurried down the wide, windswept main street, past the Queen's Hotel, Chinese restaurant, butcher shop, drugstore, hat shop, and Dutch bakery. I opened the door of the newspaper office as if I were entering a cave full of hibernating grizzlies.

The dimly lit front room was deserted. I was about to tiptoe out again when I heard a crash from the rear followed by a roar. "Bloody bleeding blasted balls!" I sidled around the front counter and down the narrow hallway to the back shop where the printing press stood.

MacTavish was crouched on his hands and knees, his bony backside sticking up in the air like a rock in a field, a circle worn on the seat of his pants by the snuff tin in his back pocket. He was surrounded by dozens of tiny nine-point lead letters that had fallen from an overturned type drawer.

"Well, don't just stand there!" he bellowed over his shoulder. "Help me pick up these buggers!"

I lowered myself to the filthy wooden floor and began to gather the type while MacTavish clambered to his feet, wiping his hands on an ink-stained rag. He was a small man — even from my crouching position I could see that he was several inches shorter than me — but he cut an impressive figure. His head was covered with matted iron-grey hair and his piercing dark eyes glared at me from under the biggest, blackest eyebrows I had ever seen.

"What the blazes do you want?" he shouted. Later I learned that he always spoke at full volume, having been partly deafened by an exploding shell, but at the time I thought he was yelling at me.

"I'd like to apply for a job," I said.

"Who's your father?"

"Tom Jolliffe."

"You're the girl who's supposed to be so bright? Well, looks can be deceiving!"

He gave a mirthless chuckle, but I wasn't sure whether to laugh so I kept my eyes on the floor. He jammed the rag into his pocket. "As long as you're here, make yourself useful! Run down to the grocery store and pick up this week's advertisement! And bring me a can of snuff! Copenhagen Long Cut! Tell them to put it on my account."

I started work that very minute. Sometimes I wondered why MacTavish hired me. He wouldn't let me cover anything except women's events, and there was little space in the paper anyway. Four pages were home print, written by clubs and sports teams and dropped through the slot in the front door. The other four pages came press-ready from an agency that supplied almost every weekly in Western Canada.

But I answered the telephone and worked the front counter, kept a pot of coffee perking, and ran errands all over town. MacTavish even taught me how to use his precious Kodak to photograph grip-and-grin cheque presentations, oddly shaped vegetables, and other subjects of intense local interest.

Each Wednesday, when the back shop was thick with the smell of melting lead and the sound of MacTavish's curses rose above the thumping, clanking din of the press, I retreated to the little bathroom where I tacked a towel over the window and developed my negatives in the sink. I printed them in the enlarger and hung them up to dry with clothespins on a piece of string. Then I hurried down to the train station and sent them to a company in Winnipeg that made the necessary engravings, small rectangular plates of blueish-coloured zinc mounted on wooden blocks. With any luck, the engravings made it back in time for the next week's issue. MacTavish laid the type and engravings onto plates, bolted the plates onto an antiquated mountain of scrap iron he called The Auld Dragon, and cranked out eight hundred copies of *The Touchwood Times*.

The first time MacTavish flew into a rage and fired me for ruining a roll of film, I rode my bicycle home weeping aloud to the fields and the skies. But the next morning I woke up and remembered everything to be done before the next edition. *He can't possibly handle it himself,* I thought. *I'll just show up and see what happens.*

I dressed and cycled to work an hour early. When MacTavish arrived, the coffee was burbling through the percolator and I was self-consciously marking up proofs on the front counter.

He banged the door, glared at me for a few seconds, and then stomped to his desk. "I like my coffee like I like my women: sweet as sugar!" he yelled. I brought him a cup meekly, although I was tempted to pour it over his head.

From then on, MacTavish continued to fire me at intervals. At first I would go home immediately and return the next morning, but once when I was in the midst of deciphering some illegible handwriting on a letter to the editor, I simply replied: "Yes, Mr. MacTavish," and kept on typing.

He stood there uncertainly for a moment, then spat horribly into the brass shell casing he had carried home from France to use as a spittoon, and retreated behind his wall of newspapers.

⁊⁊⁊

I leaned over the handlebars and swung toward home. At the top of the east hill I stopped to catch my breath. The late afternoon sun poured its peculiar saffron light over the landscape and the ripening grain smelled like yeast. From a nearby fencepost I heard the meadowlark's song: "I see, I see, I see your petticoat!"

The east hill was really no more than a long slope, but compared to the immense grassy plain to the south, this part of the world was considered hilly. If an outsider remarked on the flatness of the rolling fields around Touchwood, he was rebuked by the locals: "You go south, that's where the flatlanders live! Down there you can see your dog running away for a week!"

The Touchwood Hills, as they were affectionately called, resembled nothing so much as an unmade bed, a random series of slanting planes and ridges before the prairie reluctantly gave way to the northern bush. At the foot of the east hill lay our homestead, three hundred and twenty acres of excellent topsoil located in the dead centre of Western Canada.

From here I could see my own home, with its red-shingled roof and triple dormers like half-shut eyes. It was set back a quarter-mile from the main road, surrounded by lilacs and caraganas, and backed by a row of weathered wooden granaries. My mother was taking the wash off the clothesline, our Border Collie, Laddy, beating her calves with his shaggy tail.

In the field beside the house, my father sat on the cultivator drawn by our team of horses, Bess and Bonnie. The summerfallow changed colour behind him as the weedy soil rolled over to reveal its ebony underbelly. White gulls fluttered around the plough like oversized butterflies.

My sixteen-year-old brother Jack stood in the dry slough bed nearby, pitching forkfuls of hay bigger than himself into the hayrack. Each time he swung his arms, a shower of golden stalks followed him like the tail of a comet.

Much as I loved the familiar scene, I secretly thought farming was a wretched business. I was tired of hearing about the glory years after the Great War, when every farmer drove a new truck and every farmer's wife wore a fur coat. I had grown up during the long drought that followed, the dirty thirties bringing one crop failure after another.

Out of the corner of my eye, I saw Charlie Stewart waving from the tractor on his father's field beside me. I raised my hand politely in return. My father had dropped a few hints about the eligibility of an only son with clear title to a half-section right across the road, but I dreaded the idea of farming — least of all with a big, good-natured beast of burden like Charlie. Instead, I cherished a secret dream of going to university.

I mounted my bicycle again, coasted down the hill, and turned onto the long driveway, lined by a double row of feathery blue spruce trees. I recalled the back-breaking trips Jack and I had made from the well, soaking the tiny saplings with pails of water while the drifting soil threatened to bury them alive.

❧

"What a blessing my parents aren't alive to see this," Mother said.

As we sat at the table eating pork sausages and fried potatoes, we studied a map of Europe hanging on the blue plaster wall. Shiny steel pins from her sewing basket marked the line of invasion. The pinheads had already marched across Czechoslovakia and into Poland, leaving behind scattered holes like gunshots.

The large kitchen was the heart of our home. In winter the wood stove kept it warm, and in summer it was cooled by a breeze that flowed through the screened windows. A bouquet of late-blooming marigolds sat on the table in a green ceramic vase. Over the kitchen door hung the first needlework sampler I had sewn myself, at the age of ten. The crooked letters spelled: "Homes weeth ome."

Dad sat at the head of the table where he could see his entire farm through the open window. A breath of air lifted the edge of the lace curtain, bringing with it the faint scent of smoke. Somewhere a farmer was burning off his stubble.

"Don't worry, Anne. There's still the English Channel between us and them." It was a sign of my father's ambivalence that he sometimes referred to the English as us, and sometimes as them.

"Did you ever see a German tank, Dad?" Jack asked, piling more sausages onto his plate. My brother was keen on weapons and his latest fascination was with the new Panzer.

"No, son, they came in at the end of the war and I'd already been shipped home. It must be quite something, like a mobile cannon with steel belts wrapped around the wheels. Apparently it can crawl over boulders, fences, anything."

We were silent as we shared the horrifying vision of tanks rolling across the bright fields, driven by foreign savages indulging their lust for conquest, as the king said in a recent speech.

My mother reached for the milk and poured it into her cup first so the scalding tea wouldn't crack the bone china. I loved to watch her eat, the way she buttered her bread one bite at a time: so gracious, so mannered, so … English.

I never called it home, at least not out loud, but I sometimes thought of England that way. I had once heard the term "ancestral pull," the yearning to return to the birthplace of your forefathers. I knew it existed. I felt it in my bones.

My mother had grown up in an English seaside village, the only child of scholarly parents who encouraged her decision to become a nursing sister during the Great War. Both parents had died suddenly during the 1918 flu epidemic. The poor girl continued her work in the military hospital where she met my father, who was recovering from a vicious shrapnel wound, and later followed him to Touchwood.

I was pleased when people told me that I resembled my mother, because she was beautiful. We were almost the same height, although in the last year I had gained an inch on her. Both of us had a thick mass of wavy dark brown hair, hers with a few silver threads, and our eyes were the same shade of hazel.

I had even inherited my mother's crooked face: the left eyebrow permanently cocked and the left side of her mouth quirked upwards, as if smiling at a private joke. MacTavish had once told me that I looked older and wiser than I deserved.

I glanced at my father gripping his coffee mug in his fist, his fingernails blackened with soil that no amount of scrubbing could remove, and asked myself again how he could be so indifferent to his own heritage.

His grandfather had come from the Orkney Islands to work for the Hudson's Bay Company and married a Plains Cree. Dad had looked up some distant Scottish cousins while he was on leave during the first war, and had come away blessing his grandfather for having the good sense to leave that godforsaken place, with its rocky soil and sleeting winds.

"Just be thankful we live where we do," he said for the hundredth time. We raised our eyes to the map again, as if in prayer. In 1939 the sun never set on the British Empire, and Canada was the biggest pink patch in the whole world.

Cambridge, England
October 20, 1939
Dear Anne,

Thank you for your recent letter and the photograph
of the children. We were surprised to see how much
they have grown. Rose is quite the young lady now.

Roger's teaching position continues, although
class sizes have dwindled since so many students have
enlisted. It's a mercy you aren't in England. I have
often felt sorry for you, so far away from civilization,
but now I wish we had emigrated when we had the
chance. Both my cook and housekeeper have joined
up and we are in an awful muddle without them.

The tin of sweets you sent was most appreciated. We are simply longing for a taste of sugar.
We don't even have marmalade for our toast now
that the oranges aren't getting through from Spain.

Will you please send me some American cigarettes? And six pairs of silk stockings.

Your cousin, Pamela Spencer

"Dear old Pamela," Mother said. "She always thought she
was better than the rest of us, but when she landed an officer
she became insufferable. After he started teaching at Cambridge,
Pamela conveniently forgot she had any relatives. It must be a real
comedown to clean her own house again. Well, I can't afford silk
stockings, but I'll send her a carton of cigarettes."

I thought my mother was being a little harsh. After all, Pamela
led the life of a real English lady. No wonder she wasn't used to
scrubbing floors.

3

"Rose!" MacTavish came into the office, shaking the snow off his moth-eaten beaver hat. "There's another bunch of young blockheads leaving on the afternoon train. Run down and take a picture!"

I hurried along the street, the snow crunching beneath my galoshes, anxious to return to my comfortable desk. But when I came around the corner and stepped onto the platform, I forgot about the cold.

A small crowd stood shivering in the clouds of steam gushing from the engine. I said hello to Laura Guthrie, who was dressed to the nines — brilliant lipstick, high heels, and fox-collared coat — but she didn't even notice me. Her eyes were fixed on her boyfriend's face as if she were trying to memorize it. Old Mrs. McGill clung tightly to her only grandson. One father whacked his son on the back as if he had something stuck in his throat. Several of my former classmates clowned around, punching each other's shoulders, pale and feverish with excitement. Their breath was ghostly in the frigid air.

They're so young. I had heard my mother's words a dozen times but never truly understood what she meant. I was the same age as these boys, and I was ready to experience life to the fullest. But for an accident of birth, I would be leaving with them.

Yet I couldn't help thinking that they did look awfully … immature. That boy's face was so smooth you could tell it had never felt a razor. The one beside him was wearing a baggy uniform whose sleeves fell to his fingertips. I remembered MacTavish's words: "The army issues their uniforms too damned big because most of them haven't even finished growing yet!"

I lifted my camera to focus on a young man standing with his mother before I realized that his chin was trembling, and he was wiping his nose with the back of his hand. She handed him a handkerchief. "Blow," she said, as if he were still a toddler. I lowered my camera and turned away before my own tears began.

"Hey, Charlie, bring me a Jerry's helmet!" shouted someone in the crowd.

I turned to see Charlie Stewart lumbering up the steps, wearing his old brown plaid jacket with the corduroy collar pulled over his ears, duffel bag in hand. "Charlie! What are you doing here?"

"The same thing as everybody else, Rose." He spoke in his usual low voice, his eyes on his feet. It had been several years since Charlie looked at me directly. "I'm off to do my bit."

My jaw dropped. "But … what about the farm?"

"I stayed long enough to finish the fall work. My cousins from town are going to help Dad with the seeding next spring."

"I'm just, just, flabbergasted, Charlie. I was sure you'd ask for a deferment because you're an only son."

"Yeah, I could have done that, but it didn't feel right. Somebody has to stop the Krauts." He squinted down the tracks toward the eastern horizon. "Besides, I've always wanted to fly."

I didn't know what to say. Charlie Stewart, of all people. We had known each other all our lives, built snow forts together, helped each other catch frogs in the slough. After Charlie's mother died when he was only ten years old, he spent a lot of time at our house. We were playmates until people started pairing us off and I suspected he was getting a crush on me. That was the kiss of death for our friendship.

I gazed at the puffing train while I tried to imagine how Charlie, so bashful and awkward, would fare across the sea, a stranger in a strange land. The poor boy was so clumsy he couldn't walk through a classroom without crashing into a desk. I couldn't picture his massive shoulders squeezing into the cockpit of an airplane.

Then I gave myself a mental shake. He should do as well as everyone else. After all, he wasn't stupid — just the opposite. He finished school with the highest mark in geometry.

I raised my eyes to find him still staring into the distance with an unreadable expression. Then he said a curious thing: "You know, Rose, I've never cared much for farming."

That was all. A gust of icy wind tore across the platform and I held my skirt down, freezing and miserable. The whistle blew and the men began to move toward the train. Behind us, a woman broke into sobs.

"Well, best of luck, Charlie!" I held out my red-mittened hand and he squeezed it so hard that my grandmother's gold signet ring cut painfully into my little finger. The pain ran up my arm and into my chest.

I felt a sudden sense of loss. For the first time in my life I wasn't going to have him in my back pocket, my ace in the hole. Now that I might never see him again, I was sorry that I hadn't been nicer to good old Charlie.

For once, he was looking into my eyes, and I realized that he wanted to kiss me. I hesitated, then stepped forward and lifted my face. Charlie's big arms came around me in a bear hug that drove the breath out of my ribcage. He gave me a noisy smack on the mouth. His lips were warm in the frosty air.

The whistle blew for the second time, and without another word Charlie bounded up the steps onto the train, hitting his head with a glancing blow on the doorframe. While I waited on the platform with the other women and children and old men, he appeared at the window, his shaggy hair flopping over his forehead and a huge grin on his face.

The last thing I saw as the train chugged away across the endless white prairie was Charlie's big hand waving goodbye. I ran to the end of the platform and waved back, almost frantically, until the train was out of sight.

‹••

At the eleventh hour of the eleventh day of the eleventh month, I joined almost every soul in Touchwood at the cenotaph, observing two minutes of silence while I shivered in my thin stockings. I envied the butcher's wife, who had the nerve to show up in trousers.

The silence seemed to go on forever. I thought about my Uncle Jack, killed at the Somme before I was born, but oddly enough I didn't cry. Usually I cried at the drop of a dead leaf. This year I remained dry-eyed, counting on my gloved fingers the number of able-bodied men who were still at home. I felt annoyed that nobody was taking the war very seriously. Farmers and townsfolk alike were so ecstatic about the recent bumper crop that war seemed no more threatening than a black cat running across a distant future.

Nothing much was happening overseas, either. The enemy had advanced as far as the French border before setting up camp. Two rows of steel pins faced each other on our map: the British Expeditionary Force and the German Army in a standoff. *No wonder they call it the "Bore War,"* I thought. I stamped my feet to keep them from freezing.

At least the women were doing their part. MacTavish still refused to allow me to cover anything except the powder-puff beat, as he called it, but this was a moot point. Women's work now jammed the home print pages as the good ladies of Touchwood sprang into the war effort with a will.

The Order of the Eastern Star launched a knitting crusade, and my mother taught me how to knit. It was harder than it looked. Either my stitches were so loose they fell off my needles, or so tight that I had to pry them off. I almost gave up, but then I imagined some soldier marching through the snow with purple, swollen feet inside his leather boots, and redoubled my efforts.

The Imperial Order of the Daughters of the Empire began to collect used clothing and blankets for bombed-out civilians. "Bundles for Britain" read posters on every store window. I ransacked my meagre wardrobe, then climbed into the attic. "I was saving these for my grandchildren," Mother said when I asked to donate a box of baby clothes. She stroked a tiny crocheted blanket. "I guess I can always make more."

The Red Cross held regular blood donor clinics. I went down to the Legion hall and gave blood so often that Mother warned me I would become anemic. But I loved lying in the chair with my eyes closed, imagining my life's blood pouring into the veins of an injured soldier.

Now the silence was broken by the mournful sound of the bugler playing "The Last Post." My father sniffed and I wondered if he were crying. I slipped my hand into his coat pocket, where he gave it a squeeze.

My jovial father rarely spoke of his years in the trenches or of his only brother. Instead he dealt with his memories of war by making a joke of them. When Jack and I were small, we would pull aside the tank top of his black woollen bathing suit and admire his jagged purple scar. "But how did you get shot in the back?" Jack asked, every time.

"Well, son, when I left home my dear old dad said to me: 'He who fights and runs away lives to fight another day.' But one day I was high-tailing it back to my trench when a hunk of shrapnel nailed me right where your finger is."

"I don't know why you tell them such bunkum," Mother always interjected at this point. "Your father was running toward the enemy when he was hit. He was so far ahead of the other men that a German shell fell behind him."

"That's what *she* thinks," Dad always whispered and rolled his eyes, putting a finger to his lips. We would laugh delightedly.

Now the town policeman Fergus Lumby launched into his annual ritual, singing "In Flanders Fields" in his deep baritone. I caught sight of my brother standing at the other side of the cenotaph with his friends, a look of intense concentration in his bright blue eyes. I knew he was praying the war would last long enough for him to get into it.

⸽

Back home the kitchen was warm and welcoming, the kettle hissing gently on the wood stove. I set the table for dinner while Mother mixed up a batch of baking powder biscuits. When I went to fetch a jar of pickled beets from the pantry, she joined me in the doorway and for a few minutes we admired our handiwork. Over the summer we had picked hundreds of pounds of berries and vegetables, boiling and bottling far into the night. The pantry dazzled like a jewellery store: pickled onions, dills, and carrots; raspberry and strawberry and chokecherry jam; rosehip and Saskatoon jelly.

"You don't think we'll get rationing here, do you, Mother?"

"I don't know, but I'm not taking any chances." She sighed and I knew she was thinking of England. I wished we could go on rations. I was itching to endure some hardship, make some sacrifice to show solidarity with the English, even if it meant starving myself.

From the living room came the sound of a plummy British accent: "This is the BBC World Service." I ran into the room and fiddled with the dial on the cabinet radio, trying to get better reception. "Listen, Mother!" I called. "It's Queen Elizabeth!"

The high-pitched feminine voice, speaking in the cultured accent I admired so much, came crackling through the airwaves.

"I know that you would wish me to voice, in the name of the women of the British Empire, our deep and abiding sympathy with those on whom the first cruel and shattering blows have fallen:

the women of Poland. Nor do we forget the gallant womanhood of France, who are called on to share with us again the hardships. and sorrows of war."

I dropped to my knees on the worn carpet.

"War has at all times called for the fortitude of women, even in other days when it was an affair of the fighting forces only. Wives and mothers at home suffered constant anxiety for their dear ones, and, too often, the misery of bereavement.

"Now all this has changed. For we, no less than men, have real and vital work to do. To us also is given the proud privilege of serving our country in her hour of need. The call has come, and from my heart, I thank you, the women of our great Empire, for the way in which you have answered it. We have all a part to play, and I know you will not fail in yours."

We have all a part to play. Across the ocean, thousands of girls even younger than me were marching shoulder to shoulder with their fathers and brothers in the fight for freedom.

Tears of frustration sprang into my eyes while the orchestra played "God Save the King." *What is my part?*

4

"Victory, my royal keester!" MacTavish shouted. "The Brits have been chased home with their tails between their legs and now we're supposed to call it a miracle!"

I studied the map on our office wall and trembled for England, the size of a pink thumbprint. The Germans had driven the Allies into frantic retreat and conquered the entire continent. The enemy was now only twenty-five miles away from Britain's shores: spitting distance, by our standards. The barbarians were indeed at the gates.

"It was a miracle that all those men escaped with their lives, Mr. MacTavish!" I was deeply moved by the way hundreds of civilians had used their sailboats, yachts, and lifeboats to help the British Navy evacuate three hundred and forty thousand troops from Dunkirk.

"Yeah, a bloody miracle that the Huns didn't massacre them when they had the chance!" MacTavish chewed his snuff so vigorously that he gagged. "They left behind their weapons, for the love of God! And don't forget forty thousand men were taken prisoner!"

"Please don't tell me you're going to call it a defeat in the newspaper." I held my breath.

"I'm bloody well not going to call it a triumph! We had enough of that cockamamie in the last war! Our readers deserve to know the bald facts!"

"Mr. MacTavish!" I ripped the cover off my typewriter, wishing it were his scalp. "How do you expect to win the war if you're going to take that attitude?"

"Do you really think people believe all this twaddle about victory?"

"Yes," I said, then hesitated. "Well, they want to believe it! They rely on the newspapers and the radio to buck them up! How can any mother's son go off to fight if he thinks he isn't coming back? And how can any mother bear to let him go? The way you talk, you'd like everybody to roll over and surrender!"

MacTavish's voice was gloomy. "I don't think we should give up the ghost, don't get me wrong. But this cursed propaganda sticks in my craw!"

"It's not all lies. There are lots of stories about heroism and human sacrifice that are the honest truth."

"And just as many in the German papers, I expect."

I was running out of arguments. "Don't you feel one spark of loyalty to the king, Mr. MacTavish?"

"Why should we swear allegiance to that stammering idiot? The royal family is nothing but a bunch of Krauts in disguise, anyway. Queen Victoria and that so-called consort of hers spoke German when they got between the sheets!"

"Please, Mr. MacTavish," I said faintly. I didn't want to imagine anyone between the sheets, let alone the crowned heads of Europe.

"All right, Miss Limey-Lover, I've had my say. I've never heard of winning a war by running away, but from now on I'll keep my opinions to the editorial page. You can spoon-feed the ignorant masses. I don't have the stomach for it."

"Thank you, Mr. MacTavish!" I tried to keep the crow of satisfaction out of my voice.

He swivelled his oak chair and bent over his desk. "Have you heard what they're calling the British Expeditionary Force now?"

"No, Mr. MacTavish."

"Back Every Friday." He chuckled. I let him have the last word.

···

With the fall of the continent, enlistment soared. Farms and families no longer kept the men from joining up, and the women didn't even try to talk them out of it. I had seen the same thing happen at hockey games. If there was a fight, every guy in the arena wanted to jump over the boards onto the ice, get right into the thick of it.

And it wasn't only the men. A group of local girls calling themselves the Touchwood Women's Militia began to meet regularly in the high school gymnasium to drill, to learn engine repair and to read maps.

I went down to the school one evening to take their photograph. "Do you think they'll ever let women enlist?" I asked their leader, Monica Fisher, a pig farmer's daughter.

"It'll be a rotten shame if they don't." She scowled. "Look across the pond, forty-five thousand girls in uniform already. All the women's militia groups across Canada are writing letters begging those old fuddy-duddies to open the doors! If I had any money, I'd pay my own way over there and join the British forces, that's what I'd do!"

With so many men away from home, the morning train was loaded down with parcels and letters, and our postmaster, Robert Day, conscripted his whole family to sort mail. His gentle wife, Vera, worked behind the wicket each morning, and Robert Junior — everyone called him Sonny — made deliveries after school. But the bulk of the work fell to my best friend, June.

"I absolutely detest it," she said, while we were sitting on her bed one evening after supper. "It's the most boring thing in the world."

I murmured sympathetically. Toiling for MacTavish was the very devil sometimes, but it was never boring.

The scarlet sunlight falling through the western window lent a rosy glow to June's bedroom. Her walls were covered with sprigged wallpaper and she had draped a scarlet chiffon scarf over her bedside lamp. I sat cross-legged on the pink chenille bedspread with my knitting needles. June, wearing pink striped pyjamas, was putting up her blond hair in pincurls.

Everything about June was curly. Her hair was the colour of fresh, golden wood shavings. Her big blue eyes were fringed with long, curling eyelashes, and her mouth curled up at the corners. She was as pretty and petite as a china doll. Her father sometimes called us Mutt and Jeff. We called each other Posy and Prune.

"The only bright spot is when Dad lets me work behind the wicket and I can visit with people," she said through a mouthful of bobby pins.

I smiled to myself. June knew everybody in town, and she would gossip for hours if given the chance.

"It *is* pretty interesting to see everyone's mail," June went on. "Jess Jones writes every single day to a sailor she met when she was visiting her aunt in Calgary last summer."

"Thank goodness we aren't in that boat. I'd hate to have a fellow, knowing I might not see him for years." By now most of the unmarried men had left town, and several Touchwood boys had already sailed for England with the Canadian army.

"I haven't had a date in ages," June said, sighing dramatically as she tied a silk kerchief over her pincurls. "By the time the war is over, we'll be old maids. If any of them ever come back, that is."

"Better an old maid than a widow," I said absently, counting my stitches. Three of our classmates had married in a rush, and one of them was already expecting a baby. I had no trouble filling the Matches and Hatches column.

"I'm not so sure about that," June replied as she uncapped a scarlet bottle and began to touch up the polish on her toenails. "At least you'd have some … experience."

I silently disagreed. I barely spoke to young men unless it was required in my job, having bigger and better things in mind. "If I ever do get married, which I doubt very much, it sure won't be to anybody from around here."

"Not even Charlie Stewart? I heard you two had quite a fond farewell down at the station."

"Don't be crazy, Prune! We used to poison gophers together, for crying out loud. I could never marry Charlie, or any other farmer, for that matter."

June fell onto her back, riding a bicycle in the air to dry her toenails. "Well, he might look a lot different in his uniform. The flyboys definitely have the edge there."

"It's the colour. Blue is so much more flattering than khaki. But it's the man inside the uniform that counts."

"I saw Clyde Gilhooley in his blues at the post office, and even he was quite presentable. If he hadn't been leaving the next day I might have gotten him to ask me out."

"That's the trouble, isn't it? They're all leaving." I threw down my needles in disgust, having just finished a six-toed sock.

"Perhaps if you were madly in love you could chase him around the world, like one of those, what do you call them, camp followers." June gazed at the ceiling as if intrigued by this idea.

"No such luck. Monica Fisher wrote to the government and asked if her militia could enlist in the British forces if they paid their own way, and the answer came back no, absolutely not. Civilian travel is forbidden. Nothing is allowed on the Atlantic now except troops and supply ships."

I hoped the disappointment in my voice wasn't too obvious. Ever since Monica had given me the idea, I had cherished the notion of paying my own way to England. My weekly salary was ten dollars. I paid Mother three dollars a week for my room and board, and put the other seven into my savings account at the post office.

"Monica and that bunch are crazy, anyway," June said. "They'd do better to concentrate on the few men that are left."

"Prune, honestly." Sometimes she could be so annoying. "The women's militia doesn't want to go overseas to chase men. They want to go for the same reasons as everybody else — to defeat the Germans."

June widened her big blue eyes in surprise. "You sound as if you'd like to go, too."

"I'd go in a minute, if I could."

It was the first time I had come right out and said it: that I was longing to be where the real war was happening. But what was the use of saying it, or even thinking it? The door had slammed shut in my face.

◂▾▸

The news from Britain was bad, but it got worse and then worse again. "Mussolini Shakes Hands with Hitler!" I hammered out the headline, pausing to stare at the wall above my desk, seeing visions of pizza and gondolas. The Italians were such a happy-go-lucky bunch. Why the dickens would they join forces with those blood-thirsty Germans?

"Nazis March into Paris!" I studied a photograph showing rows of grey-clad soldiers goose-stepping past the Eiffel Tower, and imagined jackboots marching down the main street of Touchwood. Could it ever happen here?

My heart bled for the English, who evacuated their children from cities, covered their beaches with barbed wire, blacked out the lights on their tiny island, and prepared to defend it to the death.

One sultry summer afternoon, I sat beside the radio in our office, listening to British Prime Minister Winston Churchill: "We shall fight on the seas and oceans. We shall fight with growing confidence and growing strength in the air. We shall defend our island, whatever the cost may be. We shall fight on the beaches. We shall fight on the landing grounds. We shall fight in the fields and in the streets. We shall fight in the hills. We shall never surrender." His voice was low and even, but hard as steel. The only word he emphasized was the word *never*.

I could see the hair standing up on my forearms. I leaped to my feet and paced back and forth. "What do you say now, Mr. MacTavish?"

"I just hope he's not talking about Canadian fields and beaches," he replied gloomily from behind his wall of newspapers. I heard him unscrew the cap of the mickey he kept in his bottom drawer, then swallow noisily.

Each morning I arrived at work gripped with apprehension. The German navy massed on the shores of France and waited for the signal to invade. But first the Luftwaffe, outnumbering the Royal Air Force three to one, attacked Britain's airfields.

"Battle of Britain Rages!" I banged out my headline and rushed back to the radio, my fighting spirit glowing white hot. The news was filled with tales of young Royal Air Force crews running to their aircraft in the middle of the night, flying suits pulled on over their striped flannel pyjamas.

The Battle of Britain became our battle, too. I wrote an obituary for Henry Stanton, the first Touchwood serviceman to be killed in action. His name appeared on the national casualty list, circulated to every newspaper. Casualty was such an odd word. What was casual about it? Did the military think that was kinder than calling it a violent, premature death?

Just when it seemed that things couldn't get much worse, the Germans did the unthinkable — they abandoned their assault on military bases and attacked cities instead. Buildings crumbled into bricks and splinters, women and children were horribly injured or burned to death. The war took a new and ugly turn.

It wasn't until the poplar leaves outside my bedroom window began to turn yellow that the Germans were either driven back by the RAF, according to the press releases, or decided to take a breather, according to MacTavish. Whatever the reason, the Luftwaffe went home at last, leaving twenty-three thousand British civilians dead.

I ran a front-page photograph of Winston Churchill, cigar clenched in his fat face, holding up two fingers in his famous "V-for-Victory" sign. "Never in the field of human conflict was so much owed by so many to so few," was his tribute to the gallant air force.

"You'll notice the Royal Canadian Air Force headquarters have been set up at Bournemouth," was MacTavish's reaction. "That's just typical! The Limeys put our boys on the south coast, so they'll be the first to get it when the Huns invade!"

◂▾▸

Somewhere in England
October 1, 1940
Dear Rose,

I have a forty-eight and nowhere to go, so I'm lying on my bunk writing letters. I arrived two weeks ago at a new station. Sorry I can't tell you where it is, or you'd probably get a letter with a nice square hole cut out of it by the censors.

It's pretty comfy, as stations go that is, and the food isn't bad. They make us eat carrots until we feel like bunnies. They're supposed to be good for our eyes. Once every two weeks we even get a real egg.

Boy, does it ever rain over here. I've never seen so much water in my life. At least we don't have to haul it from the well; all we have to do is stick a pail out the front door! We Canadians joke about the moss growing between our toes. Not very funny, but anything for a laugh.

My first crew has been assigned and they're a swell bunch. Our second pilot is a Dane who escaped just before the Huns arrived. He'd be a pilot himself if it weren't for his accent.

I'm flying a Vickers Wellington, we call it a Wimpy after the Popeye character. It's a twin-engine bomber, a real workhorse. Since I'm the pilot, I got to name her. I picked *Prairie Rose*, hope you don't mind. My crew thinks it isn't ferocious enough, but I don't care.

Jerry has been giving it to us hot and heavy ever since I got over here, but I'm happy to report we haven't been lying down ourselves. Enough said.

We don't have a lot of free time, but they bring in some good picture shows. Last weekend we saw *His Girl Friday*, with Cary Grant and Rosalind Russell. It's a comedy about a newspaper, so it reminded me of you. Has it come to Touchwood?

Dad sends me the *Times* every week, but I'd sure like to hear from you. Mail call is a big occasion. If you can send me a spare picture of yourself, that would be grand. Then I can show the other fellows how pretty the girls are in my hometown.

As always, Charlie

5

I didn't have much to compare it with, but Touchwood was the loveliest town I had ever seen. It lay gracefully along a high river bluff overlooking the sandy valley bottom where the shallow Tim River meandered into the deeper and swifter Mistatim. From this summit, there was a striking view of the two rivers and the low, rolling plains.

Early settlers soon discovered that the rusty clay along the riverbanks was ideal for making brick. The red-brick post office with its stately clock tower, the town hall, the high school, and the courthouse were a source of local pride. Beside the red-brick train station, two russet grain elevators soared against the sky: prairie cathedrals, some called them, or prairie sentinels.

There were handsome three-storey wooden homes, painted in pastels, distinguished among the dark spruce that grew thickly along the ridge. Farther back the smaller houses were laid out in a surveyed grid as precise as a checkerboard. On the sweep of flat prairie west of town, thanks to a former mayor with a passion for flying, was an airfield with three grass landing strips.

One Sunday evening after supper I saddled my pony, Buckshot, and went riding down to the Tim, which flowed through the rolling prairie two miles south of our farm. The delicate edges of the willow leaves, tinted with gold, were mirrored in the smooth, swift-flowing silver water. A late tiger lily was scarlet as a drop of blood in the dense yellow virgin grass along the banks.

As the sky darkened, I watched the changing panorama in the four corners of the heavens: purple streaks of rain falling to the south, towers of white clouds piling up in the east, ruby twilight in the west, a few early stars sparkling in the north.

The pony ambled along while I thought enviously of all the girls who were leaving Touchwood. One of my classmates had gone to New Brunswick to stay with her new husband until he was shipped out. Two others were in Vancouver working in factories, one welding some mysterious piece of equipment — I couldn't remember what it was called, but it sounded impressive — and the other sewing uniforms.

The women at home were behaving differently, too. Now that they were filling the jobs left by men, I saw them downtown, shopping for new clothes, eating lunch in restaurants, chattering and laughing, flushed with newfound independence.

Even I had mustered up my courage to ask MacTavish for a raise. "I suppose you think you can take advantage of me now that all the men have left!" he shouted.

"I'm worth as much as Pete Anderson," I retorted, having learned painfully over time that my boss enjoyed a good argument. "He didn't even know how to spell accommodation!" MacTavish grudgingly raised my weekly salary to fifteen dollars.

"It's amazing what the war has done for the women around here, even Freda Schultz," June had remarked the day before. "They dragged her father off to prison camp because he painted a swastika on his barn door, and he was so worried about losing the farm that he transferred the title into Freda's name before he left. She came into the post office and told me she and her mother are going to run the farm themselves."

"Good for her!" I said. "Old man Schultz should have gone to jail for the way he treated them, not because he was a Nazi. Remember the time Freda came to school with a black eye? She said she ran into a branch, but nobody believed it."

"Do you think they'll make a go of it?"

"I don't know why not. They've been doing all the work for years anyway, while the old man sat around drinking in the Queen's Hotel."

I certainly didn't want to take over anyone's farm. I didn't want to be a man, or even to be treated like one — at least, not all the time. I tried to imagine holding my father's rifle and pointing it at another person, pulling the trigger. I knew what the carcass of a gut-shot deer looked like. I shuddered as I turned the pony toward home.

But I did wish with all my heart that Canada would allow women to enlist and go overseas. I kept reading stories about the courage demonstrated by British girls, and it couldn't all be propaganda, as MacTavish claimed. Every time I thought about it, my stomach was squeezed by a jealous fist.

◆▼◆

I arrived at work the next morning in low spirits. The office seemed more dismal than ever. Dust motes floated in a shaft of weak sunlight that penetrated the grimy front window. I sat down heavily and began to slit open a stack of mail with my bone-handled letter opener.

Five minutes later I was racing down Main Street toward the post office as fast as I could run in my high heels and pencil skirt. "Guess what!" I practically shrieked when June's golden head appeared behind the wicket. "You can get out your dancing shoes, Prune!"

"You don't mean they picked Touchwood!" June staggered back, both hands clutched to her throat.

"Yes! We just got the press release in the mail!" I waved a sheet of paper over my head. On it were listed dozens of Canadian towns, most of them on the sky-and-dry prairies, chosen to train Commonwealth aircrews for the Royal Air Force.

"The men destined for Touchwood have already finished their first two phases of training," I read aloud. "Only the pilots and ground crew will take the final six-month phase called Service Flight Training School. Those pilots with steady nerves will be streamed into bombers, the heavy aircraft that carry tons of bombs into enemy territory. Those with keen eyesight and lightning reflexes will learn to fly fighters, the smaller aircraft that shoot down the enemy in mid-air." I lowered the paper. "It sounds pretty serious, doesn't it?"

"Pilots!" June sighed rapturously. "I must be dreaming!"

I returned to the office and found my boss in high dudgeon, having discovered the front door standing open and the place deserted. "Read this, Mr. MacTavish," I said, thrusting the paper under his nose.

He snatched it from my hand. Then he broke into a rare grin, revealing snuff-stained teeth. Without another word he went to his desk and wrote an editorial entitled "Let Them Come."

"If there's one thing Canada has in abundance, it's blue skies and wide open spaces," he wrote. "Now our great nation can honour its commitment to Britain without the shedding of Canadian blood!"

Within days, a contractor arrived from Ottawa to expand Touchwood's airport. "What's wrong with our local guys?" MacTavish fumed. "We have to pay through the nose so some crook from down east can suck the public tit!"

"Not to worry, Mr. MacTavish. He's already signed up every working man in the area, and he's paying top wages. I haven't heard any complaints."

"He'd better get the lead out, whoever he is. There'll be a hard frost one of these days. By the time he gets the foundations poured, the Thousand Year Reich will be over!"

But even MacTavish couldn't complain too loudly. Over the winter signs of a booming economy showed up in the newspaper: the "Help Wanted" ads tripled, and two new restaurants were already in the works.

With my camera slung around my neck, I clambered onto a stack
of packing crates so I could have a better view of the biggest crowd
I had ever seen. One of the most significant events in our history,
and Mr. MacTavish had stayed back at the office. There was no limit
to the man's pig-headedness.

The rest of Touchwood had done itself proud. Six Royal
Canadian Mounted Police officers stood at ease on the station
platform, gold buttons glittering on their scarlet tunics. Chief
Sam Whitefish, with his feathered headdress, was nothing short of
regal, surrounded by his party of young braves in beaded buckskins.
Ladies in their best hats wove through the crowd, handing out cups
of coffee and homemade cookies. When the band played "Roll Out
the Barrel," several people linked arms and danced a lively polka.

I saw a hand fluttering from the upstairs window of the post
office, kitty-corner from the railway station. Torn between seeing
and being seen, June had decided to take up a vantage point where
she wouldn't miss anything. I waved back.

As the train pulled into the station, the crowd broke into a
cheer. Every window was filled with a dozen blue-capped heads as
the men strained to see their new surroundings.

The new air base commander came down the steps and posed
in a frozen handshake with the mayor while I took their photograph. Chief Whitefish stepped forward and raised his right hand
in greeting. "Crikey, a Red Indian," I heard someone mutter from
a window on the train.

The doors banged open and began to disgorge the airmen in
a steady stream. Blue uniforms carrying kit bags overflowed the
platform and swelled into the parking area, and still the doorways
continued to empty and fill again.

The crowd of civilians, which had appeared so large a few minutes
earlier, seemed to shrink before the flood. The townspeople were still
smiling but they looked a little staggered. Touchwood's population
was only four thousand on a Saturday afternoon when the farmers
were in town. Now twelve hundred strangers had swelled their ranks.

From my position on the packing crates, I surveyed the sea of blue caps, many of them bearing a strip of white fabric tucked into the brim that meant they were aircrew rather than ground crew. A few of the newcomers were eyeing my legs, while others stared down the main street with an expression of disbelief. But most of them were looking up, squinting into the sunshine. Surely they couldn't ask for a better training field than this. Above their heads lay a blue dome so vast and empty that even the prairie dwindled in comparison.

But as I focused my camera on their faces, I couldn't help feeling a little disconcerted. I had expected members of the Royal Air Force to look more like fighting men. These boys were pale and exhausted, their faces just as youthful and timid as all the others that had left from this very spot.

"Well, I hope you're satisfied," MacTavish shouted when I got back to the office. "Now we've got the cursed Brits in our own backyard!"

I was far from satisfied. Over the next few weeks I was gripped with feverish anxiety. The whole town went plane crazy. The skies were filled with the buzzing of bright yellow training airplanes and everyone for miles around knew the difference between a Harvard and an Oxford.

Much to MacTavish's horror, the presence of the Royal Air Force caused local enlistment to skyrocket. "The air training plan, meant to substitute our land for our lifeblood, is nothing more than a thinly disguised recruiting scheme by the RAF!" he thundered in an editorial. "Canadians are outnumbering the British recruits two to one!"

I tried in vain to reason with him. "But Mr. MacTavish, everybody is on the same side at last. We haven't heard a word about those idiot politicians or those arrogant Easterners lately. And our local boys want to do their part, too!"

"Bushwa! Nothing but a bunch of sheep following each other off a cliff!"

Sheep or not, I knew how they felt. I had hoped that the presence of the base would lessen my desire to go overseas, but the opposite was true. Boys hardly older than me were being trained under our very noses, then sent away to fight while I was forced to stand and wait. It was sheer torture.

⋅▾⋅

The summer days lengthened. There was another flurry of excitement when Hitler declared war on Russia. Now Germany was facing a war on two fronts. Chortling, MacTavish sat down and banged out an editorial: "Hitler's Ego Has Lost the War!"

Unfortunately Russia wasn't making any progress. Instead, it was losing ground. However, the Russian people were fighting back furiously in what Stalin called his scorched earth policy, burning their own crops and villages rather than leaving them behind for the Germans.

"Even Russia allows women into the armed forces," I told June one evening, returning to my favourite subject as I put the last knot in a pair of socks. "I saw a photograph today of a woman driving a tank."

"You're knitting beautifully now, Posy."

"Well, you know what they say. You can take up either knitting or drinking, and so far I've stuck to knitting."

I found the rhythmic clacking of the needles helped my jitters. Besides, I didn't want to be the only woman in Canada who wasn't knitting. Even female convicts and mental patients had learned to knit. Thousands of socks formed a blue mountain at the town's collection depot. After June finished each pair, she tucked a good luck note into one toe. "Sort of like putting a message in a bottle," she said.

The town launched a metals and rubber drive called Scrap Hitler with Scrap. I photographed a team of horses hauling away the souvenir cannon from the Great War Memorial. It would be melted down and used to fight the Germans again.

One morning Jack came downstairs with his beloved collection of lead soldiers and asked me to drop them at the depot. "Jack, surely not your soldiers," Mother said sadly.

"I reckon I'm too big to be playing with toys now. I'd rather they were part of a tank than sitting in my bedroom." After he left, Mother put the lead general in her apron pocket.

‹▾›

Touchwood
July 1, 1941
Dear Charlie,

I was thinking about you today and decided to drop you a line. Remember that Dominion Day when we lit the firecrackers and almost burned down Dad's haystack? I hope you're enjoying it, wherever you are.

Touchwood is the same — boring as ever. The last two boys in our class have joined up, all except for Jake Jacobs. I guess he has flat feet. Funny, isn't it? He was always the big baseball star and now he has to stay home and milk the cows.

I was admiring your oat field yesterday on my way to work. It's the best crop I've ever seen, about shoulder high, must be forty bushels to the acre. Your father says those two young cousins of yours are good workers, but of course they're just itching to join up, too. Jack has a calendar in his bedroom and he's crossing off the days with big red Xs until his eighteenth birthday. I think it's giving Mother the heebie-jeebies!

I'm still working at the newspaper and saving up to go to university. My job is okay, but how I envy you! Are you doing any sightseeing? I would love to hear all about England.

Best of British luck, Charlie, and keep your head down.

As always, Rose

6

I sat at my dressing table, wishing I had something new to wear. The wartime motto was "Make it Do or Do Without," but I was tired of doing both.

Oh well. At least my clothes were all new to the boys in blue. I stepped into the dark red taffeta circle skirt I had sewn myself and slipped a string of Mother's garnet beads over my white rayon blouse. Pinning back the sides of my hair in a Victory Roll, I applied bright red lipstick, trying unsuccessfully to even out my crooked mouth.

When June and I arrived at the hangar an hour later, we could hear the beat of the music and the laughter streaming out across the dark tarmac, overhung with millions of bright stars. "Who's playing?" asked June, snapping her fingers.

"It's a group from the base called The Blue Aces." I admired the way June's new ankle-strap shoes set off her shapely calves. I wanted a pair, but Mother wouldn't hear of it. She thought they looked cheap.

As soon as we set foot inside the door, we were nabbed for a tag dance. The cavernous hangar with its bare walls and concrete floor was crowded with hundreds of blue tunics, their brass buttons glittering in the light from the bare bulbs dangling overhead. The scent of men's hair pomade, so popular among the British flyers, thickened the air. I changed partners nine times before the number was over.

Panting, June and I sank into two metal chairs at the end of a long table. A young man named Chopper who had attached himself to June went off to buy drinks. While he was gone the band struck up again, a fast number. Couples surged onto the floor. Six or seven airmen headed toward our table.

"Dance?" A smallish flyer reached me before the others. The top two buttons of his tunic were undone and he was flushed, unsteady on his feet. I guessed he had already been drinking. In my high-heeled pumps I was several inches taller, my shoulders just as broad.

The airman led me into the crowd. Grabbing me roughly, he swung me so hard that my skirt belled out and my feet left the floor. He pushed me away with one hand, then yanked me back again and twirled me around. He was surprisingly strong. My blouse began to work out of my waistband.

"Come on, put some life into it, girlie!" Placing his hands on my waist, he lifted me into the air with a visible effort and dropped me heavily. The sweat poured off his forehead and a few drops flicked me in the face. His feet kicked wildly out from side to side, and he wasn't following the music at all.

Spinning me around backwards, he put his shoulder blades against mine and hooked his elbows through my bent arms. "Wait a minute!" I cried, but it was too late. He threw himself forward and lifted me into the air. I knew I was expected to roll upside-down over his back and land on my feet, but mid-point during the roll he hesitated.

I had a split second of excruciating embarrassment as I realized that my legs were pointed straight up into the air and my skirt was around my waist, exposing the tops of my stockings, my garters, my bare thighs, and even my white cotton underpants. Then I felt the airman buckle underneath me. He went down with a crash and I landed on his back. I heard him grunt as the air left his body.

Instantly I leaped to my feet, smoothing down my skirt. I bent over the airman. "Are you all right?" He shook his head and groaned. His friends gathered around and helped him limp off the dance floor. I stalked back to my chair, cheeks burning. As I passed the band, the saxophone player winked at me.

June and Chopper were seated at the table, convulsed with laughter. "I say, you're supposed to entertain them, not render them unfit for service," Chopper said. I took a sip of my drink and tried to look nonchalant. People were peering over at our table and snickering. The airman had disappeared.

When the band leader announced a break, the musicians set aside their instruments and headed for the bar. "That fellow wants his head punched for treating a girl like that." I raised my eyes and saw the saxophone player. He was tall and thin, with a narrow face and a droll expression.

I smiled at him. "I hope I didn't break his back."

"He bloody well deserves it. Can I buy you a drink?"

"Thanks. A lemonade."

When he came back with the drinks, June had gone outside to have a nip from Chopper's hip flask and three airmen had already taken the chairs around me.

"Shoo, flies!" The sax player waved them off with long, elegant fingers and pulled an empty chair close to my side.

"You're an Aussie," I said, stating the obvious. He was wearing passionate purple — the dark blue uniform of the Royal Australian Air Force.

"Actually I'm a Tazzie, from Tasmania. That's an island south of the Australian mainland, in case you didn't know."

"Yes, I did know."

"You must be one of the few. I've had to explain hundreds of times."

"I must confess I have no idea what it looks like, though."

"It's marvellous." His comical face became animated. "Forests in the interior, with waterfalls and flowers as big as your head. Beaches along the coast, with white sand like powdered sugar."

"You sound like a tourist guide."

"That's because I am one. I worked for the tourist board in Launceston, that's the capital, before I joined up."

"My name's Rose Jolliffe."

"Max Cassidy." We shook hands. Max had a firm grip and he didn't try to hold my hand too long as some of the others did.

"If it's so beautiful there, you must miss it."

"It's not so bad for me. I've been away from home for six months now. But most of the Brylcreem boys, this is their first time out of merry old England."

"And they have their families to worry about."

"Too right. Some of the boys — when they see all the food in the mess, they just break down. People aren't eating very well over there right now. There's one bloke who cries himself to sleep every night in his bunk."

"What do the others think of that?"

"Usually someone tells him to put a sock in it. We'd all end up blubbering if he went on!" Max laughed.

The band members began to resume their places on the stage. Max drained his beer. "Do you ever go into the canteen?"

"I'm there Tuesday and Thursday evenings. That's when Mother and I do our shift."

"I'll see you there, then. Cheerio!"

I danced every dance. Whenever I caught Max's eye, he was watching me. I noticed the airman who had dropped me jitterbugging wildly around the floor with a slip of a girl. He scowled at me as he bounded past.

◄▼►

The following Tuesday, Mother and I entered the former downtown furniture store that had been converted into a servicemen's canteen. Every woman in town took her turn behind the small lunch counter, serving sandwiches and cake and providing a friendly shoulder for the homesick boys.

Someone was playing the piano expertly while several airmen and girls sang less expertly, but with great enthusiasm. The pianist performed a jazz version of "Don't Sit Under the Apple Tree," with plenty of rippling chords. He finished with a flourish and spun his stool around to face the room. It was Max.

Immediately he jumped up and came over to me with a big grin on his face. "Hello! I was hoping you'd turn up!"

"Mother, I'd like you to meet Max Cassidy."

"How do you do, Max? Will you help us make coffee?"

"Sure thing, Mrs. Jolliffe." He began to run water into the coffeepot. "It's a right treat to have real coffee again. I used to drink gallons of the stuff back in Taz."

Robbed of their accompanist, the singers drifted off to play ping-pong or darts. Someone had pinned a cartoon of Hitler's face over the dartboard. Applause broke out whenever a dart pierced Hitler's nose or eye.

"Do you live around here?" Max asked.

"No, we live four miles out of town. My father's a farmer."

"Funny, you don't look like a farm girl." He squinted his eyes as if examining a rare butterfly.

"How many have you known?"

"Come to think of it, none. You'll set the standard."

While the coffee was brewing we returned to the piano. I leaned over Max's shoulder while we sang all of my favourites. He had a clear tenor voice.

"There must be a song about Rose," he said at last, trailing his long fingers over the keyboard and smiling up into my face.

"My father named me after his favourite song, 'Rose Marie.'"

"That's a lovely song. It suits you." Max played while we sang together: "Oh, Rose Marie, I love you, forever thinking of you...." Mother's soprano joined in from the kitchen.

I finally dragged myself away long enough to wash the dishes, but Max followed me into the kitchen and insisted on tying an apron over his uniform and drying them. When the last saucer was put away, it was time to go.

"See you on Thursday?" Max asked.

"I'll be here." I glanced over my shoulder as we left the canteen. He winked and waved.

◂▾▸

Unlike June, who had already fallen in love half a dozen times, I tried to keep my distance from the airmen. I knew there was an uncertain future in store for these boys, not to mention anyone who cared about them. And I shrank from the way some girls openly pursued the pilots, bagging them like trophies. Their mothers weren't much better. Mrs. Cooper, for instance, never invited anyone but officers to her house, practically shoving her unmarried daughters in their faces.

But I knew I was in trouble one sunny Saturday, when Max made the long walk out to our farm. While Mother baked cookies in the kitchen, Max and I fooled around on the piano. I could play, although not nearly as well as Max, and he was showing me a new duet. We had never been alone in the house. In fact, we were never alone at all unless we went out for a walk. Mother was quite firm about that.

"Are you going back to the tourist business when the war is over, Max?"

"I'm hoping to conduct."

"Conduct?" I asked, thinking about trains.

"Righto, conduct an orchestra. I practise all the time."

"How do you do that?"

"Give me a piece of paper and a pencil, and I'll show you." He took the paper, tore it into bits, and wrote on them.

"Now some pins, please."

I fetched my mother's sewing basket. Max pinned the pieces of paper in neat rows along the back of the blue mohair chesterfield.

"I need some music. I'll take a gander at your records." Max bent over the wind-up gramophone in the corner and searched the small record collection. "Hmm … Harry Lauder, John McCormack. Here's a good one: Glenn Miller, 'In the Mood.'"

He put the record on the turntable, wound up the machine, dropped the needle onto the edge of the record, tapped his pencil on the back of a chair, and stood poised in front of the chesterfield, arms raised to shoulder height. I came closer to see what he had written: First Strings. Second Strings. Clarinet. Saxophone. Drums. Then his paper orchestra began to play.

I stood beside him, entranced, as Max conducted the Glenn Miller Orchestra flawlessly. When it was time for the saxophone, he pointed his pencil at one piece of paper and the saxophone came in right on cue. When the music hushed and the piece seemed to be over, his pencil was still. Suddenly he raised his arms again and the instruments rushed back in a crescendo of sound for the grand finale.

He stepped back, turned to me and bowed from the waist. I clapped until my palms stung. "Max, that was terrific! How did you learn to do that?"

"Every night I put my bits of paper up on the wall and have a gay old time. The problem is that I don't have any records so I go through the pieces I already know. Once in a while I even try a new arrangement."

"Can you actually hear the music in your head?"

"If I'm not too fagged out from studying. Then all I can hear when I go to bed is the sound of the engines in my kite. We're coming up for finals, you know."

I knew Max would return to England and begin flying operations soon. "Do you think you'll pass your exams?" Suddenly I wanted him to say no.

"I expect so. I'm doing quite well in most of my classes."

I reached out my hand and drew him down beside me on the chesterfield. We sat silently for a few minutes, me thinking of the half-life that awaited Max in England, far from home and family, risking his life for freedom.

His arm slid around me, and we kissed. My cheeks flushed and the strength drained from my limbs. Even my fingers felt weak, the way they did sometimes when I woke up in the morning and couldn't make a fist.

"I never wanted this to happen, you know." My voice was trembling. "I didn't want to … to … you know, get attached to somebody who was going away."

"You'd better not, then."

"I can't help it." We kissed again.

"When the war is over, I want to take you home to meet my mother and my sister, Kathleen, and show you all over Tasmania."

"I'd like that, Max."

Neither of us spoke for a moment. "I'm very lucky, you know," he said suddenly. "I once won five pounds in the mess. I'll probably live to be the most dreadful old man. You'll have to throw me down the stairs to get rid of me."

⟐

I awoke with a tremendous start, my eyes wide open and staring. I had dreamed that German Panzers were rolling across the farm, but the real nightmare was waking up and remembering that Max was nearly ready to leave for England.

I buried my face in the embroidered white pillowcase while my mind roved over some unlikely possibilities. Disguising myself as a man and enlisting. Smuggling myself aboard Max's ship. Arranging an accident that would leave him unfit to fight. A wave of shame engulfed me and I groaned into my pillow. Millions of women all over the world were sharing this same dread. What gave me the right to be so selfish?

I jumped out of bed and began to dress. I was so restless that I couldn't sit still. At the breakfast table my father asked me if I had St. Vitus's Dance. At the office, I did my work in five-minute bursts, pacing between my desk and the front counter.

"You're worse than a flea on a dog!" MacTavish said. "It serves you right for getting mixed up with one of those guys. He'll be gone in a few weeks, and then you'll be moping around here with a face like a wet dishrag."

Every evening I went over to the airfield after work to watch the pilots practise. I asked Max so many questions about lift and drag and altitude that he finally told me to knock it off. "I'm a good pilot, Rose. If you don't believe me, I'll get my commanding officer to write you a letter," he joked.

I was only partly reassured. I knew Max's quiet confidence would make him a good bomber pilot. It was the rest of the air force I wasn't so sure about.

◀▶

At last a press release arrived that practically transported me out of my chair with joy. The Canadian government had caved in, but only after the British government requested permission to send members of its own women's air force to work on our air training bases.

Embarrassed and beleaguered, Parliament finally voted to allow women into the Canadian armed forces.

I rushed out of the office and rode my bicycle out to the Fisher place, where I found Monica in the barn shovelling pig manure, an expression of rapture on her face. When she saw me, she dropped her pitchfork and gave me a hearty embrace that almost knocked me off my feet.

Her drilling and letter-writing had borne fruit. She had already received a telegram from Ottawa asking her to train as an officer in the newly formed women's division of the Royal Canadian Air Force.

"Are you going to enlist, Rose?"

"I'm not old enough yet, but I'll join up on my twenty-first birthday next May if I can go overseas!"

"I wouldn't count on it. Every girl in the militia is hankering to get over there."

"What are the chances, do you think?"

"Not so good. We know the government only wants us to scrub

floors at air bases. It could be years before we convince them to let us out of the country."

I pedalled back to the office, my face streaming with tears. When I came through the door, MacTavish asked me why the waterworks. "I figured you'd be happy!" he shouted. "If there are going to be females on stations, God forbid, they might as well be Canadian!"

His words were infuriating. "There's no reason to assume women can't do the job, Mr. MacTavish! Even the supreme British air commander supports women in uniform. Listen to this press release: 'Members of the women's air force have raised the standard of efficiency, discipline, and morale on air bases all over England!'"

"Well, the poor devils are in a different boat, aren't they? They have to use every warm body, like it or not!"

✦✦✦

Time was the enemy now. Each red dawn brought Max closer to the day he would leave for England. I felt frantic inside, the way I had when Buckshot ran away with me.

There was frost at the beginning of September. "I say, is it almost time for the snow to come?" Max asked. "I can't wait to see that. It must be fantastic, everything covered with white. Kathleen made me promise to send her a snap of myself standing in a big pile of it."

"I wish you'd been here last winter. It was so deep you could climb right onto the roofs of the granaries."

"I wish I'd been here every winter." He squeezed my hand.

"Where do you think you'll be stationed?" Lately I was torn between never mentioning it and talking about it constantly.

"I hear they're sending a lot of us wild Colonial boys out of England. The Brits want to be at home, defending their patch of God's green earth, and I can't blame them. I just want to be where I can do the most good, so we can get this thing over with."

✦✦✦

I was brushing under the wavy ends of my thick hair, getting ready to go to the picture show with Max, when the telephone rang. *Captains of the Clouds* was showing at the Empress Theatre, starring Jimmy Cagney as an RCAF pilot.

"Rose, it's for you!" Jack called from the bottom of the stairs.

"Coming!" I tied the sash of my housecoat. I ran down the stairs two at a time and lifted the heavy earpiece off the wall.

"Hello?"

"Rose, it's Jimbo." His voice sounded faint and distant.

"Hi! How are you?" Jimbo was a friend of Max's on the base, one of the boys who liked to pull practical jokes.

"Is your mother there?"

"Yes, do you want to talk to her?"

"No. I'm afraid I have some bad news." He paused. "Max isn't coming tonight."

"Don't tell me his leave has been cancelled again!"

"It's not that. Rose, there's been an accident."

"Oh, sure." I laughed. "Pull the other one, Jimbo."

"Listen, I'm not joking." Jimbo's voice broke. "His Harvard went down this afternoon."

I didn't reply. If this was a joke, it wasn't funny.

"It was the ruddy kite, Rose. He told me it was acting up, but the mechanics couldn't find anything wrong. It pranged ten miles out of town."

My legs felt weak and I sat down on the bottom stair. There was a draft coming under the door. I tucked the hem of my robe around my bare feet, which were suddenly cold.

"Is he hurt?"

"He bailed out, but not soon enough. His chute didn't have time to open. A farmer saw the whole thing. He reached Max a few minutes later. But he said Max was … was … dead as soon as he hit the ground. I'm awfully sorry, Rose."

For a moment I felt, heard, saw nothing. Then I gave a harsh, guttural cry. I didn't even recognize my own voice. The kitchen door flew open and Mother came running into the hall. "Rose, what's the matter?"

The receiver fell from my hand and banged against the wall. I flung myself into Mother's arms, crying like a child with my mouth wide and square.

♦♦♦

For a long time, I could not forget the image of Max falling through the sky, his soft body striking the hard ground. It was shocking how grief felt, how crushing and how relentless. "I'll grind his bones to make my bread," said the giant in the fairy tale, and I felt as if giant hands were grinding my bones.

"He never saw the snow," I wept every night. Snow symbolized everything that Max and I had wanted to do together. He would never see the leaves fall on the Touchwood Hills, would never feel the touch of snowflakes on his warm skin.

It still hadn't snowed when they buried Max in the stone cold ground. The young airmen stood at attention, pale and solemn in their dark blue greatcoats, as the twenty-one-gun salute rang out over the cemetery and echoed back from the hills across the river.

When the first snow fell, I stayed home from work and locked myself in my bedroom. In the long, silent hours, I wrote a letter to Max's sister, whom I would never meet. I thought about the thousands of other women who would share this pain before the war ended. But mostly I thought about Max's talent and courage and how they would never be used in the way he had hoped. The sense of waste was unbearable.

Three days later I came home and told my parents I had found a way to go overseas.

Book Two

November 1941–June 1944

7

I opened my eyes to darkness that was blacker than the inside of a black cat, as Dad would say. My bed was tilted to one side. An unpleasant odour of diesel fuel mixed with perfume hung in the air. And what was that thundering sound? A thud, thud, thud like muffled drumbeats from a distant pow-wow.

Then my mind cleared. It was the sound of marching feet. Troops were boarding the ship in Halifax Harbour and I was far below, lying on the upper bunk of a triple-decker bunk bed, crammed with eight other girls into a cabin built for four.

A drowsy voice spoke. "Anybody know what time it is?"

A match flared and a second voice said: "Seven hundred hours. Better get dressed."

"How long does it take to load fifteen thousand men, anyway? They've been at it all night."

A third voice, shriller than the others: "Fifteen thousand? The notice on the wall says there are only enough lifeboats for three thousand."

"Well, for once being a woman might do some good, eh?" another voice chimed in. "At least we get first crack at the lifeboats when the torpedo hits!" Suddenly I felt an urgent desire to get upstairs on deck.

We took turns washing in the cubbyhole called a head. Shivering with excitement, I pulled on my Harris Tweed trousers and rooted around in my suitcase until I found the crimson cable-knit cardigan that Mother had knitted as a goodbye gift.

As I buckled on my life preserver, a knock sounded on the steel doorframe. The door itself had been replaced with an army blanket to prevent us being trapped if the ship went down. It was Mrs. Simpson and a burly naval officer who would accompany us everywhere.

"Girls, the men are under orders not to speak to you, or even look at you," Mrs. Simpson said. "Please behave yourselves, and don't go anywhere without an escort."

We ascended to the dining room on slanted stairs. The rhythm of marching feet finally came to a halt as the last man boarded and the ship levelled off.

When we finished our scrambled eggs, we went out on deck, accompanied by our officer, and stood at the rail watching the docks below. Bands were playing, hundreds of brightly dressed women and children were waving and calling, their voices carried away by the salty breeze that burned my cheeks. I had seen dozens of farewell scenes in the last two years, but this time it was different. Finally, I was the one going to war.

The throb of the engines grew louder and vibrated through our feet, the horn sent forth an ear-splitting blast, and the sullen grey water below us heaved as the tugboats pushed the ship away from shore. The crowd waved and wept. One mother picked up her baby's arm and flapped it back and forth.

I wondered when I would see my beloved country again. My heartstrings felt stretched to the breaking point, as if they were attached to dry land. The hot tears overflowed and trickled down my icy cheeks. Gradually the watery gap widened, the cries grew fainter, and the faces became indistinct. I stayed at the rail, straining my eyes until the shore shrank into a distant black line.

Then a mighty roar sounded overhead as three Sunderlands appeared to port bearing the RCAF insignia. The troops let out a yell, almost trampling each other in their hurry to get to the port-side rail, and the women weren't far behind.

These were the strangest airplanes I had ever seen. Their heavy bellies made them look like pregnant cows with wings. Despite their odd shape, they flew as gracefully as eagles, circling low across the white-capped waves as they searched for the dreaded German wolf packs.

All morning I remained on deck, watching them wheeling and swooping, until my face was numb with cold and my hair was a tangled mass. But eventually they circled the ship one last time and waggled their wings farewell and good luck before turning back to shore.

We had now entered the Atlantic's black pit, too far for aircraft to reach from either side of the ocean. If the ship went down here, there would be little chance of survival. We were very much alone on the vast sea.

Suddenly there was a tremendous lurch and the deck tilted sharply. The girl next to me screamed and grabbed my arm to keep from falling. "Nothing to worry about," our officer said. "The captain is just taking evasive action." A few seconds later, with another jerk, the ship swerved in the opposite direction.

The decks fell quiet while everyone clung to the rail and tried to accustom themselves to the zigzagging motion. I had a funny feeling in the soles of my feet as I imagined a German submarine below the ship, aiming a torpedo at our massive hull. It was the first time that I, Rose Marie Jolliffe, was in personal danger from the enemy. It would take some getting used to.

As I gazed down into the churning wake, unrolling behind us like a length of gigantic white rick-rack while the ship staggered drunkenly from side to side, I remembered how much my parents had wanted me to stay at home.

•▾•

"But why can't you join the Canadian air force?" Dad asked me again, as we sat around the kitchen table after supper.

"I don't want to peel potatoes at some air base in another prairie town just like this one. I want to go overseas and work on a real operational station. Canada might never send women to England, and even if it does, it might take years. But I can't stay here any longer. I just can't."

"My dear girl, are you sure this is how you want to spend your hard-earned money?" Mother asked sorrowfully.

"You know I was saving for university, but that will just have to wait until after the war."

Dad shook his head. "I still don't understand how you wangled this."

"It was the most amazing stroke of luck. The British Women's Volunteer Force stopped at the train station this afternoon on their trip across Canada, and their leader, Mrs. Simpson, said as long as I pay my own way she'll arrange my passage to England and let me travel with them. Once I arrive, I'm free to enlist in the British air force."

"You're positive the air force wants you?" Dad was persistent.

"I'm a British subject, and besides, they can't afford to be choosy! Dad, they're taking every woman over sixteen!

"You're so lucky, Rose." Jack broke in. "I'll be over there myself pretty soon." Dad and Mother turned to him with a sick expression on their faces, and for a moment I suspected they had forgotten all about me.

"I'll be perfectly safe," I repeated. "There's no danger since the Blitz ended. You know we're going to win the war — it's only a question of when. If people like me join up, it'll be over that much sooner!"

•▼•

Oxford, England
November 19, 1941
Dear Mother and Dad and Jack,

I arrived here yesterday, imagining myself a world
traveller already. The trip across Canada was gorgeous until we reached Ontario, and then it was
nothing but huge boulders and huge tree trunks.
In Quebec City we stopped for an hour while a
party of French Canadian soldiers boarded, and it
was so funny to hear our boys in uniform speaking
a "foreign" language. We finally arrived in Halifax
and saw the ocean for the first time. Yes, I stuck
my finger in the water and tasted the salt, just like
all the other land-lubbers!

Our crossing was uneventful. I spent most
of my time on deck, peering into the water for
periscopes. One girl even got a reprimand for
throwing up over the side, in case the contents of
her stomach were spotted by a U-boat!

I can't tell you where the ship docked, but
it was a ghost town: old Georgian houses along
the waterfront, windows boarded up, no vehicles
on the streets, no people except for a few in uniform. On the beach were the most gigantic rolls
of barbed wire, each one big enough to fence our
whole farm!

The next day Mrs. Simpson put me on a
train for Oxford, and Roger and Pamela met
me at the station. They persuaded me to spend
a few days getting my bearings, as we sailors

say. Pamela looks like Joan Crawford — black eyebrows and red lipstick, and silk scarves fluttering behind her like flags. She even uses an ivory cigarette holder. Dad would say she wears the trousers in the family. And she *does* wear trousers, all the time.

Roger reminds me of the Duke of Windsor — the first person I've ever seen wearing a silk ascot. He makes fun of me because I say bitter instead of bittah. But then he says Canader instead of Canada!

This house is colder than a morning in January, and as damp as a root cellar. Three days ago I washed my socks and hung them up in my bedroom, and this morning I squeezed water out of them. I keep imagining I can see my breath.

Pamela's first words were: "What did you bring me?" Thank goodness I had chocolates. She's still complaining about the lack of servants. It's true she isn't much of a cook. Last night we had cabbage soup and tinned meat. I tried to keep my fork in my left hand so they wouldn't think I was a proper barbarian.

After supper — they call their noon meal "luncheon" and their evening meal "dinner" — we ladies "withdrew" to the drawing room so Roger could smoke his pipe. While we were sitting there, the cat, Fanny, jumped onto the windowsill, and five minutes later the air warden banged on the door and yelled at us because a crack of light had flashed out when the cat moved the curtains. (Pamela sewed the blackouts herself, and you should see them, Mother — the hems are so crooked.)

Pamela says a few times the front door opened at night and a strange red-haired man walked in. "Sorry, wrong house!" he'd say, and off he'd go. Then one night, she opened what she thought was her front door and found the red-haired man sitting in front of his own fire! He lives one street over, and it's easy to get confused. You never saw anything like the blackout here on a cloudy night — you can hold your palm an inch from your nose and see absolutely nothing!

You're going to think I'm crazy, but the biggest surprise is hearing little kids on the street speak with an English accent. They sound so darned strange, as if they're putting it on.

I miss you so much. The first thing I saw when we came down the gangplank was a poster that said: "Homesickness is like seasickness — it soon wears off." It isn't true. I wasn't a bit seasick, but oh, I am terribly homesick!

Give Laddy and Pansy a hug from me.

All my love, Rose

❧

I spent hours walking the streets, memorizing details for my letters home. The dreaming spires, the church towers, and the ancient monuments were beautiful, but I was forced to admit that England wasn't quite what I expected.

Maybe it was the dirt. The stone statues were filthy, their heads and shoulders stained with pigeon droppings. The elaborate brickwork on the buildings was pitted with age and the cobblestoned streets were littered with rubbish.

Or maybe it was the damp. One afternoon I stood on an arched bridge while university students dressed in white punted down the river. It was a lovely scene, but the wind cut through my coat like a blade. Even the sun shone weakly, a pale imitation of the sun back home, more like the prairie moon.

I was disoriented, having lost all sense of proportion. This must be how Alice felt when she ate the toadstool, growing bigger and smaller by turns. The sky had shrunk to a patch of pale blue overhead, its horizons covered with rooftops and trees so enormous that I felt like an ant scurrying through a vegetable garden. The leaves that drifted to the ground were bigger than dinner plates. Yet in spite of the monstrous trees, everything was made of brick.

Other objects were so tiny that I felt like Gulliver in the land of Lilliput. Pamela's narrow brick house shared walls with the homes on each side, as if the buildings had been squeezed together like an accordion. The front yard, lined with ugly spiked railings, was the size of my old sandbox.

"Where do you keep everything?" I asked in genuine amazement, when Pamela showed me the kitchen, no bigger than a pantry with a small porcelain sink. That was just after I had cracked my forehead on the low beam over the doorway.

And England was strangely primitive, lacking in the amenities I took for granted. Here, in the midst of one of the world's most civilized cities, there was no telephone. I couldn't understand it. Even old man Thorpe who lived on the bald prairie ten miles out of Touchwood had a telephone.

Pamela and Roger weren't quite so appealing at close quarters, either. I had been so eager to meet my English flesh and blood — especially my glamorous cousin and her husband, a real university professor. But Pamela wore a perpetual smear of cigarette ashes down the front of her blouse, and Roger was always putting his arm around me in a way I didn't quite like.

Three days later, when we had exchanged all the family news and the effort to make conversation was wearing a bit thin, Pamela and Roger exchanged a long look over the dinner table. "Shall we take her to the Green Boar tonight?" Pamela asked, blowing jets of smoke through her nostrils.

"Righto, I'll fetch my cap and stick."

Stumbling though the pitch darkness and accompanied by Pamela's curses, we found the doorway with difficulty and came into the warmth. I was eager to see a real pub, since women weren't allowed in bars back home. Sometimes when I had walked past the Queen's Hotel in Touchwood, the doors opened and a smoky, yeasty smell blew out. I always tried to peek inside.

But I guessed that this English pub was quite different. It was delightful in the cozy room, with wooden timbers and stone fireplace where a blaze was crackling. Blackout curtains covered the door and windows.

There was one drawback. To keep the light to a minimum, the bulbs were painted blue. I had never seen anything so ghastly as Roger's face in the blue light. His large, crooked teeth were stained yellow by pipe smoke, and when he smiled the blue light turned them a sickly green colour. As for Pamela, her thick pancake makeup enhanced the blue valleys under her eyes.

I sat uncomfortably between them on a red leatherette bench. "She has marvellous hair, hasn't she, Roger?" Pamela said. "Just feel the weight of it."

He lifted the bottom of my heavy pageboy with his liver-spotted hand. "Yes, indeed."

"Go and fetch us another round, would you, dear boy?"

"Quite." Roger sauntered over to the bar.

Pamela leaned forward, dropping cigarette ashes on the table. "Attractive, isn't he?"

"Who?" I glanced around.

"Roger, of course. He was a fine-looking man when we first married, and he's still quite dashing, wouldn't you say?"

"Yes, he's very handsome," I said politely.

"I don't suppose you'd like to sleep with him, would you?"

I turned to Pamela with a frozen smile, thinking this was some kind of British joke. "Sorry, I don't understand."

"Sleep with him — you know, do the dirty deed." She smirked and waggled her eyebrows.

I was aghast. Surely she didn't imagine I had designs on her husband. "Believe me, I don't think of Roger that way."

"Well, I'm asking you to, you silly gel. He's taken quite a fancy to you. I like him to have a bit on the side now and then — it keeps him young. There are girls falling all about themselves at the university, but we have an agreement that he won't touch any of them unless I've vetted them first."

My head swivelled toward Roger, who was leaning against the bar while the bartender drew his pints. He gave me a green leer.

"When you arrived, we agreed at once that you'd be perfect. You know, keep it in the family, what?" She squinted at me through a cloud of smoke.

"Pamela — I'm sorry, but it's out of the question." I had to refrain from a shudder of revulsion, although part of me wanted to scream with laughter.

"Oh, well, just a passing thought." Her voice was cool.

Roger returned to the table, bearing three pints of beer.

"It's no go, I'm afraid, Rog," his wife said.

I thought he looked a little relieved. He reached over and patted my hand. "Perhaps another time. No hard feelings."

The next day I woke early and found my own way to the nearest recruiting office.

8

I sat on my cot in the drafty wooden barracks and pulled on a pair of woollen bloomers called passion killers that hung to my knees. A pale pink cotton brassiere followed, with wrinkled, oversized cups. Over that, a woollen undervest.

I pulled up the ugly grey lisle stockings one at a time, and fastened them to the garters dangling from my suspender belt. Then I buttoned my shirt and slipped the black necktie over my head, still knotted from yesterday because I hadn't learned yet how to tie the knot.

Next I scrambled into the scratchy blue woollen skirt and battle-dress tunic, belted around the waist. The wool had the texture of an old horse blanket, but I was pleased that the air force allowed me to wear my Canada badge on each shoulder, thanks to Mackenzie King.

Tucking my thick shoulder-length hair into a roll, I secured it with bobby pins before putting on my peaked cap. Rather than cut off my wavy hair, which was maddeningly unmanageable, I had decided it would be simpler to keep it pinned out of the way. Finally, I tied up the laces on my thick black leather shoes.

"Where are you from?" asked an English girl, in the midst of the same procedure at the next bed.

"Touchwood," I said, as I slipped a string around my neck bearing two metal identity discs. "That is, I mean Canada."

"You have a boyfriend over here, I suppose."

"No, I don't know anyone in England, except my mother's cousin in Cambridge."

"I say, you are a plucky one. The Women's Auxiliary Air Force has become very unwaffy since conscription came in — the last stragglers flocked to volunteer so they wouldn't be sent to work at a factory or a farm. This scruffy lot would rather be in the pub, most likely."

She gestured to the photograph one girl had hung above her bunk: wearing brief shorts and a midriff-baring sweater, she was making the V-for-Victory sign by lying on her back with her legs spread-eagled in the air. "I mean, really. So common."

I secretly agreed. Nothing had prepared me for the vulgarity in the barracks. I had never rubbed shoulders with the English working class, whose manners were quite different, to say the least, from those of my mother.

I literally gasped when I first heard several girls singing, to the tune of the "Colonel Bogey March": "Hitler has only got one ball; Goering has two, but very small; Himmler has something similar, but poor old Goebbels has no balls at all!"

Even that paled compared to the song I heard the following week, a parody of the popular "Bless Them All," in which the word "Bless" was replaced with a word starting with F that I had seen only once before, after Ernie Snyder carved it on the barn door and was soundly strapped by our teacher.

"What about you?" I asked the friendly girl.

"I've wanted to volunteer ever since the war started, but I had to take care of my mother. She's gone to live with relatives in Ireland now, so I took my chance. No matter how bad it gets in the service, it can't be any worse than home life."

I thought sadly of my own happy home. Having never spoken to a woman in the armed forces before, I had no idea of the humiliations that were in store. The first was a medical inspection, stark naked, for "scabies, babies, and rabies." And my life was now controlled by a bell or a bugle or a shout. Going to lecture, going to grub, going to briefings, going on parade; it was like being a trained poodle in a circus.

And that first awful night, the sound of muffled sobs all over the room after lights out. *Homesick is a good word*, I thought as I wept into my pillow, *because I've never felt so sick in my life, not even the time I had blood poisoning from stepping on a rusty nail.*

I remembered that dreadful two weeks each spring when Dad weaned the calves by penning them into the barnyard. The cows lined up along the fence, groaning in pain and frustration, while the poor calves gathered on the other side and cried: "Maa, maa, maa!" The din lasted for several days and nights while we covered our ears and suffered along.

In fact, I heard someone sobbing "Mama, mama," in the bunk below me. It was Daphne, the frightened child I had met on my first day. *She doesn't look a day over fourteen*, I thought, feeling almost matronly now that I had left my teens behind.

Poor little Daphne had made herself into a laughingstock by entering the showers in her bathing suit. I didn't blame her. I showered quickly in a room full of naked girls, my eyes averted. Even worse, the toilets had no doors. The ablutions, as they were called, faced the entrance so that anyone could see you sitting on the toilet. I was deeply offended. I may have grown up using a biffy, but at least it had a door.

After breakfast we lined up in crooked rows on the parade ground for our first marching exercise. The burly, red-faced RAF drill sergeant looked as if he enjoyed his job even less than we did. Maybe he was being punished for something.

"Swing them bleeding arms — they won't drop off!" he yelled at Daphne, who was mincing along self-consciously as if she were strolling through the park. She stopped dead and burst into sobs, which made the ready tears spring into my own eyes.

"Jesus bloody Christ!" he yelled. "What do we have here, a bunch of crybabies or members of the King's Own? Get back in line or I'll put you on notice!"

Don't cry, don't cry, don't cry, I told myself fiercely. I stared straight ahead, trying to harden my face into a mask of stone. Fortunately, thanks to Mr. MacTavish, I was accustomed to being yelled at. Unfortunately, thinking of him made me want to cry again.

⟨•⟩

The next six weeks were the worst I had ever known. Time after time I asked myself whether I was crazy. Most of the other girls thought so. "You want your head examined," said a coarse-looking girl, when she found I had come from Canada to enlist. "I plan to fall pregnant on my next leave. That's the only way out of this hell hole."

I suffered from fatigue, sore muscles, blisters on my feet, and a gnawing homesickness that was worse than physical pain. I woke each morning with my eyelids swollen from weeping. After five weeks, I checked the calendar and discovered that I had skipped my period. Off I went to the medical officer.

"No chance that you're expecting, I suppose?" he asked.

"None, sir!"

"You do know where babies come from?"

"I have a pretty good idea, sir," I replied stiffly. "I grew up on a farm."

"Well, I have to ask. It's surprising how many girls don't have a notion. Anyway, it's nothing to worry about. The combination of hard work and emotional stress causes many girls to stop menstruating. Carry on."

I was surprised he didn't mention the food. It's enough to throw anyone off.

⟨•⟩

Somewhere in England
December 15, 1941
Dear Mother and Dad and Jack,

The meals here are disgusting. You hold out your
tin plate, and slap goes a piece of liver with a
greenish tinge. Then a ladle full of Brussels sprouts
is piled on that, then a helping of stewed prunes,
and finally runny custard poured over the whole
thing. Breakfast today was pancakes with one
lonely sardine on top!

In spite of the horrible food, I scrape my plate
clean. After marching ten miles I'll eat anything.
Our parade drills are quite professional now. I'll
bet I could take a step exactly twenty-seven inches
long if I were walking in my sleep! I can also snap
out quite a smart salute. I'm not sure who deserves
one, so I salute everyone in uniform just to be on
the safe side.

You should see the shocking way some girls
behave. They "go out saluting" for the fun of it —
marching up and down the street, giving the officers the old one-two, because it forces the officers
to salute back! They swagger around with the top
two buttons on their tunics undone, copying the
pilots. And they hate our regulation hats, so they
wear their tin helmets instead whenever they can
get away with it. It looks like a shiny halo, a lot
more flattering than the standard pie crust. Most
of them don't even want to be in the service, but
of course we aren't allowed to quit now. I can't
wait to finish my training and get out of here. I'm
praying for an operational station.

Did Mr. MacTavish put a banner headline

on the front page after Pearl Harbor? He'd better have, or I'll write him a stern letter. Everyone here is just giddy with delight. I think some of the Brits would like to send thank you letters to Hirohito for forcing the Yanks into it at last! Everyone is saying how Uncle Sam will show the Krauts a thing or two.

I'll spend Christmas Day here in the barracks. Those of us who can't go home will have a special dinner and show provided by a London troupe, but I'll be thinking of you every minute.

All my love, Rose

‹▾›

I tried to make my letters cheerful. Terrified that I would humiliate myself by crying, I found a trick that helped: I placed my hand to my throat, fingers spread, and bore down with my thumb and index finger just below my collarbone, pressing hard enough to cause pain. The tears still came into my eyes, but they didn't overflow. After a few seconds, the impulse to cry went back to its hiding place.

‹▾›

Touchwood
December 28, 1941
Dear Rose,

I hope you had a happy Christmas, my darling daughter. Did you receive my parcel in time? It was the one with soap and stockings and fruitcake. I'll mail one parcel each month and number them, so you can count that as number three.

We did our best to make merry, but it wasn't the same without you. On Christmas Day we listened to the King's message and felt pretty gloomy when he said the war might go on for several years. George Stewart came over for turkey dinner and I sent him home with a big box of leftovers. He's very lonely. Charlie was invited up to Edinburgh to spend Christmas with his navigator's family, so that's a relief as I hate to think of you young people so far from home at this time of year. His father is very proud of the boy, as we all are.

On Boxing Day we heard about the fall of Hong Kong. Bill Allen is over there. I saw him at home on leave before he sailed. The Allens are in a bad way but they are hoping that if Bill is alive, he will be treated well by the Japs. Sixteen hundred Canadians were taken, poor boys.

Last week the Touchwood girls decided to challenge the Australian airmen to a hockey game. Of course they could skate circles around the boys — most of the Aussies couldn't even stand up on skates. Finally they just gave up and scooted around the ice on their behinds. We almost died laughing.

Mr. MacTavish has hired a lady named Ida Flint. She's a widow, with one son in the navy. I met her when I dropped into the office last week to give Mr. MacTavish his fruitcake. She's a stout lady, quite red in the face, but pleasant enough. She said she'll type, answer the phone, and make coffee for "the old man," as she called him, although I doubt if he's older than she is.

We read in the *Times* that Anthony Davis was awarded his stripes, a nice Christmas present for his parents. But when I congratulated his mother

at Red Cross yesterday, she said her husband —
who was a conscientious objector in the last war
— is ready to disown Anthony. "Nothing will convince him that Tony isn't a coward, running off
to join the air force like the other lemmings," she
said. It takes all kinds, I guess.

It's minus thirty but I see that your father
finally got the truck started so we can drive into
town to pick up the mail. It really brightens
our day when June hands over a letter from you.
We think of you so often, Rosie, and miss you
so very much.

All our love, Mother XXOO

From the very first, I loved to march. It was like dancing, planting
my feet in measured lengths, swinging my hips a few inches to make
my skirt sway back and forth, lifting my arms to shoulder height.
When I caught a glimpse of the other girls, wheeling and turning
together like a ribbon tied to a stick, I saw their shining eyes and
rapt expressions.

On this frigid January day, we drew up before the examining
stand in perfect formation. My eyes were full of tears but my head
was high, my jaw clenched and my arms ramrod straight by my
sides. When the last pin was presented, I whooped and tossed my
hat into the air along with the others.

"Oh, Rose, you've been a brick." Shy little Daphne hugged me.
"I wish we had gotten the same posting." Daphne had been assigned
to work as a laundress, but she was ecstatic because her new station
was only three miles away from her home.

"Don't remind me, Daffy."

Yesterday the other girls had ripped open their envelopes with
feverish haste. I heard cries of glee and dismay around me as I

fumbled with the flap. My heart sank as I read the terse message: I was ordered to take another three months of training.

"But nobody else in the class has their props already," said Daphne, referring to the tiny set of propellers, which as Leading Aircraftwoman, I was now entitled to sew on my shoulders. "You skipped a whole rank! And nobody else had 98 percent in the technical exam! Lots of other girls wanted to train in photography."

"I guess so," I said doubtfully. "As soon as they found out I could use a camera and develop my own film, I was sunk."

◄▼►

This is only a temporary setback, I told myself. The men posted to air bases had to train for months. And there was certainly a lot to learn, just to become a lowly darkroom technician.

We began with instruction in the assembly of a camera, characteristics of film, types of paper, and properties of light. Then we went to work in the laboratory, illuminated with a dim red light, called the "screaming room" because of the women's reaction when their film didn't turn out. I remembered how I had cried when MacTavish once fired me for spoiling a roll of film. I could laugh about it now, just barely.

My newspaper experience was helpful, because I already knew how to remove the film from the camera in total darkness and develop it in a tank of chemicals, rotating the tank by hand with a crank. I knew how to print photographs, too, placing the negative in the enlarger, exposing the paper to light and bathing it in hydrochloric acid before rinsing it with water. Here I didn't hang the wet prints to dry, but fished them out of the tank with rubber tongs and flattened them against a huge revolving heated drum.

The new skill for me, and one that I enjoyed the most, was piecing together aerial maps. All the photographs were printed four inches square, and overlapped in a diagonal pattern to form an aerial view of the landscape below, as if a deck of cards had fallen over sideways. The edges were almost invisible, and the scale so accurate that the entire thing could be superimposed over a map with all the roads and railways matching.

I was so absorbed during the day that I didn't think about anything but my work. At night, I was tired enough to fall asleep before the homesickness really sunk its teeth into me.

9

I tore open the envelope and pulled out my orders. Closing my eyes, I said a silent prayer before unfolding the stiff white sheet and reading: "Report to the Central Interpretation Unit, RAF Medmenham, 1300 hours, April 1, 1942."

My disappointment was so intense that I felt dizzy. I raised my hand and pressed my fingers under my collarbone. Now I understood what that final interview was about, when they asked all those questions concerning family and friends. They were going to park me in some stuffy intelligence office. I'd never even heard of a place called Medmenham.

I requested a meeting with my commanding officer.

"You know it's bad form to question a posting," he said with a stern expression. "You should consider yourself lucky indeed to be assigned to this position. For one thing, it will put you in line for promotion. Many British girls would jump at the opportunity." There was a faint emphasis on the word "British."

He looked at my face and seemed to relent. "Don't take it so hard, Jolliffe. It's quite an honour to be selected for intelligence work. We can't all fight the Hun, you know."

⋆▾⋆

The journey to my new headquarters, located in the Thames River valley forty miles northwest of London, took place on a typically sodden spring day. The landscape shimmered under a sheet of rain like a watercolour painting.

As the train jogged along, I closed my eyes against the deluge that poured down the windowpanes of my compartment and visualized the farm at this time of the year: new calves frisking around the pasture on legs like spindles, flocks of geese honking their way north, Dad's rubber boots sticking out from under the tractor.

With my eyes closed, I fingered the set of propellers on my shoulder. My new rank made me feel a little better. Every recruit began as an Aircraftwoman 2nd Class, called an Acey-Deucey, and after basic training was promoted to Aircraftwoman 1st Class. I had gone straight up to the third rank: Leading Aircraftwoman, or LAC. There were still nine ranks to go ending with wing officer, but I was glad to have made it this far.

As the train jerked to a halt, I opened my eyes. "Is your journey really necessary?" asked a threatening message on the wall. How I wished it weren't. All signs had been removed to thwart the invading Germans, but I had counted the stops on my fingers and knew this was my destination, the town of Marlow.

I slung my gas mask container over one shoulder and struggled off the train with my kit bag. Why did they make us carry so darned much stuff? A canvas tube tied around the top with a rope, the kit bag contained my shoes, clothing, rain cape, and ground sheet. When my helmet fell out of the bag, I resisted the impulse to kick it across the platform.

"LAC Jolliffe?" A young transport driver with acne was walking toward me. I dropped the heavy bag on my foot and winced as I returned his salute.

"The lorry is around the corner, ma'am. Let me help you with that." He picked up the bag and set off while I trotted along behind him, then hoisted myself into the cab of the transport truck while he loaded several boxes from the train.

We left the town and headed west along a winding road that followed the northern bank of the Thames River through a dense forest. The showers ended abruptly, as they often did in England, and the sun broke through the clouds, piercing the dark green leaves and dappling the road with golden coins of light.

As always, the sunshine lifted my spirits. Through an opening in the trees, I caught a glimpse of the Thames, the opalescent water gliding past the low riverbanks dotted with flocks of woolly sheep like huge fluffy dandelions gone to seed.

After a few miles, the driver turned off the main road and changed gears as the truck laboured up a steep, narrow incline. We broke through the trees at last and my new home came into view. The driver glanced at me with a smile. "Here we are, ma'am."

Standing on the brow of a hill overlooking the river was an enormous white two-storey mansion, topped with red brick chimneys and a row of crenellated stone teeth. Square towers rose from both ends, and a wing ran straight back from each tower so the house formed a three-sided rectangle, open at the back. Across the full length of the ground floor, a series of arched openings gave it a Mediterranean appearance.

Emerald lawns surrounded the house, sloping down to the river's edge. Magnificent beech and willow trees were scattered across the grass. Long flowerbeds bursting with Wordsworth's yellow daffodils lined the pebbled driveway.

"We don't really work here, do we?" I asked in amazement, looking around for the ubiquitous metal huts.

The driver chuckled as the truck pulled to a stop at the front door. "Yes, ma'am, there's room for offices and living quarters as well. The darkroom technicians bunk in the north wing, under the clock tower."

I sat motionless, still staring in disbelief. "Is it very old?"

"No, ma'am, it was only built around 1900." The driver put the truck into neutral and leaned back in his seat, assuming a self-important expression. "Danesfield House was built by the heir to the Sunlight soap company. He hired an architect to design this place in the Italian Renaissance style. It went through two or three owners before the war broke out, then the RAF requisitioned the house and all sixty acres."

"It's gorgeous."

"It's pretty," he said scornfully, "but it isn't great architecture or anything. There are follies all over England — that's when some-body with plenty of dosh decides to build a monument to himself. Locals call this one The Wedding Cake."

I tried to view the house critically, but I still saw a fantastic fairytale castle. "Why is the stone so white?"

"It's chalkstone, a type of rock native to this area. The entire village of Medmenham down the road is made of chalkstone."

He pointed toward the door. "Your section officer is waiting for you, ma'am."

I clambered out of the truck, hoisted my kit bag over my shoulder, and mounted a set of broad white stone steps to the grand entrance where a woman stood, a pleasant-faced officer about forty-five years old with steel-grey hair and spectacles.

"Welcome to RAF Medmenham. I'm Section Officer Hamilton." She returned my salute and led me into a front hall the size of our barn. I had another one of my Alice sensations as I felt myself shrinking to the size of a mouse under the twenty-foot arched ceiling.

Up the curved mahogany staircase we marched, and down a long hallway leading to the north wing. Upstairs most of the carved wood panelling was draped with sheets, and the furniture had been removed. The walls showed lighter rectangles where paintings and tapestries had once hung. There were no floor coverings, and our heels clattered on the large square flagstones.

Mrs. Hamilton turned and headed down another long hallway before opening the door to a palatial bedroom. Even the metal bunk beds along the walls didn't diminish the elegance of the room, with its ornate mouldings and leaded glass windows.

"You'll kip over there," Mrs. Hamilton said, pointing to a lower bunk. "The others are on shift in the darkroom. I'll brief you after you've put away your things. You've already been added to tomorrow's duty roster."

After dumping my meagre belongings into the military chest at the foot of my bunk, I was taken into Mrs. Hamilton's office where I signed The Official Secrets Act. I was not to breathe a word about my work to anyone — not loved ones, friends, or acquaintances — neither in letters nor in conversation. If I breached this oath, I would be court-martialled.

Then Mrs. Hamilton briefed me on RAF Medmenham. When the war began, photo reconnaissance was rarely used. But after the continent fell, there was no way to find out what the enemy was doing except to spy on them from the air.

To minimize the usual wrangling among the army, navy, and air force, a single Photo Reconnaissance Unit was created to fly the planes and take the photos, and a Central Interpretation Unit to decipher the results. The flying unit was located on the nearby riverbank and this luxurious house was fitted out with all the necessary photographic equipment.

The head of the interpretation unit was RAF Group Captain Martin Shoreham, a First World War veteran with a sterling reputation. I met him when Mrs. Hamilton escorted me to the south wing, down more hallways as long as runways. "He has an artificial hand," she warned, before opening his office door. "Please don't stare at it."

Although simply furnished, the commander's office was an elegant chamber with an elaborate plaster frieze around the ceiling, and a pair of French doors that opened onto a stone balustrade overlooking the sweep of the Thames.

"Glad to have you on board, Jolliffe," he said. A vigorous man with a chest like a rain barrel and a huge RAF moustache, he rose to his feet with his left hand behind his back, smiling at me like a friendly uncle.

"We're completely swamped. We've doubled our staff in the past year — we have forty interpreters now, and we could probably use another hundred. It's very difficult to find the right people. What part of Canada are you from?"

"Western Canada, sir. The prairies."

"Excellent. I haven't been farther west than Ottawa, myself. Perhaps after the war. Welcome to Medmenham. Mrs. Hamilton will take good care of you. Dismissed."

We returned to the north wing, where a monstrous bathroom had been converted into a darkroom by removing the toilet and bathtub and adding several large sinks. On the floor was an intricate Grecian key pattern of dark blue and white mosaic tiles, repeated at waist level around all four walls.

I forced myself to concentrate as Mrs. Hamilton began my briefing. "As soon as a recce aircraft lands, the rolls of film are rushed here straight away, and we develop and print two sets of photographs." At first I was confused, thinking she had called them "wrecky" aircraft. Then I realized this was air force slang, short for reconnaissance.

"One set of prints goes to the first phase interpreters for a quick once-over. Next they are passed to second phase interpretation for the next twenty-four hours. If something suspicious is found, the photos go to third phase. That requires the most intense scrutiny by subject specialists, who are divided into fifteen sections: aircraft, bomb damage, camouflage, and so forth."

I listened intently, trying to remember everything.

"We also receive negatives and prints from every air base in the country. These are filed here in our central library, and reviewed frequently. For example, if a new factory is detected, the industrial section will request all the cover from that area be brought out for another examination."

Mrs. Hamilton examined me over her spectacles. "I'm warning you, it can be very high-pressure. You'll know what I mean when you have two or three officers hanging fire outside the darkroom door. In a crisis, they may want to see the negatives first. Or they may want a quick-and-dirty. That's when we print the wet negatives under cellophane, without waiting for them to dry."

"Yes, ma'am." I felt charged with duty and responsibility.

"These rolls were brought in last night. I'll walk you through the procedure."

◆▼◆

Touchwood
April 27, 1942
To my very own Sweetheart of the Forces,

We saw the first robin today — that's ten days earlier than last year. The road is pure mud so we've been sticking close to home until it dries up. I cut a bouquet of pussy willows and your mother has them on the kitchen table.

I'm hoping to get an early start on the seeding since Jack isn't around to help. I wanted to keep him here, but I couldn't say no when all of his friends have gone. He's hankering to fly a Spit, but I told him not to count his chickens. His last letter was from Trenton, Ontario. He's not much for writing, but he dashes off the odd postcard.

George Stewart and I have worked out a plan to help each other this year. We'll use both seeders on his place, then come over to ours. He said Charlie has been posted to a new station in the north of England. Charlie isn't allowed to say where, but before he left they worked out a rough code. I can't tell you what it is, or the censors will be cutting holes in this letter, too.

There are planes buzzing around all the time now that the new relief airfield went in next to the Stewart place. The base built a hangar and radio shack there, even a barracks building. I was worried about the cattle but they've gotten used to the racket now. Two airmen came over this morning looking for something to do, so I gave them a couple of .22s and told them to shoot gophers. I hope they don't shoot each other.

Did the British newspapers report anything about our plebiscite on conscription? Everyone in English Canada was in favour but the Quebeckers voted no almost to a man. MacTavish tried to defend them in an editorial, but he made himself pretty unpopular down at the Legion hall, not that he cares.

I wish you could describe your work but we know it's top secret. We're glad you've been posted to a safe place away from London. That's where the balloon will go up if things get worse.
Your loving Dad

⸎

Somewhere in England
May 1, 1942
Dear Mother and Dad,

Today I met a real lord! His name is Lord Alfred March. One of the public relations officers was showing him around, and he introduced me by saying: "Leading Aircraftwoman Rose Jolliffe is a real asset to the Commonwealth." For the life of me, I didn't know whether I should salute, shake hands, or curtsy! I gave a nervous nod and said how do you do.

He didn't look very lordly. Tall and thin, with a bowler hat and a fusty black suit, satin waistcoat, and bow tie. Maybe he was trying to imitate Churchill. He had lots of room for a bow tie because his neck was so long and skinny.

After they left the room, one of the other girls told me that Lord March has contributed his entire fortune to the war effort and turned his estate in Devonshire into a home for war orphans. I felt awful then, judging him by his appearance!

I go for long walks whenever I'm not on duty. The countryside around here is so pretty. I amuse myself by trying to identify the unfamiliar flowers. The barrage balloons look like big silver jackfish floating in the sky. I sat on a stile last night to watch the sunset, and the bottoms of the balloons turned the loveliest shade of pink.

All my love, Rose

10

My pupils felt permanently dilated, like a cat's eyes in the night. I now spent most of my daylight hours in the windowless darkroom, and emerged only after sunset into full blackout.

I remembered the old saying about a soldier's life: *10 percent hell, the rest sit around and wait.* When the weather was good and the recce pilots were flying, the lab people were working under intense pressure. Either we were making prints, extra prints, and then more prints because another section wanted copies, or the pilots were weathered out and we were killing time by cleaning equipment and checking chemicals.

Today I was in the print library, filing a batch of photographs with purple fingers. All the girls had them, because the developing fluid stained our skin a gentian colour. Since our work was secret, if anyone asked us about our hands, we were supposed to say we had been dyeing the curtains in our quarters.

My thoughts were as dismal as the black, roiling clouds covering the sky. The Allied situation was grim. Our troops in North

Africa were being driven back, fighting fiercely for each yard of sand. The Germans had penetrated deep into Russia. The Japanese had conquered the entire British Empire in the east, and the Americans were battling for supremacy in the Pacific.

I had quietly celebrated my twenty-first birthday the previous day, in sharp contrast to the joyful occasions at home with cake and presents. I had allowed myself the luxury of shedding a few tears into my pillow before falling asleep.

If I had stayed in Touchwood, I would now be old enough to join the women's air force. The Canadian women were doing a stellar job, but none of them had been allowed to leave the country yet because of fears for their safety.

Nobody mentioned it — the subject was taboo — but I couldn't help secretly wondering what would happen if the unthinkable happened and Germany won this war. Would the conquerors allow the Canadians to return home? Or would my uniform mean spending years in a prison camp, or even worse? It was too terrifying to contemplate.

I heaved another deep sigh and picked up the next stack of photographs. They weren't top priority — a pilot had used the last of his film on his way home across northern France. The photos had been examined and were going into a cardboard filing box, where they would stay until after the war.

The European fields were most unlike the neat squares back home. They were a hodgepodge of shades and textures: a crazy quilt, with rivers, hedges, and roads featherstitching them together like dark and light embroidery floss.

These photos were obliques, taken from a side angle as the plane banked at low altitude. I wondered how our own farm would look from the air. I could see rivers and roads, trees and roofs. The bare fields showed the parallel marks of cultivation where the blades had cut into the earth.

As I placed each photograph in the box, I studied it closely. I had a niggling feeling that something was out of place — what was it? Spreading the photos out on a wooden table, I took up a magnifying glass.

An hour later, I was standing in Mrs. Hamilton's tiny office. "Excuse me, Section Officer, but I couldn't help noticing something odd when I was filing these photographs."

She listened to my explanation, then pushed back her chair. "I don't know what you're talking about, quite frankly, but any discrepancies should be noted."

We marched down the long hallway to Shoreham's office. Mrs. Hamilton gave a gentle knock, and we were told to enter. Shoreham was seated at his desk in front of the oversized French windows. The dark clouds had parted, and a shaft of pale afternoon sunlight fell over his shoulder.

Two other people were present. One of them was the head of the camouflage section, a tall, dark-haired officer in his mid-thirties named Gideon Fowler. I knew him by sight, and only because he was so handsome it was impossible not to notice him. He reminded me of the actor Robert Taylor, right down to the pencil-thin moustache, the cleft in his chin, and the sleekness of his glossy black hair. Several girls in the darkroom pretended to swoon behind his back whenever he walked past.

The other was Janet Withers-Brown, one of the officers who worked in camouflage, a fair-haired woman with large front teeth. I had taken an instant dislike to her when she came into the darkroom asking for a set of prints. She had spoken to me quite rudely, as if I were one of her servants.

"Leading Aircraftwoman Jolliffe found something unusual, sir. I thought you should be informed."

"Quite right, Section Officer. You may return to your duties." She saluted and left the room.

"Let's have a look." Shoreham took the sheaf of photographs from me and placed them on his desk.

I could feel my face beginning to burn. Bad enough explaining to Shoreham, but making a fool of myself in front of two other officers as well? If only Janet what's-her-name would wipe that smirk off her face.

I pointed at the photograph on the top of the pile. "It's this farm here, sir," I said in a low voice. "His rows aren't straight."

As soon as I spoke the words, I knew I sounded ridiculous. Janet made a snorting sound, then pretended to cough.

Shoreham leaned back in his chair and smiled at me with his usual avuncular expression. "All right, let's hear what you have to say. Start at the beginning."

Standing rigidly at attention, I took a deep breath. "Well, sir, you can see that the farms in this area are prosperous."

"How do you know?"

"Because of the size of the barns, and the number of outbuildings. And the trees and bushes are larger, which means this area probably has more moisture. The soil is different, too."

"In what way?" Shoreham didn't even look down at the photographs; he was still watching me.

"I compared these photographs with some others that were taken farther south a few minutes earlier. It was close to noon. I could tell by the short shadows. Since they were on the same strip of film, the exposure would be similar. But the colour of the soil on these farms to the south is quite a bit lighter. Probably it contains more sand. In this area to the north, the soil is black. It's likely very good topsoil."

The eyes of both men were fixed on me now. Janet was examining the sole of her shoe. "I might be completely wrong, sir. I'm sure you have people who can give you this kind of information. I just couldn't help noticing ..."

"Go on." Shoreham's tone was encouraging.

I pointed with my purple fingertip. "Well, on every farm, you can see the furrows quite clearly in the cultivated fields. Here, on this farm, the one with the really large barn, the rows aren't straight."

"And what do you think that indicates?"

"All the farms except this one have perfectly straight furrows. That takes a bit of skill. I don't know if it's the same in France, but where I come from, it's a matter of pride to make your rows as straight as possible. On this farm, sir, the one with the biggest barn, the furrows are really cock-eyed. They are wobbling all over the place, as if a complete amateur ploughed this field."

There. I had said it. Now he could tell me to go and jump in the river, and I would gladly go.

Shoreham took up a magnifying glass in his right hand and braced the photograph on his desk with the piece of flesh-coloured celluloid that had replaced his left hand. I tried not to stare at it while he studied the photo.

I spoke again, to cover my awkwardness. "You won't be able to see it in a couple of weeks, because the grain will have grown up by then. It's just after seeding, when the earth is still bare, that you can see the rows. That's when the farmers back home like to drive around the countryside and look at each other's fields, to see what kind of a job the others have done." I knew I was talking too much and stopped abruptly.

"As you said, perhaps an inexperienced farmer sowed this field." Shoreham angled the photograph toward the shaft of sunlight slanting across his desk.

"That would be the logical explanation," I hastened to agree. "Perhaps the farmer is away, or unable to work. But in a farming community, usually if the man of the house isn't fit, the neighbours would help out by doing the seeding."

Shoreham lowered the magnifying glass. "Anything else?"

"No, sir. Well, there is one thing, but there could be a dozen reasons for that. You see this road to the farm is a bit wider than the other roads in the area — as if it's been built up."

He shuffled the photographs into a neat pile and rose from his chair. "Righto. We'll send these back to the experts again and see what they can make of them. Thank you for your observations, Jolliffe. We'll keep you posted."

We exchanged salutes and I left the room without glancing at the others. I hurried down the hall toward the darkroom, thankful to escape. I imagined the others were examining the photographs and laughing. Probably Janet was making some snide remark right now.

◆▼◆

For the next few days, I paid close attention to developing my prints and didn't even allow myself to glance at the results before distributing them to the various sections.

Late one afternoon there was a knock on the darkroom door and Gideon Fowler's head appeared around the corner. "You were right about that farm, Jolliffe. We diverted an aircraft yesterday to take another dekko, and we found a convoy of trucks heading toward the barn. Apparently the Jerries are using it as a fuel depot. One of them must have cultivated that field and botched the job." I noticed how much younger he looked when he smiled, despite the furrow between his eyebrows.

Summoned to Shoreham's office the next afternoon, I walked down the hall slowly. Even though I had been right once, I wouldn't be surprised if he warned me to remember my rank.

When I knocked and entered the room, Shoreham gestured to a chair. "Sit down, Jolliffe. Did Fowler inform you about your crooked rows?"

"Yes, sir." I sat down stiffly on the edge of the wooden chair, knees and heels together in military precision.

He consulted a buff-coloured file folder on his desk. "What you did constituted fairly elementary interpretation — are you aware of that?"

"No, sir."

He squinted at me, as if trying to read my mind. "Interpretation requires a distinct set of skills. The primary difficulty for most people is learning how to see the world by looking straight down on it. In order to reorient themselves to do this, our interpreters have to be reasonably intelligent, and also quite imaginative."

He studied my file again. "I think we can assume from your examination results that you're intelligent — do you also have imagination?"

"I don't know, sir."

"We don't want too much imagination, you understand. We don't want people thinking they see tanks under every hedgerow."

"Yes, sir."

"And we need people who have an excellent memory, and an eye for detail. Half the battle is remembering things from a previous set of photographs — things that didn't make sense at the time, but take on new meaning when they are seen again."

"Yes, sir."

"We want people who can work under pressure, a great deal more than you are experiencing now. Many of our photographs are interpreted while important officers are waiting for the results. But we can't rush through our work, or lose our concentration. Do you think you are capable of that?"

"Well, sir, I was accustomed to deadlines when I was working for a newspaper." I stopped and bit my lip. "Of course, that wasn't nearly as critical."

Shoreham smiled. "No, although your newspaper work was probably more exciting. The thing is, photo interpretation is boring, sometimes quite deadly. You have to spend long hours hunched over a desk — it can be very tiring. The blink of an eye, the lapse of attention for a single second, seeing without understanding — any of these could result in a vital element escaping detection."

"Yes, sir."

Shoreham seemed to be thinking aloud as he stared at the file in his lap. "Still, you may have the one quality that we can't do without, and that's intuition. Our best interpreters can sense when something is not quite right — much like the feeling you had when you saw your crooked rows, Jolliffe. Those rows were what we call a hot item — that is, a bit that doesn't belong."

"Thank you, sir."

"I'll give you an example. Last year one of our interpreters picked out a hot item — a field of craters. He noticed that the earth wasn't scattered to one side, as it is when the shell hits the ground at an angle. Instead, the earth was thrown out evenly around the holes, making them look like doughnuts. Jolliffe, the enemy had occupied that area without our knowledge. They had shovelled out the craters by hand and were using them as foxholes. By counting the holes, we were able to estimate the size of their division."

"That's amazing, sir."

"Indeed." He sat for a few minutes, studying the file. To keep from staring at his hand, I admired the view out the long windows while I reflected on the cleverness of the Germans. It was an overcast day but the river reflected its ghostly light through the green trees.

Shoreham spoke again, a little awkwardly. "Jolliffe, naturally I'm aware that your home is in Canada. You didn't enlist to, er, join a boyfriend or anything of that nature?"

"No, sir! I enlisted because I want to win the war, sir!"

"Excellent." Shoreham slapped the file folder shut. "How would you like to take our three-week photo interpretation course? I'm warning you, it's quite difficult."

"I would like that very much, sir!"

"We have a new course beginning the day after tomorrow. It's a good opportunity for you, since our interpreters are commissioned officers. If you pass the course, you'll receive an automatic promotion to assistant section officer and be assigned to camouflage, under Gideon Fowler. His department is very short-staffed."

"Thank you for the opportunity, sir! I'll do my best, sir!" I jumped to my feet and snapped out a salute. I couldn't keep my face from breaking into a grin. Shoreham returned my salute, smiling back at me.

11

"Class, please be seated."

I pulled out a chair at the end of a long wooden table where five other women were taking their places. I had woken long before reveille to polish my buttons and shine my shoes. Unfortunately, they were already covered with mud after I had rushed through a downpour to the metal Nissen hut where the class was being held. Since the unit had swelled, dozens of these huts, looking like giant corrugated metal pipes cut in half lengthwise, covered the green lawns behind the house.

The instructor passed sets of aerial photographs down the table. As I took them from his hand, I noticed that mine wasn't quite steady. The other women were older than me, and, as my father would say, a different breed of cat. I listened to their accents as they chatted and knew they were among the upper class, typical of most people who made it into intelligence work.

I could hear MacTavish's voice as if he were growling into my ear. "Those hush-hush boys are all peers of the realm and what-not because they have the brass to buy their way out of the dirty fighting. You won't find Lord High Cockalorum up to his balls in mud!"

If MacTavish could only see me now, I thought with an inward chuckle, *rubbing elbows with high society.* I straightened in my chair as the instructor spoke. "Right, let's begin by learning the difference between roads, railways, and rivers." Although all three showed as lines, roads had right angles, railways were curved, and rivers were crossed with bridges.

Then we turned to airfields, and counted airplanes, including those hiding in the shadows of hangars. "How many have you found?" the instructor asked the young woman next to me, her auburn braids arranged in a coronet.

"Six planes, sir!"

The instructor frowned. "Six is correct, but give that answer in front of a flying man, and he'd have your head. The word 'plane' is strictly for civilians. We call them 'aircraft.'"

I was at a distinct disadvantage, since the others had travelled on the continent and were familiar with the European landscape. I shook my head when the instructor handed me a photograph and asked me what country it came from.

"Anyone else?"

Several hands shot up. "It's England, sir, because traffic is travelling on the left!" I blushed with shame.

We learned to count ships by size, being unable yet to recognize types. Again, I floundered when it came to ships, having never laid eyes on one until I sailed to England. The instructor clicked his tongue with disapproval when I referred to the back of a ship instead of the stern.

But I redeemed myself the next day when he asked whether a train was moving or stationary. I knew it was moving, because I had so often seen the way the shadow from the smokestack trails against the snow.

Shadows were vital, the instructor explained. And since reconnaissance photographs weren't taken unless the weather was fine, every single one of them had shadows.

I learned to place the prints with the shadows falling toward me. Strangely, if the photographs were turned in the opposite direction, so the shadows were falling away from me, an optical illusion made rivers look like ridges, and hills look like valleys.

On the third day we were introduced to the most significant tool of photo interpretation — an odd little device called a stereoscope that resembled a pair of eyeglasses set in a rectangular piece of metal and supported by four legs.

"Look at me and close one eye," the instructor said. "Now do the same thing with the other eye. You see the same thing, but from a slightly different angle. Look at me with both eyes, and the two images are fused together.

"Stereo photography is based on the same principle. The two photographs are taken from the aircraft a split second apart. When we put them under a stereoscope, the left eye looks at the left photograph and the right eye at the right photograph. Together the images blend together and you'll see it in three dimensions, just as you do in real life."

I placed a pair of prints under the stereoscope, but I continued to see two separate pictures. "Keep jiggling them back and forth," the instructor said. Almost simultaneously, several women exclaimed aloud.

I pushed my photographs around miserably. *I'll never be able to do this,* I thought. Just then, the prints merged into one, and the buildings leaped up toward me so powerfully that I gasped and jerked back my head.

The instructor gave a rare smile. "Extraordinary, isn't it?"

"Yes, sir!" I said. "It's like standing on a cliff and looking down into a valley!"

The stereoscope opened a new world to me. I began to see the earth the way a bird might, a sparrow fluttering over the treetops, or a heron swooping over a lake. More like a hawk, searching for its prey in the long grass.

But it wasn't until the third week that reconnaissance really came alive. "Today you will meet one of the men who is risking his life to bring these photographs to us," the instructor said. "Pilot Officer Adrian Stone is one of our chief recce pilots. He's older than average, because he acts as his own commander. He must have both the steady nerves of a bomber pilot and the reflexes of a fighter pilot."

The instructor spoke very seriously, as if to impress us with the importance of his words. "The recce pilot's only defences are speed and altitude. If the enemy spots our man from the ground, their fighters can't get up fast enough to catch him. But if he runs into a fighter in the air — well, there's not much he can do since he flies unarmed. His aircraft has been stripped of all weapons in order to store extra fuel for the long flights."

The classroom was very quiet. When the door opened, all eyes turned toward the man who entered. Adrian Stone was a stocky Englishman with blue eyes, a blunt nose and the thick-skinned, ruddy complexion so common in this country. He was a teacher by profession, which explained why he appeared so comfortable in the classroom. He perched one hip on the desk.

"What we do isn't glamorous," he began. "Half the time the bomb boys are ticked off because our photos show they missed the bloody target and blew up a farmer's field instead. And the rest of the time, the interpreters are annoyed at us because we wobbled our wings."

Several women chuckled and the instructor shot them a stern look.

"When I first receive my assignment, intelligence informs me exactly what needs to be covered. In most cases I don't know the significance of my target, so I can't reveal any secrets if I'm captured."

I hadn't considered this aspect of reconnaissance. A horrible vision arose of the Gestapo trying to extract information from the poor man. How long would it take before they concluded that he didn't know anything?

"When I reach the target, I likely can't even see what I'm shooting. From twenty thousand feet, the earth resembles a pale green blur. On a clear day, I can see entire countries. If there are aircraft down below, they look like silver minnows darting around at the bottom of a pool."

He walked across the front of the room. "I suppose you've studied stereo viewing?"

We nodded our heads and murmured yes.

"To obtain the photos needed for stereo, the pilot must fly absolutely level across the target, holding his wings straight and accounting for wind drift. If the target is crooked, a shoreline for example, we shoot it in legs."

He picked up a piece of chalk and drew a zigzag pattern on the blackboard. "We make one run across a straight length of shoreline, turn the camera off to save film, circle around and come back along the next leg, and so on.

"The most difficult target is a point target, which is essentially a single spot on the map." He ground the chalk into a circle. "Unfortunately it's the point targets like factories that are the best defended." The chalk snapped in half. Adrian picked up the pieces and brushed the chalk off his hands.

"Any questions?"

The auburn-haired girl, whose name was Sally Fairbairn, raised her hand. "What if the enemy sees you?"

Adrian smiled. "Then you bloody well head for mother! Seriously, the main drawback with reconnaissance flying is that you only have one pair of eyes. Have you heard of recce neck?"

We shook our heads.

"It's a stiff neck that we get from swivelling our heads around like a pinwheel in a strong wind!"

There was general laughter. Even the instructor chuckled.

"We're fortunate to have the best aircraft. We use Spitfires for the most part, but the new Mossie — that's the Mosquito — it's an incredible piece of work, faster than the Spit and double the range. The other day I took some photos of a German fighter who was trying to claw his way up to me, but I just sat on my tail and walked away."

I raised my hand. "Isn't it awfully cold up there?"

Adrian glanced at the Canada badges on my shoulders and smiled again. "You'd better hope your heating system doesn't fail, because it's seventy degrees below zero up there. Once my heater conked out, and when I got back to base I looked like Jack Frost with a beard of icicles hanging off my oxygen mask. The worst part was that my windscreen frosted over and every time I scratched a hole in the ice I thought I saw a Messerschmitt!"

A couple of women chuckled. I didn't laugh, thinking that it made a funny story but must have been terrifying at the time.

"We wear protective flying suits called Sidcots, named after the Australian who invented them, Sid Cotton. He was a real reconnaissance pioneer. It was Sid who believed women would make excellent interpreters because, as he put it, they need the patience of Job and the skills of a good sock darner."

I glanced at the other women, who were beaming with satisfaction. It was a nice change to be told that we could perform this job as well as men. Even around my station, there were more than a few disgruntled male officers who firmly believed that women should be confined to the typing pool.

"Have you ever done any dicing?" asked the instructor.

"Only when I first started flying reconnaissance. Then one of my best friends learned the hard way, and I decided there was no point in going after him. Does everyone know the term?"

We shook our heads.

"Dicing with the devil is a gambling expression. It's slang for low-level flying, strictly against orders, but you can imagine how frustrating it is when clouds cover the target. Sometimes they're so low even the birds are walking! It's very tempting to stick your head under the blanket. Unfortunately, that's when you're likely to have it blown off. We've lost more pilots through dicing than any other way." For the first time, a hint of sadness crossed his face.

"Don't you wish you had guns, so you could defend yourself?" one woman asked.

He shook his head. "Speaking for myself, no. This is one of the few front-line jobs in which we are not required to kill."

"How many missions have you flown?" asked Sally.

"Oh, I'm considered an old man now, because I've been flying recce since the war started. Probably taken a thousand rolls of film." He bent over and pointed at his bushy head. "See this grey hair? It wasn't here when I started flying."

More laughter. I appreciated the way he kept the mood light, although everyone knew the subject was deadly serious.

"How do you know if you've flown a successful mission?" someone else asked.

"You never know for sure until you see the photos at your debriefing, about two hours after you land. Sometimes you get a nasty shock. Once I brought back a full roll that was perfectly aligned over the target, and there were black streaks over the negatives. I was in the darkroom cursing out the techs when my mechanic informed me that I had an oil leak spraying right across the lens."

"Do you ever have any pleasant surprises?" I asked, forgetting to hold up my hand.

Adrian nodded. "Yes, although not as often as I wish. One day when clouds wouldn't let me cover the target, I used up my film coming home over the Channel. Now here's where you interpreters can take the credit. Some clever chap spotted a man on the open sea in a rubber dinghy! He had lost radio contact before bailing out of his fighter. He was picked up several hours later, practically frozen stiff, but damned lucky to be alive. The chances of finding him were next to nil." He glanced at his watch. "I must shove off — I'm headed out this afternoon on a mission over Brest, to see what they're keeping in dry dock. Brest or Bust, as the saying goes."

He made it sound so easy. I knew Brest was one of the most heavily defended seaports in German hands. While the instructor thanked the pilot, I gazed at him in open admiration.

I won't let him down, I vowed silently. *I'll study those photos until my eyes wear holes in them, if that's what it takes.*

◀▼▶

The final examination loomed. I took my aircraft and ship identification manuals to bed with me every night and crammed until my eyes danced. "I'm beginning to see ghostly shapes floating in thin air," I told Sally.

"I say, are you any good at jigsaw puzzles?" she asked.

"My mother and I have probably done hundreds. Why?"

"I was talking to one of the interpreters, and he said that's a sure sign. Apparently interpretation doesn't have anything to do with intelligence — it all depends on whether you have the mind of a jigsaw puzzler! I do hope he's right."

12

I was bone tired at the end of my shift, but not too weary to put away my instruments, caressing each one as I did.

How happy I had been to get them — soft lead pencils, grease pencils that showed white against the dark photographs, scissors, small knife, compass, protractor, slide rule, and my very own stereoscope, all carefully packed into a hard-sided leather case. I was almost as proud of them as I was of the thin stripe on my sleeve.

I had been a photographic interpreter for one month. The work was far more demanding than anything I had ever done. We worked around the clock in shifts to keep up with the flow of photographs, which rolled in unceasingly from reconnaissance units across the country. By the end of my shift, my eyes sometimes blurred and the images dissolved into meaningless shapes.

It was generally accepted that the camouflage section had one of the more difficult jobs. Not only did we have to calculate the significance of a tiny speck on a piece of paper, but it was a speck disguised by all the cunning resources of the enemy.

And they were cunning. Runways painted with dark green stripes to look like hedges on a flat field. Shipping docks draped with seaweed. Aircraft hidden inside fake houses, complete with window boxes full of flowers.

Although I had a lot to learn, my skills were growing. I counted on the support of my commanding officer, Gideon Fowler, who stopped by my desk a couple of times a day. "Everything all right here, Jolliffe?"

I knew he spoke to everyone in our section the same way, but I always smiled when I answered, "Yes, sir." It was so nice to hear a friendly voice. His was deep and warm and rich, what Sally called a BBC voice.

"He's a career officer, a real pukka sahib type," she said. "Went into the air force straight out of Cambridge, then married well. It doesn't hurt to have an RAF air commodore for a father-in-law. He and his wife have a country estate, two sons whose names were put down for Eton before they were born, you know the sort of thing."

I didn't know the sort of thing, but I could guess. Apparently MacTavish was right — you had to have connections to become an intelligence officer in the British armed forces. If I hadn't noticed those crooked rows, I'd probably have spent the war up to my elbows in purple developing fluid.

Take Janet Withers-Brown, the only other woman in camouflage. Before the war she had spent two years at a finishing school in Switzerland. Even her uniform was posh, with a silk tie and gold cufflinks bearing her family's crest. Not that she was under-qualified. Her interpretation had uneven results, but she was occasionally astute. It was Janet who determined that a dozen aircraft sitting in a snowy field weren't aircraft at all — just the shapes of wings and tails and fuselages carved into the snow by those diabolical Huns.

Janet barely spoke to me unless it was to insult me. Fortunately she wasn't around all the time since her family estate was only a dozen miles down the river, and she went home at every opportunity to visit her prize-winning thoroughbred Arabian horse,

Crusader. Janet even looked like a horse. Her dishwater-coloured hair was cut in an ear-length bob that made her long face look longer. When she laughed, she drew back her upper lip and showed her gums in a way that reminded me of Buckshot when he shied at a rock on the road.

"How's our little Colonial?" Janet would ask in her nasal voice when I came into the room. Or, with a theatrical laugh: "Find anything suspicious in the manure patch today, Jolliffe?"

"Don't pay any attention to her," Sally advised. "Every woman in the place knows Miss Over-and-Under is an absolute horror."

"Why do you call her that?"

"It's her hyphenated name, darling, like a double-barrelled shotgun. And she isn't terribly clever. She must have been the inspiration for that waffy song, you know the one." She sang loudly, and off-key:

> I'll sit on the commander's knee,
> I'll make him endless cups of tea,
> That's how I'll get my LAC,
> It's crafty but it's done!

I laughed. I couldn't picture Janet sitting on anything except a saddle, but Sally's jokes always made me feel better.

Sally was twenty-six years old and came from a wealthy family, although she didn't put on the dog like Janet. She had attended art school in London before the war, and now worked in the model section downstairs, creating scale models of towns, seaports, and other military targets. Since the first day she had been at loggerheads with the brass, who were deeply suspicious of anyone possessing an artistic temperament. They referred to the artists as "mouse-milkers" because of their fascination with miniatures.

"Soames peered at me through his monocle the other day and asked me if I'd ever done any nude modelling in art school!" Sally said. "The dirty-minded old sod! He's your typical First World War officer — all bum and eye-glass."

I laughed again. It was a standing joke that former cavalry officers had child-bearing hips from years of riding horses. But I wasn't surprised that Sally attracted masculine attention, with her beautiful violet eyes. One of the few women in service who hadn't cut her waist-length auburn hair, she wore it in a braided coronet. She had even convinced her commanding officer that she be allowed to grow her fingernails past regulation length.

"It was simple, darling. I told him my nails were the tools of my trade. I need them to pick up those teeny little houses and railcars. It's bad enough having to wear this scratchy uniform and keep my hair braided like an old rug. I made up my mind I wasn't going to cut my fingernails, come Huns or high water."

There were two other interpreters in my section. Sam Blackwell was about thirty years old, a good-natured chap with sandy hair and a face like a bulldog, covered with freckles from forehead to fingertips. He was one of the educated poor who had attended university on a scholarship and owned a photography studio in Brighton before the war.

Sam devoted his off-duty hours to keeping the peace between his widowed mother and her twin sister, who had moved in together during the Blitz and were now engaged in what he called the second Battle of Britain. He was refreshingly unaffected compared to most of the other officers.

"Here's a question!" he would shout to the rest of the room. "How do you estimate the size of a camp by the number of latrines? My guess is one man per hole if they're officers, twenty per hole if they're enlisted men!"

Irving Leach was an American, and therefore exempt from the class structure present in British service life. He had joined the unit six months earlier when Americans began to pour into England by the thousand. Leach had deep-set black eyes and a deathly pale face that looked as if he had spent his life in a darkroom. A brilliant mathematician from Massachusetts, he was the only one who had no trouble determining the speed of a moving ship by measuring the distance between cusps, the peaks of each wave cast out by the ship. I worked at it for days before I mastered the technique.

I was painfully aware that I was the weakest member in camouflage, and hadn't yet distinguished myself with any important discovery. Moreover, I was unable to shake off my image as a jumped-up farmer's daughter. Just last week I had been given another task that Janet told everyone in a loud whisper clearly suited my limited abilities.

"I have an unusual assignment," Fowler told me. "It's unofficial. You'll have to do it off duty."

"Yes, sir." I was eager to prove myself to the team, and even more anxious to make an impression on my handsome commander.

"One of the high-ranking officers here has friends in the village. Their aunt has been staying with them since war broke out. She's from Holland, doesn't speak a word of English. She's convinced the Germans have destroyed her farm. She's taken to her bed and her nephew says she's literally dying of grief."

"I'll see what I can do, sir. It depends on where her farm is located, and whether we have cover on it."

This was one of the lucky ones. Without much trouble, I found recent negatives of the area around Leiden and asked Mrs. Hamilton for permission to use the darkroom.

As I printed my photographs, I hummed to myself. It was good to be back in the darkroom. I experienced again the familiar magic of making pictures with bits of celluloid and flashes of light and sheets of white paper. I dried the prints and took them back to the section room, where I bent over my stereoscope.

The following day when my shift was finished, I ventured into the nearby village of Medmenham, our station's namesake, reached by a footpath along the riverbank. It was a tiny village, with a church made from the local chalkstone, a shop that sold stamps and cigarettes, and a sixteenth-century pub called The Dog and Badger, popular with locals and air force alike. I was lucky enough to find a Dutch airman in the pub to translate the printed report before I delivered it to Mrs. De Jong.

The old lady, who appeared very frail, was bewildered when I appeared at her bedside. I handed her the paper, nodding and smiling in reassurance. There was a little flurry of activity as she found her reading glasses and put them on. With blue-veined hands, she took up the report.

I had written: "All farm buildings are intact and the roofs appear to be in good repair. The barley crop stands twelve inches high and eight large haystacks in the field indicate that forage is plentiful. Individual cattle numbering one hundred and thirty-seven were counted in the pasture. There are no signs of bombing or shelling in the immediate area. In conclusion, this farm has not suffered any ill effects from the war to date."

Mrs. De Jong came to the end of the page, took off her glasses, wiped them on a corner of the sheet, and started again at the top. When she finished reading for the second time, she dropped the paper on the bedspread and turned to me with her old eyes full of tears. "*God zij dank!*" She wrung my hands and pulled my face down so she could kiss me on both cheeks. Naturally the tears sprang into my eyes, too, and we had a little cry together. She was already getting out of bed when I left.

Only a farmer, I reflected as I returned to my station along the path, *understands how strongly one human being can be attached to one piece of earth.*

◆▶

It was midnight, and I had spent the better part of my shift determining that a row of black points along the edge of a French apple orchard were gun barrels. Wearily I descended the mahogany staircase. I was too tired to remark to myself, as I usually did, on what must be the most luxurious officers' lounge in England. Green leather sofas and armchairs were clustered around a massive marble fireplace with bronze ornamentation, modelled after a fireplace in the palace at Versailles. *Punch*, the *Daily Mail*, and the *Illustrated London News* were scattered on the carved oak side tables. Purple brocade draped the two-storey windows, and the cathedral ceiling arched high above my head.

I lit the gas flame in the butler's pantry next door so I could make myself a cup of tea before falling into bed. Reaching up to the overhead shelf, I took down my teacup, which everyone knew belonged to me because it had roses on it. With a surge of anger I noticed that the rim bore a trace of Janet's sickly mauve lipstick. *That woman would stoop to anything,* I thought. I scrubbed my cup savagely, poured the tea, and carried it up the stairs to my room, closing the door behind me with a sigh of relief. Oh, the blessed gift of solitude after a long day's work.

A nun would have been at home here. It was just large enough for a metal cot covered with grey woollen army blankets, a straight-backed wooden chair, and a small bureau where I kept my flashlight, Bible, fountain pen, and bottle of ink. My uniforms hung on three wooden coat hangers inside a cubbyhole, once considered adequate closet space for an upstairs maid.

But my quarters weren't devoid of personality. The ceiling was so high it gave the impression that the little room was standing on end. Over the bed was a tall, narrow window with leaded glass panes and wavy glass. A pair of green velvet drapes, heavy enough to serve as blackout curtains, were tied to each side with tasselled cords.

The red sweater knit by Mother, one of my few civvy garments, hung over the chair. On the bureau was a photograph of my family in a silver frame, a candlestick, and an ivory cream pitcher containing flowers and twigs that I gathered during my daily walk in the country.

My most precious possession also stood on the bureau. It was a pretty blue-and-white coffee tin containing several ounces of earth from the farm that I had carried with me across the ocean. Sometimes, when I was feeling particularly homesick, I twisted off the lid and smelled the rich blackness.

Now I sat down on the bed and opened the tin to enjoy the fragrance of home. Without thinking, I wet the tip of my forefinger and touched the dirt, then licked it off.

I had always loved the taste and smell of earth. When I was a toddler, I had eaten it by the handful, much to Mother's dismay. As I buried my nose in the tin and closed my eyes, a wave of longing rose in me. How terribly I missed the prairie around Touchwood.

With a sigh, I put the lid back and picked up a letter from June that I had been saving to read before lights out.

◂▾▸

Touchwood
July 15, 1942
Dear Posy,

We've been sorting mail, mail, and more mail — and I'm sure creating my share. I'm writing to eight guys, at last count. After they've been around for a few months, it's hard to see them go. One of them cried like a baby when he said goodbye to Mum last week. I've sewn on so many sets of wings I have a sore thumb. I'm even named as a beneficiary in several wills. The boys have to fill out their forms before they go overseas. I wish they wouldn't — it gives me the willies, ha, ha.

Sonny has joined the air force. He always hated the idea of going into the post office, so this is a happy postponement of his fate. Mum and I are worried about his rebellious streak, but Dad thinks it will make a man out of him.

The big news is that our family has taken in a war orphan! She's named Daisy, six years old and a real handful. She went to the Corrigals first but they couldn't cope with her, so of course my dear sweet mother stepped into the breach. Daisy has no table manners, just yells: "A piece! A piece!" if she wants a slice of bread. She even bit me on the arm yesterday, but I warned her that if she did it again I would bite her back!

I can't help feeling sorry for the poor little blighter, though. The other night we had a big lightning storm and Daisy woke up and had hysterics trying to persuade us to go to the bomb shelter. After the storm passed, she was convinced that it was quiet because the Huns had gone home. Very sad to think what she has been through.

Speaking of Huns, we had two flyers from Alsace-Lorraine home for the weekend. Since German is their first language, they have a real thick accent. Before they arrived Dad took his hunting rifles and hid them in the root cellar! Mum said even if they were German spies they wouldn't likely murder us in our beds, but he said he wasn't trusting any Krauts no matter what.

You'll never guess who came into the post office to show off his new uniform — Willie Cuthand, from Redfeather Reserve! Dad asked him why he joined up, and Willie said: "My grandfather signed a treaty with Queen Victoria, and it is my patriotic duty to go to her country's defence." Dad was beaming — you know he's always bragging about how his parents were United Empire Loyalists — and then Willie said: "Besides, when am I ever going to have another chance to shoot white men and get paid for it?" He laughed, but poor Dad was speechless!

One of the Free French boys named Claude who was here last spring was posted to a northern station for gunnery training and he sends me love letters written on birch bark. Even the envelopes are made out of bark. I guess he thinks it's quaint. Dad says: "Tell that young fool to quit killing our trees!"

I've been learning to play cricket. The boys have formed a couple of teams and I must say it's a boring game to watch but I have no shortage of instructors who want to show me how to hold the bat. I now know what a sticky wicket is.

Monica Fisher is working on me to join up. I took one look at her uniform and said not on your life. That hat! She could hide a bag of potatoes under it.

Our old pal Charlie Stewart is doing very well for himself. I was reading in the *Times* this week that he's gotten a promotion from Pilot Officer to Flying Officer. Maybe he's not such a clodhopper after all. You may have to eat your words.

So when are you going to write and tell me all about the fellows you've been dating? I'm dying to hear about Covent Garden. How I envy you, being so close to the fun!

Mum just came into my room and told me to quit burning the midnight oil so I'd better close now. Write soon. Love, Prune

I folded the letter and slipped it back into the envelope. Had I ever been as young and innocent as June? I felt as if I were still on the ship that had borne me away from home, and every day it sailed farther away from everything I had known.

I undressed and lay down on my cot. As I reached out to turn off the lamp, I glanced up and saw the Rhine River. *No,* I thought, shaking my head on the pillow. *It's only a crack on the ceiling.* But the dark line ran across the red colour inside my eyelids for a long time before I fell asleep.

13

It was after Dieppe that I started to smoke.

Officially, no one at the station knew the name of the target. But it wasn't hard to figure out. The model section created a huge scale replica of the beach, ten feet long and six feet wide, complete with minutely detailed streets, houses, trees, and cliffs. Most of the other interpreters had holidayed on the French coast, and they knew exactly where it was.

If we knew where, we also knew when. The signs were obvious: extra reconnaissance flights and extra shifts marked up on our duty roster. A date was chosen, then cancelled due to weather. Another date was red-circled: August 19. There was a sense of excitement around the station as everyone waited eagerly for the outcome of the first full-scale Allied attack on the continent.

I woke early that morning and pulled open my drapes. The sun was rising in a watery blue English sky. I recalled the names of several Touchwood boys who had been cooling their heels at Aldershot since the war began two years ago, waiting to be called into action. It would be the Canadian Army's first taste of battle, and they were chafing to prove themselves the equals of the Brits, not to mention the Yanks. As for the Germans, that went without saying.

I dressed and went to the mess for breakfast. I wasn't hungry, but I forced myself to eat a slice of toast and margarine and drink a cup of cocoa thickened with powdered milk.

As the day wore on, I fidgeted at my desk, which in reality was a large wooden table. Our section room had been converted from one of the spacious bedrooms on the second floor, large enough for each of the five interpreters to have an individual table with a wooden tray for paperwork and a swivel-necked lamp.

The room was filled with natural light from a row of multi-paned windows that began at waist height and rose up to the high ceilings. I rose and paced the room, stopping to stare unseeingly at the spectacular view of the river.

The reconnaissance photos from Dieppe weren't printed until early afternoon. I came off my regular shift at four o'clock and practically ran down the hall to the army section. When I came in, a couple of interpreters glanced up from their work and quickly lowered their eyes again.

"Hello, everyone! I just dropped in to see how my countrymen fared in their first battle."

There was a short silence. The army section head, a bespectacled little man with an unhappy expression, cleared his throat. "Not too well, I'm afraid."

The smile left my face. "What happened, sir?"

"The landing craft ran into a German convoy. They were supposed to arrive in darkness, but by the time they reached the shore the sun was already up and the Hun was ready for them, poor devils."

A feeling of dread like ice water ran down my spine. "May I take a look, sir?"

He hesitated, then nodded. I picked up a magnifying glass and bent over the photographs.

For a moment I was disoriented. During my months as an interpreter I had studied only photographs taken from high altitudes, the recce aircraft well above the reach of German anti-aircraft guns. From that height the buildings below were no bigger than punctuation marks. But these photos were low obliques taken by some daring pilot during the raid itself, the horizons slanted as he jinked from side to side to avoid the flak.

They showed a scene of utter chaos: aircraft flying in every direction, white fountains erupting from the sea as shells burst in the water, the beach covered with a pall of black smoke. Near the edge of the water, I could see half-submerged tanks, disabled before they reached the shore. A few tanks had made it as far as the beach, but they were burned-out shells wedged up against a massive wall of concrete.

With growing horror, I scanned the defences along the top of the steep cliff: concrete pillboxes, mortars, and machine guns. The invaders had been met by a blizzard of gunfire.

I turned to the dark squiggles scattered along the narrow, pebbled beach below the cliff and floating in the water without realizing at first what I was seeing. Then I gasped. These could only be bodies, arms and legs crookedly outflung.

I set down the magnifying glass, leaning on the table with both hands. "What are the estimated losses?"

"We don't have the final numbers yet." He hesitated again, as if reluctant to speak. "Of the five thousand Canadians who took part, about two-thirds were lost, either killed or taken prisoner. It's a damned shame."

I thanked him, and left the room. In the hallway I leaned against the wall, wiping my damp palms down my rough woollen skirt. The pressure in my chest was building and I knew if I went to my room I would cry. Instead I walked unsteadily down the long stairs toward the lounge. The light-coloured paving stones seemed to jump and chatter under my feet.

When I entered the room, I saw several officers standing around the fireplace, talking in hushed voices. I marched straight up to an officer I knew only slightly. "May I cadge a cigarette, please?" I asked in a deliberately hard, bright voice.

He offered me a Woodbine from his silver monogrammed cigarette case, and ignited it with a matching lighter. I turned my back to the group and took a deep drag, coughing slightly. The nicotine rushed into my bloodstream and my knees went weak.

I collapsed into a nearby armchair and picked up a magazine, staring at the same open page and pretending to read while I smoked the cigarette right down to the stub with quick, determined movements. Every time I inhaled, it felt as if my throat were on fire.

I had never questioned the decisions of my British military superiors, but now my confidence was rocked to the core. Either they had sacrificed the Canadians in a pointless exercise, or they had been dead wrong. How else to explain the futility of trying to breach those monstrous defences? Had MacTavish been right about the British commanders after all?

At last I dragged myself upstairs. After undressing, I went down the hall to the women's bathroom and tried to vomit. The images of dead bodies bobbing on the waves floated before my eyes, but I retched dryly without finding any relief.

◆▼▶

That night I woke with a tremendous start, my whole body electrified. Lately I had been having the same nightmare. I called it the red, white, and blue dream.

Jack and I were kids, playing in the snow-covered pasture at home, laughing and throwing snowballs. Then Nazi soldiers with swastikas on their helmets came running over the east hill, their black boots leaving black footprints in the virgin snow. The soldiers were hunched over, firing their rifles as they charged. Jack fell spread-eagled as if he were making a snow angel, and the blood poured out around him.

There was no colour in the dream except the brilliant blue of the sky, the dazzling white snow, and the scarlet blood, soaking into the snow until it formed a huge lake, with me in the centre, screaming.

I lay in the darkness with my pulse racing, waiting for the dream to fade. My grandmother had told me that looking into light would blot out the memory of a nightmare. I fumbled in my drawer until I found a box of matches and lit my candle.

The glow cast black shadows into the corners of the high ceiling. I sat on the edge of my cot, blanket clutched around my shoulders, and stared into the flame, willing the dream to disappear while my mind returned to the bodies on the pebbled beaches of Dieppe.

Until now I had taken a clinical approach to my work, as if the photographs were no more than a different type of jigsaw puzzle. Now I realized this was no longer possible. Like it or not, I was playing a deadly game, not with inanimate metal ships and tanks, but human beings — their young bodies full of life and energy and bright red blood.

◂▾▸

The winter of 1942 was a dreary one. There was snow — not glittering and majestic like the snow at home, but flakes the size of pinheads that melted into grey slush, as pathetic as dust on a windowsill. The damp cold seeped into the marrow of my bones. *If only we were making some progress*, I thought as I pushed back my sleeve to check for goosebumps. I recalled everyone's excitement when the Americans had joined the conflict a year earlier, believing the tide had turned. Now it seemed as if the war might drag on forever. I remembered the Hundred Year War between England and France. Was the world locked in a stalemate that would last the rest of my life?

Some headway was being made by the Allies, but at a terrible cost. The German Army was surrounded by the Russians at Stalingrad and more than one million people, soldiers and civilians, died in the burning arctic cold that I knew only too well. One million. When I tried to imagine one million dead bodies, my mind went blank. The entire population of Canada was only eleven million.

Worse yet, there were rumours trickling back from the Pacific that the Japanese were fanatical fighters who would be difficult to defeat — if not impossible.

◆▼◆

It was the middle of the night, and dead quiet. I hated the overnight shift, since I had to rush straight to the mess if I wanted to eat breakfast before beginning the arduous task of trying to fall asleep in broad daylight.

I took a break and rubbed my eyes. They were often tired, even when I woke. I tried to remember to rest them every hour.

Sam's face showed dimly at the edge of the lighted half-circle made by his desk lamp. He looked up at me and winked, tossing a print across the space between our desks. "How about this one? Think it will make the Blue Book?"

The photograph showed a colossal column of black smoke billowing skywards from the landscape below. It was impossible to know what lay below the smoke.

"Very impressive," I said dryly. We both knew clouds of smoke indicated nothing, yet looked spectacular when reprinted in newspapers with a headline: "Bold Strike Over Germany!" Or words to that effect.

I handed it back. "What do you mean by the Blue Book?"

"It's Bomber Harris's personal album. Apparently he puts on his velvet smoking jacket after dinner and takes his guests into the study to show them photographs of Germany's destruction. The public relations department sends extra prints to the prime minister and Buckingham Palace. Even Stalin gets copies so the old boy can see we're not lolly-gagging on the Western Front."

I didn't know anything about Arthur Harris, the head of Bomber Command, except that the bomber crews were devoted to him. I had heard a couple of interpreters refer to him as Butcher Harris, but I assumed they were just being funny.

"One of his favourite shots was taken when we bombed Rostock. It shows German civilians running for cover. Unfortunately, they're no bigger than grains of pepper. He'd probably like it better if he could see the terror in their eyes."

I shrank back in my chair. I was still struggling to treat the subjects of my photographs as lifeless matter, the way an astrologist would examine a dead planet though a telescope.

Let the photographs speak to you. I remembered the instructor's words. Sometimes they spoke to me of blood and death, but at other times they spoke of the beauty and wonder of creation. Landing craft heading toward the beaches, each leaving a streak of white wake, like a galaxy of shooting stars. Tank tracks in the snow, twisting like hundreds of fox-and-geese games. A pillar of steam, rising from a factory chimney in a great white feathery plume. Once I asked the darkroom technicians to make me an extra print for my own: the delicate shadows of a suspension bridge reflected on the still water below, like Belgian lace draped over a mirror. I found it almost unbearably lovely.

I changed the subject. "I'll keep an eye out for Blue Book material, but right now I can't concentrate because of this blessed heat."

It was a frigid night in February, but Medmenham was scorching hot. For some reason the heating system was malfunctioning, running at full blast. Central heating was considered one of the station's greatest charms. Since our mountains of film had to be kept at a constant temperature, we didn't have to ration our fuel like the wretched civilians who spent the winter huddled around fireplaces and wood stoves.

But tonight we were suffering more than we would have in the cold. My jacket was hanging over the back of my chair and my tie was loose, but my shirt was damp with perspiration and my hair was sticking to my scalp.

I leaned over and studied the photograph once again. I had been working on it for two hours, yet I couldn't interpret the strange pattern of light-coloured circles against a darker background of grass.

I was becoming adept at identifying surfaces based on tone and texture alone. Earth, grass, sand, rocks — each had its own distinctive shade of grey. By now I was skilled at reading a photograph, squeezing out every drop of information like the pulp of an orange.

What had made those strange spheres? No weapon or vehicle that I recognized. I stuck out my lower lip and blew air upwards over my flushed face.

Fowler came into the room and stopped beside my desk. "Everything all right here, Jolliffe?" It had become a private joke, his using the same words every day.

I looked up at him and smiled. "Yes, sir, except for the heat. The problem is the exposure on this photograph. Maybe if it were darker I could make out some detail inside these circles. I'll check the others and see if they're any sharper."

"Very good, Jolliffe." He smiled back at me and I felt a frisson of excitement. *Don't be a fool,* I told myself. Lately I couldn't help noticing that even in the midst of my deepest concentration, if Fowler walked past my desk it took me a few minutes to recapture my focus.

I went down to the library and told the duty clerk what I needed.

"Sorry, Assistant Section Officer. The prints are checked out to someone else."

"Is anyone on duty in the darkroom?"

"No. We aren't expecting any new photos tonight. Mrs. Hamilton said to call her if anything arrived unexpectedly."

"Well, don't bother her. Just give me the negatives. I'll pop into the darkroom and make a print. It should only take me twenty minutes."

"If you're quite sure —" She eyed the stripe on my sleeve and handed over the negatives.

I turned on the red warning light outside the entrance to signify no admittance, and slipped between the heavy floor-length curtains. Gosh, it was sweltering! The interior room without windows was like a steam bath. The reddish-coloured safe light seemed to pulse with an unearthly glow.

I found the negative and slipped it into the enlarger. Almost faint from the heat, I made a decision. Quickly I slipped off my shoes, then my skirt. I pulled my tie over my head, and unbuttoned my shirt. Finally, off went my stockings and garter belt, leaving me in my underwear.

I felt lighter and cooler, my bare feet damp with sweat on the stone floor. I lifted a piece of paper out of the cardboard box and slipped the edge into my mouth, identifying the emulsified side when it stuck to my upper lip. After sliding the paper between the sheets of glass, I flicked the switch on the enlarger.

I burned in those puzzling circles by allowing the light to fall on them directly, protecting the rest of the photo by dodging my hand back and forth under the beam, and slipped the print into a tray full of developing fluid.

While I watched the dark image rise from the white paper, I splashed clean water from the rinsing tray over my shoulders and throat. It felt delicious on my hot skin. When the photo was ready I picked it up with a pair of rubber tongs and slid it into the tray of fixing solution.

As I gazed at the image, my mind wandered. Suddenly I had one of those rare sensations of flight. I almost felt myself lift physically from the floor and soar high above the tray, seeing it through a bird's eyes.

Of course! I knew what those circles were — nothing to do with any type of warfare. "It's goats!" I said aloud, and laughed. The circles were the grazed patches made by goats on tethers, walking around the stakes in mathematically precise spheres.

I returned to my own skin and my feet touched the stone floor just as a shaft of light entered the darkroom. I whirled around. Gideon Fowler was standing inside the blackout drapes, staring at me. For a couple of seconds both of us were transfixed.

"Terribly sorry," he muttered, before vanishing again.

I looked down at myself. My arms and shoulders glistened with drops of water, gleaming in the rosy light. My modest white cotton brassiere and underpants were more revealing than any bathing suit. I wished I had been wearing my standard issue bloomers, but they had been replaced long ago.

Why hadn't he seen the warning light? Everyone at the station down to the lowliest cleaner knew that opening the curtains could ruin the precious film. I scrambled into my uniform, my temperature rising again.

Quickly I ran a rubber squeegee over the photo and stepped outside the darkroom. I looked up and saw that the warning light overhead had burned out. I marched down the hall and handed the negatives back to the filing clerk.

"Did Flight Officer Fowler find you, ma'am?"

"Yes, he did," I replied, pretending to study the photograph in my hand. "The warning light outside the darkroom needs replacing. Could you do it right away, please?"

I walked down the long hallway, my footsteps slowing as I approached the camouflage room. Outside the door I squared my shoulders, then went straight to my desk without glancing left or right. Sam's face was glued to his stereoscope and Fowler was sitting with his back to me, reading a file held open on his lap. No one spoke for the rest of the shift.

14

It was almost spring. How I missed the thaw at home — the way it arrived on the wings of a chinook, breaking winter's back overnight, shattering the frozen landscape. Here the seasons changed almost furtively, like fog creeping through the crack under the door.

Since the darkroom incident, Fowler was rigidly professional, although on several occasions I caught him staring at me when I lifted my eyes from my stereoscope. I blushed ferociously, remembering his gaze on my half-naked body. It was difficult to maintain my composure when he spoke to me.

He really had the loveliest voice.

Janet continued to ignore me. Sam was friendly enough, but he spent his leaves off the station. Leach refused to talk to anyone unless it was related to work. I tried to make conversation with the interpreters from other sections, but it was heavy going. After answering their predictable questions about the weather in Canada and the size of my farm, I sat quietly and listened to their gossip about mutual acquaintances and parties.

I was often amused by their expressions. One has to keep up appearances. It won't do to let the side down. Not quite the thing, old boy. Once I laughed out loud, thinking they were joking, only to be met with a freezing silence.

It didn't help that my fellow officers were frighteningly well-educated. The entire geography department from Cambridge University had been seconded to interpretation. Fowler himself had graduated with a first in history. There were professors, geologists, archaeologists, botanists, and engineers. One of them had even climbed Mount Everest. Compared to them, I felt like some kind of colonial idiot savant.

Even my rank was a mixed blessing, since it prevented me from mingling with my former darkroom colleagues. Sometimes I overheard the girls in the library chattering, but they fell quiet when any officers, including me, entered the room.

I knew that the darkroom technicians had a secret pet, a cat named Wisteria who climbed the vines at night and crept through their windows. How I envied them that cat. I missed my pets almost as much as I missed my family.

Touring around the country was discouraged, and without any signposts, I was afraid of getting lost. Regardless, I spent my forty-eights cycling down the narrow country lanes that wound through the trees, their branches showering me with icy droplets.

Once I had taken the local bus to the cinema in Henley, seven miles away. I felt morbidly self-conscious sitting alone in the theatre, but I wanted to see the film *Waterloo Bridge*, starring Robert Taylor. I imagined Gideon Fowler playing the role of the handsome officer, and myself as his sweetheart Vivian Leigh.

The people with whom I might have found common ground, the village residents, kept their distance from women in uniform. One evening I tried to join several villagers seated around the fire at The Dog and Badger. It was a picturesque scene — the men with clay pipes between their teeth, the thick blue smoke curling under the low wooden beams, two Border Collies and a Bull Terrier lying under the tables.

Their conversation was familiar to me: crops and weather. I longed to talk to them about farming. I also wanted to pet the warm, furry dogs observing me with friendly eyes. I edged closer and smiled when anyone glanced my way, but they soon pushed back their chairs and left.

The only woman with whom I had any personal contact was Sally, but since the model section had gone to three shifts she was often sleeping when I was awake. Occasionally we visited the pub, but one of us was usually yawning before midnight. There were dark circles under her violet eyes and, like me, she was smoking constantly.

Writing home was a painful duty. If only I could have described the red, white, and blue dream, and let Mother soothe my fears. Or tell Dad the truth about Dieppe. I knew from their letters that everyone in Canada believed the raid was a great success. Instead I was forced to write about trivialities — the weather, the food, the difficulty in finding decent shampoo.

With great determination, I forced my thoughts into two separate compartments. Sometimes they went kicking and screaming, but, ultimately, they went.

On duty I thought of nothing but work.

Off duty I thought of nothing but Gideon Fowler.

When I closed my eyes at night I didn't see camouflaged roads or bridges or factories — I saw his beautifully manicured hands. When I woke after my nightmare, I lit the candle and recalled the way his dark hair grew on the back of his neck. When I felt the terrible homesickness rising, I imagined his voice, as rich and mellow as that of a professional crooner.

It's only a fantasy, I reassured myself, to keep me from being homesick or dwelling on the war. And it had the added benefit of helping me in my work. I was so anxious to earn every scrap of attention from my commanding officer that I worked long hours, exerting myself to the utmost.

I came into the section room an hour early to start my afternoon shift. Sam and Leach were off duty and Janet was at her place in the far corner. I experienced the usual throb of excitement when I saw Fowler's head bent over his work.

"Good afternoon, Jolliffe."

"Good afternoon, sir."

He came over to my desk, his uniform crisp and immaculate as always, his dark hair as sleek as if he had just lifted his head from under water. As he bent over me, his shoulder nearly touching mine, I noted the faint scent of cologne.

"Here's new cover on Bruno, the radar station near the French coast. I've already reviewed these, but I'd like you to compare them with the ones taken last week."

"Yes, sir." I tried to keep my voice steady. "What am I looking for?"

I knew this radar station was wreaking havoc with RAF bombing missions. German and British scientists were locked in what was called "the battle of the beams," a race to develop the most sophisticated use of radar. So far the enemy was one step ahead of us. Their early warning system detected our bombers as they passed over the French coastline. Then their night-fighters rose up like vampire bats in the darkness and picked off our aircraft one by one.

"The radar station is located in a farmyard on the edge of a sea cliff. When it gets dark, an aircraft will drop several of our paratroopers on the field, here." He pointed to a flat expanse east of the farm. "They'll make their way into that grove of trees and hide there until the dead of night, then creep out. Their mission is to overpower the German guards, dismantle the radar dish, and bring the key pieces home so our scientists can examine them. A boat will be waiting on the beach."

"Isn't that dangerous, sir?" I asked foolishly. Of course it was dangerous — anyone could see that.

Fowler smiled. "Yes, but it should work if everything goes according to Hoyle. A recce aircraft was sent over at dawn today to take these shots, just as a precaution."

He returned to his desk and I began with the earlier photos. Lining up the first pair under my stereoscope, I waited for the sensation that had now become familiar — there it was. I lifted straight up into the air like a bird rising from the branch of a tree, leaving my stomach behind for a split second. Then I was high above the ground looking down, wheeling in a long, slow turn.

The photos showed a tidy farmstead, with a two-storey house, two large barns, and several smaller outbuildings. Between the house and the cliff was a thick grove of trees, sheltering the yard from the strong offshore winds. A faint track led through the trees and down the face of the cliff to a flat, pebbled beach.

What was obvious even to an untrained eye was a gigantic bowl-shaped device made of wire mesh, twenty feet in diameter, smack in the centre of the farmyard. A footpath led from the dish to the house. Luckily for our side, there was no way to disguise a radar dish. Since its function required wide open spaces, it couldn't be hidden in the trees. Although coated with white camouflage paint, it was clearly visible against the snow.

A single vehicle track led between the farmstead and the main road to the rear. The Germans had made an effort to eliminate the track by brushing the snow, probably with brooms or tree branches, but it was fairly elementary interpretation to see the sweep marks.

I turned to the new photographs, low obliques taken early this morning. They didn't show any sign of life except a wisp of smoke from the chimney of the farmhouse where the radar technicians were quartered. The brush marks were hidden under a fall of fresh snow. Even the footpath between the radar dish and the house had vanished.

I spent an hour studying the new prints. There was something odd about those farm buildings, but darned if I could think what it was. I leaned back, closed my eyes, and tried to let my mind go blank. It didn't work.

I pushed back my chair and strolled over to the window. A farmer had let his cattle out onto the banks on the far side of the river, and I watched them with affection as they stood grazing peacefully and switching their tails.

They were the familiar red and white Herefords. I admired the way they were scattered across the sloping hillside, their colourful hides contrasting with the green pasture. *Our Herefords at home are cousins to the English cattle,* I thought. *Just like us, the same bloodlines on both sides of the ocean.*

I could almost smell them. I never understood why the others complained about the fragrance of manure that occasionally wafted through the open window. To me, it was nothing more than the natural, rich smell of chewed grass. I remembered the feel of a cow's warm flank against my cheek as I bent to do the milking, the heat of its grassy breath, the stuffy coziness of the barn on a cold winter's night.

I ran back to my desk, pressing my face to the stereoscope.

"Excuse me, sir!"

Fowler was at my side in a moment.

"Take another look at these buildings," I said in a low voice. "The whole area is covered with fresh snow, except for the roof on this small shed nearest the house."

Fowler bent over the photo. "The sun was up when these were taken. It must have been warm enough to melt the snow."

I consulted the attached notes. "It's true the southern side would start to melt shortly after dawn, sir, but the northern side should still be covered. Besides, the other roofs are still white."

"Could this roof be made of a different material? More conducive to heat?"

"I doubt it, sir. In the earlier set, the bare roofs are identical, even to the weathering of the wood."

"Well, what do you think it means?"

Janet was gazing over at us with narrowed eyes, obviously straining to hear. I lowered my voice. "I always notice the barn roof from my bedroom window at home. If the cattle are out in the pasture, there's snow on the roof. If they're inside, the heat of their bodies warms up the barn so much that the snow melts off. Their bodies are like furnaces."

Fowler's forehead was furrowed. "Go on."

"We know there can't be animals inside, sir. We would have seen some sign of them. So there's only one reason that shed would be warm enough to melt the snow off the roof. I think there are people inside."

"What!" His voice was loud in the quiet room. "Let me see those again." He bent over the stereoscope while I waited. The more I thought about it, the more I was convinced.

"I'd better inform Shoreham," he said, raising his head at last. "The paratroopers are leaving right after dark." He snatched his hat off his chair and hurried out of the room.

Janet was scowling at me. I returned to the photographs, trying to come up with another possibility. As the sun sank below the trees, the cattle across the river turned with one mind and plodded single file along the river path and out of sight. I drew the blackout curtains, and our goose-necked lamps shed their circles of yellow light in the darkness.

Could I be mistaken? Why would the Germans hide in their own shed? Finally the section room door opened and Fowler came in. He beckoned with his head.

"Come with me, Jolliffe." His face was expressionless.

I followed as he strode down the long hallway, descended the elaborate wooden staircase, and went outside. Our steps crunched on the pebbles as we walked around the corner of the house and stopped under a large, overhanging willow.

The spring air was cool and thick as cream, fresh with the scent of budding leaves. In the twilight I could see only the outline of Fowler's head and shoulders. It was the first time we had been quite alone.

There was a brief pause, and then he spoke in a different voice, younger and higher. "Rose, I don't know how you do it. You must be some kind of a witch!"

"What do you mean, sir?"

"We contacted one of our French agents by radio. He confirmed that two troop trucks went into the farm yesterday, just before it started to snow. We suspect there are Germans hiding in that shed, waiting to ambush our men. It's a trap!"

I didn't understand for a moment, then I gasped. I had a vision of our paratroopers creeping across the farmyard, crumpling as the bullets drove through their bodies, their crimson blood gushing into the snow.

Fowler's arms came around me and I automatically leaned into them, the way a dog leans against his master's legs, conscious only of the blessed comfort of being held. I felt his hand under my chin, raising my face, and then his mouth on mine.

It was a long kiss, unlike anything I had ever experienced. His moustache tickled my upper lip. I didn't know how to respond, so I stood as stiff as a fencepost and held my breath until I felt faint. When he released me and stepped back, I gasped for air. My knees were trembling and I steadied myself by clutching an overhead branch with my right hand.

"Rose, you're the most fascinating girl." His deep voice was husky with emotion. "I never imagined anyone like you existed. I can't stop thinking about you. In fact, I may very well be in love with you."

My heart, which had been beating hard before, now felt as if it were going to burst out of my tunic. I couldn't utter a word.

"God knows I've tried to keep my distance, but I desperately want to see you alone, away from all this nonsense. Would you, could you find it in your heart to meet me in London?"

"Yes, sir." My voice was no more than a whisper.

"Brilliant. I'll be counting the hours until then." He reached for my left hand in the gloom and caressed it with both of his. "I know this is absolute folly, of course. But I just can't seem to help myself. You're such an enchanting little creature."

Nobody had ever called me enchanting before, and certainly not little. My head was spinning and I felt slightly nauseous, as if I were on board ship during a heavy sea.

It had suddenly grown very dark. I heard Fowler take a deep breath and sigh heavily. It was almost a groan. "Look, my darling, I must go back inside before Janet gets suspicious. Why don't you knock off early? You've been going at it awfully hard."

He raised my hand to his lips and kissed it passionately, then released it. My arm fell lifelessly to my side as if it belonged to a rag doll. I heard his footsteps recede down the gravel path.

He was in love with me. I couldn't comprehend what that meant, what would happen next. It was as if a pair of giant hands had picked up my world like a snow globe and given it a vigorous shake, sending everything familiar spinning into the air.

Touchwood
March 15, 1943
Dear Posy,

It's a gay, mad social whirl around here, as usual. I was down at the station yesterday and I saw four real live Germans, prisoners of war going through town on the train. Some kids flashed them the V sign, and they gave it back upside down! Of all the nerve! A couple of them were sure cute, though.

Speaking of prisoners, guess who blew into town — Freda Schultz's father. The government got sick of the old coot, so they sent him home. He wanted Freda to return the deed to the farm, and she told him to get lost! So he took a swing at her, and she rang up the Mounties. They came out and read her name on the title, fair and square, and drove Schultz to the train station. Good riddance to bad rubbish.

The most awful thing happened to Evelyn Starling, the one the boys called Evening Star. She tried to give herself an abortion with a knitting needle, and she bled to death. I guess she was crazy in love with one of the pilots who left two months ago and got shot down his first time out. The funeral was just tragic, and nobody knew what to say to the poor Starlings. I still cry buckets whenever I think of her.

My little brother was two weeks away from getting his wings when he fell off a horse and broke his arm. You know what a daredevil he is. He won't be flying again for six months. He had a long leave at home, and the girls hung around the house like flies. You can imagine the wounded hero, all pale and noble, with his arm in a cast.

We've been hearing rumours about Jews being murdered wholesale. Dad says you can't believe the newspapers, but even so. I met a Jewish pilot who showed me his identity tag — they usually say Catholic or Protestant, but his reads UCC for Unorthodox Christian of Canada. That's so he won't be identified as Jewish in case he gets captured. Scary stuff!

I wish you could see Daisy now. She was such a scrawny little thing when she arrived, but she's cute as a button since Mum fattened her up. She wears her favourite hat all the time — a children's replica RCAF wedge cap that Sonny ordered from Eaton's catalogue for thirty-nine cents. She even sleeps in it.

Dad brought home a couple of new kittens for her. She named them Bubble and Squeak. She had a cat back in London, but it had to be put down. One of the English boys from the base told us that most family pets had to be destroyed when the war started. People couldn't feed their pets, couldn't find homes for them in the country. And you can imagine how the poor things reacted during the bombing. He said the lineup at the local vet stretched around the block.

Better dash now — I'm working at the canteen tonight.

Love, Prune

15

Oh, to be in England, now that April's here. I remembered the line of poetry as my train chugged across the green, fragrant countryside, and came out into the enormous glass-domed Paddington Station.

The blood was rushing through my veins like whitewater rapids. My uniform was impeccable, my hair washed, and I had painstakingly applied lipstick and powder. I had even opened a rarely used box of mascara and blackened my eyelashes with the little brush.

Preparing myself mentally was more difficult, as I had no idea what to expect. Was Fowler — perhaps I should call him Gideon now, although it sounded ridiculously presumptuous — planning to take me to a restaurant? Or perhaps a picture show, or one of those famous attractions like Piccadilly Circus that people were always asking me if I had seen yet?

Through the crowd I caught sight of Fowler — Gideon — standing under the big station clock with a rolled-up newspaper under his arm. I felt a surge of pride that such a distinguished-looking man was waiting for me. I gave him a tremulous smile and saluted, in case anyone was watching. He returned my salute briskly and marched toward the exit. I was at a loss momentarily before realizing that I was expected to follow. I trotted after him. Without looking back, he turned left down a side street, and right again at the next corner. He was so far ahead that I had to jog to keep up with him.

He vanished through a doorway leading into a block of flats. I followed and found a flight of shabby wooden stairs. I began to climb after him. I could hear his footsteps, but it wasn't until I was mounting the third flight that I saw him on the landing above me, unlocking a door. When I reached the open door, he was waiting inside the room.

"Rose, my darling," he said in his deep voice, his arms outstretched. I stepped inside, and he kicked the door shut and began to kiss me so hard that my jaw cracked. I turned my face away. "Please, sir, just let me catch my breath."

We were standing in a small attic bedroom under the eaves. The walls were painted white, the floor battleship grey. A sagging double bed dominated the room. Through another open door, I saw a tiny bathroom with a toilet and sink.

"Where are we?"

"This place belongs to a friend. Here, let me help you with your jacket." He reached toward me with his beautiful hands and unbuttoned my tunic, drew it from my shoulders, and tossed it over the room's single wooden chair.

When he sat down on the bed, it emitted the sound of creaking springs. "Come over here, darling." I perched on the edge of the bed beside him. Without another word he reached for me again, loosened my tie, and began to unbutton my shirt.

With a shock that struck me like a lightning bolt, I knew what was going to happen next. We weren't going to have a long chat, or even a drink. This was what we were here for — at least, what he was here for.

My body stiffened as I mentally reviewed my options at the

speed of light. I could put on my tunic and leave. That would be humiliating for both of us, and would create repercussions back at the station that I couldn't begin to imagine. He was my commanding officer, after all.

Or I could tell him I wasn't ready yet. I opened my mouth, but I was still trying to think of something to say that wouldn't make me sound childishly pathetic, when he started kissing me again.

He had my shirt unbuttoned now, and was pushing me gently but inexorably backwards onto the pillows. By the time he reached under my skirt and began to stroke the bare skin above my stockings, I decided it was too late to object.

I finished undressing myself quickly, almost paralyzed with shyness. Leaving my clothes on the floor, I managed to scramble into bed and cover myself with the sheet before Fowler finished laying his trousers and shirt neatly over the chair.

Without his uniform, he looked thinner, and somehow older. His legs were long and bony. The muscles in his upper arms were ropy, his wrists narrow and delicate. A sprinkling of black hair covered his milky-white chest and stomach. After one quick peek, I averted my eyes.

The sheets had that peculiar dampness common to English linens, as if the bed had been made before they were fully dry. I clenched my jaw to keep my teeth from chattering.

Fowler opened the top drawer of the small wooden bureau and fumbled with something that made a rustling sound. "We don't want any accidents," he said, turning to me with a confident smile.

I couldn't look anywhere but at his familiar hands: not much larger than my own, with slender fingers and manicured nails. He had removed his wedding ring. The soft, white skin was tinged with blue, as if they were cold. They were cold. I shivered when they touched me.

A few minutes followed during which I exerted every ounce of will to avoid crying out in pain, and it was over. Fowler detached himself, rolled over on his back, and put his arm across his forehead with a deep sigh. I was surprised. Somehow I had thought it would last longer.

I lay perfectly still, not wanting to say or do the wrong thing, conscious only of the throbbing pain. A mournful train whistle from Paddington Station sounded in the distance. It reminded me of home. I felt the familiar constriction in my chest that meant I was about to cry.

Suddenly Fowler rolled over and took me in his arms. He gazed at me searchingly with his fine dark eyes. "My darling girl. You don't know how much I wanted that, how much I needed it."

"Really?" I whispered. My chin was quivering. I raised my left hand and pressed my thumb and finger into my collarbone. I wondered if I should tell him that it was my first time. It hadn't seemed to occur to him. Maybe I had already lost my virginity galloping around the prairies on Buckshot.

Fowler went on. "I'm under the most tremendous pressure, darling, you've no idea. No matter how hard I slave away, Shoreham simply won't cough up a promotion. And there's no joy on the home front, either. Frances is so busy with her precious charity work we're like ships passing in the night."

I involuntarily flinched at the mention of his wife, but he didn't notice. I hadn't even known her name.

He touched his finger to the tip of my nose. "It's simply bliss to be here alone with you. In fact, that's what I'm going to call this place — Bliss. Nothing exists outside that door. No Germans, no generals, no wives. It's our own little escape hatch from reality."

I forgot my pain in a sudden surge of emotion. What an enchanting fantasy. To be here in a private world, alone with my handsome English prince, the object of my dreams. It was better than the most romantic novel. I imagined how I would cherish this day, recalling every word and touch when I was alone.

"How often do you think we can visit ... Bliss?" I asked.

"Every chance we get."

◀▼▶

Three days later I studied my face in the small folding mirror I kept in my bureau and remembered June's cousin Myrtle, who had been married in white lace and lilies.

Myrtle didn't like the photograph taken on their wedding day, so after the young couple returned from their honeymoon at the Banff Springs Hotel they dressed in their bridal finery and were photographed again.

June and I had studied both photographs, trying to decide if anything had changed in Myrtle's face. June was of the opinion that the bride looked more knowing and womanly after her wedding night; I maintained that she looked exactly the same.

Would anyone think my face had changed? I examined my eyes in the mirror. No, I couldn't see any difference. Perhaps that was because I had never looked very innocent, with my crooked mouth and raised eyebrow. Or maybe I just didn't want to see any difference. My jigsaw-puzzle mind had become adept at setting aside the pieces that didn't fit into the big picture. Now I made up my mind quite deliberately to lock away the knowledge that Fowler was a married man.

I had been raised to respect the sanctity of marriage. But that was real marriages like the ones I had observed back in Touchwood, not the hollow legal marriages of convenience that people contracted in this archaic culture. I had a hard time picturing Frances, who seemed as flimsy as a paper doll. I thought of Mr. Rochester, hopelessly married to a crazy woman in the attic, and imagined myself as Jane Eyre.

◀▼▶

On duty, I was punctiliously courteous toward Fowler. The section had become more informal and it was tacitly agreed that we didn't have to call him sir except when outsiders were present. But I was so afraid someone might suspect our new intimacy that I continued to use 'sir' almost to excess.

There was no opportunity for private conversations, other than a few whispered words here and there, but we did have our own secret signal. When he wanted to tell me he loved me, he touched the tip of his forefinger to his nose.

The only relief I had from the grinding work was my daily walk. I found a route that took me down the footpath to the river, past the airfield, and beyond. After climbing over a stile, I entered a William Constable landscape, through a meadow filled with wildflowers, and past a stone gate smothered with climbing roses where an old brown-and-white speckled English Setter lay sunning himself. As soon as he saw me coming, the dog would lift his head and thump his tail feebly on the ground. I always stopped to stroke his thin flanks and fondle his grey muzzle.

◆▼◢

I had now seen the European landscape through all four seasons and this made my job much easier. I knew the colour of a cultivated field when it was frozen with ice or ripe with mud; the shapes of the trees when they were in full leaf or stripped bare.

My discovery of the radar trap marked a new German approach to photographic reconnaissance. Rather than simply try to camouflage the important targets, the enemy now began to create dummy targets called decoys, drawing the Allied bombers to drop their loads in the wrong locations.

I was reminded of the crudely carved wooden decoys with dark green painted heads that Dad set out on the slough during hunting season. They didn't look enough like ducks to fool anybody, let alone a duck. Yet every fall they drew hundreds of trusting mallards out of the sky.

Bomber pilots were as helpless as those poor ducks. The camouflage didn't even have to be very good to fool them. They had only a glimpse of the scene below, usually in darkness and often covered with clouds. How easy to mistake one river or town for another, especially if the aircraft was off course due to wind drift or navigational error.

In spite of my best efforts, I still made mistakes.

Once I interpreted a mined field, showing the typical pattern of dots. The Germans were so orderly that they even laid their mines an exact distance apart. To my chagrin, the field proved to be nothing more than a graveyard, with rows of tombstones. *I should have known that,* I scolded myself. Hadn't I noticed what an amazing number of dead bodies there were in Europe? The whole continent was one vast burial ground.

Another photograph baffled me for the longest time: an aircraft hidden in a small clearing, surrounded by trees. But how did it land or take off? There was no runway through the forest, not so much as a footpath.

I puzzled over this one for hours and finally set it aside. That night I dreamed I was a bird flying over the clearing, my shadow flickering through the leaves. The next morning, I went straight back to the print and laughed. There was nothing there except the shadow of the reconnaissance aircraft, which had crossed the angle between the sun and the clearing just as the shutter clicked.

I told the joke on myself to the other interpreters. Janet found it hugely amusing. "I declare, if the shadows were right, you could tell the difference between a cow and a bull."

I was offended. I repeated the remark to Fowler in a rare private moment, but he merely laughed. "Janet can be a little toffee-nosed sometimes, but she's all right," he said. "I was at school with her brother. You girls should really try to get along."

•❦•

I was seated in the camouflage room one morning, trying to block out the sound of Janet's voice. She was describing the ease with which her precious thoroughbred took a high hedge. An ornately framed photograph rested on her desk, showing herself seated on Crusader, holding a silver trophy. She often gazed at it adoringly, and once I saw her kiss her fingertips and press them to the glass.

Everyone's going a bit barmy, I reflected, not for the first time. Sam's joviality had undergone a sea change, and he was now as irritable as a hornet. He seemed to have developed an unreasonable dislike for Fowler.

Leach looked like a walking cadaver, his eyes burning with an unholy light. Everyone hated the Germans, but Leach would gladly have torn them apart with his bare hands. I felt sorry for him, ever since Sally had told me he was Jewish. Some disturbing rumours about the treatment of Jews in Europe were drifting through the unit, although nobody quite believed them.

Perhaps the whole world was going crazy. Surely the Germans must have undergone a massive brainwashing experiment by that monster Hitler. An entire race, including scientists and musicians and mothers and ordinary farmers like the ones in Touchwood, couldn't have gone collectively mad.

One thing was certain. They wanted to conquer the rest of the world and become the master race, and they would stop at nothing to reach their goal. My darkest thoughts were confirmed a few minutes later when Fowler entered the room.

"New orders, everyone. A report from Bletchley Park says the Germans are working on a long-range weapon that can be fired on England from the French coast."

A cold hand clutched at my chest. How could we hope to win this war when their scientists kept inventing better weapons? Was it possible that they could attack from such a distance? If so, our small advantage — the narrow strip of water, heavily defended by our navy and air force — would be lost.

"It just gives me the gruesomes!" Janet said. "Imagine them taking aim while we're sitting here, utterly helpless and unsuspecting!"

"How did they find out about this weapon, sir?" I asked. Bletchley Park, located forty miles north of Medmenham, was the head of British intelligence and had a network of tentacles reaching around the planet.

"One of our agents in Norway. Whether to believe him is the question. The boys and girls at Bletchley spend more time trying to sort out the hoaxes from the genuine article than we do searching for decoys."

"What do they know about it?" Sam asked.

"The weapon is being tested at an experimental station called Peenemünde, which translated means the mouth of the Peene River, on the northern coast of Germany. An object resembling a rocket was fired from Peenemünde into the ocean four months ago, on Christmas Eve. We've been ordered to examine every photograph of enemy territory within one hundred and thirty miles of London."

There was a pause while we waited for further instructions.

"What are we looking for?" Janet asked.

Fowler looked down at the paper in his hand and frowned. "There's not much more, I'm afraid. The orders say: 'This weapon may or may not be shaped like a tube, a gun, or an aircraft. Size unknown.'"

The orders were so vague as to be laughable, but no one laughed.

"That's what I hate about this bloody job," Sam said. "The brass expects you to find a needle in a haystack! In fact, that would be easier, since we know what both needles and haystacks look like!"

I came on shift the next day to find that the entire unit, now with more than one hundred interpreters, had been pulled off their regular duties to search for the mystery weapon. Not everyone was convinced that it even existed. It sounded like one of those crazy rumours that went round the station now and then. One whisper said the weapon was capable of reaching all the way to Canada. I had a horrible vision of Halifax being bombed into rubble.

Slowly I opened my leather case and unpacked my instruments. I didn't even know where to begin.

Settling down to work, I first examined the photographs of Peenemünde. The naval base was located on a peninsula, surrounded on three sides by the ocean, attached to the mainland by a narrow neck of land, and covered with dense forest. The only unusual items were several large circular hollows in the earth, the size of sports stadiums. Inside them were large inexplicable black smears. I then turned to the long coastline along northern France, Belgium, and Holland, seeking the tiniest clue that might indicate a site where a rocket could be launched.

I tried all my personal tricks. I allowed myself to become a bird, soaring over the landscape, my bright eyes registering every leaf and shadow. Nothing.

I took frequent breaks from my work, letting my mind go blank before going back to my desk. Nothing.

I tried scrutinizing every square millimetre of a photograph, setting it aside and returning to take a quick overall glance, hoping a hot item would reveal itself. Nothing.

The section room was quiet as everyone else jumped through the same visual hoops. There was nothing to see, nothing to find. Or if there was, we didn't recognize it.

New photographs arrived daily as the recce unit was sent out again and again to photograph the coastline. I ran into Adrian Stone one afternoon as he came downstairs after a meeting with Shoreham. Over the months we had become quite friendly. I had even met his wife, Grace, and his two little boys when they visited the village.

"We're covering hundreds of square miles, taking shots of absolutely nothing," he said. "Well, good luck. I hope you find it — the sooner the better."

My jaws were aching. I had developed the habit of grinding my back teeth in frustration. This was like a game of Blind Man's Bluff, hearing rustles and whispers, tripping over unseen obstacles and running blindly into blank walls.

◀▼▶

It had been three long weeks and Fowler hadn't suggested another meeting at Bliss. Outside the camouflage room, he made himself scarce. I knew he was just being cautious, but still. He said we

would visit Bliss at every chance, but apparently those opportu-
nities — at least for him — were thin on the ground. Now that I
had committed myself body and soul, it was deeply painful to be
treated like a virtual stranger. I was beginning to think that I had
made a complete fool of myself.

Late one night I returned to my room exhausted and dispirited.
Shoved under my door, along with a couple of letters from school
friends, was a plain white envelope with a typed address and a
London postmark.

Curious, I sat down on the edge of my cot and slit open the
letter. There were two pages of handwriting, in a flowing script that
made me catch my breath. It was familiar because I had seen it so
often in my own section room.

❧

London
April 30, 1943
My own darling Rose,

I'm writing this at my desk, and seated across
the room from me is an angel from heaven in a
blue suit. It would be easier to meet the enemy in
hand-to-hand combat than undergo the exquisite
torture of seeing you each day, and knowing that
you are untouchable. When I see your head bent
over your work, a tiny frown on your adorable
face, I want to jump across my desk and take
you in my arms.

It's been nineteen days since we were alone —
you see, I am counting — and not an hour has
passed when I haven't thought of you. My dreams
make the long days pass more quickly. I long to
visit Bliss again, in every sense of the word.

Don't be distressed if I seem distant when I
am near you, my sweet. Know that I have our
best interests at heart. We must be very cautious.
Discovery would mean the end of my career.
Until we meet again, I send you all my love.
Gideon
P.S. Please destroy this letter after reading.

My world was instantly transformed. I read the letter two, three,
four times before clasping it to my breast. No other gesture could
have meant so much. What had begun to tarnish around the edges
was illuminated once again with a brilliant glow.

16

I was struggling to stay alert one sultry afternoon when Leach gave a low exclamation and handed round a pair of photographs. They showed a thick vertical column about forty feet tall and four feet thick, standing on the shore at Peenemünde between the high and low water marks.

"That looks exactly like a rocket!" I said.

"We aren't allowed to call it a rocket." Leach's scientific background made him impossibly precise sometimes. "It's just a tall cylinder at this point."

"Don't split hairs, old man!" Sam said. "I'll wager those black streaks are scorch marks, made when the rocket was fired! You found the bloody thing!"

Fowler rushed upstairs with the good news while the rest of us leaned back in our chairs, practically weak with relief. With the exception of Janet, who requested a twenty-four-hour leave to visit Crusader, we walked down to The Dog and Badger to celebrate. I was thrilled when Fowler agreed to accompany us because I so rarely had the chance to feast my eyes on him outside the section room. The four of us huddled together at a corner table where we couldn't be overheard and congratulated ourselves on a job well done.

"Now that we know where the blighters are, our bombers can wipe them out. You may very well have saved the world for democracy, my dear chap!" Sam slapped Leach on the shoulder, and even Leach allowed himself a small smirk.

By the time I had finished my second pint, I felt very merry. We had thwarted the Third Reich once again. I was only twenty-two years old, an officer in the British air force, in love with a handsome man who was counting the hours until we could be together again.

I smiled as I met Fowler's eyes. Instantly he leaped to his feet. "Well, I've got to push off and make my report to the powers-that-be in London. Have another round on me."

◂▾▸

That night, I went through my bedtime ritual. First I recalled everything that Fowler and I had said to each other during the day. That was easy since we rarely exchanged more than a dozen words.

Then I remembered his arms around me, the feel of his rough uniform against my cheek, the smell of his cologne. I never went so far as to imagine the part where we climbed into bed together. Standing safely in the circle of his embrace was a perfectly satisfying fantasy, an end in itself.

Finally I knelt beside my cot, not to pray, but to stretch my arm under the mattress all the way to my shoulder and pull out the letter he had written to me. I read it two or three times each night, although it had been committed to memory long ago. I couldn't bear to burn it, even if that meant disobeying a direct order.

◂▾▸

Three days later, I came into the lounge and sat down in a leather armchair to drink my morning tea. I was lighting my first cigarette of the day when I spotted the front page of the *Daily Telegraph* lying on the table at my elbow.

With a shock, I recognized the reconnaissance photograph I had interpreted the previous day, with the headline: "RAF Blows Up Three Key Dams in Germany."

I picked up the newspaper and read: "With one single blow, the RAF has precipitated what may prove to be the greatest industrial disaster yet inflicted on Germany...."

The photograph showed the great Möhne dam bearing a ragged hole three hundred feet wide, the water smooth on top, foaming at the edges where it tore at the rough edges of the shattered concrete and boiled down into the valley below.

As I finished reading the article, Fowler appeared. I was so intent on the photograph that I didn't experience my usual surge of delight at the sight of him.

"Where did the paper get this?" I asked, without even saying hello. I was afraid it must be some appalling mistake. Ordinarily reconnaissance photographs weren't released to the papers, other than the odd column of smoke meant to illustrate bomb damage.

Fowler leaned over my shoulder. "The public relations department decided to play this one up big. They even have a name for the bomber crews who participated — The Dam Busters." He smiled broadly when he saw the huge photograph. "Makes a pretty good show, doesn't it? That should give public morale a real shot in the arm."

I was a little shaken by his offhand tone. This was only one view of the disaster. We had both seen the other photographs — the wreckage of villages, the broken church steeples peeping from the foam, the splintered houses, the bodies of cattle and horses and people being borne downstream in a raging torrent.

Touchwood
May 23, 1943
My dear girl,

It's your birthday today, and my own anniver-
sary as a mother. You arrived on a lovely spring
morning, the kind of day that makes you believe
the whole world is being born again. Tom took
one look and said: "Her face is like a little rose."
We'll be thinking of you all day, my darling. I
hope you received your birthday parcel, marked
number twenty.

Jack will be home next week for his final leave
before being shipped out. He'll write and tell you
where he's stationed as soon as he gets to England.
It makes us feel so much better to know his big
sister will be nearby.

George Stewart received the most tremendous news yesterday. Charlie has been awarded
the Distinguished Flying Cross! Here's what it said
on the front page of the *Times*:

"Flying Officer Charles Edward Stewart has
proven himself to be a gallant and courageous
pilot. On April 15, 1943, his aircraft was detailed
for an attack against Kiel. On the return flight his
bomber was damaged by anti-aircraft fire and fire
broke out. Flying Officer Stewart ordered his crew
to abandon the aircraft by parachute. All the members did so, except the mid-upper gunner who was
wounded and unconscious. Flying Officer Stewart
chose not to abandon the aircraft himself, but
successfully accomplished an extremely difficult
emergency landing, and assisted the gunner to
escape from the fiercely burning aircraft, thereby

saving his life. Flying Officer Stewart's magnificent courage, exceptional skill, and devotion to duty are worthy of the highest praise."

George is just bursting his buttons with pride. He's especially happy because Charlie has been given a six-month leave from flying, so we don't have to worry about him for now.

George and Tom have finished seeding already. We had so much snow this winter that the ground is moist so we're off to a good start. The fields are already greening up. Since the war started, crops have never been better — nature's way of compensating, I sometimes think.

Robert Day drove up one evening last week and asked me to come out to Mrs. Boyd's farm with him. He had a pile of mail for her and she hadn't been into the post office since her son Harry left Canada. When we came into the yard, we knew right away that something was wrong. The blinds were down and the dog looked awfully thin and hungry.

Robert broke the lock on the door, and we went in and found Mrs. Boyd in a terrible state. Her hair was wild, and she even had marks on her hands and arms where she had bitten herself. "He's dead, he's dead!" she kept shrieking. We showed her a letter from Harry, but she wouldn't believe us, so we took her into the hospital and sent a telegram to her sister in Regina. Poor woman! I've written to Harry and told him his mother is poorly, but there's nothing he can do now except to keep writing.

Hank Oswald's mother received a letter from him last week, after he was badly wounded in Africa. She said Hank opened his eyes in hospital and there was a patchwork quilt over him. The first thing he saw was a piece of his old pyjamas! When he was a little boy he'd filled in all the printed arrowheads with a coloured fountain pen. Hank said he thought he had died and gone to heaven. Then he turned over the edge of the quilt and found a label: "Canadian Red Cross, Touchwood." Hank figures it was a sign that he will come home again.

I saw June in the post office yesterday, and she mentioned that Daisy is calling her parents Mummy and Daddy. They have written to ask the Children's Service if they can adopt her. She's a dear child, so bright and lively. It makes me wish I had another little one of my own.

Well, I must go and work in the garden — with both you and Jack away we don't need as much food, but it's always a comfort to put my hands in the soil. I'll plant your marigolds again this year, as it makes me feel closer to you to see their sunny faces whenever I look out the kitchen window. God bless you, dear girl.

Love, Mother XXOO

Finally we visited Bliss again. Once again, I groomed myself with meticulous care, hoping that this rendezvous might unveil the mysterious pleasure that other women experienced in the embrace of their lovers.

But this time was no better than the last. Making love lasted only moments before Fowler jumped out of bed and began to dress. He was on his way to a meeting in central London. After the marvellous letter he had written, I was sure that he would have arranged to spend more time in Bliss. I knew my forlorn expression said it all.

"Look, darling, it's like this," he said, sitting down on the side of the bed and taking my hand. "I'm in this for the long haul. It's not just the war I have to think about, it's my whole career. There are thousands of men younger than me in uniform, waiting for the main chance. And the Yanks are handing out medals left and right. They even get gonged for surviving the voyage to England! One false step and I could jolly well find myself at the back of the queue."

"But you're the best leader in the unit," I said loyally.

Fowler stroked my hand. "I have to be better than the best, my sweet, especially since I haven't any combat experience. There's a stigma attached to flying a desk instead of an aircraft."

I was aware of this handicap. Fowler was what was known in the air force as a penguin — without the double set of wings proudly worn by the aircrew, he could flap but not fly.

"Do you really want to fly?" This wasn't the heartfelt conversation I had wanted, but at least it was something.

"Well, obviously, darling, every man would prefer to be out there giving the Hun his due, but then who'd organize the troops?" He tried to withdraw his hand, but I clung to it.

"Doesn't running the camouflage section count for anything?"

"It certainly helps to do intelligence, but I could use a really substantial discovery — like that radar trap of yours. That was a wizard piece of work." He patted my hand again. "You'll receive a letter of commendation for that. It's lying on my desk. I just haven't passed it up to Shoreham yet."

I felt warmed by this piece of news. My personal life may have been lonely and barren, but I took pride in my work. I imagined how thrilled my parents would be when I told them, but then I quickly pushed them out of my mind. This wasn't the time or the place to think about my family.

Fowler was staring at the floor and frowning slightly, a gesture that deepened the lines around his eyes. He isn't young, I noticed again. I felt a rush of sympathy for him, thirty-eight years old, his youth far behind him. I was overcome by the desire to help his career, to prove the depths of my love. I blurted out the words without thinking. "Why don't you say you discovered the radar trap?"

He looked at me sharply. "What do you mean?"

"No one else knows. The only other person on shift that night was Janet, and she didn't hear anything."

There was a brief silence as Fowler knitted his brow and pondered the idea. Having made the offer, I now found myself wishing he would refuse. Instead he turned to me, his dark eyes shining. "Are you positive, darling?"

"Of course!" I spoke too loudly, trying to take satisfaction in the adoring expression on his face.

He put his arm around my shoulders and squeezed them affectionately. "That's my girl! After all, it can't mean that much to you. You'll be going home after the war, and I'll be left to clean up the mess over here."

His words stung. Did he really think we would go our separate ways after the war ended? Or was he referring to a temporary separation? I opened my mouth to ask him, just as he checked his heavy gold wristwatch. "Bloody hell, I must dash!" He jumped up and began to pull on his shirt.

I lay back on the pillows while I waited for the pain to subside, and for the first time I considered the future. I assumed that Gideon would divorce his wife after the war: difficult but not impossible. These days divorce didn't carry the same stigma, and his was clearly a loveless marriage. I could leave the service and find work in London, and we could continue our great love affair until his divorce had gone through. But then what?

I shook my head against the pillow and mentally shoved the future into a box. The future was as impenetrable as the heaviest London fog. Surely our love would carry us forward when the time came. First we had to win the war. Everything else came second.

Fowler finished tying his shoes and kissed me goodbye with great enthusiasm. I heard him whistling as his footsteps clattered down the stairs.

I lay in bed for a while, too despondent to rouse myself. The small room looked more tawdry than usual with its rumpled bed-clothes and stuffy smell. Gideon had brought me a small bouquet of violets — I was touched by this gesture, although I knew he had bought them for ten pence from the old woman at the flower stall in Paddington Station — but already they were hanging their heads and turning brown around the edges. A spiderweb dotted with dead flies hung across one corner of the ceiling. I felt as if there was a stone lying on my chest, making it hard to breathe.

I forced myself to rise and gaze out the dirty window. The sky was blue — not the hard, glassy blue of the prairie sky, but the soft azure of an English sky that always looked as if you could reach up and punch a hole through it with your fist. I pulled myself together and decided to see something of London before returning to the station.

My romantic vision of this fabled city had long since been shattered by the smoke, the squalour, and the industrial sprawl I saw from the train. Soot spewed from the chimney pots, and I hadn't walked far before my face and hands felt grimy.

But I bought a ticket and took a red double-decker bus to Buckingham Palace. Despite the rubbish blowing in the streets, the palace was as imposing as it looked in photographs, and the flag outside showed that my beloved royal family was still in residence. They had remained in London, despite the risk.

The white swans were swimming gracefully on the calm waters of the pool in Hyde Park. Any other bird would have been killed for food long ago, but the Londoners were sentimentally attached to their swans.

I strolled along the bank of the Thames, stopping to admire London Bridge. Having become something of an expert on bridges, I could appreciate the stately twin towers and the single span cross-ing the river between them.

I walked farther down the river toward the docks with their thicket of ship funnels. Several of the ships sported dazzle painting: streaks and whorls of black-and-white paint from stem to stern, supposed to disguise them as they moved through the waves. The interpreters knew that the technique made little difference in reality, but it was good for the sailors' morale.

By the time I returned to Paddington, it was late afternoon. The station wasn't busy; civilian travel had fallen off, and service personnel were discouraged from travelling for pleasure.

I was on my way to platform five when I heard shrieks of feminine laughter. I turned to see a dozen teenage girls coming up behind me in red tartan kilts, bagpipes and drums slung over their shoulders. They looked like large, rosy-cheeked children in their green tams topped with white pom-poms.

I felt a patriotic thrill when I recognized the red maple leaves on their armbands. "Hello, Canada! What are you doing so far from home?"

"Hello, Canada yourself!" said one pretty, dark-haired girl. They clustered around me, chattering and giggling. "We're the Canadian Girls' Pipe Band. We just docked in Liverpool yesterday. We're going to travel around merry old England, entertaining the troops."

She pointed to the train pulling into platform six beside us. "That train is full of wounded Canadian soldiers, just back from Italy. We're going to give them a real show, aren't we, girls?"

I looked at their bright eyes and felt very old. "Good luck. I'll cheer you on while I'm waiting for my train."

As I stepped to one side with the other passengers, the girls formed into rows under the direction of their pipe major, an older woman with a harassed expression.

The flag-bearer hoisted the Canadian Red Ensign and the bagpipes began to fill with their peculiar wailing sound. A blast of steam from the incoming train blew their kilts up to one side and a couple of girls laughed and screamed delightedly.

Canadian Red Cross nurses were coming down the platform and moving into position. Three of them pushed trolleys bearing steaming urns and platters of cookies.

The drum major turned to the girls and signalled them to stand ready. The door of the nearest railcar opened and soldiers in khaki uniforms began to step down.

These were the walking wounded: arms in casts, heads wrapped in blood-stained bandages. A couple of them hobbled along with sticks. One soldier's head was swathed in white; only his eyes and mouth were visible. He flung his arms around a nurse. She gently detached herself and handed him a cookie.

I looked over at the band. The drum major raised her arms and gave the signal to begin playing. The girls weren't laughing now. Their eyes above the pipes were wide and staring. The strains of "Scotland the Brave" rose into the air, but it was a dismal effort. Rather than a rousing march, it sounded like a dirge.

Now the men with missing hands and arms began to step down. Some had an empty sleeve, others had two empty sleeves, pinned across their chests. Their faces and bodies were so young and healthy that the missing limbs seemed like petals torn off a blossom in full bloom.

The pressure started to build in my chest and I put my hand to my collarbones. The band was still playing, although several bagpipes had petered out and the music was barely audible.

A ramp was lowered to the platform, and orderlies dressed in white began to push a line of wheelchairs off the train, bearing the soldiers who couldn't walk. The pipes died away, although the drummers continued to pound their instruments, slightly out of synchronization. The pipers had their mouthpieces between their lips, but they weren't making any sound. A few of them had tears on their cheeks.

Then two orderlies squeezed through the doorway carrying a boy in a woven basket. He had no arms or legs, just a body and a handsome young face, blond hair lifting off his forehead in the breeze. The legs and sleeves of his khaki uniform were neatly folded under him.

This time the music stopped and the girls broke down completely. All of them began to weep, pipers and drummers alike. "About face! Quick march!" The drum major led the distraught group down the platform.

The wounded soldiers were too busy clutching at the nurses or gazing up at the domed glass roof to notice. A few wore blank expressions and didn't seem to know or care where they were. I couldn't hear anything above the noisy trains, but I could see the drum major shouting at the girls, her face contorted with anger. Several of them were clinging together, wiping their eyes and blowing their noses.

A young mother walked past, leading her little boy by the hand. When she saw the wounded men, an expression of mingled horror and sadness crossed her face. She quickly covered the child's eyes and pulled him away.

After two or three moments the band formed up again, wheeled around, and marched smartly in formation toward us. When the drum major gave the signal, the joyful strains of "The Maple Leaf Forever" burst into the air.

A couple of soldiers shouted "Hurray!" and waved at the girls. One man whose eyes were bandaged turned toward the sound and began to sing along. A soldier in a wheelchair buried his face in his hands, his shoulders shaking.

The girls were working hard, blowing the pipes as if their lives depended on it, tears trickling down their cheeks. The drummers pounded away with grim determination. The skirl flew out of the pipes, wild and free, and was swallowed up in the noise of the steam engine.

I looked at the soldiers again, the human wreckage of what had been Canada's finest, our pride and joy, our native sons. I came as close to crying then as I had for the past two years.

17

"All right, everyone, heads up." Fowler strode into the section room. As usual his bearing was so military it looked like he had a hockey stick taped to his spine. "We're going to be crater chasers for the day."

Sam groaned. I was silent but dismayed. I hated assessing bomb damage, but it was a rule that all sections would assist when required in what was called a surge effort. Pooling our resources was the unit's greatest strength.

It was the bomb damage section that had the toughest job, in my opinion, although many interpreters considered it the easiest. There was no mistaking the crater left by a bomb. But neither was the evidence of destruction of homes and civilians.

"Where's the target?" asked Leach.

"Hamburg," Fowler said. "Operation Gomorrah. The first wave of bombers returned early this morning."

We turned back to our work, waiting for the film to be brought in. At noon Fowler went down to the darkroom with the other section heads to fetch the prints, and an hour later he came into the room and began to pass them around.

The typical night photo looked like a white spiderweb on a black plate. Searchlight beams criss-crossed the blackness, bomb bursts showed as blazing stars, and tracer bullets from fighter planes formed arcs. Huge balls of fire called scarecrows, sent up by the enemy to simulate exploding bombers and terrify our air crews, dotted the dark sky. Anti-aircraft fire looked like straight white lines, changing to blurry zigzags when the pilots jinked wildly back and forth.

I lined up the first pair of photographs under my stereoscope and bent my head. As they came into focus, I felt my body lift and soar above a picture of destruction unlike any I had ever seen. Although these photographs had been taken long before dawn, the glare from the inferno below created an effect of daylight. Billowing smoke plumes covered half the city. Even from this altitude, a good mile above the ground, sheets of flame licked at the edges of the smoke.

For a few moments I experienced the powerful sensations of a bird in flight. Fear swept through me as I dodged and darted through the searing, shimmering heat waves. Percussion blasts from exploding bombs knocked me from side to side. My heart fluttered rapidly in my chest, my eyes stung with the smell of gunsmoke, scorched wood, and human flesh. Between the explosions I heard faint screaming.

My sensory impressions were so powerful that I had to lift my face from the stereoscope. I looked around to see how the others were reacting. The room was hushed, except for the rare sound of Leach's laughter. "That'll show the bastards," he muttered.

I picked up another set of prints and slid them under the stereoscope. This one showed hundreds of incendiary bombs raining from the bomb bay of a Lancaster like handfuls of straw tossed into the wind. Small fires had started all over the city below wherever the incendiaries landed. The bombers circling the perimeter glinted against the black smoke as vividly as a flock of white seagulls against a black thundercloud.

The smoke plumes from the smaller fires leaned toward the central blaze as if being sucked into it. Sparks, cinders, and chunks of burning wood went spinning through the air into the hungry mouth of the flame. The force of the sucking wind was so powerful that it had uprooted trees and ripped buildings from their foundations. The flurries of ash were as thick as snowflakes in a blizzard.

"Righto, let's take our measurements," Fowler said. "The Yanks have decided to horn in on the action — they're making a daylight raid against Hamburg right now. You can expect another batch of photos by tonight."

It was a hot summer day, and I was perspiring. The wisteria from the vines outside the open windows scented the air. At eight o'clock the new photographs were brought in.

It didn't seem possible that the fire could have grown worse, but it had. A huge spiral column of flame the size of a tornado swirled a mile high from the centre of the city. No air raid shelter could protect human life against that conflagration. The roads leading away from Hamburg were clogged with vehicles and people on foot trying to escape.

"It must seem like hell itself," I said aloud, to no one in particular. There wasn't any point in measuring the fire in acres, the way bomb damage was usually assessed. After a brief discussion, we agreed to put the blaze at four square miles.

"The RAF is going out again tonight," Fowler said. We raised our heads, startled. "They won't even need the Pathfinders — that fire will draw them like a candle in the window. And the German defences have been eradicated. It'll be a piece of cake." I heard the note of satisfaction in his voice.

"I don't see how dumping another load of bombs is going to accomplish anything." My voice broke slightly, and I put my hand over my chest in the familiar gesture.

Fowler grinned, his white teeth gleaming. "Ours is not to wonder why. Just enjoy it while it lasts. Bomb damage is standing everyone a pint down at the pub later."

After my shift ended, I went straight to my room. Fowler looked surprised when I said I wasn't coming. Without taking off my uniform, I threw myself onto my bed, still overcome by the phantom sensations of heat and smoke and suffering.

The faces of unknown women and children rose before my eyes, being roasted alive in concrete shelters as surely as if they were ovens. I remembered how horrified everyone back home had been when German bombs had killed twenty-three thousand British civilians during the entire three-month Battle of Britain. The civilian deaths in Hamburg alone, in a single raid, must be twice as high.

This was terror bombing, pure and simple. I rolled over onto my stomach and pressed my face into the pillow, wishing I could cry. I hadn't cried for over a year. I wondered if I would ever cry again. Hours later, I undressed without even reading Gideon's letter and fell into a restless sleep.

It wasn't until three days later that the assessment was completed. The fire had burned itself out, although a pall of smoke still hung over the city. Sunlight was reflected from the gigantic pools of water lying in the streets, remainders of a futile effort to contain the blaze.

I had seen burned buildings before, their walls still upright, looking like charred honeycombs. In Hamburg, even the walls had burned to the ground. Nothing remained but a flat, black surface, marked with giant smoking heaps of rubble.

As I scrutinized these smouldering piles, I became aware of a more sickening reality. These were not the typical pathetic sticks and stones that remained of people's possessions — these were the remains of people themselves. Thousands of blackened corpses had been stacked into gigantic funeral pyres.

⁌⁘⁍

"Hello, stranger!"

"Sally! Come in and pull up a cot." I was pressing my spare uniform, standing in my little room with the ironing board

166 · ELINOR FLORENCE

propped against the bed. It was the first time I had seen her in weeks, and I was longing to talk to someone who could take my mind off the war.

The room was so small that I had to step into the hallway while Sally clambered onto the bed. She leaned against the wall, curled her long legs under her gracefully, and lit a cigarette. "You look like hell," she said, eyes narrowed against a cloud of blue smoke.

I had begun to wear a severe bun at the back of my head, pulling my hair so tightly that my scalp hurt. My family photograph and my coffee tin were mathematically aligned. My uniform was spotless, brass buttons polished until I could see my reflection. Once I had even gotten out of bed in the middle of the night to rearrange the contents of my bureau. I didn't know why, but I felt more in control if my surroundings were in order.

Sally was still frowning. "Are you getting enough sleep?"

I shrugged. "I have nightmares. Who doesn't?"

"Maybe you should try Churchill's trick. Apparently he puts his head on the pillow, says: 'Bugger everything!' and then sleeps like a baby."

I chuckled. I couldn't remember the last time I had laughed — the sensation was almost as unfamiliar as crying.

"What's this I hear about you and Sam?" I asked, changing the subject.

Sally shook her head. "This place is a bloody gossip mill. You can't get away with a thing. But that's what I came round to tell you. We've been spending some free time together, outside the station."

"Sam's a wonderful man, Sally. I admire him so much."

"He even took me down to Brighton a fortnight ago so I could meet the terrible twins."

"Do tell. I've always been curious about them."

"They're a couple of old dears, although Sam says things can get nasty. Whenever there's a raid they nearly come to blows. One of them thinks the cellar is the safest place, and the other is determined to go into the attic."

I laughed again. "As long as they approve of you, that's the main thing."

"Oh, I can charm the birds off the trees. But there's another wee problem. I have some overdue leave, and I want to take Sam home with me. I'm worried about Daddy's reaction. Sam's not exactly what he'd call top drawer."

I lifted the iron off my sleeve. "Top drawer? Whatever do you mean?"

"Sam was a scholarship boy, so he went to the right schools, but before the war he operated his own business. I can hear Daddy now: 'My daughter with a shopkeeper? Egad!'"

I stared at her. "Surely that sort of thing doesn't still exist outside of Jane Austen. Your father must be a throwback to the eighteenth century!"

Sally's expression was serious. "I know it seems foolish to you, Rose. It does to me, too, especially when I see it through your eyes. It's a treat to find someone who doesn't care that my grandfather's sister was married to a baronet. Daddy's a bit stuffy, but he's no different than any of his friends. The rules of class are invisible until you run up against them. Then they're like steel bars."

I was silent while I thought this over. "I guess that explains Janet's attitude toward me."

Sally snorted. "Janet's probably never been forced to rub shoulders, let alone share the same rank with someone whose father is a farmer, and Canadian to boot. She's a pretentious twit — but you have to remember that she's not an exception, she's the rule."

I couldn't help asking. "What about Gideon Fowler? He's a member of the upper class, but he always treats me as an equal."

Sally looked at me sharply. I lowered my eyes and became very concerned with getting a wrinkle out of my collar.

"Fowler's probably more set in his ways than my father. His entire life has been directed toward taking his rightful place — the best marriage, the military career. He's a very able administrator and he has a reputation of working well with all kinds of people. He has what's called 'the common touch.' If he keeps his nose clean, he'll wind up with a promotion before the war is over."

I tried to speak lightly. "You make it sound so cold-blooded, Sally."

"It's utterly heartless, I'm afraid. That's why I'm nervous about taking Sam home to meet my people. He has enough brains to know when he's being insulted, even in the nicest possible way."

◂▾▸

August 1, 1943
London
My darling Rose,

I have never before considered a Canadian accent to be attractive, quite the opposite in fact, but coming from your lovely lips it is the sweetest sound on earth. I particularly enjoy the way you say the word "pudding." For some reason it makes me want to kiss you.

I am spending the next three days here in London, huddled around the table with some very important men, but I find myself struggling to concentrate as my thoughts constantly find their way back to you. I close my eyes and imagine you seated at your desk, a pencil tucked behind one shell-like ear, penetrating the mysteries of the European continent.

I know it is difficult for you, as it is for me, to be separated for so long. Life is full of trials that test our inner strength, and our devotion to each other. You are indeed my good fairy, my muse, my inspiration. You must have been sent to me from

the wilderness for a reason. With you by my side,
even the dark clouds of war have a silver lining.
All my love, Gideon
P.S. Please destroy this letter after reading.

◂▾▸

Touchwood
July 30, 1943
Dear Miss,

I wonder if you love the limeys so much now
that you have to live with them. My guess is they
aren't quite so charming at close quarters. They'll
do their damnedest to make you feel like two
bits, so I'm dropping you a line to say don't you
believe them.

The lady who's working for me now doesn't
know the first thing about newspapers, but neither
did you when you started. One thing is for sure,
she isn't going to let me train her and then take a
notion into her head to run off and join up.

I met your father at the livery stable the other
day and he says nobody has the faintest what
you're doing over there but I will say one thing:
you're a smart girl and catch on fast and as long as
you don't take any guff from those two-faced rat-
tlesnakes they call officers you'll be all right. Just
remember where you came from and who your
real friends are.
James MacTavish

◂▾▸

RCAF Middleton St. George
August 2, 1943
Dear Rose,

Your mother sent me your address, since I wanted
to drop you a line and see how things are going
"down south."

I've transferred into the new Bomber Six
Group. We're all Canadians here, so that's a nice
change, although I made some real good pals
while I was flying with the RAF. The Yorkies are
a swell bunch and make us feel right at home. I
meet up with a couple of guys from Touchwood
now and then. Mostly we talk about the old days.
I saw Teddy Jones last week, he just arrived. I
don't know how come he didn't wash out with
that squint of his, but maybe they aren't as fussy
now as when the war started.

Until recently I've been grounded, training
the rookies. Some of these boys need all the help
they can get, only eighteen years old and green
as grass. You can't hold their hands up there, you
just have to knock some sense into their heads
and then send them off into the wild blue yonder.

But anyway, I pestered the powers-that-be so
many times that they put me back in action, and
now I'm flying one of those new Avro Lancasters.
Boy oh boy, what a beaut of a plane! Fast, heavy,
and high. It can fly on three engines, manage on
two, and limp away on one, so we feel as safe as
houses up there. Her name is *Prairie Rose Two*.
The first one caught fire and was put out to pasture
after bringing us home safely more times than I
care to remember.

Dad has another bumper crop on the way, and he's building two more granaries to hold it all. I wish I were there to see it. I always miss being at home this time of the year. I wouldn't even mind doing the swathing, something I always hated because of the grasshoppers.

Well, I hope the pommies are treating you okay, Rose. I sure would like to hear from you. As always, Charlie

18

"Rose, we have a serious problem." I was roused from my concentration as Tommy Thompson, head of the target section, stepped up to my desk. He dropped a sheaf of photographs at my elbow. "I'm blessed if I know what to make of these."

Lately I had begun to work more closely with the target section. Their task was formidable: whenever a bombing mission was laid on, they prepared a target folder for each of the seven men in a bomber crew. In a large raid, this amounted to thousands of folders. Each folder contained a map, an information sheet with every scrap of knowledge about the route and the enemy defences along the way, and a photograph of the target itself, sometimes using one of Sally's models.

"What's the matter, Tommy?"

"There was a raid last night on a factory manufacturing aircraft parts, located in a German town called Walburg. It's a deucedly dangerous target, because the bombers have to run the gauntlet through a path of anti-aircraft guns. The town itself is well-marked by a bend in the Walburg River. The weather was clear last night, unfortunately, and the bombers were sitting ducks. Quite heavy losses, both going over and coming home." He ran his hand through his thinning hair. "Now here's the odd bit. The boys claim they dropped their bombs right on target. But today's assessment from bomb damage says there's no sign of an explosion in Walburg. The town's still standing, the factory chimneys smoking, everything is business as usual."

I thought for a minute before asking the obvious questions.

"There's no chance the recce aircraft took photos of another town instead?"

"None whatsoever. You know the recce pilots are far more reliable than the bombers. They don't even need landmarks. They just set their instruments and fly straight to the target like a bullet."

"You've checked with the darkroom — could bomb damage have gotten an earlier batch of negatives?"

"That would probably be a hanging offence, but I've confirmed with them, yes. This was the film they were given this morning, straight out of the magazines."

"And there's no chance the bombers missed the target altogether, and tried on a bit of a cover-up." I hesitated. "You know how they do sometimes."

"Who can blame them, poor chaps?" Tommy shook his head. "But in this case, I don't think so. Dozens of aircrew have the same story — they reached the target, dropped the bombs, and headed for home. If somebody's fudging, they usually spout tales of fighters coming out of nowhere, or unexpected lightning storms, or some other excuse. Besides, even the Pathfinders agree: they arrived on schedule, identified the target, and dropped the flares."

When Fowler returned from lunch, I requested permission to devote the rest of the day to Walburg. First, I studied the early photos included in the target folders: they were months old, and not the best images, but perfectly readable. There was the bend in the river, and the tall, distinctive smokestacks of the aircraft factory visible on the northern edge of town. In the town square was the graceful spire of a church.

Then I lined up the photographs taken the morning after the raid. As I studied them, pair by pair, I noted the bend in the river and the smokestacks. The church spire was clearly visible.

I lifted my head from the stereoscope and rubbed my eyes. Well, bomb damage was correct: there wasn't a sign of destruction. The roads, the roofs — even the grey tones of the grass and trees, usually the first to show any change resulting from exploding bombs — were absolutely intact.

Sometimes if I left things alone for a bit I could see them with fresh eyes. I pushed back my chair and went downstairs to the model section.

Unlike my own section room, this was a lively and colourful place. Pots of paint and rolls of paper littered the room; the floor was dotted with bits of plaster.

Sally was at work, looking quite at home. Her sleeves were rolled up and her tie was crooked. Wisps of hair had come undone from her coronet of braids, and there was a smear of green paint on her chin. She was bent over a huge model, holding a tool that resembled a cake decorator.

"Hello, Rose! Hang on, I'll be finished in two ticks."

Today she was completing a model of Berlin, eight by ten feet on a plywood base with contoured hills, buildings, and miniature trees. The skin of the model — photographs of the area, shot to scale — was glued over the contours; then the model was delicately painted by hand. Since the photos were black and white, the colours had to be guessed, based on tone and texture.

"What on earth is that thing you're holding?"

Sally flourished a canvas bag with a nozzle on one end. "We call it the hedger. We use it to squeeze green paint onto all the hedgerows. We were jolly grateful when some bright spark came up with this one, I can tell you! I never knew there were so many hedges in Europe until I had to paint them by hand."

She leaned over and gave the hedger a gentle squeeze while I strolled around the model, making admiring sounds. "It's good, isn't it?" she asked. "See those wee sailboats on the lake? I couldn't figure out what to use for masts until Tommy came along and I had a brainstorm and I said, 'Yank out a couple of those gorgeous bristly moustache hairs and hand them over!'"

"Brilliant." I envied her enthusiasm. Sally was often able to forget the war and pretend she was still in art school.

"Stay right there and I'll show you something." She ran around the room, closing the blackout drapes and shutting off the overhead lights, then flicking on a yellow floodlight in one corner. The golden light streamed over the model, filling the contours with shadows.

"That's what our boys will see when they fly over the city under a full moon." The model was eerie in the dim glow. I could almost imagine how the aircrews felt when they saw their target from miles above.

"This morning we ran a movie camera hung on a clothesline across the ceiling, as if it were flying through the sky, and showed the film to the air crews. We made it more realistic by using a smoke machine to fill the air with little black puffs of smoke, just like flak."

I studied the model. "How much of it is guesswork? I mean, how do you know where the tramlines run?" The model showed tiny tram cars sitting on rails along the streets.

"We used photographs of Berlin, about two thousand of them, and we collected tourist snapshots, maps, anything we could scrounge. One fellow even brought in a couple of postcards from the 1936 Olympic Games."

I didn't answer. I was studying the model, lost in thought. Suddenly I headed for the door. "See you later, Sally, I must run. You've given me an idea."

I dashed up the stairs and down the hall to the print library. "Do you have anything on Walburg, Germany?" I asked the reference clerk.

While I waited for her to check, I gazed around the room, marvelling at the vast quantity of printed information stored on the floor-to-ceiling shelves: maps, guidebooks, newspapers, and reference books. We had often been able to enhance our findings here — even an old theatre ticket, with a sketch of an opera house, had been added to a target folder.

The clerk handed me a slender file. "Not much here, I'm afraid. It was just a sleepy little town before the war."

I thanked her, and took the file back to my desk. I opened it and began to sort through the scanty information. Here was a map, showing the town of Walburg. Nothing I didn't already know — it showed the distinctive bend in the river, the town tucked into the curve.

Here was a brief description, cadged from some pre-war British textbook: "The village of Walburg was founded in the eleventh century. Like many others, it was settled near the river to allow for ease of transportation. Walburg was incorporated as a town in 1473, and has not grown significantly since that time. The population is around three thousand."

I picked up the next sheet of paper. This was a newspaper advertisement for a winery, located on the edge of the town. It contained no useful information.

The fourth and final item in the file was a postcard of Walburg's main street, taken during some sort of festival. The two-storey buildings with their dark crossed beams swept down to the river's edge, where a narrow bridge supported by three stone arches stretched across the water.

In the foreground were two laughing women wearing dirndl skirts, and a little blond boy in lederhosen. I studied the postcard, wondering how the good folks of Walburg were coping with the bombing. On the other hand, perhaps they weren't having to cope at all. If the reconnaissance photographs were correct, they hadn't experienced so much as a scare.

I closed the file. Not much to go on here. I'd better examine the photographs again. I bent over my stereoscope.

By five o'clock my head was throbbing. I hadn't found any explanation for the discrepancy. There were two options: either the bomber crews or the reconnaissance pilots were mistaken.

I knew the recce pilots were far less likely to make an error. They weren't dodging flak, and they had time to do pinpoint navigation. The bombers must have dropped their loads on a town that resembled Walburg. But where?

I returned to the library and requested cover of the area around Walburg. It had been photographed months earlier, before the Germans had installed their heavy defences.

I pored over the photographs. The river flowed straight as an arrow through the countryside, leading to Walburg like a shining path. Another town called Neustadt stood on the riverbank, about twenty miles west of Walburg and closer to Britain, but it wasn't located in a river bend.

It was inconceivable that the bombers weren't even close to the target. Yet that must be what had happened. They must have bombed another town — in another part of Germany, perhaps even another country, heaven knows where.

I walked slowly down the hallway to the target section. Tommy looked up when I came in. "Anything?"

I shook my head. "Afraid not. I can't come up with a single reason except pilot error. If you like, I'll go over to the airfield with you when you meet Fanshawe."

"Would you, Rose? I could use the moral support."

We went down the broad mahogany staircase and hailed a transport vehicle parked outside. On our way over to the recce unit, we didn't speak. The atmosphere was heavy with dread.

Within minutes we entered the office building next to the main runway where two men were waiting: Adrian Stone, and the formidable Group Captain Albert Fanshawe of Bomber Command. Fanshawe was an officer of the old school: full military moustache, medals pinned across his barrel chest, spine as straight as a plumb line.

Hesitantly, Tommy explained to Fanshawe that photographic interpretation concluded the bombers had missed the target. The captain's face darkened.

"Balls!" he shouted. "Are you trying to tell me that even the Pathfinders missed the target? Followed by more than one hundred skilled pilots and navigators? What the hell were they aiming at, then?"

Tommy's voice was tense. "We've examined the photographs at great length, sir. We haven't been able to find an alternative target. There's nothing in the area that resembles Walburg, not even slightly."

Fanshawe literally bared his teeth in a snarl. "Then obviously it must have been Walburg!"

"No, sir. The reconnaissance photographs are quite clear on that subject. Not a blade of grass has been disturbed."

The group captain began to pace back and forth, hands behind his back. He appeared to be struggling to get a grip on himself before he spoke. When he did, it was in a low voice.

"I don't think you people quite realize what's at stake," he said. "We must take out that factory unless we want the whole bleeding sky filled with German fighters.

"But there's something else, something I feel even more strongly about. I have three hundred airmen under my command, and every one of them goes through a daily struggle — with emotions which I won't even attempt to describe — in order to strap himself into that aircraft when his name comes up. The one and only thing that keeps him in the war is the conviction that he's making progress! Do you understand?" Fanshawe stopped and glared at each of us in turn. His gaze rested on me longer than on the others.

"If I inform them that sixty-seven of their mates lost their lives in an absolutely futile gesture, a navigational error or some other balls-up, I'll tell you what will happen. Those men will be angry and bitter. Within a week, some of them will lose their nerve and declare themselves unfit to fly. Or, if they want to avoid the shame of court martial and spare their families, they'll ditch their kites over the Channel and we'll cover up by calling it an accident." Fanshawe's voice was rising. "I cannot, and will not, tell them — contrary to the evidence of their own senses — that you so-called experts sitting over there in your ivory towers have come to the brilliant conclusion that they dropped their bombs on a town that doesn't exist!"

The room was hushed. Adrian spoke first.

"Group Captain, I don't know how to explain the mystery, but I will personally volunteer to fly another mission over the area to see if we can't throw some light on the situation."

Tommy rose from his chair and stood at attention. "Speaking on behalf of the interpreters, we understand your position, completely. All we can do is redouble our efforts."

The meeting broke up with an exchange of salutes, very half-hearted on Fanshawe's part. Darkness was falling, and the air outside the smoke-filled office was warm and scented with flowers.

During the silent trip back to the station, Fanshawe's words repeated themselves inside my head. Once again, I was reminded that we were dealing with frightened boys far from home, risking their lives each night, eager to defeat the enemy, counting on us to send them in the right direction.

Had I been too quick to judge pilot error? Had I overlooked some tiny clue? I returned to the section room and began to study the photographs again.

❧

RAF Medmenham
August 10, 1943
Dear Charlie,

It was so nice to hear from you after all this time. I don't write many letters. They keep my nose pretty close to the grindstone here. I wish I could tell you about my work because I know you would be interested.

My heartiest congratulations on getting the Distinguished Flying Cross. You're a credit to dear old Touchwood. I read the account in the *Times* and it made my blood run cold. Please be careful and don't take any chances, Charlie. I guess that's a silly thing to say, but I mean it.

I don't have much free time, but I love walking in the countryside. The hay fields are so lush, and the cattle are so sleek and fat. At least the animals aren't suffering from the food shortage! The English farmers sure make the most of every last acre. I'd like to see what they could do in Canada with our farms. We have an embarrassment of riches.

I'm glad you're happy in the new Canadian group. I hear the food is a lot better in the RCAF. Frankly, I never want to see another baked bean as long as I live! I don't know how I would survive if it weren't for Mother's parcels.

The Americans here eat at their own mess. The Brits are still mad at them for coming into the war so late, but I think the real reason they resent the Yanks is that their food is so much better. The American mess even has steak and ice cream!

Jack's been over here for a couple of months, but we haven't been able to coordinate our leaves yet. June says her brother will be the next in line. Hard to believe he's old enough to join up, he seems like such a kid. Well, I guess we are all a little older and wiser now.

As always, Rose

19

Two weeks later, I looked through the leaded panes in the section room at a blurry green landscape and fervently thanked God it was raining again. Rain: how precious it was back home on the dusty prairies. When the clouds gathered and delivered their priceless cargo, our family ran outside, splashing through mud puddles until we were filthy, opening our mouths so the life-giving water fell into our throats.

Now I wanted it to rain for an entirely different reason: so airmen wouldn't lose their lives searching for a phantom target.

Tommy entered the room and came straight to my desk. "Bomber Command has targeted Walburg again."

"Oh, no." I had been expecting this, but hoped something would happen to prevent it. "When?"

"As soon as the weather clears. Fanshawe isn't happy about it, and I don't blame him. He's putting his men's lives on the line based on our sorry skills. And the hell of it is that we don't have any new information. All we can do is give them the same target folders again and let them take another run at it."

Tommy's face was a picture of misery. The small, bespectacled man, a bank manager in civilian life, cared deeply for the bomber crews and suffered agonies when the losses were high. He had earned their devotion when he persuaded Bomber Command to let him ride along on a mission.

Later they were glad they did. Everyone knew that rivers in moonlight form luminous arrows on the dark landscape below. But Tommy saw more than rivers. He saw that the tiniest pool had a pearly reflection, mud puddles resembled silver coins thrown on the ground, and standing water in ruts looked like twin silver threads. Now even the smallest streams were plotted.

That was a bad day. I was sure the bombers had dropped their loads on another town, but I had now reviewed old photographs of an area one hundred miles around Walburg without finding another town in a river bend.

That night the crack between my blackouts gleamed with moonlight, and I knew the bombers would be out. Early next morning I went directly to the target section without eating breakfast. Tommy was already at his desk.

"What have you heard?"

"It was a bloodbath." He shook his head. "The ack-ack guns were ready and waiting. Fanshawe sent over two hundred bombers this time, and their losses were 10 percent, twice the average. Please God, the strike was successful."

We went down to bomb damage to wait for the new photographs. When they arrived, I snatched them out of his hands. Bending over the stereoscope, my heart sank. Nothing on the first pair. Quickly I grabbed another pair. Nothing.

By the time I got to the third pair, I knew the truth — Walburg looked as pretty and peaceful today as it had two weeks ago: houses intact, church steeple rising above the green fields, river flowing smoothly past — and the factory chimneys smoking in full production.

Tommy looked at me and shook his head. There were tears in his eyes. "I'd better get over to Fanshawe's office. He'll be pacing the floor."

"Do you want me to come with you?"

"No, thanks. Nothing has changed, except the enemy has another hundred fighters in the air, and we've lost another hundred good men."

⋆▾⋆

Walburg wasn't the only target that night. The next morning there was news that lifted my spirits slightly: six hundred bombers had made the thousand-mile round trip to Peenemünde and destroyed the experimental station.

But when I learned that German night fighters had shot down forty of our bombers in the bright moonlight, once again the weight of responsibility fell like a cloak of lead.

Besides, I wondered if the sacrifice had been justified. The Germans were unbelievably resourceful. Surely they would keep copies of their rocket plans at another location. It might not take them long to return to full production.

The other interpreters didn't share my anxiety. Janet barely glanced at the photos before resuming her study of a book about show horses. The phlegmatic Leach, on the other hand, was positively gleeful. "That ought to set back their dirty little plans," he said as he studied the twisted wreckage.

Fowler agreed. "That's one for our side, chaps!" It crossed my mind that he was hoping for a promotion, but I felt a spurt of disloyalty for questioning his motives.

My thoughts turned to Charlie. I knew his station had taken part in the raid. Had he been shot down in that bloody moonlit battle over the Baltic Sea? The idea pierced my heart like a sharpened stick. I sat back with my hand over my chest as I remembered with great sadness how he had kissed me goodbye in Touchwood. I might never see him again.

⋆▾⋆

That night I examined myself in my small folding mirror. The lopsided tilt to my face was more pronounced than ever. My eyes were sunken and shadowed. The regulation striped flannel pyjamas that had once fit perfectly were loose around my waist.

I crawled into my cot and lay wide-eyed in the darkness, fighting a wave of homesickness. It was now four long years since the war began, two years since I had seen my family.

I tried to console myself with the good news: the Allies had finally gotten a toehold on Italy's boot and begun to battle their way north, inch by bloody inch. Canadian soldiers had acquitted themselves brilliantly in Sicily, their first campaign. They had struggled through hundreds of miles of rugged, mountainous terrain and borne a large share of the fighting.

And the Russians had turned back the tide on the Eastern Front at a little town called Kursk. There the biggest tank battle in the world had ended in defeat for the Germans. I recalled MacTavish's glee when Hitler had declared war on Russia. Well, the editor had been right about that, just as he had been right about so many other things — including the fact that the war would go on for years.

"It can't be much longer now, do you think?" I had asked Sam yesterday.

"The Hun won't give up that easily, Rose. He'll take a stand in Italy and hold us up for the winter — but when he feels the push, he'll move north and concentrate everything in France. That's where the real battle will be fought."

◄▼►

Two days later Fowler asked me to meet him in Bliss.

It had been so long since our last visit that his letters were worn thin with handling. I reminded myself sternly that many lovers were separated by war, sometimes for years, without losing their passion for each other, but the argument sounded feeble even to my own ears.

I caught the morning train and found him waiting at the station. As we turned down the narrow side street, he caught me by the arm. "What's the rush? I thought we'd have lunch first."

"Oh, Gideon!" I was elated. We had never been out together in public.

"There's a rather nice restaurant on the next street called the Marlborough. I'll go ahead and you can follow."

When I entered, a waiter showed me to the table where Fowler was already seated. I could see why he had chosen this restaurant. The front entrance was hidden behind a potted palm, and the plush-backed booths were so high that the other customers were invisible.

I was too excited to finish my omelette, which was made of the typical powdered eggs but served on a Royal Albert china plate with thinly buttered toast and two slices of fresh tomato. *This is a real date,* I told myself.

Fowler paid the bill and we slipped away to Bliss. The happiness I felt in the restaurant evaporated like smoke as soon as we were alone. It was so easy to justify our affair when I was lying in bed at Medmenham. But when we visited Bliss, the haste, the fear of discovery, and the guilt dampened what little pleasure I took in his embrace.

And it was little. I didn't know what was wrong with me and why I couldn't respond. The sheet that covered us might as well have been between us, since all sensation on my part was deadened. Fowler didn't appear to suspect anything, and I was loath to bring it up.

As usual, the best part for me was the aftermath, when I lay in his arms and enjoyed the warmth of his skin. Today Fowler smoked a cigarette and seemed in no hurry to leave.

I finally began to relax. My limbs felt heavy, and my eyes closed. "You have the loveliest golden skin," he said as we lay close together, my arm flung over his milky chest.

"Must be from my Cree great-grandmother," I said, without opening my eyes. I felt him pause in the act of dragging on his cigarette. "Your what?"

"My great-grandfather came out from Scotland in 1870 and married a Cree." I was pleased that he had finally asked me something about myself. "There were no white women around back then. But they were married, fair and square, in a mission church."

I opened my eyes to find him staring down at me with an inscrutable expression. "I say, I shouldn't mention that around the station if I were you."

"Why not?"

"It might give some people the wrong idea." He butted out his cigarette in the saucer beside the bed. "Well, I must toddle off. Big parley downtown."

I made my way back to Medmenham in a state of despair. Our meeting had been so unsatisfactory that I felt worse than if we had not met at all. But the next morning, I received another white envelope with a typed address. Eagerly, I tore it open.

London
August 28, 1943

Oh, my love is like a red, red rose
That's newly sprung in June
Oh, my love is like a melody
That's sweetly played in tune.

As fair art, my bonnie lass
So deep in love am I
And I will love thee still, my dear
Till all the seas go dry.

Till all the seas go dry, my dear
And the rocks melt with the sun;
And I will love thee still, my dear
Though the sands of time be run.

And fare thee well, my only Love
And fare thee well a while!
And I will come again, my Love
Though it were ten thousand mile.

All my love, Gideon
P.S. Please destroy this after reading.

I knew he hadn't written the poem himself — I was familiar with the works of Robbie Burns — but it could easily have
been written for me, especially the reference to ten thousand miles.
Gideon was telling me that we would be together some day.

As I lay in bed that night, I tried to imagine our future. The
best option, I decided, was for him to emigrate to Canada. I had
overheard other officers talking about leaving England after the war,
breaking with the past and beginning a new life overseas.

With Fowler's education and administrative ability, he could
make his mark anywhere. I thought he might do very well in
Victoria, the head of the provincial government in British Columbia,
with a large community of loyal Brits. Although a long way from
Touchwood, at least it was in Western Canada. I could probably
visit my family every year.

Gideon's boys were almost teenagers now. They lived at boarding school, and they could spend their summers in Canada. They
would love the mountains and the ocean. *Besides, there would be
other children soon*, I thought.

At this point my vivid dream began to break up around the
edges and splinter into fragments. In all honesty, it was difficult to
imagine living in a city, even one as lovely as Victoria, even in a
charming, Tudor-style cottage on the seashore. My fantasy was so
ethereal that it seemed like a fairy tale.

❧

Touchwood
August 30, 1943
My dearest Rose,

I'm sitting at the kitchen window looking at our beautiful crop. The wheat is as high as my waist and the heads so heavy they're hanging down. Your father would dearly love to buy a new combine, but farm machinery isn't being manufactured now, so he'll have to make do with the old one. The government wants us to produce more grain with our broken-down equipment, and then raises our taxes to boot!

I have some news — Jock MacTavish and Ida Flint went to Calgary last week and got married. It was quite a shock to everyone. Ida is a tough cookie — one day the chimney caught fire and she climbed up on the roof with a pail of water and put it out. Jock seems quite taken with her.

Harry Boyd was killed. The telegraph agent said his mother took the news quite calmly. "I knew my boy wasn't coming back," she said. "I shed all my tears a long time ago." Remember how she carried on when he left home? Somehow her mother's intuition knew he wouldn't survive.

If she moves into town, the Boyd place will be empty. There are so many deserted farms around here. The Parker house has been boarded up. It makes me so sad to drive past, remembering those twin boys, both lost at sea. Mrs. Parker gave up farming after she was nearly crushed against the stall when she was feeding the bull. The animals are making trouble for the women now that the men aren't around. One of the Smart girls was thrown out of her buggy last week when her team ran away, but she was only bruised.

Mrs. Barrington has gone quite strange since her son Barry was killed. She wanders around town with a poem that she reads to every woman she meets. It goes something like this: "Sisters, take the oath: We will go barren to the tomb, rather than breed sons to die in battle!" She has moved in with her sister and says she won't live under her husband's roof until the war is over.

Enough bad news. The Allens finally got a note from the Red Cross, saying that Bill is alive in a Japanese prison camp. It's been eighteen months since he disappeared, but Mrs. Allen never gave up hope. There was no word of his condition.

Your father was over at the Jamison place yesterday and he says the field looks like it was taken over by badgers — holes everywhere! When war was declared Malcolm and Morris Jamison flipped a coin to see who'd enlist and who'd stay home, and Malcolm lost. Before he left, he took his money and buried it in a tobacco tin so his brother couldn't drink it up. Morris has been digging for that tobacco tin ever since!

Well, I must go and peel some potatoes. We can't wait until you are home again, safe and sound. I don't know if I will be able to let you or Jack out of my sight again!

Love, Mother XXOO

P.S. The last parcel was number twenty-three.

20

"It isn't a case of us missing the bomb damage, sir," Tommy explained to Group Captain Shoreham. "There's nothing there to find." In the bright daylight from the long French windows, I could see the twin lines of strain etched down his face like the tracks of tears.

Shoreham's expression was sympathetic, but his voice brooked no argument. "Fanshawe's raising holy hell with the War Department, trying to launch an internal investigation into the interpretation unit. You simply must come up with a feasible explanation." We saluted and left his office.

Back at my desk, I took the familiar file folder out of my wooden tray and studied the postcard of Walburg's main street again, although I had it memorized: the laughing women and the little boy in leather shorts on the cobbled street leading to the Roman bridge, the triple stone arches casting three curved shadows onto the glassy water below.

Once again, I examined photos of the bridge, which showed only as a thin, dark line leading south across the river, joining a narrow country road on the other bank. Neither the bridge nor the road to the south was of tactical importance, since the new aircraft parts were taken away to the north to be assembled elsewhere. The northern route was much wider, built up to support military supply vehicles.

I stared through the lenses and tried to become a bird again. I hadn't had much success with this trick lately. It seemed as if my heart were too heavy to let me leave the ground. But as I sat in the quiet room with my forehead pressed to my stereoscope, I felt a gust of wind beneath my wings, lifting me above the earth, and I soared like a hawk riding an updraft.

I was flying east down the long, straight stretch of river. It was shallow at this time of year. I could see reeds sticking out of the water and mud flats along the shore. A town came into sight — not Walburg, but the nearer one called Neustadt.

As I flew over it, I could see that it was the same size as Walburg, with streets laid out on the traditional pattern. There was a church steeple rising from the town square, and a bridge across the river. No aircraft factory, though.

I flew on. The sun gleamed against the flat water. After a few minutes, I saw the river form a half-sickle, with Walburg tucked into its curve. Then the smokestacks of the factory, and the church steeple. There was the arched stone bridge.

I came back to earth with a thud. "May I run over to the recce unit?" I asked Fowler.

"Of course." He winked and touched the tip of his forefinger to his nose. I was so preoccupied that I barely noticed. I dashed down the hall, my heels clattering on the stone floor. There were no transport vehicles at the front door. Too impatient to wait, I scurried down the path along the river toward the airfield.

Fifteen minutes later, I threw open the door to Adrian Stone's office without knocking. He was seated behind his desk, shuffling through a stack of the endless forms required by the military. A row of windows overlooked the tarmac, where two Spitfires were parked. A couple of mechanics were tinkering with one of the propellers.

"About Walburg." I was panting slightly. "I have an idea."

Adrian motioned toward a chair. "Why come to me?"

"If I tell anyone in my section, Shoreham will have to know, and then Fanshawe. Everybody will get the wind up. You'll think it's completely far-fetched anyway. Please, can't we keep it between ourselves for now?"

He leaned back in his chair. "Go ahead."

I sat down and took a deep breath. "Could the town upstream from Walburg have been mistaken for the target? They're exactly the same size, and Neustadt lies on the same flight path."

Adrian looked skeptical. "You know as well as I do that Walburg is situated in the river bend."

"But what if the Germans duplicated the bend in the river?" I sat forward, eagerly waiting for his reaction.

He stared at me as if I had lost my mind. "Rose, it's a great bloody bend about a mile wide."

"It wouldn't be that difficult." I remembered how easily the shallow Tim River changed course in spring when the melting ice narrowed the channel.

Adrian shook his head. "I know we're all under a lot of pressure, but I think you're clutching at straws."

"I brought some enlargements." I came around behind him, setting down the photographs and leaning over his shoulder. "Look, here's Neustadt. If the Germans blasted right here, and sandbagged the river a few hundred yards downstream, the water would swing round the town through these low-lying hayfields."

Adrian picked up a magnifying glass and studied the photograph without speaking.

"The last time your boys photographed Neustadt was three months ago — plenty of time for the Germans to have diverted the river. You see how similar it looks to Walburg. In the darkness, that curve would show like a silver scythe. Obviously the bombers are relying on the biggest watermark this side of Russia to guide them to the target."

Adrian finally spoke. "Since Neustadt is just upstream from Walburg, the bombers would reach it first. They'd drop their loads and head for home without knowing how close they were to the real target."

"Yes, and who's going to do accurate navigation when they're getting shot at left and right?"

Adrian set down the magnifying glass and leaned back in his chair, gazing at me without expression. "How do you suggest confirming this theory of yours, as if I didn't know?"

"We must have photographs of Neustadt in daylight."

"Do you suppose I can order reconnaissance without letting anyone know? I'm not exactly a one-man air force."

"Please, Adrian. I know your pilots don't always stick to the rule book. Can't you wait until you have an assignment in the area, and then take a little detour?"

He laughed shortly. "You're talking about deep penetration into Germany. The reason we haven't photographed Neustadt in the last three months is because the area is so heavily defended. The fighters are out day and night. Not only that, but they have flak guns up and down that valley that can reach to forty thousand feet — that's as high as we can fly."

I had been so excited that I hadn't considered the risk. I was appalled at myself for even suggesting it. "I'm sorry, Adrian — I have no right to ask you to do anything that dangerous."

He went on as if I hadn't spoken. "Besides, we'd have the same problem as the bombers." He stared out of his small window at the runway, thinking aloud. "If they look the same from high altitudes, how would we convince the brass we were photographing Neustadt rather than Walburg?"

"I think I know how." I hesitated, almost reluctant to pursue the discussion. "But it would mean flying at low altitudes, and that would be even riskier."

"Let's have it."

I launched into my explanation. "The Germans can decoy another town to imitate Walburg pretty easily. Those church spires are much the same in every town in Europe, especially the ones built around the same period. And it's not difficult to mock up a factory — just build a plywood shell, paint it, and add some chimneys stuffed with burning straw to make them look as if they're in full production.

"But they couldn't recreate the bridge over the river. There's a bridge in Neustadt — but I'll bet you a shilling it isn't a stone bridge with triple arches. Those Roman bridges aren't that common. A recce pilot would have to fly low enough to photograph the arches."

Adrian sat silently, studying the photographs.

"There's something else." I didn't want to pressure him, but he was bound to find out. "There's another raid scheduled on Walburg Friday night."

Adrian scowled. "Christ. We'd better get our finger out, then."

"Does that mean you'll go?" I was afraid he would say no, afraid he would say yes.

"I can't take off on my own hook — I still have to file a flight plan. But if I can wangle a mission over Germany within the next few days, I'll take one of the Spits and divert over Neustadt. There'll be one hell of a yo-ho if anyone finds out."

"Are you quite sure?" An image of his little boys popped into my head.

He was still talking to himself. "If there were two birds, it would increase the odds. I'll ask my chum Barney Blake if he'll sign on. He's always good for a lark."

◂▾▸

I arrived in the section room Friday morning before breakfast and opened a sealed envelope on my desk. Inside was a slip of paper with the brief message: "Birds in flight. A.S."

For the next few hours I paced around the room, stopping at the windows to peer out at the cloudless sky. The weather was fine, which meant the bombers would be preparing to take off at dusk.

I smoked three cigarettes, went to the bathroom and brushed my teeth, then smoked another four.

"What's the matter with you today?" Sam asked. "You're as jumpy as a scalded cat."

"I have a headache." I wasn't lying. My head was throbbing and my nerves were at the breaking point.

Fowler looked up from his stereoscope and touched his finger to his nose. "Take the rest of the day off and go sick. Everything's under control here."

Without another word, I left the building and rushed down the path to the airfield. Although the skies were clear, it was damp and cool. A faint mist was rising from the river. The breeze rustled the leaves and sent a shower of droplets down my neck. When I reached the airfield, I sat down on the wet grass along the edge of the tarmac.

The breeze picked up and I saw streaks of clouds begin to drift across the sky from the east. There was a stronger gust of wind, and the yellow windsocks lining the runway filled until they were as stiff and pointed as if concrete had been poured into them. I clasped my hands around my knees and shivered.

Although I dutifully attended church parade every Sunday, I had given up praying as a waste of time. Now I found myself whispering, "Please, God. Please, God. Please, God."

At last I heard a faint drone. A single camouflaged Spitfire appeared, painted the distinctive reconnaissance shade of dark blue mixed with grey, the colour of the sky at high altitudes. It circled and landed, taxiing to a stop beside the hangar.

I scrambled to my feet and strained my eyes into the sky, searching for the second Spit. Where was it?

The pilot climbed out of the cockpit and unzipped his leather jacket. He unbuckled his flying helmet and pulled it off, the wind ruffling his dark hair. It was Barney.

As the ground crew emerged from the hangar, he spotted me and began to walk across the runway. I squeezed my hands together so tightly that my signet ring cut into my finger.

Barney came up to me and stopped. One look at his pale face, his mouth twisted in a grimace, and I knew the worst.

"I'm sorry, Rose. Adrian didn't make it."

"What happened?"

He put his arm around my shoulders. "Here, you look a bit wobbly. Let's sit down and I'll tell you everything." We dropped onto the damp grass.

Barney pulled a pack of cigarettes out of his jacket and offered one to me, but I shook my head. He bent over his cupped hands to shelter his match from the stiff breeze, then took a long drag.

"At first everything went like clockwork. When we crossed into Germany, we were flying at twenty thousand feet. The clouds started to build, so we went lower. It was clear sailing for a while until we hit another patch of clouds. Adrian was leading the way. We dropped to ten thousand."

Barney gazed into the sky as if watching the events unfold. "The clouds were getting heavier. When we reached the target area around Neustadt, it was completely obscured, close to ten tenths. Then, through a hairline crack in the clouds, we saw the river. There was no way of knowing exactly where we were. Adrian suddenly dived into the hole and disappeared."

Barney took another long drag on his cigarette.

"I was shocked, quite frankly. We all know how Adrian feels about dicing. We were maintaining radio silence so I couldn't ask him what the hell he was doing. Then I heard his voice on the radio: 'Target still obscured. Going down to five thousand!'

"I was getting a bit windy. We both knew the place was lousy with Huns. Then he called: 'I've been spotted!' The guns opened up below and flak started to come through the clouds and burst all around me. I yelled: 'Come up here, man, or you'll get your tail shot off!'

"I didn't hear anything for a few minutes. I was circling, trying to keep my eyes peeled for fighters and waiting for Adrian to come through the floor. Then he called: 'Too late. I'm holed up! About to bail out! See you on the other side, Barney!'"

I moaned and dropped my face onto my knees. Barney put his arm around my shoulders.

"There's one more thing. His last words were so faint I could barely make them out. He said: 'Tell Rose there are no arches. Repeat, no arches. Over and out.'"

21

Adrian was listed as missing in action. Both he and Barney received formal written reprimands. Then, in a typical example of military inconsistency, an emotional and grateful Group Captain Fanshawe of Bomber Command pulled all kinds of political strings and had them both cited for bravery.

At his disciplinary hearing, Barney explained how the decoy had been identified and I received my letter of commendation at last. This time it came straight from Shoreham's desk. Sam hugged me, Leach grunted, and even Janet muttered her congratulations — but everyone in the camouflage section knew we had received a harsh lesson in enemy tactics.

"Not only did they divert the river, but they must have evacuated the entire population of Neustadt," Sam said. "For Fuhrer and Fatherland, what? I'll tell you, chaps, we'd better be on our toes from now on."

Although my reputation was now as sterling as the British pound, it was a hollow victory. Adrian's loss was a serious blow to the reconnaissance unit. I wrote a letter of condolence to his grieving wife and sons with the deepest regret, feeling responsible for the role I had played in his fate.

Two days later Bomber Command successfully located the real Walburg and destroyed the aircraft factory. I looked once more at the postcard of the laughing women and the little boy, closed the file, and returned it to the library.

The man whose opinion mattered most to me was silent. "Why the hell didn't you tell me about that bridge?" he whispered the first time we were alone.

"I didn't want to compromise you, Gideon. I knew you'd have to take my theory higher up the line. If I had been wrong, it would have come down on you. Please try to understand."

But he didn't understand. Gone were the whispered conversations and meaningful glances. He didn't touch his finger to his nose once. There were no more letters.

The grey November closed in and my spirits faded with the dwindling daylight. Only my growing confidence in my skills as an interpreter gave me the strength to press on.

◂▸

"May I have your attention, please?" Fowler spoke in a brusque voice. He rarely joked with the interpreters anymore, and the furrow between his eyebrows had deepened. He looked ten years older. We set aside our work to listen.

"As you know, our bombers removed the risk of the rockets at Peenemünde, but according to an absolutely reliable double agent, there's another threat."

"What are those devils up to now?" Sam asked.

"Apparently the Germans are working on two completely different jet-propelled weapons. They're called V weapons, short for Vergeltungswaffe."

"What does that mean in white man's language?"

"It means revenge weapons."

"Revenge! What bloody cheek!" Janet cried. "We're the ones who should be seeking revenge!"

I sighed, thinking once again of Hamburg. I continued to hope that some major event would draw the war to a close. Instead, the conflict was escalating. Each side seemed more determined than ever to bring the enemy to its knees, even if both were destroyed in the process.

Fowler continued. "From now on we refer to these revenge weapons the same way the Germans do: the rocket is called the V-2, and the new weapon is called the V-1."

"We searched for those bloody rockets for weeks," Janet said. "Please don't tell me we have to start all over again."

Fowler nodded. "I'm afraid so. But we have a bit more to go on this time. The V-1 looks like a miniature aircraft. It has a wingspan of about twenty feet, and flies without a pilot — sort of a flying bomb with wings. Apparently the Germans are already building launch sites in northern France."

"Christ Almighty," Sam said in a low voice, behind Fowler's back. "I'm surprised the brass doesn't want us to interpret the headlines on the newspaper Hitler reads while he's drinking his morning coffee."

New reconnaissance photos delivered the following day made it clear that the Germans were hiding something. Eight construction sites had been carved out of the forest. In each clearing were several long, narrow, windowless buildings: only ten feet wide but two hundred and sixty feet long, sharply curved at one end. The aircraft section determined that the tips were curved to protect the building against shock waves when the flying bombs were fired. Because they resembled huge skis laid on their sides, we began calling them ski sites.

"Just think of the tremendous amount of resources the Huns are pouring into these weapons," Leach said. "Hitler must be putting all his faith in them."

"Here's what's really alarming," I said, setting down my slide rule. "They're pointing directly toward London."

Everyone was silent for a moment.

"We've been ordered to review previous cover of northern Europe for more launching sites," Fowler said. "The War Department is taking the threat very seriously. A special committee called Operation Crossbow has been formed to coordinate the search."

When a filing clerk brought round several large cardboard boxes, we set to work. Hundreds of photographs lay piled on a central table. We took turns going to the table and pulling them out in batches. After three days of intense scrutiny, we had whittled down the pile and identified nineteen ski sites.

My bones felt as if I had been beaten. Searching for fragged items — fragments rather than overall patterns — was the most tiring form of interpretation. Dozens of times I probed a spot the size of a pinhole, or a mark no bigger than the streak that appears when a lead pencil is thrown onto the desk.

"Sir, may I review previous cover of Peenemünde?" I asked. "The last time we examined it, we were searching for the rocket. Maybe the flying bomb was there, but we missed it."

"Please yourself," he said, without meeting my eyes. "I'm going down to London to give the committee a progress report. So far all we have are the nineteen launching sites, but no sign of the flying bomb itself."

I went to bed early and fell into a troubled sleep. The next morning after breakfast, I went straight to the print library and requested back cover of Peenemünde. I carried the photographs down to the section room, opened my leather kit, arranged my instruments and began to review them, pair by pair. I gazed again at the photograph of the V-2 rocket that had caused so much excitement, but I couldn't find anything that hadn't already been noted.

I slid the photographs into their manila folders and put them back into the cardboard box. At the bottom of the box was a loose pile of random photos of the area around Peenemünde.

I picked up one of them and studied it through my magnifying glass. It showed a road leading to the edge of the seashore, ending in a ramp banked with earth.

I found the matching pair of photos and slipped them under my stereoscope. The ramp had a pair of rails that inclined upwards and disappeared off the edge of the photo. I consulted the attached notes. The industrial section had determined the ramp had something to do with dredging the shoreline to increase the usable land area.

I picked up the next pair and aligned them under the stereoscope. At the end of the ramp, sitting on a platform stretched out over the water, was a midget aircraft. It looked like a fly sitting on the photograph, its tiny wings clearly visible.

"I found it, I found it!" I leaped to my feet, knocking my chair over backwards. The others came crowding around my desk. Sam bent over my stereoscope.

"It's an aircraft, all right! Give me that ruler!" He made some swift calculations. "Twenty-foot wingspan, just what the doctor ordered!" Grabbing me by the waist, he swung me around in a wild polka. "You amazing girl, if only you were English, you'd be perfect. Wait until Shoreham hears about this!"

"Shouldn't we hold off until Fowler comes back?" I felt apprehensive about revealing my discovery while he was off the station.

"Assistant Section Officer, you know I'm in charge of camouflage when he's away. Write up your report like a good girl. That's an order!" I sat down without another word and prepared my report.

By the time Fowler returned, the report had gone upstairs. I shrank from the expression on his face when Sam told him the news. "Congratulations, Jolliffe," he said, with a curt nod. I felt the perspiration break out under my woollen tunic.

Sam shot me a look. "Rose wanted to wait, but I knew you'd insist that the report go up straight away."

"Yes, quite right. Excellent work."

I went back to my desk with a sense of foreboding. Should I have kept quiet about my discovery until I had a chance to tell him?

I had been so excited when I saw the flying bomb that it hadn't even crossed my mind.

But then my sense of fair play kicked in. No, I did the right thing. Surely Fowler didn't expect me to tell him privately every time I made a discovery, presumably so he could take the credit.

A week later a lone Mosquito found Berlin socked in with dark clouds, and returned to England by crossing the Baltic coast. As the pilot flew over Peenemünde, he switched on his camera and photographed the station that had been smashed beyond repair — or so we thought.

The new photos showed a ramp extended over the water's edge, pointing straight toward London. On it was a flying bomb, looking like a tiny, malevolent angel of death.

Shoreham ordered a surge effort involving hundreds of interpreters. We went back to the tiresome search, this time with the assistance of every section. By the end of November, ninety-six ski sites had been located in northern France, all with their tips pointed toward London.

If each site launched one hundred flying bombs a day, that meant close to ten thousand flying bombs landing on London around the clock. Immediately, the heavy bombers of the U.S. Eighth Air Force were dispatched to wipe out the ski sites.

"Thank God that's an end to this bloody chapter," Sam said, echoing our collective sentiment. "I'm tired of searching for mystery weapons. We have enough problems finding the ones we already know about."

◆▼◆

Gideon ran up the dingy stairs, dragging me by the hand. Before the door had slammed behind us, he started to kiss me. I almost swallowed my chewing gum.

Without another word, I began to undress in the chilly room, draping my skirt and blouse across the iron rail at the foot of the bed and quickly unfastening my brassiere.

As usual, Fowler undressed more carefully, pausing to fold his pants and hang his jacket on the back of the chair. He disappeared into the bathroom while I jumped between the chilly sheets. As he opened the bathroom door, I fluffed up my hair and stuck my gum on the seat of the chair.

"Darling!" He bounded into bed. Immediately he was on top of me, kissing my neck and pushing my legs apart. I twisted my face to one side. "Wait a minute, please."

"You're so beautiful, I can't help it. God, what a day I've had. All I could think about was getting you alone." Just as my cold hands and feet were beginning to thaw out, it was over.

"Thank you, darling, that was splendid," he said, smiling into my eyes and showing his even, white teeth. "I honestly don't know how I would carry on without you."

His words didn't generate the same torrent of emotion as they had in the past. In fact, it was more of a trickle. If he was so crazy about me, why couldn't he arrange to spend more time in Bliss? After not seeing him alone for weeks, I badly needed to build up my stock of threadbare memories. More importantly, I wanted to discuss our future.

"I would love to stay longer, you know that," he said, as he saw me open my mouth. "There's a meeting at two o'clock — the brigadier ordered me to be there."

I wished he had mentioned it beforehand so I could have steeled myself for the usual disappointment. I watched without speaking as he put on his shirt and tie, then picked up his trousers and pulled them on.

He glanced over at my face as he straightened his tie. "The thing is, darling, we simply must find more time." He sat down on the chair beside the bed to lace up his shoes. "This hole-and-corner business isn't good for either of us. I'm trying very hard to get leave so we can spend a couple of days together in the country." He turned to me, smiling. "Would you like that?"

"Oh, that would be heaven!" I threw my arms around his neck. He gently took my hands away. "I'm going to miss you, my darling," he said, the familiar preamble to his goodbye. I sank back on the pillow.

As he stood up, my horrified eyes saw a long string of gum follow the seat of his impeccably pressed blue pants into the air. He felt a slight tug, turned his head, and saw the long, grey elastic thread. "What the hell! Rose, my trousers!"

I laughed. I couldn't help it. He looked so funny standing there like a vaudeville comedian, an outraged expression on his face and a string of gum drooping from the seat of his pants.

He began to unlace his shoes, hopping up and down while he balanced himself on one foot and then the other. His handsome face was brick red with rage. He tore off his trousers and rushed into the bathroom.

I jumped out of bed and followed him. "Let me help," I said timidly, not wanting to make him angrier. "I have a nail file in my bag." He stood in his underpants, breathing heavily through his nose and glaring at his wristwatch while I scraped away the white patch. "Look, it's almost gone."

He pulled on his trousers for the second time. I picked up his jacket and helped him into the sleeves. "It doesn't show," I reassured him. "Your jacket is just long enough to cover the spot."

I felt guilty about leaving the gum on the chair, and even worse about laughing at him. Fowler stood at attention near the door, as if his military bearing would cancel out the recent mortification. He bent his head just far enough to allow me to kiss him on the cheek, and the door slammed behind him.

I crawled back into bed, trembling with the same frustration that I always felt after our meetings, half emotional, half physical. I took a deep, shuddering breath, close to tears.

Suddenly I remembered the gum hanging from the seat of his pants and burst into hysterical laughter instead.

22

The fourth wartime Christmas approached. Fowler was going home to his estate in Kent. Sally, whose family owned an extraordinary number of houses, was off to Scotland. Pamela had invited me for the holidays, but I had declined with a polite note.

The mantle of dreams I had embroidered around Fowler, fabricated from a grand total of four visits to Bliss, plus an exchange of significant signals and whispers, was wearing as thin as my body. When I pinned up my hair in front of the mirror, my upper arms looked like white sticks. Sometimes I felt nearly transparent, as if the essence of Rose was fading into the English landscape.

A week before Christmas, I was standing at the windows in my section room watching the clouds race along. At home the clouds drifted so high above the earth they were almost stationary, slowly and majestically changing into fantastic shapes. Here they hung so low over the landscape that the slightest breeze sent them scudding past like flocks of wild birds.

Barney Blake appeared in the doorway, his face beaming. "You'll never guess who the cat dragged in! Adrian Stone!"

I turned toward him with a cry.

"The lucky bugger wasn't even taken prisoner! He followed the river downstream to the French border and landed in the laps of the local resistance. They smuggled him ashore in a fishing boat last night. He has to spend the day in hospital so the quacks can check him over, then he's going home on leave to the wife and kiddies."

"Oh, Barney! What a marvellous Christmas present." I was unable to say anything more. I turned back to the window. Suddenly the sun burst forth from behind the clouds and the greyness disappeared in an explosion of colour. Each blade of grass sparkled with diamonds. Masses of birch leaves, hanging from their magnificent branches, dripped with thousands of liquid rainbows.

◄▼►

RAF Tangmere
December 20, 1943
Dear Sis,

I finally have a two-day leave to see the Big Smoke. Don't give me any of that hush-hush business, you must be able to twist a few arms and meet me there on the twenty-third. I've been over here for months and haven't laid eyes on you. Write to my digs at 16 Holyfield Crescent. Can't wait to see you.
Your loving brother, Jack

◄▼►

I took the train to London and found the address Jack had given me without any trouble. Hesitating outside the wrought iron fence, I felt almost afraid to bring the two different parts of my life into contact.

"Rose!" The front door flew open and Jack caught me up in a bear hug. I hardly recognized the tall, blond stranger in the crisp blue uniform.

He stood back and held me at arm's length. "Rose!" he said again, this time with dismay. "What have you done to yourself? You're nothing but a rag, a bone, and a hank of hair, as Dad would say!"

"Wait until you're on British rations for a while." I tried to laugh it off. "Jack, you must have grown three inches!"

"I probably have. How long has it been? And now we're together on this side of the pond! Who'd have thunk it?"

He put his arm around my shoulders and squeezed. I hugged him back, burying my face in his shoulder. How wonderful to smell my own familiar flesh and blood.

"Let's go out on the town, I mean really do it up brown. Have you been to Covent Garden yet?"

"No, I haven't. I've been waiting for a tall, handsome Canadian to take me there, and so far I haven't run across any."

"Your luck's about to change. I'm pretty flush, too. I hear the British pay is chicken feed."

"It's your treat, then. Let's find a cab."

I felt more like a serving girl than a princess, arriving at the famous ballroom in my faded uniform, but the setting was magnificent. The huge dance floor was shaped in a figure eight, and a twelve-piece orchestra filled the room with sound. Layers of balconies rose up to an enormous arched rooftop overhead.

Hundreds of uniforms, dark blue and light blue and khaki, revolved around the floor, mingling with the colourful dresses. The pant legs of the men's uniforms were streaked with makeup from the women's bare legs. The air was hazy with cigarette smoke and filled with the scent of a dozen perfumes.

Jack looked a little dazed. "It's a far cry from the Touchwood hall, eh, Posy?"

We found a seat near the dance floor, and Jack fetched us a couple of watery gins. I drew a cigarette out of my crumpled package and tapped it on the table.

"Don't tell me you smoke those foul Woodbines!"

"I have no choice. I can't get American cigarettes unless Mother sends them to me, and she isn't too happy about me smoking."

"Good Lord. I have a whole raft of Sweet Caps stuffed in my overcoat. I'll give them to you later — call it your Christmas present. You can put them in your gas mask container."

"Thanks, Jack. It's so funny to think of you being old enough to smoke, let alone drink."

He took a long swig from his glass. "The Limeys have one thing right, anyway — old enough to die, old enough to drink."

I gave a shudder. "I don't care about the English right now. I want to hear all about home, and Mother and Dad. I miss them so much. I miss Laddy and Pansy. I even miss the cows."

"Let me get another drink first. Then we'll have a real old chinwag. I want to tell you something."

While Jack was away at the bar, my eyes wandered around the room. Every man there was in uniform, and many of the women. Some of the civilian girls looked cheap, heavily made up with low-cut blouses. Others were conservatively dressed, probably there with their boyfriends or brothers, like me.

I watched a couple dancing near our table. The woman with her back to me had a luxurious mane of blond hair hanging over one eye, Veronica Lake style. Her pale blue satin dress was cut low in the back and the hand of the air force officer she was dancing with was so large it almost encircled her naked waist.

The couple rotated again and this time I looked straight into the officer's eyes. It was Charlie Stewart.

I leaped to my feet as Charlie abandoned his partner in the middle of the floor and bounded over to our table. "Rose Jolliffe! I can't believe it! After all these years!" He grabbed my hand and wrung it painfully. I was laughing but speechless. I had forgotten how big he was. The blonde came up behind him. "Who's your friend, Charles?"

Charlie introduced us, shaking his head and staring at me as if he couldn't believe his eyes. I kept smiling, although my chin was trembling. Just then Jack came up to us carrying two glasses.

"Jolly! You here, too!" Charlie burst out.

"Well, if the bad penny hasn't turned up again!" Jack was pounding Charlie on the back. "I'm finishing up my training on the south coast at Tangmere. Where are you?"

"I'm up in Yorkshire, with Six Group." He looked into my eyes again, still smiling. "I can't believe running into you. It's the first time I've been down to London in the past year."

The blonde looked pointedly at her dainty gold wristwatch. "Charles, I hate to break up this little party, but I'm on duty at ten."

"Righto, Vicky. I'll see you to the door." Over his shoulder, he called: "Don't move a muscle! I'll be right back!" Within minutes he came shoving through the crowd, head and shoulders above the dancers, his grin covering his face.

It was a magical evening. The three of us couldn't talk fast enough. I drank more than I ever had before. I could feel my cheeks burning. We laughed hysterically at each other's jokes.

I danced with Jack, then Charlie, then all three of us danced the butterfly. We joined a long chain of people doing the Lambeth Walk, whooping along with everyone else. After several more drinks, Jack and Charlie, feeling no pain, danced a polka together while a crowd of onlookers clapped and cheered.

I had a hard time keeping my eyes off Charlie. His shaggy hair was close-cropped, revealing a nicely shaped skull. He no longer stammered, and he danced not only without stumbling, but down-right gracefully.

The boy of nineteen who had left Touchwood was now a flight lieutenant on his second tour of operations as a bomber pilot, responsible for a crew of six other men.

As we sat together, I admired the silver Distinguished Flying Cross on his chest, hanging from a violet-and-white striped ribbon. Charlie unpinned it so I could study it more closely. "You'll notice it even has a little rose engraved on it, my lucky charm," he said.

I pointed to the wound stripe on his shoulder. "What happened, Charlie? You didn't mention that in your letter."

"Oh, that. I caught a piece of flak a couple of months ago. It came right through the cockpit and took off my finger. I was grounded for a few weeks while it healed, but it's fine now."

He held out his left hand, bearing a stump instead of a ring finger. I didn't even flinch. I was accustomed to fingerless farmers who were prone to accidents with their machinery.

"Whenever I look at my hand, it reminds me of Andy Pavlik back home," Charlie went on. "I once asked him how he lost his finger, and he said: 'One day me and my brother were out chopping wood. I was showing my brother where to chop — but he already knew!'"

Jack and I almost fell off our chairs laughing. I wanted to laugh and laugh and never stop. I wanted to be young and carefree again. Whenever I looked at Charlie, I felt my face stretch into an involuntary grin. *This is the first time for ages I've felt like myself and not like some stranger,* I thought.

The evening wore on, and we got even sillier. I found myself jitterbugging wildly with Charlie. He put his big hands around my waist and lifted me off the floor as if I were a feather. Sometime after midnight, Charlie and Jack decided to stand on the table and sing "The Maple Leaf Forever," while I laughed until my sides ached. Then I climbed onto the table, and we put our arms around each other and shouted our high school yell:

> Poke 'em in the eye!
> Kick 'em in the jaw!
> Touchwood! Touchwood!
> Rah! Rah! Rah!

When it was finally time to leave, my voice was hoarse from shouting and singing. A taxi pulled up, its headlights dimmed to slits for driving through the blackout. Charlie and Jack stood on the pavement, wringing each other's hands. "Good luck, old man!" Charlie said. "You have my address, so stay in touch! Merry Christmas!"

I held out my hand and Charlie squeezed it so hard that my grandmother's signet ring cut painfully into my finger. I remembered the last time we had said goodbye. I looked into his eyes and knew he remembered, too.

"Goodbye, Rose. It was terrific to see you again. I don't get down this way too often, but I'll write — if you promise to write back."

"I promise, Charlie. Have a very happy Christmas." My hand seemed to have a mind of its own and I practically had to tear it out of his warm grasp.

I looked out of the rear window as our taxi pulled away. Charlie was still standing on the sidewalk watching us leave, a big solid shape in the night.

⋆⋆⋆

Touchwood
December 29, 1943
Dear Rose,

Please excuse the blots on the paper, as I can't write for crying. I have terrible news. My dear brother Sonny was killed last week in a training accident.

Mum and I were both at home, expecting him for Christmas. It was his last leave before getting his wings. When a taxi stopped in front of the house, and Dad got out with a slip of yellow paper in his hand, we knew the worst at once. Mother was kneading bread dough. She fell backwards into a chair and put her hands up to her face, and the tears made tracks through the flour on her cheeks.

Sonny was low-flying down the river when he hit a power line. He must have seen it in the setting sun at the last minute, because a nearby farmer said he heard the engines roar as Sonny tried to pull up the plane. He ran outside and saw the plane break up when it struck the ice. He said Sonny must have died instantly.

As you might expect, Mum is being very brave. She said: "We'll have a memorial service — not just for Sonny, but for all the boys in Touchwood." We invited every family in town who has lost someone, and the crowd overflowed the church and filled the yard. The minister called Sonny and the others "bright young soldiers who are now in the army of Christ."

Only once in the past week have I seen Mum angry. Auntie Violet wrote and said that God sends us these tribulations to try our faith. Mum crumpled up the letter and threw it into the stove. She said: "If I thought my God would do such a thing, I'd never set foot in church again."

Mum and Dad asked me if I would go down to Saskatoon to accept Sonny's wings since they weren't strong enough. It was a beautiful Wings Parade. The boys lined up in rows of three, but they left an empty place where Sonny should have been standing. I couldn't tear my eyes away from that spot.

Afterwards the commanding officer gave me Sonny's wings and I wrapped them up in my lace handkerchief. He said Sonny was one of the best pilots he'd ever seen.

Dad keeps saying: "If he had gone overseas, at least his death might have counted for something." He goes down to the river every evening and stares at the ice. Mum watches him like a hawk, and when she sees him leaving, she calls: "There goes Dad! Run after him quick and keep him company!" Daisy always follows him and holds his hand, and I think her presence comforts him a little.

Rose, until now the war was something that happened to other people. I never dreamed it would happen to me.

Love as always, June

⁂

War was a ravenous monster, tearing chunks out of happy families, leaving them crippled and bleeding. I had seen the suffering of other women, I had heard the weeping at night in the waffery, I watched my companions at Medmenham disappear on compassionate leave and return to their duties, shrunken and pale with misery.

Now it was my turn to live with the daily dread. Jack had begun flying operations.

23

"Say, Rose, I checked the duty roster and we both have a forty-eight next weekend. Would you like to run down to London?" Sally asked, stopping by the camouflage section room one dreary winter morning. "Daddy keeps a flat in Kensington, so we can camp out there overnight."

We caught the Friday afternoon train and entered the underground tunnel into central London. It really was a tube, round on three sides and flat on the bottom, where the tracks ran. When we stepped down from the train we saw hundreds of cast-iron bunks stacked three high along the underground platform.

"You should have seen this place during the Blitz," Sally said. "Thousands of people slept down here. It's freezing cold and absolutely filthy. In the morning you'd see all these tykes on their way to school, faces black with soot."

"Why haven't the bunks been removed?"

"Some people are still sleeping here because their homes have been bombed, and others simply refuse to sleep above ground until the war's over. There's still the odd raid, although I don't think we have anything to fear."

As we emerged from the station, I looked around with keen interest. Signs of the Blitz, that terrible winter of 1940, had begun to heal. Huge mounds of debris were covered with grass and even the occasional clump of snow.

However, there were still plenty of signs that this was a city at war. Vacant lots dotted the streets like gums after the teeth have been pulled, the empty places raw and sore. Many buildings had blinded eyes, their windows boarded over. Shop windows had little to display except a few tins of food and bits of clothing. Tattered posters exhorted people to buy bonds, shut your mouth, and keep the home fires burning.

"Do you fancy a drink?" Sally asked. "This is Daddy's favourite watering hole, or should I say was. It was bashed pretty badly, but the owners have patched it up."

The sturdy oak door led into what looked like a pile of rubble, bearing the sign: "Yes, we are blasted well open!" I followed her into a dark, cave-like room, the sagging interior walls shored up with timbers.

The decor was festive, as if the owners had dragged out every bit of colour to cheer up the place. Bright red tablecloths covered the tables, and shiny pewter beer mugs lined the shelf behind the bar. Travel posters were tacked around the walls. One of them showed Heidelberg Castle. Some wag had used a pencil to sketch an RAF aircraft in the sky overhead, bombs falling toward the ramparts.

We found an empty table in the crowded room and studied the hand-written menu. "Not much to choose from, I'm afraid," Sally said. "We used to get a decent fish and chip in here, but I can't vouch for anything now."

When the meal arrived, it was mostly greasy chips, sprinkled liberally with malt vinegar, and a sliver of plaice. We washed down the salty food with glasses of beer.

"Let's have another," Sally said. "Can't fly on one wing, you know." As the waiter approached our table, the sound of an air raid siren filled the room.

"It's Moaning Minnie!" Sally scowled. "Wouldn't you know the Jerries would spoil our little holiday!"

Immediately the room began to clear. Several people tossed back their drinks and rushed out, while others continued to chat as if there was nothing to worry about.

"There's a shelter on the corner," Sally said. "I can't sit through a raid without batting an eye, like some people. I never believed that stupid theory that says if your name is on the bomb, you'll get it."

As we snatched up our hats and joined the throng of people moving toward the exit, a bomb fell nearby. The rush of air caused the door to fly open, and then it was sucked shut again with a loud slam. "Jesus, that was close!" Sally looked shaken. "Let's get out of here!"

The street was in full blackout now, and the searchlights were beginning to flash back and forth across the sky in a frenzied search for the German attackers. There were running footsteps around us, someone swearing, and a baby crying with an outraged howl as if he had been snatched from his crib. "Come along, Dad!" A woman's voice came from the darkness beside me. "Just a few more steps!"

As we stumbled down the street, the first wave of bombs began to explode in the distance like muffled drums. *Crump! Crump!* Then the ack-ack guns on the nearby rooftops opened up with a thunderous sound. A surge of terror swept over me. Sally was running now, half-dragging me behind her.

I looked up. It was brighter than all the fireworks I had ever seen, compressed into one night sky. Hundreds of streams of bullets and tracers raced upwards before burning out, turning the sky as pink as a prairie sunrise. Two German bombers were coned in the searchlights, others flickered like bats in and out of the snowy beams. A white flash, brighter than lightning, illuminated the street around us and revealed the ashen faces of people racing toward the shelter.

Suddenly a series of booms pounded our eardrums. I gave a faint scream, soundless in the din. "It's Big Bertha, the anti-aircraft battery in Hyde Park!" Sally screamed in my ear. "Come on, Rose, hurry!"

I ran, although I wanted to throw myself on the ground and cover my ears. A bomb fell directly in front of us. There was a huge, splintering crash as a block of flats collapsed inwards, followed by the sound of pieces of wreckage raining down on the pavement around us, and then the whoosh of flames as the gas main at the end of the street exploded in a giant fireball.

In the orange glow, bright enough to read a newspaper, we plunged down the concrete steps into the entrance of the shelter and around the L-shaped corner that protected the interior from shock waves. We threw ourselves onto the hard wooden benches lining the walls. A young woman and an old man sat down beside me. People were streaming into the shelter and we kept squeezing down the bench until we were packed as tightly as kernels of corn on a cob.

An air raid warden stuck his head around the corner: "That's it, folks, we're full up! It looks like we're in for a pretty good thumping tonight, so steady on!"

He slammed the exterior door, but the sounds diminished only slightly. Inside the shelter one woman was praying, her head bowed. When there was a particularly loud explosion, another woman shrieked and the baby cried louder. A cloud of greyish-white dust fell from the low concrete ceiling and settled on our heads and shoulders. Someone had hung a kerosene lamp from a hook overhead and it swayed from side to side, casting everyone's faces alternately into glare and shadow.

I looked at the woman sitting across from me, so close that our knees were touching. For a moment I wanted to scream with laughter. The woman had pink rubber curlers in her hair, and over them a saucepan turned upside down like a helmet. "Look at me frock," the woman said in a shaking voice. "I was that rattled, I put it on inside out."

The noise grew louder. The spent bullet casings from the anti-aircraft guns rattled off the shelter's concrete roof as they rained down from the sky. It sounded as if the attackers were banging the sides and the roof of the shelter with sledgehammers. It reminded me of the times Jack and I had run into the steel culvert in the dry creek bed as the train was approaching, huddling inside the metal tube while the train pounded overhead.

Big Bertha ceased firing and there was a brief lull. The exploding bombs sounded louder and closer than ever.

"Why did Bertha stop? What's the matter?" A young woman began to sob aloud and her husband put his arm around her shoulders.

"Hang on, dearie."

The old gentleman next to me was becoming increasingly agitated. His hands moved restlessly from breast pockets to pant pockets and back again. "I can't find my bits," he muttered. "I can't find my bits."

I glanced over and caught the eye of the girl beside him. "It's all right, Father. Your bits are safe at home. Change places with me so you don't bother the lady."

She moved next to me and whispered in my ear. "He's getting soft in the head, you see, ducks. Can't remember anything. He writes it all down on bits of paper — birthdays, appointments, historical dates, and such. He carries them everywhere. Calls them his bits. We ran outside so fast that he left them behind. He didn't used to be like this. When Mother got killed in the Blitz, his memory just left him, like."

Sally was staring at her hands. She was motionless, but a tear ran down her pale cheek. "Look, Rose," she said in a quivering voice. "My nail." One of her long, beautifully manicured fingernails had torn off.

I stared straight ahead. There were two babies howling now. The voice of the praying woman had an undertone of desperation. The old man repeated more loudly: "My bits! My bits!" The entire shelter full of people was on the verge of hysteria, myself included. The roof was so low, and we were as cramped as rats in a cage. I was panting in shallow breaths, and I could see the brass buttons on my chest jumping up and down.

Suddenly the woman with the saucepan threw back her head and opened her mouth wide. *Here it comes,* I thought, gripping the edge of the bench with both hands and opening my mouth to scream, too.

But instead she started to sing, in a raspy voice: "Oh, God, our help in ages past, our hope for years to come." The sound was so faint it could scarcely be heard above the guns.

Automatically, I sang the next line. "Our shelter from the stormy blast, and our eternal home!" The young woman began to warble along. The crowd was still shifting and murmuring. Then a man in a naval uniform sitting farther down the row heard our voices, and let go with a booming baritone that made me jump. A few others joined in.

The song gained in strength, rising above the noises outside. The praying woman didn't open her eyes, but she stopped chanting and started to sing. One crying baby hushed, then the other. I reached over and covered Sally's broken nail with my hand. She began to croon, dreadfully off-tune.

When the song ended, a hush fell and the terrible sounds outside rose up again. "Come on, then, what's next?" shouted the lady with the saucepan hat.

Someone struck up with "It's a Long Way to Tipperary." By this time, everyone in the shelter was singing. I could hear the old man's voice, cracked but in perfect pitch. Whenever there was an explosion, our voices faltered for an instant and then roared out stronger than ever, as if fighting back. The sailor sang defiantly, daring the Germans to drown him out.

I was overtaken by a kind of fierce joy. The faces around me were exultant, as if the human spirit would not be daunted. People looked into each other's eyes as they sang, smiling through tears, nodding their encouragement. The sailor began to stamp his feet and clap his hands and we joined him. The atmosphere became more boisterous, and the songs wilder. We sang "The Quartermaster's Store" and "Don't Sit Under the Apple Tree" and

"You Are My Sunshine." "Pack up your troubles in your old kit bag and smile, smile, smile!" We were practically screaming.

The sailor jumped to his feet and stood at attention, almost hitting his head on the low ceiling, holding his cap over his heart. "There'll always be an England!" he sang the first line, and the next line burst out of our throats like a battle cry. "And England shall be free, if England means as much to you, as England means to me!"

Finally the anti-aircraft fire grew intermittent and the sounds of bombing passed away like thunder receding across the lake. The "All Clear" siren began to wail. The door opened and the warden's voice called: "Everyone all right down there?"

"Good night! God bless!" The crowd filed out of the bunker and hurried off in different directions, anxious to see if their homes were still standing. Some of them hesitated, trying to get their bearings. Even Sally had to stop and think, as the familiar landmark on the corner — a large stone statue — had toppled off his perch and was lying in fragments.

We practically staggered to Sally's flat, arm in arm, leaning against each other in exhaustion. Fire trucks and ambulances raced past us. Books, clothing, and pieces of furniture lay in the street. Broken glass crunched under our feet. An odd smell filled the air — a combination of smoke, wet plaster, coal gas, and broken sewers.

"Remind me to ring Daddy in the morning before he sees the papers," Sally said in a voice hoarse from singing.

As we dragged ourselves up to her building, we saw a couple of dark figures clamber through a broken window on the ground floor and run into the night, arms full of bundles.

"Bloody looters!" Sally said.

24

The big show is coming! The party's on!

Rumours had been circulated for years that the Allies were preparing to take back the continent. People whispered and winked and tried to look knowing, but I knew it was wishful thinking. The dwindling rations, the patched clothing, the fatigue on everyone's faces — these told the real story. England was a nation exhausted and impoverished by war.

But now the invasion rumours began to circulate thicker and faster, and the streets and shops in the village had an air of suppressed excitement. *This time it's the real thing!*

Civilians would have to be blind not to guess what was happening. Convoys of battleships were moving from Scotland to the south. Every field and farmyard was crammed with military vehicles, hidden under hedges and parked in the shadows of barns. The island was so weighted down with troops and weapons that jokers said only the barrage balloons kept it from sinking into the sea.

Then our unit received the official word. We no longer had to speculate like everyone else. The party was indeed on. Our job was just beginning, and it would be the most formidable task we had ever faced. Invading an entire continent from one tiny island would require every ounce of strategic support we could provide.

Everyone looked grim. There were no jokes now. We knew this invasion was a one-shot deal. The Allies would give it everything they had — but if they failed, they would never be able to muster the resources or the will to repeat the attempt. They would have to go crawling to Germany and beg for some kind of conditional surrender.

On the other side of a narrow strip of water were one million fighting men and an armoury of the deadliest weapons ever invented. To my eyes, the task looked impossible.

◆▼◆

"Jolliffe and Blackwell, report to Shoreham's office." Fowler's lips were clamped in a thin line. Everyone was tense, but he was wound up as tight as a mechanical toy soldier.

When we entered, Shoreham was seated at his conference table in the corner with two army officers, both wearing the visors with gold braid called scrambled eggs. We exchanged salutes and were ordered to sit down before Shoreham began to speak.

"This is General Cage of the United States Army, and this is General Stevenson. The two of you are being taken off your regular duties to assist with a special project. Code name: Operation Fortitude. Would one of you gentlemen like to brief them?"

"Certainly." The American general was tall and gaunt, with long legs that unfolded like a tripod as he rose from his chair. He might have been comical were it not for the piercing grey eyes that he fixed first on Sam, then on me.

"The key to the success of our invasion is to confuse the enemy over when and where it will take place. There isn't much hope of a full-scale deception — there simply isn't anywhere to hide hundreds of thousands of troops on this island." He grimaced, no doubt thinking of the wide open spaces on his vast continent, and mine.

"We know the Germans have their own spies, their own photo reconnaissance, although we don't know how good it is. So we plan to throw dust in their eyes with mountains of false information, forcing them to thin out their defences by scattering them along the coastline. There's an old military saying: 'He who defends everywhere, defends nowhere.'"

I couldn't resist taking a quick peek at Sam. We saw the question in each other's eyes. What had the generals come up with this time?

"Operation Fortitude will be the greatest hoax ever perpetrated. We intend to create a decoy army on the coast around Dover, to deceive the Germans into assuming that we'll invade across the shortest point of the Channel, to Pas-de-Calais. Instead, the invasion will take place — elsewhere."

A detailed image of the French coastline sprang into my mind. Everyone in the room knew there was only one other alternative route, from the southern coast down to Normandy.

But Calais really makes the most sense, I thought. *It's so much closer to England. Not only that, but Calais lies on the direct route to the Ruhr valley where most of Germany's armaments are manufactured.*

I leaned forward in my chair, gripping my knees tightly with my hands. *I hope to God these people know what they're doing*, I thought for the hundredth time.

Now the British general spoke, in his clipped upper-class accent. "Operation Fortitude will involve people from all branches of service. We'll use every type of jiggery-pokery to bamboozle them — faked wireless messages, false rumours, air and sea manoeuvres, whatever our most brilliant minds can come up with."

He stopped and looked at us as if weighing our abilities. "A team of camoufleurs, many of whom were theatre set designers in civilian life, will create a decoy army called the Fourth Army. In reality, there's no such thing."

The difference between designing a stage set was so different than mocking up an entire army that the concept was almost laughable. Still, I had seen what magic Sally and her cohorts were capable of manufacturing.

"Now, this is where you interpreters come in. We need people trained in the art of camouflage to study aerial photographs of our own decoy army, to see it through foreign eyes, as it were. You will review the photographs on a daily basis and point out anything, no matter how insignificant, that doesn't look quite right. We must find the inconsistencies and correct them before the enemy spots them. Do you understand?"

"Yes, sir," we replied in unison.

The American general pinned us with his steely gaze again. "You'll be engaged in a battle of wits with the finest minds in Germany. And make no mistake: this is the turning point. He who wins the coming battle will win the war."

"Yes, sir," we chorused again. My mind was grappling with the enormity of the task.

"The camouflage squad is already at work. With any luck, we'll begin to amass tanks and trucks in the Dover region by the end of the month. These will be artificial tanks and trucks. It is your responsibility to tell us whether they are realistic enough to deceive a trained interpreter."

⁊

The Fourth Army began to form up on the south coast, moving its fake weapons into position. Sam and I examined every square inch of the area, searching for pieces that didn't fit the puzzle. Most of the time, the fictitious army used faked items that would fool even the most expert observer.

I moved aside to let Sam look through my stereoscope. "Would you believe those are spoofs? Tanks made out of rubber?"

Sam studied the photos. "No. They're identical to our

Shermans. Even the shadows match. How did they manage the tank tracks in the dirt?"

"They pull around a special two-wheeled trailer with treads specially made to imitate tank tracks."

"I'm impressed. It just proves those artistic types can still teach the army a thing or two."

"But there aren't enough truck tracks. The whole camp should be filled with those double-V tracks that trucks make when they come to a stop and then reverse."

"Good thinking, Rosie."

"How does the coastline look?"

"Not bad. Their interpreters would be damned professional if they could see anything wrong with these plywood landing craft. There's an oil spill next to one of them, floating on the water, and smoke coming out of the funnels. There's even laundry on the rail, as if a sailor's hung his knickers out to dry!"

There were a few hiccups. Although the work was supposed to be carried out under cover of darkness, one day I spotted a glaring error — two uniformed soldiers in broad daylight, carrying a realistic-looking rubber tank on their shoulders. I picked up my pencil and scrawled a hasty note of warning.

The airfields around Dover began to fill up with wooden bombers and canvas gliders. Piles of empty fuel containers grew in neat stacks. Fake campsites showed hundreds of empty tents flapping in the breeze, defended by dummy weapons.

"There isn't as much traffic as there would be at an army base," I told Sam. "I'll suggest that they run extra Jeeps up and down these roads." From then on photographs showed lorries and Jeeps turning off at signposts marked "Fourth Army Bivouacs."

The greatest deception involved professional actors called ghost soldiers. One thousand men acted the parts of thirty thousand. They constantly marched in and out of tents and buildings, hastily changing hats and uniforms, swapping or removing their badges and military insignia to give the impression of large numbers of soldiers with various ranks.

The ghost soldiers did more than mime the appearance of real soldiers. They created a flurry of bogus radio exchanges, their words carefully scripted to fool the eavesdropping Germans. They visited local pubs, pretended to drink too much, and spilled vital information about the fake army in loud voices, hoping that spies were present.

I was impressed to read a marriage notice in the London *Times*, between Miss Helen Alice Dawson of Hertfordshire and Sergeant Colin Edward Brownlee of the Fourth Army. I was beginning to believe this might actually work.

◆▼◆

It was the darkest hour of the night. All five of us were on duty in the section room when the familiar drone of a reconnaissance aircraft was heard overhead. I raised my head and glanced toward the long windows. We never bothered to close the blackouts anymore, and the full moon shone through the bare branches of the beech trees and reflected the river as it flowed smoothly toward the sea.

"I say, he's out rather late," Janet said.

The roar of the aircraft grew louder. "That's no recce bird," Sam said. "That sounds like a bleeding great bomber. He must have gotten lost on his way back to his station."

Before the last word was out of Sam's mouth, a thunderous blast shook the room. Through the window I saw an electrifying sight — a great silver bomber, shining in the moonlight, with a pair of black crosses standing out on its wings, the insignia of the German Luftwaffe.

A dark cylinder plummeted from the belly of the aircraft into the river. There was another explosion, louder than the first. A column of foaming water shot into the air. The river divided in two like the parting of the Red Sea, and the water surged up on both banks.

"It's a bloody Hun!" Sam yelled. "Hit the deck!" Janet leaped to her feet, where she stood wringing her hands and screaming one long scream. Leach ran toward the window and wrenched the black-out curtains shut while I threw myself under my table. I peeped out to see Fowler dashing through the door into the hall.

Janet was still screaming. I didn't know how she could keep it up so long without taking a breath. "Shut up, for God's sake!" Sam shouted as he tackled her. They crashed to the floor under the heavy wooden map table against the wall, just as a third explosion shattered the light fixture on the ceiling and broken shards of glass rained down. Janet took a deep breath and began to scream again.

Another blast followed, this time farther down the river, followed by the clatter of the anti-aircraft guns around the reconnaissance airfield as they opened fire.

After a few moments, all grew quiet. Leach and I were still huddled under our desks while Sam shielded Janet under the map table. She had stopped screaming. I wondered where Fowler had gone.

Running footsteps were heard in the hall, and a defence officer stuck his head in the door. "You lot can come out now. No harm done but a couple of broken windows. One lone Jerry must have followed the Thames, but he's gone back where he came from. And from now on, keep your bleeding blackouts shut!"

We clambered out rather sheepishly from our hiding places. Everyone looked pale and shaken. Janet collapsed into the nearest chair. I picked up a wastepaper basket and began to brush the broken glass from the surface of my table with a sheet of cardboard. Leach walked to the window and, with careless disregard for the defence officer, yanked open the blackout drapes and shook his fist at the sky, swearing savagely.

I went to the doorway and looked down the dim hallway. It was deserted. Where was Fowler? He must have gone up to Shoreham's office. Or perhaps he had dashed over to the airfield.

"What we need is a good strong cuppa," Sam said. "I'll go and fill the kettle." *He's a good man to have around in a crisis,* I thought. *Sally is one lucky girl.*

I found a whisk broom in the cupboard and began to sweep the broken glass on the flagstone floor into a neat pile. A few minutes later Sam came back into the section room with the kettle in his hand, shaking his head and grinning.

"I was standing at the sink in the men's room and I heard a voice say: 'Is it over yet?' Guess who was crouched in the bathtub? Our own Fearless Fowler!"

Everyone burst into laughter except me.

◄▼►

London
February 14, 1944
My darling Rose,

Happy Valentine's Day, my own true love.

How I long to run away with you to the ends of the earth. I close my eyes and imagine us together on a desert island, far away from the horrors of war, the relentless pressures of society, and family demands. Long before birth, my life was laid out for me, predictable in its rigidity. My thoughts of you are like a beacon of radiant sunshine, beaming through the prison bars and warming my darkest hours.

I can't help dreaming of what might have been. If only we had met in a different time and place. There will be a future together for us somewhere, my darling Rose, perhaps not in this world but in the next. You are my destiny.
All my love, Gideon
P.S. Please destroy this after reading.

◄▼►

Slowly I lowered the piece of paper and sat motionless on the edge of my cot. For once I wasn't overcome with the usual surge of emotion at being told I was Gideon Fowler's destiny. Instead I had the prickling sense that I always experienced when I spotted a hot item, something that didn't feel right.

His words were so removed from his actions that it was like having an affair with two different people. The charming lover who wrote me these passionate letters was a phantom. These letters, as erudite and romantic as they were, had as much substance as the dark smoke hanging over the decoy targets.

He said he wanted to see me, but never found the time. In all these months, we had been together in Bliss just four times. And even those four meetings were brief and profoundly unsatisfying. He said we were meant to be together, but never mentioned the future except in the most abstract terms.

Because we both spoke English, I thought we were speaking the same language. How wrong I was.

I closed my eyes. Without even trying, I felt myself rise above the bed and soar like a bird. Now I was flying across the ocean, over the hills and valleys and across the wide prairies, straight back to Touchwood. I could see the farmhouse below, my parents sitting at the kitchen table.

My dear father's face came into view, and I saw his lips moving. He had once spoken scornfully about a local politician who was all talk and no action. "Never listen to what a man says," he told me. "Always look at what he does."

With blinding clarity, I realized that Gideon was all talk and no action. He carried on his love life the same way as his service life: a penguin who could squawk and flap, but never fly.

To my eternal sorrow, I hadn't heeded my father's words. What would he think of Fowler? Most likely, he would take his hunting rifle down from the rack hanging above the back door and run him off the place.

The swirling mists that had been obscuring my vision of the

solid ground beneath my feet cleared away, and the big picture came sharply into focus at last.

With great deliberation, I assembled the handful of letters I had received from Gideon and burned them, one by one, over my candle flame.

25

Always inventive, the wily Germans had now gone to earth. They hid their aircraft in tunnels on the Autobahn, able to take off and land with no need for a runway. They transported their aircraft parts under cover of darkness and assembled them in deep caves. We could see the entrances but had no idea what they were doing underground.

I felt like a medical researcher bent over a microscope, trying to find the hidden virus that would poison the human race if undetected. The tiresome nature of the job was wearing down my mental resources as surely as water dripping on rock. I wasn't the only one. Everyone on the station down to the lowliest filing clerk was haggard and exhausted.

Then Fowler arrived one morning with the most unwelcome news possible. "Intelligence says the Germans have stepped up work on their flying bombs. To avoid detection they've scrapped the ski-shaped buildings and modified the launching sites to make them smaller."

"What did I tell you?" Sam said. "There's no stopping the buggers!"

Wearily, we examined new photographs of the same territory,

beginning with the area around Calais. This time there were no cries of discovery or shouts of jubilation. We doggedly searched for any clue that might lead to a camouflaged launching site — a faint footpath, even an odd arrangement of shrubs.

It was Sam who found fresh tracks leading into a pile of wreckage, and twigged onto the idea that some of the bombed-out ski sites had been secretly reoccupied.

Further study revealed that the original damage had been left in place, and the German crews carried on working, under and around the wreckage, without moving so much as a charred plank or a twisted girder.

Once again, we were both impressed and alarmed by the shrewdness of our enemy. An exhaustive search identified sixty-six potential launching sites. Fowler took the information to Operation Crossbow, and came back shaking his head.

"It's been an utter waste of time," he said. "Our side can't spare the resources to attack the launching sites. After the invasion, the Germans will be forced to abandon them anyway."

There was a brief silence. "Jesus," said Sam. "The invasion had damned well better come off, then. If those sites are operational, we'll have flying bombs simply raining down."

◂▾▸

I lit a cigarette, drew the smoke deep into my lungs, and released it. As I exhaled, the knot of pressure in my chest lessened slightly.

It was ten o'clock in the morning and I was lying back in a comfortable armchair in the lounge, taking a short break from my stereoscope. As usual, I hadn't slept well and my eyes were gritty. The lounge was empty except for Janet, who was sitting on a green leather chesterfield with a magazine up to her face.

I heard a sniffle from behind the pages. Another sound, distinctly like a sob. Janet — whose single attitude was one of haughty grandeur — was actually crying.

I thought about leaving the room, but instead I stood up and went over to her. "Anything I can do, Janet?"

She lowered her magazine and burst into tears. I sat down beside her, wishing I had minded my own business.

"What is it?"

Janet cried louder.

"Is it your family?" I tried to ask as gently as possible, knowing her brother was in Burma.

"No," she wailed. "It's Crusader!"

"What's wrong with him?" I asked, not quite so gently.

"He's ruined." Janet broke into a veritable storm of loud weeping. Through hiccupping sobs she managed to gasp: "Daddy rang to say they're putting him down this afternoon."

Although he was only a horse, I knew how much he meant to her. We all had our lucky charms, and Crusader was Janet's talisman. Without him, she would be devastated.

"That's awful, Janet. Did he have an accident?"

"His wind is broken," Janet pulled a handkerchief out of her battledress tunic and held it to her streaming eyes. "That's when their lungs get little holes, and they join together and form a big hole, so they can't breathe properly."

"I know what broken wind is. What are his symptoms?"

"He started coughing about two weeks ago. He coughs all the time, even when he's resting. It's worse when he's eating. The poor darling!" She howled again.

"Has he started heaving — taking two breaths to fill his lungs instead of one?"

Janet lowered her handkerchief and looked at me through streaming eyes. "Yes, but what do you know about heaves?"

"I've been around horses all my life, Janet." After two years, it was annoying that she knew so little about me. "My pony was diagnosed with broken wind, but it turned out to be something else altogether."

"What do you mean?"

"Poor Buckshot had all the symptoms: coughing, double gasping. It's terrible to hear them when they can't get enough air into their lungs, isn't it? Just like a child with asthma. We decided the poor thing had to be put out of his misery. But my father couldn't bear to shoot him, so he told me to take Buckshot over to a neighbour's farm and ask him to do it."

"What happened?" Tears were running down her cheeks but her eyes were fixed on me.

"I tied a halter on him and started to lead him down the road — me crying my eyes out, and Buckshot wheezing as if he were crying, too. About a mile away, I noticed that he wasn't gasping so much. We went a little farther and he started to breathe quite normally. By the time we arrived at the neighbour's, about two miles away, he was fine."

Janet was hanging on every word. "What was the matter with him?"

"It was a simple case of hay fever. A Polish immigrant owns the field next to our pasture, and that spring he planted a new type of oilseed called rape. It bloomed in July — the most brilliant golden flowers, the colour of wild mustard. But the pollen irritated Buckshot's lungs. It was odd because the other horses didn't mind a bit. Dad says some horses are more sensitive, just like people."

Janet's eyes darted rapidly back and forth between my pupils, a habit I had always found extremely irritating. "You're sure the symptoms were exactly the same as heaves?"

"Yes, exactly. My father is an expert on horses, and he said he'd never seen it before. We kept Buckshot at our neighbour's until the crop stopped blooming, and then brought him home again, right as rain."

"Did it ever happen again?"

"Never. A month later we had an early frost and the rape froze solid. That was the end of the experiment. The growing season where we live is too short. But I've noticed a few rapeseed fields around these parts."

Janet leaped to her feet. "I must ring Daddy straight away." She rushed out of the room without another word. I didn't see her again for the rest of the day. *Surely they wouldn't award compassionate leave for a horse,* I thought.

The next morning, Janet came into the section room and approached my desk. Sam looked up in surprise at the unfamiliar sight, and winked at me. Janet's homely face was mottled with emotion but her eyes were shining. "I wanted you to know — Crusader is better today. After I rang yesterday, Daddy had him taken up north to my uncle's place."

"So it was hay fever after all?"

"Apparently. Daddy said this crop you talked about — rapeseed — it's being grown on our estate. They're using the oil to lubricate battleships."

I smiled up at her. "I'm so glad, Janet, truly."

"Thank you," she said, with an effort. It was an awkward moment. "I won't forget this."

"It's quite all right," I said, dropping my eyes. I certainly wasn't going to let a good horse get shot for no reason.

⁕

One sunny morning in April, the exhausted interpreters were rewarded for their efforts by a visit from Queen Elizabeth. Nobody seemed excited about the prospect except me, but I remembered how she had inspired me with her radio speech to women back in 1939.

When the visitor arrived, the entire station was on parade, buttons polished, standing at attention in crisp rows behind Shoreham. The camera crew set up on the grass at one side of the marshalling area, preserving the precious occasion on film.

Queen Elizabeth stepped out of a black Rolls Royce. Shoreham marched forward to meet her. She spoke a few words with a dignified air, and presented him with a plaque. He saluted with his artificial left hand and accepted the plaque in the other.

The queen was small in real life, no different in appearance from the ladies who attended my mother's church auxiliary meetings back in Touchwood, although her pale yellow frock and matching coat were very smart. Her smile under the flowered hat was warm and pleasant.

I tried to memorize every detail so I could describe the event in a letter to my parents. *I have a good mind to write a gushing letter to MacTavish,* I thought, *just to annoy him.*

The visit lasted only moments before she climbed into her limousine again and sped away. It was hardly worth the fuss of a full-dress parade, just a photo opportunity for the newsreels.

That evening we assembled in the lounge to view the movie film. Rows of chairs were lined up in front of a projector screen, the camera crew eager to show off the latest technology.

We settled down and the lights dimmed. A rather blurry picture appeared, showing our rows of uniforms and the white towers of the house in the background. The limousine pulled up and Shoreham approached. He stood at attention, saluted, and accepted the plaque from the queen's hands.

Suddenly the film gave a jerk and began to run in reverse. Shoreham stiffly handed the award back to the queen, saluted, and marched rapidly away, backwards.

The room erupted in laughter. It was as funny as any Charlie Chaplin movie — the jerky movements, the solemn faces, the royal insult. I fell forward with my head on my lap, laughing uncontrollably. Out of the corner of my eye I saw Sam's head thrown back, and heard his hearty "Haw! Haw! Haw!" On the other side of him Janet was emitting a high-pitched whinny. Even Leach on my right was gasping and snorting. All around me I heard the semi-hysterical laughter of people whose nerves were near the breaking point.

Someone flipped the switch and the room was flooded with light. "Play it again, Sam!" a voice yelled. Fowler stood at the front of the room, a look of murderous rage on his face. "That's all for tonight! Dismissed!"

✦✦✦

A week later I climbed the narrow stairway to Bliss and unlocked the door. The room smelled of stale cigarette smoke.

I had arrived early to prepare myself for Gideon's visit, not to fuss with my appearance, but to steel myself for a confrontation. I was about to tell him that our affair would not, could not continue.

I ran cool water into the sink, rinsing my flushed face. While I was drying my hands, I heard the door open. I gave myself a bracing look in the mirror and stepped into the bedroom with a fixed smile that quickly dropped from my face. A strange air force officer with stripes on his sleeves was embracing a blond woman in a skin-tight skirt.

He caught sight of me over the woman's shoulder. "Good Lord!" He dropped his arms and stepped back. The woman turned around. She was wearing dark lipstick and showing a lot of cleavage.

"What are you doing here?" the officer demanded. "Gideon distinctly told me the place wasn't being used on Tuesdays!"

"I'm sorry, but I guess it is."

The officer straightened his tie and took the woman's arm. "Come along, we'd better be off," he said in an annoyed voice. "But do tell Giddy that he's frightfully disorganized."

After the door slammed, I dropped onto the chair. Bliss was our place. How dare he share it with strangers?

Then I noticed an envelope and a brown paper package on the bureau with my name on it. I tore it open and read the brief note: "Forgive me, my darling. I've been unavoidably detained. All my love, Gideon."

I was disappointed, but not for the usual reason. I had spent days working up my courage to tell him it was over. How long would I have to wait before there was another chance?

I reached for the parcel, untied the string, and pulled open the brown paper. Inside lay a pool of snowy white silk. I lifted it by the shoulders and it fell from my hands like a shimmering waterfall. It was the most beautiful nightgown I had ever seen, with a close-fitting bodice, long sleeves, and a bias skirt that floated to the floor.

It was a nightgown fit for a Hollywood starlet. I knew I would never wear it. I could see, as though looking down from above, what a pathetic picture I made, sitting in a shabby bedroom with a fancy nightgown, waiting for a married man who wasn't coming.

At that moment I hated myself.

I refolded the nightgown carefully and repacked it in the brown paper. I didn't want to leave any evidence of myself in that room. I put the note in my pocket, tucked the package under my arm, and locked the door behind me for the last time.

·•·

April 15, 1944
Touchwood
Dear Posy,

Just a quick note with my big news: Mum and Dad have reluctantly agreed to let me join the RCAF Women's Division. Dad spends more time than ever at the post office and Mum is busy with Daisy and her volunteer work. I'm the one who's having trouble settling down to anything. Mum says I wander around the house like a lost soul.

I wish I had died instead of Sonny. Mum says I'm not to think that way, but I can't help it. I'm longing to help bring an end to this ghastly war. Surely the air force will find me something better to do than sorting mail.

Love, Prune

26

In the last weeks and then days before the invasion, we worked constantly, snatching a few hours of precious sleep whenever we could be spared.

The Allies were using every available aircraft that could be fitted out with cameras to do reconnaissance. Fifty-thousand photographs a day rolled in from around the country — more than one million in the month of May alone.

We were practically overwhelmed trying to glean every last scrap of information: not only the army, navy, and air force sections, but also plotting, communications, wireless, industry, and camouflage — all had their work cut out for them. The target section was swamped.

The interpretation unit had tripled in size. I was now one of six hundred officers and twelve hundred other ranks. The wooden cricket pavilions behind the house were converted into living quarters, metal Nissen huts filled the surrounding forest, and every house in the village had a lodger.

Sally's section worked feverishly to construct hundreds of models. The largest was a contoured map of the beach at Normandy, sixty feet long, made of four hundred individual panels. When the panels were fitted together, the model was so huge that officers could walk around on the surface as they discussed their strategy.

Scientists analyzed the beaches of Normandy, identifying tide patterns, currents, and underwater reefs. The coxswain of each landing craft had detailed photos of his beaching point. Every infantry commander had photos showing the landscape lying in his path.

Dicing was no longer forbidden to the reconnaissance pilots. They were doing a heroic job, pulling dozens of dangerous missions along the shore from Brittany to the Netherlands. Most of these were decoy flights — the pilots flew hundreds of miles over heavily defended beaches where no one had any intention of landing.

"Take a gander at this." Sam moved aside so I could look through his stereoscope. German soldiers were running for cover down a sandy beach as the recce aircraft swooped daringly low overhead. One of them was shaking his fist at the sky.

The Germans were building beach defences at low tide, so they would be concealed under the water at high tide. These were wooden structures about five feet high, each topped with a mine that would explode on contact. Higher up the beach were hundreds of wooden devices called hedgehogs that looked like giant jumping jacks, angled toward the water to pierce the hulls of incoming landing craft.

"Since we're gathering so much information about them, what do they know about us?" Sam asked.

Everyone looked thoughtful. From time to time, we speculated on German reconnaissance: just how good was it? Until recently, the enemy hardly needed to bother with aerial photography. They had the entire continent under their thumb.

I was hopeful that the Germans hadn't made much advance in photographic intelligence. Surely they could tell by flying over their own factories and airfields what was so obvious to us.

But what if I were wrong?

Operation Fortitude appeared to be hoodwinking the Germans so far. Enemy aircraft had even carried out a couple of hit-and-run bombing raids on the phony shipyards. The camoufleurs quickly repaired their plywood ships.

"Just be thankful that we aren't working for the other side," Sam said. "They must be staggering under the mountain of information we've heaped on them. And their intelligence people have to figure out what's real and what isn't. They have so many clues and false leads they must be driven mad by this time."

"They aren't the only ones," Janet said.

Tempers were scrappy as everyone in the unit grew more irritable. It wasn't unusual to walk into any section room and find someone with his or her head on the desk, sound asleep.

In the final hours before D-Day, I was running on nervous energy. It had been three months of anticipation, working up to a crescendo of excitement. I made my way back to my room at night feeling light-headed and weightless, as if I spent more time soaring like a bird than I did with two feet on the ground.

My mind and body were near the limit of their endurance. I was reminded of Dad's old John Deere tractor, which chugged along until it came to the east hill. Then it moved laboriously up the slope, straining every cylinder. I sometimes felt myself falter and stop, miss one or two beats, and then forge ahead.

The clock was running against us. Just one more day, one more night, one more hour, one more batch of photographs, please God, let us find anything that might slow or halt our invading forces.

◄▼►

In the early hours of June 6, I glanced into my little mirror before crawling into bed. My eyes looked like bomb craters. The quirk on the left side of my face had hardened into a grimace, as if I had suffered a slight stroke.

I pulled the covers up to my chin and prayed, as I knew hundreds of thousands of men were doing all over England tonight — writing their last letters home to loved ones, hoping they might be among the lucky ones who would survive the next twenty-four hours. I had no idea what part Jack would play in the battle, but I prayed for him — and for Charlie, and all the others.

A few short hours later, I was wakened by a deep rumble, solid and steady as an endless roll of thunder. It was still dark outside. I grabbed a blanket off my cot without getting dressed and ran down the long staircase and through the front door onto the lawn. A small group of people stood on the grass.

The sky above shone with the pale grey light of dawn, but it was blotted out by thousands of aircraft, rising from every airfield in England and flying wingtip to wingtip toward Germany, like a horde of locusts filling the sky. No one spoke. One officer standing nearby was reciting the Lord's Prayer in a low voice, another woman was quietly weeping.

I went inside, but I couldn't go back to sleep. I drew aside my blackout drapes. It was raining in earnest now, lashing against my windowpanes. The tops of the beech trees were bending low in the wind. I prayed again, almost unconsciously.

After I washed and dressed, I steeled myself to wait for the first reconnaissance photographs to come in. Restless people filled the halls, counting off the hours.

I wasn't hungry, but I went down to the mess and forced myself to eat a big meal — the usual grey meat and gravy, dehydrated potatoes, and bread pudding — and washed down the stodgy food with three cups of tea. I wanted to give myself all the energy possible before the long day began.

Throughout breakfast, the rumble in the sky went on. I envisioned Jack flying over my head, then Charlie, then the other flyers I knew. When I came upstairs, the sky outside was still black with aircraft. I didn't know the Allies had so many aircraft. The numbers were unbelievable. Not a single soul in Britain could fail to be aware of what was happening.

In the lounge, everyone was gathered around the radio. The BBC was broadcasting live. Now and then a ragged cheer broke out, but no one knew what was happening, really. Wind and rain were whipping the French coast: some said this was bad, others weren't so sure. I thought it was good, on the whole. The Germans wouldn't expect an attack in such poor weather.

The passage of time was painfully slow. To kill the hours, I went outside in my rain cape and walked down the river path. The countryside seemed strangely deserted under a light drizzle. A cuckoo sang from its hiding place in the trees. Violets and bluebells covered the mossy undergrowth along the path. The cattle on the riverbank chewed their cud, careless of the blood and destruction just a few dozen miles away.

I made my way into the village. The streets were empty. Through an open window I saw the shop owner, sleeves rolled up and suspenders hanging loose, hunched over his radio set, the announcer's voice loud and excited in the stillness.

It must be time now. As I walked briskly back to the station, I passed frenzied activity at the airfield. Recce aircraft were taking off and landing. Air crews dashed across the tarmac with magazines of film.

After I entered the section room, running footsteps could be heard in the hall. Fowler burst through the door and began handing out the photos, still damp.

"All we need to know is what's over the next hill or the next bridge. I want a sheet of paper from each of you describing the enemy defences. A messenger will return them to the recce unit and bring back the next batch.

"The ground troops will move forward until they run into the enemy's defences. They'll sit tight until new plans are formulated, based on our reports. The Luftwaffe is nowhere to be seen, so the recce planes have an all-clear."

He stood at attention and spoke in his deep, commanding voice. I was moved in spite of myself. "It's called blitzkrieg reconnaissance, my friends. Let's make this our finest hour."

Closing my eyes, I took a deep breath. The Luftwaffe hadn't appeared yet. That meant that if Jack and Charlie were in the air today, they must be safe. Then I took up my magnifying glass and set to work.

As I examined the first photographs, I thought I had never seen so many implements of warfare in one place. Thousands of landing craft floated in the surf and nosed up to the shore like piglets to their mother, packed so tightly it looked as if you couldn't get a pin between them.

Transports, barges, tank carriers, corvettes, cruisers, and battleships — the entire Allied navy was together in one place for the first time, bobbing and churning on the choppy waves.

The landing vessels were invading at low tide, rather than risking the appalling consequences of the underwater obstacles. It seemed to be working. Flak from the coastal defences spouted flame, but it was thin and wasn't having much effect.

Minesweeping vessels moved along the coast in formation, dragging wires to explode the buried mines. The sappers were already at work on shore, clearing the path for the battalions of men behind them. Hundreds of tanks crawled up the beaches, leaving double tracks behind them in the pebbles.

Despite the low cloud and rain, the sky was darkened with three thousand Allied fighters and nearly as many bombers, each painted with black-and-white invasion stripes on their wings and fuselage to distinguish them from the enemy aircraft. In one photograph, a stream of aircraft was towing gliders, stretching from horizon to horizon. Parachutists fluttered to earth like leaves falling from a poplar tree in a high wind.

This was no Dieppe. I could see that in spite of the obvious casualties, the bodies dotting the sandy shores, troops were pouring inland and tanks were rolling down country roads away from the beaches.

"By God, it worked!" shouted Sam. "There aren't nearly as many Panzers as we expected! They're still in bloody Calais!"

We worked rapidly, making notes of crossroads ahead of the invading soldiers, bridges that might be mined by the retreating enemy, church steeples where German snipers might be lurking.

The intense occupations of flying and interpreting went on throughout the night. I threw myself on my bed fully dressed and slept for a few hours, then returned to my desk.

By noon the next day the photographs told the story: beach heads had been established along the Normandy coast. Supplies and men were pouring ashore in a widening stream and dropping from the sky. Best of all, casualties were running at 3 percent, far lower than the most cautious estimate.

After three long years, the Allies were back in France.

27

"Here you are, darling. It's all yours." Sally handed me the key to her London flat, hugged me goodbye, and departed for her uncle's estate in Scotland.

Almost overnight, our job had changed from critical to meaningless. As the Allies inched their way deeper into the continent, the fighting units couldn't wait for interpretation results from Medmenham.

Instead, mobile labs, each with several dozen men, were set up at the very edge of combat zones. They operated around the clock, tracking the enemy's movements and searching for hidden targets. There was no question of women joining them — it was far too dangerous.

After the unrelenting workload of the past few months, the exhausted interpreters were finally given leave. They dispersed to the homes of family and friends with only a few muttered words of farewell.

I spent the first night of my leave staring into the darkness, my mind whirling with visions of ships and tanks and aircraft. Toward dawn, I fell into a sluggish slumber but was soon wakened by the sound of repeated knocking. I pulled my blanket around my shoulders and stumbled to the door. A young batwoman was outside.

"What is it?" My voice was a croak.

"This came for you." She held out a telegram.

My mind pulled itself hand over hand to the surface. "Are you sure it's for me?"

I couldn't imagine who would send me a telegram. Perhaps Fowler was asking me to meet him? As my palm touched the flimsy envelope, I was jolted awake. I tore it open. My eyes fell on the words, but registered only fragments.

"We regret to inform you ... John Thomas Jolliffe ... killed in active duty ... for King and country ... deepest sympathy."

I raised my head and stared at the batwoman unseeingly.

"Shall I send for someone?" she asked. "Your commanding officer?"

"No. Not yet. No." I closed the door in her face.

As I walked back to my bed, I noticed my legs were as stiff as wooden crutches. My knees wouldn't bend. I sat down heavily on the edge of my cot, holding the telegram. My hand felt as if it were on fire. I opened my fingers, and it fluttered to the floor and lay there, staring up at me. I reached out my foot and shoved it under the bed.

There was a red mark on my hand, as if the telegram had scorched my skin. Odd. *I can't feel anything. I must be in shock.*

I stared at the tall, narrow rectangle of grey light behind my window. A few raindrops slanted across the glass. I forced myself to focus on those raindrops. I sat there in a state of intense concentration for several minutes. Or perhaps it was several hours. Eventually I became aware of little tendrils of pain wrapping themselves around the edges of my consciousness, like snakes trying to force their heads out of a box.

When I begin to feel this, nothing will ever hurt so much, I thought with a sense of panic. I wanted something. I wanted someone. I thought of my mother and father. I gave a cry of agony. I forced my mind away from them. I couldn't think of anybody ... except Fowler.

I fumbled into my uniform and went down the hallway. I descended the broad staircase with difficulty. The soles of my feet couldn't find the treads, which fell away beneath them.

Stumbling into the dark recess under the staircase where the telephone was located, I asked the operator for Fowler's home number in Kent and waited while someone — a servant, I supposed — summoned him.

It took all my strength to move my numb lips. When I spoke my name, his voice became stern and professional. "Yes, Assistant Section Officer, what can I do for you?"

"My brother. Has been killed."

There was a pause, the sound of a door slamming, and then his voice came back, this time in a whisper. "My poor darling. What can I do?"

"I need you." My voice sounded so strange that I hardly recognized it. "Will you come to Bliss?"

"I wish I could, but it's simply out of the question." His voice was warm and comforting, as always. As always, his words carried rejection. "I've been called into a top level meeting with the brass at six o'clock. I expect it will be an all-nighter. Can't you ring up Sally or someone?"

"Yes, of course." I ran my tongue around my dry lips. "Goodbye, then."

I hung up on the sound of his voice and dragged my wooden legs up the stairs, found my way to my room, and sat down again on the edge of the bed.

For a long time I concentrated on a knothole in the floor. When I looked up again, the rain had stopped and the late afternoon sun was shining.

The long, dark night stretched ahead of me like a pit. I was already growing weary with the effort to resist the fist of knowledge. I didn't know how long I could avoid thinking of — the thing.

I cast around for some alternative. My only comfort might be found in the fantasy world that I had created. I would go to Bliss on my own.

I focused on one simple task at a time. Put on my rain cape. Pick up my gas mask. Close the door behind me. Down the hallway, steady myself with one hand against the wall, manoeuvre the staircase, out the front door. I passed a couple of uniforms without glancing at them. The sun was shining weakly, casting long shadows on the soaking grass.

Walk down the path to the village and board the train for London. Watch the scenery. The cattle on the riverbank lifted their heads as the train smoked past. That was a bad moment. The thing came very close then, but I shut my eyes and pushed it away. I didn't dare open my eyes again, like a child who doesn't want to look under the bed.

Paddington, next stop. I clasped my cape around my shoulders and descended to the platform. On the busy street outside, I stopped to collect my strength. I was suddenly terrified of being alone.

The restaurant where Gideon and I had lunched on our one memorable outing was only two streets away. I decided to go there first. In a crowd, it might be easier to keep the thing away.

The waiter guided me to a booth at the rear, the high seat hiding me from view. I faced a large mirror on the back wall that reflected most of the room. The restaurant had the typical wartime odour of stale food and wet wool.

"Tea, please," I said, but when the waiter served me I found that I couldn't bring the teacup to my lips. It wasn't my hands that trembled, but my head. My neck had no strength in it, and when I lifted the cup my head wobbled so violently I was forced to set it down without taking a sip. My eyes were fixed blindly on the mirror, watching but not seeing the customers come and go.

All at once my heart gave a lurch that lifted me to my feet. In the mirror, a familiar set of shoulders, dark hair, a slender face — Fowler! He had come after all!

I didn't stop to wonder how he knew where I was. I lifted my hand in greeting, then dropped it again when I saw his reflection helping a woman off with her coat. I sank into my seat, eyes glued to the mirror. Fowler and the strange woman were ushered to a table in the bay window.

She was very striking, with a slightly oversized nose and a flawless English complexion. Her pale blond hair was swept back into a chignon. She wore a well-cut dark green suit and silk stockings. I knew immediately it was Frances.

A family emergency, I thought. But the couple didn't appear worried — in fact, they were chatting and smiling. Once Fowler threw back his head and laughed.

I couldn't force my eyes away from the mirror. Fowler leaned across the table and took his wife's hand. Together, as if seeking an audience, they glanced around the room. I slid down a few inches in my seat. Their eyes returned to each other. Well-dressed, well-bred, well-matched. He reached across the table and touched the tip of his wife's nose with his forefinger.

I left through the kitchen without paying for my untouched tea. I simply picked up my cape and marched past the cooks and out the rear door into the alley.

I walked for a long time. The sun had gone down and there was a full moon, a bomber's moon. The shadows of the surrounding buildings, black and silent behind their heavy curtains, fell like wooden blocks alternating with stripes of white light across the street.

A bat swooped overhead. I wondered what I must look like to the bat — a black dot on the white pavement, my long shadow pointing like a finger. I could see everything beneath my feet quite clearly, yet I staggered along as if drunk.

I would never return to Bliss again. I found myself on the street leading to Harlington Mews. Had I remembered Sally's key? I reached into my pocket.

As my fingers touched the cold scrap of metal, I heard a faint droning sound overhead. A couple of running figures disappeared around the corner, leaving the street empty in the moonlight. Their footsteps died away in the distance. I didn't feel like running. It was all I could do to remain upright.

The droning sound grew louder. It sounded like my father's tractor, coming in from the field at suppertime.

As I drew closer to Sally's flat, I saw the dark shape of a woman standing on the front steps. She was knocking repeatedly. When I was only a few feet away, the strange drone above turned into a swishing sound. The change penetrated my trance, and I looked up.

Against the moonlit sky was etched a small, stubby-nosed miniature aircraft. A red light at the nose of the toy aircraft flashed twice. For an interval of one, two, three seconds, my mind registered the image without recognizing it.

Then it came to me. The last time I had seen this funny little aircraft was on an aerial photograph of Peenemünde. As I watched, the flying bomb grew larger and the swishing sound increased. It was plummeting straight toward us.

My will to live flickered. Then a blue-eyed baby looked over the woman's shoulder and into my face, one tiny fist waving in the air.

Instinctively, I leaped forward and grasped the woman by the arm. "Run!" I screamed. She didn't even turn her head. She started to pound her fist against the door.

The swishing sound changed into the scream of a whistling teakettle. I pulled at the woman's arm. "It's a bomb! Run!" The woman deliberately braced her feet and refused to budge. Without thinking, I reached over her shoulder, snatched the baby from her arms, and darted away.

I had taken only a dozen running steps when the street exploded and the percussion blast coming from behind lifted me high into the air. Trying to cushion the baby in my arms, I came down hard on the pavement on my right side. The air left my body like a blow from a sledgehammer. I gagged for breath, hearing the baby's muffled screaming against my breast.

Weakly, I lifted my bruised cheek off the pavement and looked back into a cloud of yellowish smoke. A crater filled the street where the woman had been standing. The entire front of Harlington

Mews had vanished. The steps to the second floor led upwards and stopped in a mass of jagged splinters.

Water spurted out of a burst pipe under the pavement and the spreading pool was icy on my stockinged foot. The roof was on fire, and sparks had already jumped to the building next door. The roaring flames lit up the street and made it seem warm and cheerful. Fire sirens sounded in the distance.

As I watched almost peacefully, a wooden beam, partly consumed by the crackling flames, broke away from the overhang with a crunching, tearing sound and fell toward me, blotting out the red glow.

Just before I passed out, the baby's crying stopped.

BOOK THREE

June 1944–August 1944

28

I watched the hands creep around the clock on my bedside table. Twenty minutes to go. I crumpled a handful of cotton sheet and pushed it into my mouth. This was the worst hour, just before the morphine arrived.

Closing my eyes, I concentrated on taking deep, even breaths through a mouthful of fabric. The pain across my back grew fiercer, sharpening from a smoulder to a searing blaze. I had never seen the burn because bandages wrapped my torso from my armpits to my hips, but it felt as if my entire body were on fire. Even my fingers and toes throbbed.

I bit down on the sheet, but a muffled moan escaped from my throat. Five more minutes. I strained my ears for the nurse's footsteps in the hall. I tried to imagine tying a rope around a burning bundle of pain and lowering it down a deep, cold well.

"Here we are, then." The young nurse's sympathetic voice came out of nowhere. "Just another few seconds, love, and you'll feel better." She skilfully plunged the needle into my thigh.

"Doctor says you should drink as much water as you can. Let me help you with the glass." I swallowed the cool liquid and dropped like a stone into blessed unconsciousness.

◦▿◦

Drifting slowly to the surface, I became aware of a light pressure on my hand. With my eyes shut, I moved my fingers slightly. There was no doubt about it — I was touching warm human flesh. I took a quick peek and closed my eyes again, having registered an image of a nurse's white cowl. I didn't want to talk to anyone, but I couldn't turn my back because I was too stiff to move. Any part of me not covered with bandages was a pastiche of black and burgundy bruises.

I lay motionless and willed her to go away. For a long time there was no sound except the distant clatter of the hospital ward. My tense body gradually relaxed. I admitted that the simple handclasp was rather comforting. Deciding to risk another glimpse, I saw a pair of grey eyes in a strong-boned face.

"Don't try to talk." Her voice was deep for a woman. "You're in a private room in St George's Hospital in London. There's a severe burn on your back that will take a long time to heal and leave a nasty scar when it does. But you'll make a full recovery. You're a very fortunate young woman."

I thought about this, dimly aware of the faint murmur of city traffic on the street below. Ghostly images loomed and receded as if my mind was swirling with thick fog. Suddenly my eyes flew open again. "The baby?" I whispered.

"The baby is fine, thanks to you. An elderly man saw everything from the cellar across the street. The mother died instantly, poor thing. She was a widow with no family, so the baby was sent to a home for war orphans."

I pondered this until the nurse spoke again. "I've written to your parents and told them you're well, but not able to write to them yourself yet. Try to sleep as much as possible. You're receiving the maximum dose of morphine, so there's nothing more we can do, medically speaking. I'll drop in each afternoon on my rounds. I'm Sister Lillian." She left the room with a starched rustle.

The days and nights ran together like ink and water. Sometimes I found the sister holding my hand, crisp and professional in her white pinafore and organdy veil. I didn't ask about the war, didn't want to know. When the morphine was in effect, there was no sensation of pain, only listless apathy. When the drug wore off, I could focus only on my own suffering.

One day I woke to find the sister's grey eyes upon me. "You haven't asked about visitors, Miss Jolliffe. But someone rang several times, a young lady named Sally Fairbairn. She's most anxious about you. I told her she could come round next week."

I turned my head away. The clasp on my hand tightened. "Miss Fairbairn told us about the loss of your brother. My dear girl, I'm so sorry. What a world this is." I squeezed my eyes shut and shook my head on the pillow. I didn't want to talk about it.

She began to stroke my hand, the way I had often petted the wild barn kittens. "Your burn will heal more quickly, my dear, if you can also heal your spirit," she said. I hoped she wasn't about to preach a sermon.

"None of us can know God, but I've observed a great deal about people's souls, spirits, whatever you want to call them. Since the war began we've treated the most dreadful cases — mothers who have lost their children, men who have lost their limbs, their sight, even their minds. Very little can shock us anymore."

I wished she would finish her speech and go away.

"Now your spirit is struggling to put itself back together. It will repair itself in time, with or without your help. And much like a broken bone, when your spirit heals it will be stronger than ever before. Believe me, I've seen it happen."

A final squeeze of my hand, and she swished out of the room. I felt vaguely resentful that she presumed to know anything about my feelings when I didn't even know them myself. Overwhelmed with the sheer fatigue of thinking, I slept.

Three days later I was dozing when I felt a perfumed cheek against my own face, and looked into Sally's violet eyes, brimming with tears.

"Blimey, Rose, let me find a handkerchief. Don't go away." She blew her nose, then leaned over and hugged me again. "I was so sorry to hear about your brother."

She wiped her eyes, placed her cap on the bedside table, and sat down beside me. I wondered why everyone felt so much worse than I did.

"I've brought flowers from the camouflage section," she said. "One of the nurses is putting them in a vase."

I spoke for the first time. My voice was as hoarse as a crow's. "I'm glad you came, Sally." Surprisingly, it was true. I thought I hadn't wanted to see anyone.

"Shoreham himself sends you his best wishes. He's writing a letter on behalf of the entire unit."

"That's good of him." I knew better than to ask if there was any message from Fowler. I placed my elbows on the bed and lifted myself a little higher on the pillows, inhaling sharply against the pain. "Can you tell me anything about my accident, Sally? The morphine makes everything seem like a bad dream."

"You were nailed by a bloody V-1. Isn't that the limit? All those weeks we spent searching for them, and we were wasting our time. The flying bombs, buzz bombs everyone calls them now, they're pouring down on London. One of them lands every ten minutes, day and night."

"So Sam was right — bombing the launching sites didn't work after all."

"Trust the Jerries. They found a way to construct all the parts for the bombs and the launching pads separately. They load them onto trucks, drive to a secluded spot, and assemble them at the last minute."

"Isn't there any way to stop them?"

"Our fighter pilots are doing their best. Some of them are able to catch up to them in mid-air over the Channel and tip them over with their wings, but not often enough."

"How are the civilians coping?"

"You can imagine, Rose — they're in a complete panic. The Londoners are fleeing to the countryside in droves again." She gave a shudder. "I even saw one myself from the train. There's something so sinister about the sound — a death rattle, then this awful hush when everyone holds their breath, then an explosion with brilliant red and orange flames, big enough to demolish an entire city street."

"Any sign of the rocket?"

"Not a sniff. Hopefully the attack on Peenemünde wiped them out. Then again, maybe the Huns are saving them for another nasty little surprise."

"What a shame to lose your flat in Harlington Mews."

"Who cares about a silly old building? Just think if you'd been inside." Sally's eyes filled again. "My family is steering clear of London until this mess on the continent is cleared up."

"How long will it take, do you suppose?"

"How long?" Sally grimaced. "How many times have we asked each other that question? How long this, how long that, how long until this frightful war drags to an end? God only knows."

She was silent for a moment. "The invasion gave everyone a tremendous lift — like a glimpse of blue sky through the black clouds. Some people are saying it will be over in a few weeks, but Sam expects the Germans will go down fighting. What's the point of guessing? We've been wrong so many times before." She gingerly patted my shoulder. "Never mind that now. Your job now is to rest and recover. St George's is an excellent hospital. I'm so glad they brought you here."

I lifted one feeble hand. "Thank you for coming, Sally."

"The pressure at work has eased off now, and I have oodles of leave stored up. I can come back next Saturday. That Sister Lillian — she looks a good sort, by the way — she said you can have all the visitors you want."

But dear faithful Sally was my only visitor. She came the next Saturday, and again the next. By this time I was sitting up in bed, still indifferent to my surroundings.

After the first few agonizing days, I had been moved from a

private room to a ward. I kept my bed curtains drawn, blocking out the view of Hyde Park right outside my window and the three patients who shared my room.

I still hadn't cried. My tear ducts had shut down. In fact, when was the last time I had cried? Was it one year? Two years? I remembered when I would shed buckets of tears over a sad song, or a lost kitten. I worried about this on the rare occasions when I thought about anything at all.

In spite of my lethargy, I did look forward to Sally's visits. Today, after the small talk had been exhausted, she pulled her chair close to the bed and spoke in a low voice. "I don't know if this will cheer you up, but there's been a big flap in your section."

"What happened?"

"Fowler has gotten a real slap-down. Janet — the hooded cobra herself — went to Shoreham and informed him that it was you who discovered the radar trap last year."

I tried to puzzle this out. My mind worked slowly, and the mention of Fowler's name made me want to turn over and go back to sleep. "Why would she do that?"

"She never liked Fowler. Always thought he was a bit too-too, if you know what I mean. Besides, she told Sam that she owed you one for that horse business. Good old Over-and-Under. Apparently she has her own peculiar brand of integrity."

Another silence while I tried unsuccessfully to view Janet in a different light. "What will it mean for ... Fowler?" I had to force myself to utter his name.

"Oh, nothing overt. But it's a definite blot on his copy book. It's simply not done to cadge someone else's finds — a bit like cribbing on an examination. I'm afraid Fowler's career has suffered a permanent setback. Shoreham will see to that. He always had a soft spot for you, since you confirmed his excellent judgment when he made you an interpreter."

"But how did Janet know about the radar trap?" I was still struggling to understand.

"Everyone in camouflage knew, I'm afraid. That's why Sam took such a dislike to Fowler. He said he could hardly resist throttling the bugger."

I mustered my courage and looked straight into her violet eyes. "Did you know the whole story — about Fowler and me?"

Sally smiled at me gently. "I had my suspicions, darling. People are inclined to overlook some of the old kiss-and-cuddle during wartime, of course. I just hoped you weren't taking it all too seriously, thinking it was a grand pash or something."

I didn't reply. That's exactly what I had believed — that my love for Fowler was the grand passion of my life. Well, it was time to face the cold facts. My great love was nothing more than a tawdry wartime fling, like thousands of others.

One last twist of the knife. "Did everyone know about us?"

Sally leaned over and patted my arm. "I shouldn't think so. I didn't breathe a word, not even to Sam. You were extremely discreet. Besides, you were never away from the station. You couldn't have seen each other very often."

"Four times." I pulled the white sheet up to my chin as if to hide myself. "Oh, Sally, I've been such an idiot."

She took my hand again and squeezed it. "Don't torture yourself. Fowler's a handsome devil. And I don't need to remind you of how much strain everyone's under. We've all acted out of character one time or another during this insane war."

29

Scar tissue gradually covered my burn. The injections of morphine were cut back, then halted — but my mind was ticking as slowly as a rusty timepiece. One day I found myself wondering where Jack's body was buried. The last time I saw him was our wonderful evening at Covent Garden. Now he was gone forever and I hadn't even said goodbye.

Still there were no tears.

My nights were plagued with dreams in which I was running and screaming, trying to escape from unseen terrors, but the long days brought little feeling. Even when Sally held out her left hand — a small amethyst engagement ring, the colour of her eyes, glittering on her fourth finger — it was difficult to dredge up the expected enthusiasm. Fortunately Sally was so happy she didn't notice.

"We've decided to emigrate to Australia after the war." Sally's eyes were shining. "Daddy's not too pleased, but I have an inheritance from my grandmother so there's nothing he can do. He doesn't realize how much the world has changed. There's nothing left in England for us now."

"I'm so happy for you both," I said, wishing I could feel happy about anything. "But it's so far away.... What will you do with Sam's mother and aunt?"

"Oh, they're coming with us! They're absolutely pip-pip and gung-ho, dusting off their pith helmets and mosquito nets from the old days when they were Empire wives in Ceylon. I'm not sure what they expect, but they're keen as mustard."

The idea of Sam taking his little harem all the way to Australia brought me close to a smile. But after she left, I subsided once again into blankness. I couldn't feel any optimism no matter how hard I tried.

And I did try. Every day I made an effort to summon my inner strength, reaching far down into myself — and finding nothing at all. It was as if the barrel had been scraped clean. The sensation of emptiness was frightening, followed by a wave of fatigue. I closed my eyes and slept again.

Sister Lillian did her best. She made me sit up each day, read me newspaper articles, insisted that I dictate a letter to my parents, tried to engage me in conversation. One day she even spoke to me quite sharply. I could see her growing more worried as I refused to respond.

"You must have done very well in the service to have been promoted," she said one afternoon.

"That was a fluke. I don't deserve to be an officer."

"Why are you so hard on yourself?"

"I suppose I'm like one of those pilots, the ones who can't fly anymore."

"What do you mean?"

"I'm L.M.F. — lack of moral fibre." I had spent some time thinking about this and convinced myself it was true. Just as the airmen were given a black mark for reaching the point at which they were unable to climb back into an aircraft, I felt utterly incapable of returning to my unit and spending my days in the same room as Fowler. But I knew I would be returned to active duty as soon as I was medically fit.

Some people were strong. I was one of the weak ones.

"Nonsense!" The nurse's grey eyes flashed with anger. "I'd like to lay my hands on the chap who came up with that ridiculous notion! Moral fibre, if that's what you choose to call it, is a finite quality, like so many others. People simply come to the limit of their endurance, and that's the end of it." She leaned over and spoke with great deliberation. "You listen to me, my girl. Sooner or later, under certain conditions, everyone will hit bottom. But you won't begin to crawl out of the hole unless you decide to forgive yourself for whatever it is you're feeling so guilty about."

My back gave a sudden throb and I shifted uncomfortably. How did Sister Lillian know how I felt?

Several days passed while her words churned around in my mind. My guilt was as thick as a lump of butter rising from the cream. One afternoon, while she was reading aloud to me from the *Times*, I suddenly burst out: "I thought I loved him, Sister, I really did!"

She looked up, folded the paper, and set it aside. "Loved whom, my dear?"

"My commanding officer." I turned my face away, afraid to see the scorn in her eyes.

"Why don't you tell me about it?"

"I had an affair with him. I knew he was married and I told myself it didn't matter. I'm guilty of adultery. And conduct unbecoming to an officer."

Speaking the words, hearing them spoken, gave my sin an ugly reality. I felt emotion for the first time since my accident: it was a scourge of scalding shame that swept me from head to foot.

Sister Lillian patted my shoulder, but I shrank from her touch. My body was sweating under the light covers. I tried to brace myself for the harsh rebuke that must surely come.

When she spoke, her voice was kind. "Certainly if you've been brought up to respect the sanctity of marriage, then what you did was wrong. But there's no need for you to shoulder the entire burden of guilt." I wasn't sure what she meant. Surely the affair was no one's fault but my own. "Did you deliberately set out to entrap him with your feminine charms?" Her tone was sarcastic.

"No." That I could be sure of.

"Did he initiate the affair, or was it you?"

"He did."

"Of course you must take responsibility for your own actions, but the lion's share is his. He's an older man, your senior officer, and married. You're a young woman, far from family and friends, anxious for approval, homesick, and lonely. Under the circumstances it would be highly unusual to resist his advances, rather than the other way around. Any girl might have fallen for it. Many of them have, sadly, often with disastrous consequences."

"But I'm not just anyone!"

"Oh, come now." She frowned at me. "Conceit is hardly a virtue."

"Conceit!" I cried, stung. "What do you mean?"

"I mean that you're too eager to see yourself as extraordinary. You're a perfectly normal girl, susceptible to the same desires and illusions as everyone else. There's no need to castigate yourself any further."

For a moment I felt faintly insulted. Then the weight that had pressed me into the bed like an invisible cannonball lifted slightly. "Do you really think I'm normal?"

"Perfectly. You're going through a bad patch right now, but you'll recover and go on to find great happiness. I'm sure of it."

After she left, I pondered her words. Was I really conceited? Looking back, I admitted that perhaps she was right. I had led a charmed life before the war, adored by my parents, praised by my teachers. In the service I had been promoted over the other officers, and, I admitted now in a moment of scorching honesty, I was secretly smug about my abilities as an interpreter.

I had even considered myself too good to go out with anybody from Touchwood. I took myself far too seriously. It all added up to somebody I didn't like very much.

I had been in hospital for five weeks and summer was in full bloom. I opened my bed curtains at last, and a breeze wafted into the room from the open window, bringing the scent of newly mown grass from the park below.

Sister Lillian finally had me walking up and down the hall. I read the newspapers occasionally, only to feel depressed again. It was difficult to imagine the vicious combat taking place across the Channel. The war had become even more savage. Battles raged all over the continent as the Germans fought like cornered animals. Once or twice I heard the sound of a distant blast as the buzz bombs continued to fall.

Several letters arrived from my parents that were almost too painful to read. They didn't know the circumstances around Jack's death, except that he was one of the few fighter pilots shot down by anti-aircraft fire on D-Day.

And still I hadn't cried.

"Would you like to have an outing?" Sister Lillian asked one morning. "I'm driving down to the Queen Victoria Hospital in Sussex to visit one of my former patients."

I was reluctant to leave my little white sanctuary, but so grateful to her that I couldn't refuse. Besides, I had to emerge from the hospital sometime, no matter how much I dreaded the prospect. She helped me struggle into my uniform and hobble down the front steps, then eased me into the passenger seat of a tiny red Morris Minor.

Our destination was a town called East Grinstead, about an hour's drive south of London. As we bowled along the green country lanes bordered with hedges, I cranked down the window to feel the warm summer air blowing through my hair.

"How much farther?" I was stiff with the effort of sitting forward so that my back didn't press against the seat. I still flinched if anything touched the burned place.

"Almost there now." Sister Lillian was driving quickly and expertly. "You might like to visit this hospital because the RCAF recently added a new wing for burned airmen. A young Canadian plastic surgeon named Ross Tilley is treating them. His methods are so revolutionary that his patients call themselves The Guinea Pigs."

"That sounds horrible!" I shuddered. "Does he really experiment on them?"

"It's not at all horrible," Sister Lillian said in her deep voice. "It's quite splendid. The men call themselves that for a joke, although some of them are hideously burned. Sadly, many of their wounds were avoidable — young men, thinking they were invincible, refused to obey orders and flew without their gloves and goggles. When their aircraft caught fire, their skin was completely exposed." We drove along in silence before she spoke again. "It's always more difficult to deal with a wound that was self-inflicted by your own conceit." There was that word again.

When the car turned into the wide gravel driveway, I gazed with astonishment. The red brick hospital sat in the midst of the most beautiful garden I had ever seen. Stone paths led between banks of shrubs and flowers, as thick as a forest, massed together in a riot of colours.

It was my first sight of a real English country garden. They had become almost non-existent since the war started. The lawns surrounding public buildings were abandoned because their gardeners were busy fighting, and the owners of private homes were using every square inch to grow vegetables.

Sister Lillian glanced over at my rapt face. "It's lovely, isn't it? The theory is that the patients recover more quickly if they're surrounded with beauty."

"Please, I'd rather not go inside. May I stay out here?"

"If you like." She parked in the gravel lot beside the hospital, then helped me into a nearby wooden lawn chair. "I won't be long."

Sister Lillian disappeared into the hospital while I settled down to wait. For years I had been viewing the world in black and white. Now the vivid colours soaked into my soul like water into a dry sponge. A bee buzzed lazily in a bed of pansies. A huge black-and-orange Monarch butterfly landed on my shoulder, then fluttered away again.

The air was thick with the mingled perfumes of a hundred different flowers. I recognized a row of pink hollyhocks, but most of the other blossoms were so large they looked nothing like their smaller Canadian cousins.

A few patients, dressed in uniforms or hospital whites, were strolling in the distance or being pushed around in wheelchairs. Some of them knelt in the flowerbeds, weeding or deadheading the blooms.

From the corner of my eye, I glimpsed a young man hobbling up the path with a stick. He settled himself a short distance away in the nearest chair. I narrowed my eyes to slits and pretended to doze. Then I heard his voice. "Excuse me, do you know the name of that flower?"

I opened my eyes and stared straight ahead at the nearest bank of blossoms. The only shrub I recognized was a rosebush. "Which one?"

"I don't know, but something has the most fantastic fragrance."

I turned to look at the young man. His head was tilted back, angled toward the sun. His face was shocking beyond anything I could imagine, a gruesome, distorted mess — lumps and ridges of burned skin, rows of stitches circling his neck, forehead stained purple with gentian violet dye. His eyes were swollen, sightless lumps. The hand that rested on his khaki-clad knee had no fingers at all, just a thumb.

I felt my own face contort into an involuntary grimace. This must be one of the guinea pigs. I was glad he couldn't see my expression. I took a deep breath and kept my voice even with an effort. "I'm sorry, I have no idea. I'm not very good at flowers."

"That's all right, I'll ask one of the nurses." He sounded quite cheerful.

I turned away again. All my budding enjoyment in the day had vanished. The airman rose and shuffled off, leading his way down the stone path with his stick. A few minutes later, Sister Lillian appeared and helped me back into the car.

"Did you like that hospital?" she asked on the way home. "I could arrange to have you transferred there. Most of my patients find it quite restful."

"No!" I practically shouted.

She glanced over at me in surprise.

"No," I said again, in a lower voice. "Sister, I know why you took me there. You want to show me there are others worse off than I am. But that doesn't make me feel any better, it makes me feel worse. How can it help to know that someone else is suffering more than I am? How can it help to be constantly reminded that I live in a world where the most sickening things happen to innocent people?" I heard my own voice rising, and I stopped speaking and turned my face toward the window.

"I see your point," Sister Lillian replied in her usual calm manner, "but I must admit I'm at a loss to know what else to do with you. Your back is healing nicely, but I cannot in all conscience recommend that you be sent back to your unit. I simply don't believe that you're mentally prepared."

"I've been thinking it over. I know what would help me, but I'm afraid it's impossible."

"What is it?"

"To be alone, to be completely alone. For years I've been surrounded by people. You don't understand how much I need to get away from everyone." My voice started to rise again. "I need a place where no one is making me wake up or go to sleep! Or talking incessantly about the war! Or asking me the names of flowers when I don't have the answers!" Hearing my own voice break, I stopped.

"I see," said Sister Lillian. "It certainly isn't recommended procedure to send a depressed patient away to be alone. But you may be an exception. Let me think about it."

30

I found an empty compartment and dropped my kit bag at my feet. The conductor blew his whistle and the *bang-bang-bang* of slamming doors sounded down the length of the platform. With a jerk, the train began to move.

I gazed unseeingly out at the dirty brick buildings, the miniature backyards with their potato patches and lines of grubby laundry. My lassitude lifted briefly when we left London behind and the green fields began to rush past, before I sank into blankness again.

At the Oxford station, I saw an RAF officer on the platform who looked like Fowler. My stomach contracted painfully, as if it had been punched. When the man turned his head, I saw he was nothing like Fowler. The train moved on.

Towns and farms flew past, passengers exchanged greetings and farewells, and finally the conductor called Steeple Aston, and it was my turn to disembark. I stood on the platform clutching my bag. A short, stout man in shirtsleeves and suspenders scurried toward me.

"Miss Rose Jolliffe?"

"Yes, that's me."

"I'm Bert Gorsuch." He touched his hand to his tweed cap, then reached for my bag. "If you want to remember it, just say to yourself: 'Gor! Such a name!'"

My back was stiff after my journey, so I allowed him to hoist my bag into the rusty van parked around the corner. It was faded orange in colour, with *Gorsuch Groceries* painted in white letters on the side panel.

"Sorry about the vehicle. It's not a thing of beauty, but we can still find the odd bit of fuel for it." He wrenched open the battered passenger door. "The missus is waiting for us at the shop. If you're going to stay at the cottage, you'll need to pick up a few things."

We drove a mile or so and turned into the village main street, featuring the typically ancient church with its square steeple, and a handful of houses built of pale golden Cotswold stone.

The van pulled up with a screech of brakes, and we clambered out and entered a small shop through a crimson door so low that I had to duck my head. It was a combination general store and post office, with racks of ancient tinted postcards, canned goods, magazines, and cheap romance novels.

A pretty young matron with a baby on her hip was standing at the counter, having her ration card stamped. Behind the counter was a lady in a blue-and-white-striped apron, even shorter and stouter than her husband. "Good morning, my dear," she said, shaking my hand vigorously and proceeding to talk for the next five minutes, barely stopping to draw breath.

"I was quite taken aback to hear a young lady was coming to the cottage. It's been ages since the Fairbairns were here. Mr. Fairbairn did love his fishing so, and Miss Sally used to come down every year for the local hunt. I gave the place a shakedown yesterday so all's ready for you. I do hope you won't be too lonely, but then, you're probably tired of all those people in London. We went there on our honeymoon. Never again! It made our heads ache, isn't that right, Bert? We splashed out at a posh restaurant and they brought the bread on one plate and the butter on another. What kind of a place is this, we asked ourselves. We're paying a pound for our dinner and they can't be bothered to butter the bread! I'll put together a few groceries, my dear, and Bert will run you out to the cottage."

"Thank you so much. I'd like enough food to last for a week. I'm looking forward to a stretch of peace and quiet."

"That won't be a problem. Mr. Fairbairn put in the telephone back in 1938 when he remodelled the waterworks, so as long as you ring me every morning and tell me you're still alive you can be alone as much as you like! If you need anything, Bert can drop it at the end of the lane when he makes his deliveries."

"That's an excellent plan." I was relieved they weren't going to insist on keeping me company.

"Miss Sally wrote and told us you'd had a bit of an upset." Mrs. Gorsuch refrained from mentioning any details. "You're very pale and thin, poor thing. And to come all the way from Canada! Such a distance. Your poor mother must be terribly worried. Now, here are a few extras."

She began to fill a large wicker basket. "It won't be like the old days, mind, but we get fresh eggs and milk from the local farmers, and here's potatoes and carrots from our garden, and tea leaves, and a bit of cheese from the dairy. We can't spare any sugar but I have a treat for you, a jar of honey from our hives down the road, and if you put everything in the icebox, it should keep nicely."

Bert ushered me into the rattletrap van once again, and off we went. Three miles east of the village, he turned into a long lane that made a series of unexpected twists, winding through the woods like a garter snake.

We emerged in front of a cream-coloured stone cottage. Small windows peered out from under the thatched roof, looking like a mop of combed hair. A path led up to the arched door, which was painted Dutch blue and almost smothered with ivy. Beside the door hung a tarnished brass plaque: SUNNY BANKS.

Bert seemed reluctant to leave until I reassured him. "I may stroll into the village if the spirit moves me, but you don't need to send out a search party. I'm a farm girl, you know. We Canadians are used to the country life."

"Aye, well, if you're quite certain." He climbed into the van and rolled down the window. "There's a bicycle in the shed, Miss!" He waved until the van disappeared around the bend.

Alone at last. I set out to explore the cottage.

Sunny Banks was straight out of an English storybook. The front door was set into stone walls at least three feet thick. The slab of rock used as a doorsill had been worn into a concave shape by thousands of footsteps.

The main room had white plaster walls and low ceilings supported by dark, hand-hewn beams. A rocking chair and a brown plush sofa flanked the brick fireplace, over which was a stuffed fish in a glass case. Shelves crammed with books lined the longest wall. An oil painting of an Irish Setter in a gilded frame hung beside the multi-paned front window.

At one side of the room was a narrow staircase, so steep and curving that I had to put my hands against the walls to steady myself as I climbed. It reminded me of a snow tunnel.

Three doors led off the landing. I opened the first to find a simple bedroom papered with blue and white toile. A brass bed with snowy white linens and a feather duvet nearly filled the room. There was a large, hairy cushion at the foot of the bed where the owner's dog must sleep. Through the round window beside the bed I caught a glimpse of blue water between leafy branches.

The second door opened into a bathroom with a white porcelain steep-sided English bathtub, sink, and lavatory with an overhead tank and a chain; and the third room was piled with shotguns, hip waders, and fishing tackle.

I stood uncertainly on the landing, awkward in my new solitude. The thought came to me that I needn't wear my uniform here. I dragged my kitbag upstairs with difficulty, unpacked my few things, and changed into a sweater and a tweed skirt that hung on my jutting hipbones. I arranged my uniform in the tiny closet, reverently placed my family photograph on the bedside table, laid out my toiletries on the bathroom shelf, and crept down the steep staircase.

Pacing around the sitting room, I pulled the rocking chair close to the front window and plumped its faded pillows. I examined the bookshelves and noted several interesting titles. There was a clock on the mantel, with a glass cloche and gold balls that revolved. I wound it up and set the correct time against my wristwatch.

It's important to keep busy, I thought, but I wasn't sure why. I had the uncomfortable feeling that something was hiding around the corner, waiting to pounce. I dismissed the idea and put my bountiful supply of groceries away in the pale green kitchen at the rear of the cottage.

The unusual sight of all that food made me decide to eat something. I filled a saucepan with water, lit the gas flame, and boiled an egg. I ate it with a slice of homemade bread and real butter. Although it was the first egg I had tasted in three years, I didn't enjoy it as much as I thought I would. I forced down the last bite and went into the front room. Dusk was falling. I touched a match to the fire already laid in the grate and sank into the rocking chair.

My uneasiness increased. I gave myself a mental shake. This was what I had longed for, wasn't it? But after years of working and eating and bathing in rooms filled with other people, the solitude was strangely uncomfortable. I wished the owner's dog were here.

I picked up my package of cigarettes, pulled one out, and tapped it against the arm of the chair. I struck a match and lit it. Before taking a single drag, I tamped the cigarette into the brass ashtray on the side table and resolved then and there to quit smoking. No time like the present.

Impulsively I snatched up the whole package, crushed it in my hand, and threw it into the fire. The flames illuminated the words "Sweet Caporal" and I remembered that this was the last of the cigarettes Jack had given me for Christmas. He had touched that package with his own hands.

For a few moments, I was absolutely motionless. Watching the package crumple and flare filled me with a tremendous, yawning sense of loss. Without an instant's warning, my mouth flew open and a harsh, guttural cry sprang out, shockingly loud in the quiet room. My body convulsed, and a second wail erupted. Before the sound died away, tears burst out of my eyes. They didn't trickle, they gushed like water from a fire hose.

I jumped to my feet, horrified by the ugliness of the sounds I was making. I took one step, then bent double at the waist as another convulsion gripped me. I fell to my knees on the faded carpet before the fire.

Now I was wailing uncontrollably. Never had I experienced such agony, not even after my accident. All my senses were focused on the overwhelming emotional pain that was squeezing the breath out of me.

I felt like vomiting, but every heave of my stomach brought forth another hoarse, growling cry. I couldn't even close my eyes. Locked open and staring, they saw the leaping flames of the fire through tears that poured in a liquid sheet over my face and onto my lap. I fell onto one side, my knees drawn up to my chest. I tried to force my thoughts back into their box, but it was hopeless. All reason was washed away in a torrent of feeling.

Images of Jack flew through my mind like bits of paper inside a kaleidoscope. I remembered the exact colour of his blue eyes and the sound of his laugh. I remembered riding horseback with him beside the river, playing cards at the kitchen table, dancing at Covent Garden. I remembered the muscles in his bare brown shoulders as he pitched hay. A vision of ourselves as children, running hand in hand down the road, hurt so much that I screamed. I was an only child now. Only, only, only.

I had never felt so alone. Bliss had disappeared like a burst bubble. My parents were a million miles away. Wave after wave of grief surged through me, each more violent as the last. The carpet on the floor beneath my face was soaked and still the tears rushed from my eyes. Several times I tried to rise to my knees but couldn't summon the strength.

The fire was burning merrily now and I could smell scorching wool as sparks flew onto my skirt. With an effort, I managed to roll away to one side of the carpet. I pressed my face against the cold stone floor. My scalding tears gathered together in a stream and ran into the crack between two flagstones.

I wept until the fire had burned down to ashes and my howls had faded into hoarse whimpers. The room grew chilly. My limbs were stiff and cramped, and my back throbbing with a steady pounding misery.

Hanging onto the rocking chair, I managed to pull myself to my feet with arms that had no strength. Still hiccupping with sobs, I switched off the light and stumbled up the narrow stairway to my bed.

31

That was the beginning of what I called The Crying Time. The next morning tears flowed from my closed eyes while my face was still pressed into the pillow. For the next eleven days I wept. Like spring breakup on the frozen river, jagged chunks of emotion crashed into each other and swept downstream, followed by gushing torrents of water. My cheeks were red and raw from salt water, and my eyes swelled to slits.

When I wasn't grieving for Jack, I cried for all the lost and damaged boys. I cried for Max Cassidy, who would never see the Tasmanian jungle again. I cried for the orphaned baby whose bright blue eyes I remembered so well. I cried for my lost innocence. I cried for the flawless body I no longer possessed. I cried for my faraway home. I cried for my father. I cried for my mother.

For two minutes each morning, I forced myself to keep my voice steady while I made my phone call to Mrs. Gorsuch. The rest of my time was spent wandering around the cottage, or slumped in a chair, weeping. There was no point in using handkerchiefs. I carried a towel over my arm, lifting it at intervals to my streaming eyes.

Once, for an entire afternoon, I sat on the linoleum floor in the kitchen and sobbed, staring at the same crack in the wall. I found it almost unbearable that the smooth, flawless plaster should have such an ugly mark running through it.

I ate very little during The Crying Time, but I drank numerous cups of tea sweetened with honey, wondering if it were possible to become dehydrated by the loss of tears. The tea went down my throat and the liquid poured out of my eyes simultaneously. Some days I was able to force down a slice of bread or a few mouthfuls of tinned peaches. Other days my throat closed, and after several attempts to swallow, I had to spit out the chewed food.

The pain never left, although it intensified suddenly and unpredictably, like spurts of blood from an arterial wound. One morning, just after I had climbed out of bed, a convulsion tore through me. Stepping forward, I grasped the brass end rail of the bed with both hands. I bent double, pressing the rail into my rib cage, trying to squeeze the pain out of my body. I rocked back and forth against the brass rail and howled like a coyote.

I abandoned any attempt to push the pain away. At night I lay awake and imagined my suffering as a physical presence, a faceless being wearing a dark cloak. It lay on me and enveloped me, pinning me heavily to the bed. I writhed and moaned as if in the embrace of a rapist, and prayed for death.

A couple of times I briefly considered suicide, but even this dreadful escape was barred. I wouldn't inflict further suffering on my parents. And I wept again because I, who wanted so much to end my earthly pain, was bound to life.

On the afternoon of the twelfth day, I happened to glance into the shiny surface of the kettle as I blotted my tears with a tea towel. The sight of my crimson face, swollen out of shape by the kettle's curved side, recalled the mirror at the restaurant where I had seen Fowler with his wife.

I was suddenly overwhelmed with memories of him — our special place, the dreams we shared. My reflection dissolved in a blur as fresh tears rushed into my eyes.

But wait a minute. What dreams, exactly, had we shared? The dreams were mine alone. What sacrifices had he made for me? Nothing sprang to mind. The only thing he had ever given me was a silk nightgown. As I remembered the nightgown, a trembling began in my legs and swept up my arms and down to my hands. This was a new emotion. For a moment I wasn't sure what I was feeling. Then I realized it was fury.

Outside the open door leading into the overgrown garden at the rear of the cottage was an axe, resting in a tree stump used as a chopping block. I dropped the tea towel on the floor and took several long strides through the back door. Gripping the axe with both hands, I tore it out of the stump and brought it down so hard that the axe's head was embedded in the wood. I strained at it with all my strength. When it suddenly tore free, I fell backwards onto the ground. My back gave a vicious stab of pain but I ignored it.

A stack of uncut logs was piled neatly beside the back door. Snatching one of them, I dropped it onto the stump and sank my axe into it with a blunt, murderous sound. A chunk of firewood flew off the chopping block, end over end, and landed in the woods several yards away. I didn't see it, didn't see anything but Fowler's handsome, treacherous face. I struck at it with every ounce of strength, grunting as the blade bit into the wood.

The doctors had warned me to be careful, but I was feeling no pain now, only a frenzied rage. I finished splitting the log, darted to the woodpile, and snatched another. Splinters of wood flew in all directions. One of them stung me in the cheek and I growled like a dog. Every time I took aim, Fowler's face rose up before me and I struck it with the axe. The sound of chopping echoed through the peaceful woods.

When my clothing was soaked with sweat and the light was too dim to see the axe, I drove it into the stump with throbbing arms

and went into the kitchen. I stopped to pick up a chunk of wood
that had flown through the open kitchen door. I hurled it into the
yard with all my remaining strength and slammed the door shut
with a satisfying crash.

☙

On the thirteenth morning I awakened after a dreamless sleep. My
eyes were dry. I lay motionless, waiting for some unpredictable
emotion to rage through my body, listening to the robins twitter
outside the window, and watching a shaft of sunlight move across
the low ceiling.

Carefully I swung my legs over the edge of the bed and put my
bare feet on the hooked rug. I sat there for a while, without any
particular sense of time. There was nobody waiting for me, nothing
I had to do. I thought deliberately of Jack, of Fowler, of the baby, of
Mother. There was only an empty hollow where the pain had been.

From the round window in my bedroom, I saw sunlight flickering on water. After fetching a bottle of pre-war shampoo and a
towel from the bathroom, I went downstairs and pushed open the
front door. Sunny Banks sat on the southern edge of a stream that
wound through the woods. Sally's father had dammed the stream to
make a trout pond, and that was what I had seen from the window.

I picked my way barefooted down the path that ran beside the
stream, still in my striped flannel service pyjamas. It was a splendid
morning; the hawthorn trees were in bloom and the air was sweet.
As I crept along, the soles of my feet tender after years of wearing
shoes, I noticed how light I felt. Even after my frenzy of chopping,
my back was less stiff and painful than yesterday, as if I had dropped
a heavy pack after a long march.

When I reached the pond, it looked so inviting that I longed to
plunge into the cool water. I didn't have a bathing suit. "So what?" I
asked aloud, just to hear the sound of my own voice. To my surprise,
it rang out strongly and clearly. I shucked off my pyjamas, waded

up to my knees in the fresh water, and made a shallow dive toward the centre of the pond. I came up tingling.

Taking a big mouthful of the clean water, I rinsed it around and spat it out. It tasted delicious. I floated face up to the sun, opening my mouth again to catch the warm sunshine on the back of my tongue. I swallowed the sunshine, wanting to fill my empty body with it. I rolled over and let the warmth pour down on my wounded back. After a long time, I swam to shore, opened the bottle of shampoo, and washed my hair. I dried myself vigorously with the rough towel, then flung myself down on the grass.

My naked body felt purified. I lay on my stomach, arms and legs outflung, taking slow, even breaths. I was surprised at how much time it took to fill my lungs completely when I inhaled, as if they had doubled in size. The sun beat down on my flesh, abnormally pale after all these years indoors.

Suddenly I could hardly wait to eat breakfast.

◂▾▸

It was late summer and the country was enjoying a spell of hot weather. Every morning I made my way to the pond for a swim, then dozed off on a blanket or worked my way through all six volumes of The Barchester Chronicles, which I had found in the bookcase. The sun soaked into the marrow of my bones and darkened my skin.

My appetite returned and I ate voraciously, relishing the fresh food after years of tinned kidneys and corned beef. I devoured homemade bread and butter, tomatoes, cheddar cheese, apples, and wild blackberries I picked beside the path.

I was immensely tired and slept for many hours, dropping off in the rocking chair after supper, then climbing the stairs to fall into bed soon after dark. The tears were still close to the surface, and several times during the day they would trickle down my cheeks.

The waves of pain were powerful, but they didn't come as often. And for hours at a time I experienced only echoes of grief, like ripples slapping against the pilings of a pier. At first I was afraid my newfound peace might be temporary. Instead I felt stronger each passing day. In the afternoons I took long rambles through the woods; in the evenings I read or knit beside the fire.

I asked Mrs. Gorsuch to send me a few skeins of wool, since they didn't require clothing coupons, and I started knitting myself a Fair Isle vest in shades of blue. It was restful to watch the stitches gather on my needles. There was a radio on the kitchen shelf, but I didn't turn it on. Nor did I request a newspaper. I was taking a vacation from war.

Finally, although it brought on another fit of weeping, I composed a letter to my parents.

⋯

Steeple Aston, Oxfordshire
August 21, 1944
My dearest Mother and Dad,

I hope you received Sister Lillian's letters from hospital. You mustn't worry about me, especially during this dreadful time. I'm spending a few weeks at a cottage belonging to my dear friend Sally Fairbairn. There is a pond nearby and I go swimming every day. Being in the country again, seeing the trees and hearing the birds sing, has done me a world of good. My back is almost healed and I'll be ready to return to duty soon.

It's so peaceful here, and I've been thinking of the wonderful times Jack and I spent together. You must believe, Mother and Dad, that we had the most loving parents in the world, and the happiest childhood, in the best place on earth.

I keep recalling memories that I want to share with you. When I was nine years old and Jack was seven, we were jumping on my bed when I accidentally put my foot through the window! Dad heard the crash and came rushing up the stairs two at a time. "Who did that?" he yelled. Jack saw that I was terrified, so he said: "I did!" Dad put him across his knee and was about to give him the spanking I deserved, but at the last minute I said: "No, Dad, it was me!" Do you remember that you were so impressed by Jack sticking up for me that you didn't spank either of us? He was always so good to me, and so brave.

One evening before the war, we drove into town for a dance. We had lots of fun, and on the way home we saw the northern lights — how brilliant they were that night! When we drove into the yard, we got out of the truck and watched for a long time. The whole northern sky was shifting and shining, changing from pale pink to green to blue and back to shimmering white. The only sound we could hear in the darkness was Laddy's tail going swish, swish in the long grass. Jack said to me: "God's in his heaven, all's right with the world."

I have a hundred memories of Jack to share with you when we're together. Until then, I close my eyes and imagine the two of you comforting each other. I'm longing for the day when I can see your smiling faces and feel your arms around me once again.

All my love, Rose XXOO

···

Three weeks after my arrival at Sunny Banks, I rode my bicycle into the village, where I posted my letter to my parents and another one

to Sally, and filled my wicker basket with fresh supplies. It gave me
no small satisfaction to pass by the cigarettes.

"Goodness, but you look a sight better than the day you arrived!"
Mrs. Gorsuch said. "You have the roses in your cheeks! It must be
the country air. Oh, here's some mail that come for you yesterday."

I didn't want any reminders of the outside world, which I pictured in my mind as a blood-soaked battlefield, but I tucked the letters into my basket and pedalled away. When I reached the cottage,
I put my groceries into the icebox and tidied the kitchen. Finally I
settled myself in the rocking chair to read them.

⸎

> RAF Tangmere
> June 27, 1944
> Dear Miss Jolliffe,
>
> As Pilot Officer John Thomas Jolliffe's command-
> ing officer I want to extend my deepest condo-
> lences to you personally.
>
> Our investigation has concluded that Pilot
> Officer Jolliffe's aircraft suffered severe dam-
> age over the coast of Normandy, and despite
> his superb flying skills, the aircraft went out
> of control and crashed near Chichester. It will
> be some comfort to you to know that he was
> killed instantly. His body was recovered from
> the wreckage of his aircraft and buried in the
> nearby village. There his grave will be properly
> cared for by the British Commonwealth War
> Graves Commission.
>
> Your brother died a hero's death taking part in
> the greatest battle in history. He was a fine young
> man who will be sorely missed, not only by his

crew but also by all who were fortunate enough to know him.

Unfortunately I must inform you that due to a clerical error, his personal effects have gone temporarily missing. We will make a thorough search and forward these to you as soon as they are located.

Victor Gerard, RCAF Wing Commander

◄▼►

RAF Tangmere
June 14, 1944
Dear Miss Jolliffe,

I flew in Jack's squadron, perhaps he mentioned me. Your brother was the best mate a man could have. It must be true that the good die young. I'm sending you this photo of him, taken beside his kite just before his last flight. It's a good likeness, since I don't remember him without a smile on his face.

You will be wanting to know how it happened. The whole squadron went to Normandy that morning. We flew around until we were almost out of fuel but we didn't see any Huns. We were circling over the coast, watching the fun down below, and a stray tracer came up out of nowhere and hit Jack's kite. He radioed back to base that he had been hit, but he said the engines were operating and the controls were responding.

He headed for home and I followed him. We were a few minutes away from the landing field when I saw his aircraft go into a spin and plunge into the coastline. Miss Jolliffe, you must believe he didn't suffer. He was telling me a joke on the radio and the last sound I heard was him laughing. You know he was like that, always kidding around. Jolly was the proper name for him, no question.

You'll be getting letters from a couple of the other men in our squadron. It won't be the same without Jolly. He kept our spirits up by making the war seem like a game. That was worth more to us than all the medals in the world.

Sincerely yours, Frank McFarlane

⹀

To: WAAF Assistant Section Office Rose Marie Jolliffe
From: Buckingham Palace
June 15, 1944
Dear Miss Jolliffe,

The Queen and I offer you our heartfelt sympathy in your great sorrow.

We pray that your country's gratitude for a life so nobly given in its service may bring you some measure of consolation.

George, Regent Imperial

⹀

RCAF Middleton St. George
August 15, 1944
My dear Rose,

I was so terribly sorry to hear about Jack. The war has taken many good men. I wish with all my heart that his life had been spared, not only for his sake but for yours.

I wrote to you at Medmenham as soon as I heard the news, but my letter was forwarded to London and it was only yesterday that I had a reply from the hospital with your address. I hope your injury wasn't too serious, and that you are on the mend.

As it happens, I have my annual two weeks of leave coming up and I'm travelling down to Oxfordshire on the train with a mate from my squadron. After spending a week with his family, I'll be at loose ends. May I visit you on the afternoon of August 23?

If you don't want company, write back to the address on this envelope. I know it's short notice but you can always do a bunk before I arrive. If I don't see you this time around, I'll write again later. Again, my deepest sympathy.

As always, Charlie

32

After hurrying back from my morning swim, I tidied the cottage, polished the silver teaspoons, and arranged a bouquet of blue asters and white daisies from the overgrown garden. Upstairs I put on my red plaid skirt, white rayon blouse, and crimson cardigan. I brushed my hair and pinned up the sides.

I ran downstairs again, checked the clock on the mantel, and began to lay out the tea things. Snapping a white linen tablecloth in the air, I accidentally brushed it against my face. Damn! There was a smear of bright red lipstick along the edge. I crumpled it up and threw it into the closet.

Suddenly I recalled my elaborate preparations for the trysts with Fowler. Annoyed with myself, I wiped off my lipstick, then took a book and sat down in the rocking chair.

As the clock chimed three times, footsteps sounded on the flagstone path, then a gentle knock. I smoothed my skirt and opened the door.

There stood Charlie. He was taller than I remembered. He took off his blue cap and the sun shining against his back gave him a halo in the doorway of the dim cottage. His face was familiar, yet I had the sense of meeting a stranger for the first time. For a few seconds we stared at each other.

"Hi, Charlie." I held out my hand and he squeezed it so hard my signet ring cut into my finger. All at once I felt like crying again.

"Rose," was all he said. He bent his head and stepped through the low doorway.

"Please come in and sit down." I gestured to the armchair beside the fireplace. After a little play of arranging ourselves, we looked at each other again.

"It's so nice of you to come."

"It's good to see you again."

Both of us smiled sheepishly. "You wouldn't think we'd known each other all our lives, would you?" Charlie grinned the old grin. After that it was easier. The kettle whistled and I made tea. We sat at the table and drank three cups each. I ate two slices of homemade bread and butter, and Charlie ate four.

"I didn't even know about your accident until I heard from that nurse, Sister Lillian. She said you'd been hit by a buzz bomb. Are you all right now?"

"Perfectly." I tried to keep my voice casual. "A piece of debris fell on me but it was nothing serious. Mostly I was just — overtired."

The talk turned to people we knew from Touchwood and where they were posted. The kitchen window passed into shadow. "It's five o'clock already!" I said. "Can you stay for supper?"

"Sure, but I'll have to catch the seven o'clock train from Steeple Aston. It's the last one tonight."

"Would you like to sleep here? There's an extra bedroom downstairs off the kitchen." I scolded myself silently, expecting him to make some excuse.

"Gosh, that would be swell!" Charlie looked a little concerned. "But won't people talk? You know, innocent maiden spends night with degenerate airman, that kind of thing."

I forced myself to laugh, although the reference to my innocence stung. "Did anybody see you arrive?"

"No, I didn't come through the village. I hitched a ride from Oxford and the lorry driver knew where Sunny Banks was so he let me off down the lane."

"Well, that's settled." A few minutes later Charlie had his tunic off and was in the kitchen peeling potatoes while I set the table. We sat down to a meal of fresh vegetables and home-cured ham from Mrs. Gorsuch's ample larder. Dessert was apple crisp made with honey and real cream, served with a generous wedge of cheddar cheese.

"That was the best meal I've had for ages," Charlie said, pushing back his chair. "Let's go into the other room and I'll make a fire to take the chill off. I'll never get used to the dampness in this wretched country."

"What I miss most is the sky," I said, as we walked into the sitting room. "I haven't seen a decent sunset in three years."

"I miss the way it smells when the sun is hot enough to scorch the grass."

"I miss the sound of the wind in the poplar leaves outside my bedroom window."

"Stop it, or we'll both be bawling." Charlie knelt in front of the fireplace. He struck a match and touched it to the paper. The flames leaped up and his face glowed in the warm light.

I stared at him, trying to decide why he looked the same and yet so different. His big feet and his oversized hands hadn't changed, except for the missing finger. Then I realized he wasn't awkward anymore. His movements as he tossed wood on the fire were strong and graceful.

He turned to me with a sombre expression. "I was so terribly sorry to hear about Jack. Do you mind if I mention him?"

"It's all right now. Even a few weeks ago I couldn't stand it, but now I'd like to hear his name spoken again. It makes it seem as if he's still alive, but just somewhere else."

"I believe he is."

"Do you really think so, after everything you've been through?" In spite of my good intentions, my voice trembled.

"Yes, I do. War can bring out the worst in people, but also the best. When I think of the goodness I've seen, the heroism and the self-sacrifice, I can't accept that we're just a freak of nature."

"That's a wonderful attitude, Charlie. I'd like to feel the same way."

"How are your parents making out?"

"You probably know better than I do. You've been through it already." Charlie had been only ten years old when his sweet-faced mother had died of heart disease.

His voice was gentle. "When you lose someone in your family, it's like being maimed. You get used to living with a missing limb. Or maybe it's more like a chronic illness. The pain never goes away, it just gets more manageable. You have good days and bad days."

"There are so many maimed families out there now. I guess ours will survive as well as all the others."

We didn't talk anymore, but it wasn't an awkward silence. We sat together, gazing into the leaping flames until the logs collapsed in a flurry of ashes. Then Charlie retired to the little bedroom off the kitchen and I went slowly up the winding staircase.

◄▼►

The next morning I stretched like a cat, smiling when I remembered Charlie in the downstairs bedroom. The early morning sunshine was pouring through the window but the cottage was quiet. I decided to let him sleep while I went for my usual swim. I squeezed into an old blue bathing suit of Sally's I had found while rummaging through the cupboards, looking for extra sheets. It was a bit on the skimpy side, but it would do.

I strolled down the path and swam across the pond a dozen times. My energy was coming back, and my arms and legs were developing muscles again. I was sitting on the blanket, thinking about making eggs scrambled with onions for breakfast, when I heard a stir in the bushes. I snatched up the towel and flung it around my shoulders before I turned my head.

Charlie stood a few yards away at the edge of the clearing. From the expression on his face, I knew he had seen the hideous purple scar on my back. I sat rigid with mortification. I didn't want his pity, and I was afraid that my back would revolt him. It was suddenly terribly important that he not be revolted.

He walked toward the blanket and lowered himself beside me, facing the water. He had left off his uniform and he was wearing a pair of grey flannels and a sleeveless white cotton undershirt. We sat without speaking. A breeze riffled the water, and a thrush sang in the trees.

Without saying a word, Charlie reached out and slid one large hand underneath my towel. I felt his palm close over the hurt place. Warmth radiated through my body. I closed my eyes and allowed myself to feel the pleasure of his touch on my damaged skin. Charlie's hand began to move in small circles, his fingertips caressing the ridges of the wound. No one had ever touched me so tenderly, not even the nurses.

Finally he spoke. "I had no idea it was so bad. I wish to God someone had told me."

Almost mesmerized by his touch, I couldn't speak for a moment. "It doesn't hurt nearly as much as it did at first. I can't do any heavy lifting yet, but I can sleep through the night now." I tried to smile. "The doctor said I'd never be a bathing beauty, but my spine wasn't injured, that's the main thing."

"I suppose that's the only way to look at it. Of course, I disagree entirely with the bathing beauty remark."

He grinned down at me. *He has the smilingest eyes,* I thought. His face was mere inches away. I could smell the faint scent of soap on his freshly shaven jaw.

Gripping the towel tightly around my shoulders, I jumped to my feet. "Well, what about breakfast?"

Too soon, too soon. I could almost hear my own voice saying the words aloud as I beat the eggs while Charlie chopped kindling outside the back door. My back was healing, and the fresh agony of Jack's death was beginning to dull. I could feel the edges of the gaping wound left by his death starting to pucker and pull together, like the burn on my back.

But my feelings were up and down like the teeter-totter in the schoolyard. And it was only a few short weeks since I had deluded myself into thinking I was in love with Fowler.

I now saw, with perfect clarity, that I was no better than a thousand other girls who had been made fools of by older men, although I hadn't completely forgiven myself yet. Guilt and remorse occasionally swam to the surface of my consciousness, like heavy-bellied fish.

It was a curious fact that I, so clever at some things, was not at all shrewd about people's feelings or even my own, come to that. It was as if all my strength of mind had been poured into my work, like a single branch that blooms while the rest of the tree remains stunted and immature.

I was certainly in no shape to give my heart to anyone. I needed bucking up, as Dad would say. But what was far more important than my own feelings was the fact that there was a war on. The last thing I needed was a romance with someone who might — probably would, given the odds — fly away one day and never come back.

And I wanted to do right by Charlie, too. He'd been lucky so far, but the fate of a bomber pilot was affected by many things, not the least of which was his ability to maintain a certain detachment from personal matters.

Still, I couldn't help wondering about Charlie's personal life. While we were having our last cup of tea, I managed to work the conversation, rather clumsily, around to girlfriends. "What do you hear from Vicky, that girl you were with at Covent Garden? What's she up to these days?"

"Who?" He looked puzzled. "Oh, that girl. I never saw her again. I haven't had much to do with women. It doesn't seem fair on them."

"But we always hear so much about the romances that go on at an airfield, especially with all those WAAFs on duty."

Charlie nodded. "Well, there are two ways of looking at it. Some of the fellows really like having girlfriends on the station. They understand and sympathize, as much as anyone can who doesn't fly. My rear gunner has a girlfriend on the station, and I honestly think that's the only thing that's keeping him sane." He looked down into his teacup. "Then there's the other type, I guess I'm one of them. Between raids, I try not to think about the danger. If I feel the need to talk, nobody knows me better than my own crew. We've been together for the thick end of a year now, and never a cross word." He set down his cup carefully. "What about you? Any boyfriends lurking in the tall weeds?"

I wondered if I should pass the question off with a joke. Then I decided Charlie deserved an honest answer. I poured lukewarm tea into my cup so I wouldn't have to look into his face.

"I've had two serious boyfriends, for want of a better word. Both times it ended badly. The first one was killed in a training accident, and the second one was — married." My voice shook in spite of myself. I set down the teapot and raised my eyes, determined to face his reaction without flinching.

He reached his big hand across the table and took mine away from the handle of the teapot, holding it in his warm grasp. "It sounds as if you've had hard luck all the way round."

For a moment I was certain I would cry again. I drew my hand away and leaned back, anxious to change the subject. "Do you have any friends off the base, Charlie?"

"Yeah, Stanley Bates. He's a farmer, lives right next to the airfield. I met him in kind of a funny way."

"How was that?" I wanted to know everything about Charlie's life.

"Last year I was coming in at dawn and I overshot the runway. It was my own stupid fault, I was just tired. Talk about hedge-hopping. I tore the tops off the trees at the end of the runway and landed smack into the neighbour's pasture. We were okay — actually we were damned lucky — but our wing clipped the neighbour's horse and killed it stone dead on the spot. It was a beautiful animal, too, a Clydesdale. Mr. Bates wasn't impressed, to say the least. The station compensated him for the horse, but I felt so badly about it that I went over the next day and offered to help him around the farm. He put me to work mucking out the barn, and after two days of hard labour he decided I was all right. We got friendly, and now I work there whenever I'm not flying. He's a widower, getting on a bit, and he really needs help."

"That's very nice of you, Charlie."

"Don't get me wrong — I'm the one who gets the good out of it. I reckon plenty of fresh air and exercise help me sleep nights. Besides, I can relax and forget about things when I'm working on the land."

Charlie hesitated. "You're probably going to laugh when I tell you this, but I never wanted to be a farmer. I was planning to leave home before the war broke out. I told Dad I wouldn't be sticking around, not even for the pretty girl across the road." He winked at me.

"And how do you feel about farming now?"

"It's strange, but spending time with Stan Bates has changed my outlook on things. I used to hate farming, but now I can't wait to get back to it. I'm sick and tired of blasting and burning some other fellow's farm. I want to bring things to life for a change, instead of killing them."

He went on in a rush. "I lie in bed at night when I'm still worked up after a raid and I think about all the improvements I'm going to make to the old place. I want to tear down the small barn and put up a bigger one, fence the back pasture, try some new varieties of grain. I want to plant a windbreak, and put in some fruit trees." He dropped his eyes to the floor. "Oh, I have lots of great ideas, believe me."

"I think your change of heart is perfectly natural. I suppose none of us really values what we have until we have a taste of the grass on the other side."

Charlie looked at me intently. "Do you feel that way, too?"

"Yes, I do. I used to think that Touchwood was such a dull little place. But not anymore. Honestly, Charlie, I can't wait to get back to dear old Touchwood and never leave it again! I know how the early settlers felt when they left this country, that Canada is just bursting with potential."

"That's it, exactly! There's plenty about England to admire, but I could never live here."

"I used to love all the British traditions. Now I see there's a lot to be said for a country without all that old baggage — the class system, for example." I was thinking of Sally and Sam.

Charlie was nodding. "And the poverty! My mate and I went to Manchester on leave and most of the houses there don't even have indoor bathrooms. A big city like that!"

"You know the expression, all the same in a hundred years, I never knew what that meant until I came here. Canada is a blank page, where anyone can make a mark. It's only fifty years older than we are! In this place you feel that you're just a temporary gatekeeper, that your life won't affect history one way or the other. Somehow it's — diminishing."

Charlie tilted back on the legs of his chair. "You know what really convinced me to go back to farming? Taking orders. I'm sick to death of getting up in the morning when someone tells me to, going to bed at lights out, polishing my blasted buttons. I want to be a free man again, never take orders from anyone — except maybe my wife."

He grinned at me, and my heart, quite literally, skipped a beat and then came down hard on the next thump. "Won't you miss the flying?"

"Well, that's the worst part — I really do love flying. You have no idea how marvellous it is to leave the earth behind and go straight up into the blue. At night when it's quiet and the stars are shining, it's like heaven. I'd give anything if I could have my own kite back home — nothing fancy, just something to fool around with — but it's expensive, and there's no place to keep it."

I stood and began to clear the table. I didn't want to talk about our uncertain future anymore. After breakfast we went for a long ramble in the woods, clowning around like a couple of kids, laughing at each other's jokes. Charlie was as excited as a boy when he found a bush bursting with wild roses. "You're a farmer, that's for sure," I teased him, "always enthusiastic about growing things."

"True enough, but these English roses can't hold a candle to our own prairie rose." He smiled at me.

"Come on, it's getting warm. Let's go for a swim. I saw some men's bathing trunks in the closet."

Charlie was a fine figure of a man, as my mother would say. I teased him again about his farmer's tan with the deep brown V at his throat. When he dived into the pond, his powerful calves contracted and for a split second I recalled Fowler's spindly shanks. We splashed and frolicked, and I was ducked three times before I cried uncle.

Finally we got out of the water and threw ourselves down on the blanket. "You have gold glints in your hair," Charlie said. He reached out and wound a lock around his finger before dropping it and turning his face toward the pond.

After we ate our hearty supper of sausages and mashed potatoes, Charlie built another fire. I came into the sitting room a short time later to see him stretched out on the chesterfield, sound asleep. He lay on his side, his left hand bracing his right arm to shield his eyes. It was a habit all servicemen got into after a while, trying to sleep under harsh overhead lights in a barracks filled with other people.

I took the opportunity to study him. His face, softened by sleep, was more like the boy I used to know.

His eyes flew open and he grinned. "Gotcha."

"I was thinking how young you look when you're asleep."

"Have I aged so much?"

"You certainly haven't changed for the worse."

"You need to put on some weight. You never used to be so skinny."

"Skinny! You're ruining my plan to become a fashion model after the war!"

"What are you planning to do after the war, Rose?" He sat up and gave me that curiously intent look once again.

"I haven't decided. At one time I wanted to go to university, but now I've realized that school isn't the only place to get an education."

Charlie opened his mouth as if to speak, then closed it again. I went on. "I have decided one thing since coming here, though. I'm going to transfer into the RCAF."

He looked at me in surprise. "Are you allowed to do that?"

"Yes. Now that Parliament has finally agreed to allow service-women over here, they're opening up their ranks to Canadians who were caught here by the war, or married Canadian servicemen, or joined other branches, like me. I want to finish the war among my own people."

The next morning, Charlie said goodbye and walked away down the lane. We didn't embrace. I think we were both afraid of what might happen if we did. At the first curve he turned and lifted his big hand, and I waved back. Then he was gone. I felt like part of myself was going with him. I had been wandering alone on a dark continent and stumbled across a shining path, the one that leads to home.

I sighed as I closed the front door. It was time to return to the war. I tidied the cottage and donned my faded blue WAAF uniform. How proud I had been to wear it. And how eager I was to put it behind me.

After I packed my kitbag, I turned on the radio. The BBC news was good, very good indeed. On that very morning — August 25, 1944 — French troops were marching down the Champs-Élysées while thousands of liberated Parisians screamed with joy. The Germans — weakened, but not destroyed — had been driven back to their own frontiers, where they prepared for a last desperate stand.

BOOK FOUR

September 1944–July 1945

33

"Good luck." I smiled at the baby-faced navigator as I handed over his target folder. His hand was shaking so badly he could barely grasp it. His first time out, I guessed.

"Good luck." I passed on to the next airman, and the next, looking each one in the eye and giving him an encouraging smile. Some of them smiled back, others barely noticed me.

When the folders were distributed, RCAF Station Commander Mark Tilbury began his briefing. "Men, this is your target for tonight." He whipped the canvas off a bulky shape on the table, and all eyes fell upon a model of Berlin.

From my seat at the head table, I had a good view of the cavernous room, the size of an auditorium. The aircraft identification models suspended from the ceiling slowly revolved in the thick cigarette smoke that filled the air. Posters urged the crews to avoid talking with strangers and to protect themselves from venereal disease.

Three hundred airmen sat on folding chairs. My eyes wandered across the rows of blue uniforms bearing the Six Group badge: the white rose of Yorkshire overlaid with the red Canadian maple leaf. Each crew sat in a group, wanting to stick close on the ground and in the air. The men formed a tight bond, reasoning that if their fellow crew members survived, so would they. If not, they would travel together to another place.

Some of the men had a glassy stare; others had the twitch — nervous tics in their faces or hands. Many of them fingered St. Christopher medals or rabbit's foot charms. A young pilot in the front row pushed back his chair and ran from the room. He was probably going to be sick. This, too, was routine.

As I watched the men, I calculated their odds. During their first few operations, when their nerves were tested as never before, the chance of survival for the rookies was one in ten.

The second group was composed of men who had lived through the first dozen operations. As their skills grew, their odds of survival increased until they were about even. These were the most confident, leaning back in their chairs and joking.

Then the odds began to turn against them once more. By the time they reached their last few missions, every man knew he was a walking statistical aberration.

My eyes fell on the chief pilot for the aircraft designated T for Tom. He had completed his first tour of thirty missions, trained aircrews for six months, and returned to active duty for another twenty missions. Those who survived the first tour were offered the choice of flying or instructing. This man had chosen to keep flying. Tonight would be his forty-sixth raid. His face was worn and grim, and he had rebelliously removed the wire from his cap to show he was a seasoned veteran.

The others were quite spruce in their natty uniforms. Both their appearance and their outlook had improved considerably after Six Group was taken over by Black Mike McEwen, who had transformed it from a "chop group" with unacceptably high losses into an expert fighting force.

My thoughts turned to Charlie. Was he being briefed tonight? The seven RCAF stations belonging to Six Group were scattered across Yorkshire, so close that their flight paths overlapped, yet there was little contact between our small worlds. Although we wrote to each other often, I hadn't seen him since those happy days at Sunny Banks. He was flying his second tour, but I didn't know how many missions he had left.

Suddenly the T for Tom pilot caught my eye and winked. Embarrassed, I looked out the window. A Halifax was parked on the tarmac being tanked up by the fuel trucks. The armourers sat on their little trainloads of bombs, waiting to load each aircraft with six tons of bombs. The erks, as the ground crew were called, were giving the transparent domes surrounding the guns a last-minute spit-and-polish.

"Godspeed each and every one of you! Dismissed!" Tilbury saluted his boys with an expression of pride and concern. The boys loved him like a father, and I could see why: his firm kindness coupled with their enormous need for a leader they could trust with their lives.

They filed out, picking up the emergency rations packed by the women on the base — waterproof khaki bags with a can opener, cheese, candy, razor blade, and fishing line, in case dawn found them hiding in enemy territory.

I followed them outside into the cool October dusk. The soft green of the countryside was fading into grey, broken only by a band of pink clouds in the western sky. The pilot standing under the nearest wing buckled his helmet and swallowed his wakey-wakey pill out of his hand, washing it down with a swig of coffee from his Thermos.

A short ladder extended from the hatch; the pilot took one lingering look at the peaceful countryside before he climbed into the belly of the aircraft. I marvelled once again at the bomber's size. When I stood on my toes and stretched my arm over my head, my fingertips still couldn't reach the propellers.

The blades revolved slowly, and then kicked forward into a blur as the engines coughed and started to roar. The hatch slammed shut from the inside and the ground crew pulled the chocks from the wheels. The aircraft lumbered away, moving around the ring road toward the marshalling point.

Within moments a green light flashed from the end of the runway. The mighty bomber began to move faster, groaning and straining to lift its heavy load of bombs off the ground, and then the tail light became a shrinking red speck that wavered upwards into the darkening sky and disappeared.

I sent up a silent prayer as I watched all forty-eight Halifaxes lift off one by one and circle the control tower, waggling their wings once for farewell. Like a flock of wild geese, they headed south for the rendezvous where they would join a giant bomber stream from bases all over England.

I climbed a set of wooden stairs to the second-floor control room. Here it was bright and almost cheerful. Windows on three sides of the room overlooked the long runway and the blackout curtains hadn't been drawn yet. No one knew what kind of a raid it was going to be; hopes were still high that it would be an easy one. Four airwomen wearing headsets were taking the departure signals and marking them up on a large blackboard.

As the drone of the last bomber passed out of hearing, it seemed very quiet. A flock of starlings outside the window twittered in the evening twilight. Two girls put aside their headsets and pulled out their knitting to relieve the tension of the long wait. "Tea, anyone?" asked the duty officer.

I slipped away to my own quarters. Since the bombers would be gone for ten hours, this was my chance to sleep.

I slept soundly, ate a quick breakfast, and was back in the control room at four o'clock when the radio began to crackle. Then the first aircraft was heard making a wide orbit overhead in the darkness, and the operation of landing the machines began.

The control officer and the wing commander stepped onto the balcony overlooking the runway, and I followed them. From the open doorway, we could hear the rattle of the pilot's voice on the radio receiver: "R for Roger at fifteen hundred, waiting permission to land."

"R for Roger, cleared for landing." The radio operator had a comforting voice, a mother guiding her children home.

I felt mingled excitement and relief as the giant birds swooped down from the night sky and taxied to a stop with a grinding squeal of brakes. Each aircraft was greeted with cheers by its own ground staff, who felt that they owned the bombers — the aircrews were just borrowing them.

C for Charlie drew up nearest the control room. The men dropped out of the hatch, stiff and cramped, slipping off their flying helmets and their harnesses, and stretching their arms. The pilot and navigator chatted for a few minutes, then went to the back of the aircraft and examined a cluster of jagged holes in the bomb door, made by the barrage of flak they had flown through.

I headed back to the briefing hut. As the crews came inside, they milled around, smoking, drinking hot chocolate or coffee, gobbling down Spam sandwiches. Most of them accepted the offer of a shot of whiskey to help them unwind.

Tonight there was little chatter, so I knew it had been a difficult mission. Whenever an aircraft was heard overhead, a hush fell as everyone listened to the sound of the engine, trying to determine if it was running smoothly or limping back to base.

Every time the door opened, all heads turned. Here was the crew from D for Donald. Here was Z for Zebra. The pink-cheeked rookie burst into the room, his eyes shining.

Finally, only three crews were missing. One of them was T for Tom, flown by the veteran pilot who had winked at me. They may have been shot down. Or they may have crash-landed, or ditched in the Channel. With any luck they had landed at another station, or made it to the ploughed field on the coastline lit with gas flares, the last resort for a badly damaged aircraft.

The wingco called for attention. "Let's begin the debriefing. R for Roger, you'll go with Jenkins and Jolliffe."

I noticed the look of dismay that crossed the faces of R for Roger's crew. They pushed back their chairs and followed us into an adjoining room.

Jenkins, the intelligence officer, wasn't any happier about my presence than they were. He smoked evil-smelling black cheroots and he wasn't careful to blow his smoke in the opposite direction when I was around. Now he leaned back in his chair and breathed a jet of foul smoke toward me. "Go ahead, Section Officer. It's your show."

I sat down behind the ink-stained wooden table, while the seven men took up the hard chairs ranged in front of me. I removed the bulldog clip from a sheaf of buff-coloured papers and began to ask the routine questions: "Were any fighters seen with an unfamiliar insignia? Was the weather as reported? Was any new tactic employed by the Luftwaffe?"

Their answers were short. I sensed their resistance at being debriefed by a woman, especially one who ranked higher than their own pilot. I didn't blame them, for I could never fully understand their feelings when in combat. But then, neither could Jenkins, who had been washed out during basic training.

I had learned that some men had near-photographic recall of their raids, as if the danger heightened their senses. Others were so frightened that they remembered almost nothing.

Now I dismissed everyone except the pilot, navigator, and bomb aimer. "Pilot Officer Jones, you were in the third wave of bombers. Where did the anti-aircraft fire begin?"

"Here." He pointed to the map and drew quickly on his cigarette, still worked up from the night's adventure.

"Do you all agree?" They nodded in unison.

"Navigator, was the target struck as indicated?"

"Yes, ma'am." I noted a slight hesitation.

"Please elaborate."

The navigator, still wearing his orange life preserver around his neck, was older than the boyish-looking pilot. He leaned back in his chair and deliberated.

"The Pathfinders went in and dropped the red flares first, and we heard the master bomber order the first wave to bomb red. The red smoke drifted away to the north, so the Pathfinders went round again and dropped yellow, and we heard the second wave instructed to bomb on yellow. We were in the third wave. We stooged around for a few minutes, and when it was our turn we were ordered to bomb on green."

I made notes while I considered. A flare burned for just six minutes, which meant the Pathfinder Mosquitoes had to keep replenishing the flares throughout the forty-minute raid so each wave of bombers could see where to aim. The aircrews were kept informed through a special number code on their radios.

"Was the flak heavy?"

"I'll say!" The bomb aimer spoke feelingly. "They were throwing up as much stuff at us as we were dropping on them!"

"Thank you, gentlemen. I'll examine the photographs and get back to you if there are any further questions. Dismissed."

The men gave half-hearted salutes and shuffled off to their beds, where hot water bottles were waiting. The photographs were already in the developing tank. By the time I finished interviewing another four crews, the prints were brought in, still damp. Jenkins and I bent over them.

These weren't the precisely targeted reconnaissance photographs I had viewed at Medmenham. These were hit-or-miss, taken by automatic cameras that rolled as soon as the bomb doors opened. After the bombs dropped, the pilot had to hold the aircraft flat and steady for thirty seconds so the camera could record where they had landed.

Understandably, the crews hated this order.

"There's a problem, Section Officer." Jenkins was the first to speak. "Some of the bombs were dropped about a mile outside the perimeter of Berlin, but all crews reported they were right on target. Do you see anything that looks like a decoy?"

"Not yet." I was still studying the black photographs, the searchlights below showing as thin silver pencils.

"It could be a simple case of creep-back," Jenkins said. Bomber crews, frantic to leave the area, sometimes dropped their bombs early and rushed away, causing a chain reaction as the aircraft coming up behind followed them.

"There's a row of white circles outside the western edge of the city. Have you ever seen anything like them?" I asked.

"No. Could they be silos or some kind of storage tanks?"

"They're definitely not silos." By now I was familiar with every type of farm building. For the next two hours, we studied the bomb damage photos. I walked back to my quarters at dawn, still puzzled.

Knowing the aircrews were allowed to sleep late after a raid, I waited until the afternoon before speaking to Pilot Officer Jones again. He was summoned from his quarters, unshaven and truculent, and sat down on the same chair in the briefing hut.

"You said that the first wave dropped on red, the second on yellow, and yours on green."

"Yes, ma'am."

"Were the target indicators very close together?"

"Yes, ma'am. We were right on top of the green flares before we saw them."

I rephrased his words. "So it seemed as if the green flares suddenly appeared underneath you."

"Yes, that's right." The pilot eyed me belligerently as if daring me to contradict him.

"Could you see any trace of red smoke?"

The pilot opened his mouth to answer and stopped. He squinted at the wall. "I caught a glimpse of red smoke a long way ahead. It was odd the red was already so far from the target. The wind drift didn't seem to be as bad as that."

There was a silent click in my brain as my suspicions fell into place. "We found a row of white circles about a mile outside the city. I suspect they're launching sites. When the Pathfinders radioed that the colour indicator was changed, the Germans immediately launched green rockets simulating the green smoke from our own flares."

"How would they know?" He sounded skeptical.

"I'm not sure." I hesitated. "Could they possibly have broken our radio code?"

The pilot's jaw dropped and his eyes widened. "Holy cats, ma'am, if that's true, it would explain a lot!" He dropped his air of antagonism and leaned forward with his arms on the desk. "This isn't the first time we've been surprised by the flares being in a different place than we expected. We assumed it was wind drift, or some kind of plotting error."

"That didn't appear on your reports." I gritted my teeth. Most of the time I had the deepest sympathy for the airmen, except when they tried to conceal evidence that would help me perform my job.

The pilot squirmed in his chair. "We were always careful to bomb smack on top of the flares. It never crossed our minds that they might not be ours! Jesus Christ. Excuse me, ma'am. Wait until I tell my navigator. He's been worried about the discrepancy — but we figured someone else must have screwed up down the line."

34

Jenkins smiled at me, but it was more of a sneer.

"I suppose you know the men are calling you a witch, Section Officer." He always pointedly called me by my full rank, making it sound like an insult.

I simply shrugged. Given the staggering level of superstition on the base, the charms and the rituals, this wasn't surprising. I didn't care if they thought I was using a crystal ball. And by now I was well aware that a number of men, both officers and subordinates, would never yield their lifelong prejudice against women.

My fellow airwomen were a different story. I had felt warmly accepted by them ever since I presented myself at the RCAF headquarters in London. I had marched into the office in my faded uniform and handed my service file to the clerk behind the desk, who flipped through it — at first idly, and then with increased interest.

A few minutes later I met Wing Officer Kathleen Walker, the queen bee herself of the Canadian women's air force. An attractive, dark-haired woman with heavy black eyebrows, she strode around her desk to shake my hand. "We'd be delighted to enlist someone with your service record! Please sit down and tell me about yourself."

When I finished, she was beaming. "Hundreds of recruits have transferred into the women's division since we arrived in England — most of them British citizens married to Canadian servicemen, who want to transfer in because we pay so much better. But occasionally we come across a gem like you, a Canadian who volunteered for the British service and has acquired valuable experience. Because you already have more seniority than any of our members, your rank will be automatically raised to section officer."

She picked up my file and tapped it with her blunt fingernail. "You come highly recommended by your group captain for your interpretation skills. Frankly, you couldn't have arrived at a better time. I'm sending you straight up to Yorkshire, to serve with Bomber Six Group at RCAF East Moor."

I caught my breath. After all these weary years, I was finally going to serve on an operational station.

The officer came around her desk to wring my hand again. If I hadn't already felt like crying, her words would have brought me close to tears: "The Royal Canadian Air Force is counting on us to form a strong second line to the fighting service. With men we are sharing the fight. With them we will share the victory."

◆▾◆

I was fitted out for my new uniform, admiring the fineness of the fabric compared to the scratchy British wool. After a barrage of complaints, the women's division had shed the bulky patch pockets, added a smart leatherette shoulder bag, and streamlined the puckered hat so it lay smooth and flat. I boarded the train feeling almost elegant in my new uniform.

But there the luxury ended. There were no marble fireplaces or mahogany staircases at my new station, which was no more than a collection of Nissen huts and rectangular wooden buildings tossed together and painted a hideous dull green.

I didn't care. Hungry for a long horizon, I gazed at the surrounding moors covered with prickly brown gorse and purplish heather and found them achingly beautiful.

Six Group had come about because so many Canadian bomb squadrons were operating within the British air force. It was finally agreed to bring fourteen of them together in a separate group, staffed and paid for by the Canadian government. Six Group accounted for 40 percent of all Canadian aircrews, while the remaining 60 percent continued to fly with the RAF.

The Canadian stations were spread in and around Yorkshire. I knew what MacTavish would say, what many others believed: Bomber Command had placed the Canadian stations farthest away from the German targets, and in the area with the worst weather conditions.

I soon discovered another difference: the Canadians were much less formal. The first time I accompanied another officer around the barracks for kit inspection, I was amazed to see stuffed animals and even dolls. When the officer had finished a cursory inspection, she sat down on the nearest cot, shoved aside a fluffy pink rabbit, and pulled out her cigarettes, chatting to the juniors as if they were her equals.

Although I was entitled to my own small room, formed by dividing one of the long metal huts into compartments, I preferred the sitting room in the wooden hut used by the female officers, known as the henhouse. Here we spent most of our time, chatting or knitting, while lacy underwear dried on a string hung from the ceiling and a pot of hot chocolate simmered on the stove. Sometimes we rode our bicycles into the nearby village called Sutton-on-the-Forest.

I had enormous respect for my fellow Canadian airwomen, who had been hand-picked for the coveted overseas postings because of their intelligence, integrity, and patriotism.

For the first time in this war, I shared the strength of a common feminine will: not the masculine desire to bludgeon the enemy to its knees, but rather a passionate longing to end the senseless waste of human life.

‹▼›

The control room was warm and almost cozy in the quiet hour before dawn.

To relieve the tension while waiting for the bombers to return from their raid on Berlin, two girls played chess and another read aloud society gossip from the *Tatler*. A tea kettle simmered on the hot plate.

I looked up sharply from my knitting needles when the gentle rain against the windowpanes began to make a scrabbling sound. "It's turning to sleet," someone said in a low voice.

The first snow had fallen on Yorkshire's desolate moors that morning, and all personnel had turned out to shovel the runways and brush off the aircraft. The homesick Canadian boys had frolicked like children, throwing snowballs and washing each other's faces.

Although I longed to join the horseplay, it was against orders to fraternize with the aircrew because I outranked them. When nobody was watching, I lifted my face to the skies, opening my mouth to feel the kiss of snowflakes on my tongue.

But this icy sleet was something else altogether.

"Update on the weather, please." The control officer turned to the meteorologist sitting at his wooden desk in the corner, surrounded by his maps and instruments.

"One moment, sir, I'll ring and see what's up." He picked up the black telephone handset on his desk and spoke briefly, then hung up with a grim expression.

"It's a ruddy ice storm, sir, blowing in from Norway."

Immediately the room was electrified. Everyone pushed back their chairs and hurried to the long bank of windows overlooking the runway.

An aircraft could ice up in minutes. Not only did this add tons of weight, but if even the very thinnest layer of ice distorted the upper curve of the wings, the aircraft's balance was affected and it became impossible for the pilot to control. Iced up, a thirty-ton bomber could tumble from the sky like a falling leaf.

The station's forty-eight bombers, now strung out over the cold, black sea, running short of fuel after ten hours in flight, some of them trying desperately to limp home with flak damage and wounded men, were beginning their descent.

"What's the forecast?" asked the control officer.

All faces turned toward the meteorologist. "Not so good, sir. The temperature's dropping like a stone."

Nobody needed the official report to see that the sleet was rapidly worsening. A cloud of icy pellets rattled off the windows and a thick white blanket descended. The parallel rows of searchlights lining the runway were no brighter than flickering candles in the ghostly fog. I saw the dim shapes of ground crew running and sliding across the icy tarmac, the crash wagons already moving into position.

The young operations clerk beside me named Nancy Palmer made a small agonized sound in her throat. I knew she was secretly engaged to one of the rear gunners. I reached out and clasped her hand as we stood at the window, straining our eyes into the whirling darkness.

Then, over the sound of the storm, the first faint engine was heard.

The familiar thunder of the engines grew louder, and a dark shape plummeted out of the sky. It struck the runway with its left wheel, staggered slightly, righted itself, and slowed, swerving off the end of the runway onto the perimeter track where it taxied to a stop. In the dim glow of the runway lights we could see a glaze of ice gleaming on the wings.

There were murmurs of relief. "That's D for Donald!" said the radio operator. *Maybe the ice storm isn't so bad at higher altitudes,* I thought. *If they descend fast enough, they can drop right through it.*

While the props were still revolving and before the hatch had opened to discharge the crew, another dark shape loomed into sight and touched down. It was obvious that the second aircraft was approaching much too quickly.

As we watched in horror, the Halifax shot down the icy runway and slammed into the tail of the first. Both aircraft exploded in a giant fireball, bits of burning wreckage tossed high into the darkness.

Screams and sobs broke out in the control room. "Get on the radio!" the control officer shouted at the operator. "Instruct all crews to head for the emergency landing strip!" My eyes were fixed on the two aircraft blazing in the darkness, the roaring flames blurred by the falling sleet. Behind me came the radio operator's voice: "Calling all crews! Calling all crews!"

In response we heard a young man's frantic cry. "This is P for Peter! Aircraft iced up and controls not responding!" Before she could answer, an aircraft appeared out of the night sky and touched down, bouncing and screeching to a stop a few feet away from the fiery collision. The ice-covered wings gleamed in the bright glow of the firelight. The crew bailed out of the hatch, practically climbing over each other in their haste, and ran away into the darkness.

Behind me I heard the angry voice of the women's commander on watch. "Pull yourselves together!" she hissed. "Remember your training!" The sobs abruptly ceased as if they had been choked off. Nancy Palmer hurried from the room, one hand over her mouth.

The rest of us stood helplessly, watching the pandemonium on the airfield. Two crash wagons slithered to a stop at the edge of the burning aircraft. Ghostly figures in white cowled asbestos suits jumped off the sides and began to run toward the wreckage, slipping and falling on the icy surface. I saw a man pedalling a bicycle across the tarmac. As he dropped the bike and ran toward the ambulance, I recognized the station's padre.

"Several crews aren't responding, sir!" Just as the operator's words left her mouth, another aircraft came out of the white gloom, his landing wheels a few yards above the runway. The engines roared as the pilot caught sight of the wreckage and tried with all his strength to pull up the nose of his aircraft. He managed to clear the crash by inches, but the heavy ice coating his wings prevented him from gaining enough altitude. His bomber overshot the runway and crashed into the trees beyond, exploding on contact.

I pressed my hot forehead against the cold glass and squeezed my eyes shut to block out the dreadful scene. Like every other woman on the station, I had learned to live with the nightly deaths, but they happened thousands of miles away. I had never seen an aircraft explode, except in photographs. I couldn't help imagining Jack being blown to pieces in this horrible way.

I heard the control officer curse and felt the woman beside me clutch my arm. My eyes opened to see a fifth aircraft touch down at the far end of the runway. As if in slow motion, it turned and skidded sideways down the slippery tarmac toward the fire. I held my breath. The room behind me was deathly still.

The aircraft slid slowly, slowly toward the wreck. For a few seconds it looked as if it would miss the burning debris altogether — but in passing, one wingtip clipped the edge of the wreckage and the force of the collision sent it spinning in circles. It revolved off the runway and disappeared into the darkness. Another explosion lit up the frozen sky.

The control officer groaned aloud. There was nothing to be done. In the background, the operator's firm voice repeated: "All crews, do not attempt to land East Moor! Icing severe and runway inoperable. Please proceed to emergency landing strip."

Her voice was professional, but I could hear the underlying panic. "Repeat: DO NOT, repeat DO NOT attempt to land at RCAF East Moor!"

Two emergency personnel wrenched open the hatch of the first aircraft, and I saw a burning body fall into their arms. Streams of foam from fire extinguishers drenched the rear gunner's turret and another body, blackened and foam-covered, was lifted out and carried away on a stretcher.

I couldn't watch any more. I went into the women's head, where I found Nancy slumped on the floor, sobbing. Without speaking I sat down beside her and we clung together. The flight officer came in then, and sent Nancy off duty. The rest of us remained at our posts, white-faced and silent.

There were no more accidents that night. The operator's voice went on and on into the morning until the remaining aircraft had been diverted to other stations. It had been a good raid: not a single crew had been lost over Germany.

I stumbled back to my quarters in the dim grey sunrise past the stinking, smouldering wreckage. I was cold and numb, and in bed I cried myself to sleep.

◂▾▸

RAF Middleton St. George
November 15, 1944
Dear Rose,

Try not to mind the casualties too much. In the beginning I was like you, angry and saddened about the deaths of men I had been drinking with in the mess just the night before.

When you first see aircraft being shot down, you come back with this compulsion to tell everyone what it looks like, to describe how the fire spreads and how they spiral down, etc. But as time goes on you come to accept those things, including the possibility that you might be next.

You asked me why I'm not afraid anymore. For one thing, I'm prepared for whatever might happen. I practise every day, sitting in my grounded aircraft with my handkerchief tied over my eyes in case I need to fly blind, and I've learned how to do every other man's job from radio to navigation.

Mostly I think courage is like a bank account. Some start with a higher balance than others, and they can press on long after they're overdrawn. Others start out at zero. I saw one poor guy return from his first operation literally scared stiff — he couldn't move a muscle. He had to be taken out of the aircraft on a stretcher. No one thought the less of him.

Your junior officer, who believes she's a jinx because every man she dates eventually dies — that's a common myth. There was a time when I thought I was a curse. I couldn't help counting on my fingers all the men I had flown with who had been killed. But one day after a few pints I managed to talk about it in the mess, and found that everyone there had the same delusion. That really cleared the air.

You always hear about the fellow who has a premonition of his own death, but the other night I had the opposite experience. We were flying over the Swiss Alps and the silver peaks and valleys were gleaming in the starlight. I've never seen a mountain except from the air, but they must be really something. Since there's no blackout in Switzerland, we could see the twinkling lights of the villages below and even the headlights of cars driving down the winding roads. It was an incredible sight. I knew for the first time without a doubt that I will survive this war and go home again.

As always, Charlie

Touchwood
November 20, 1944
Dearest Rose,

We had a very sad Armistice Day service this year.
So many families have lost someone that it seems
pointless to observe two minutes of silence, as if
we don't remember them dozens of times every day.

The Legion Ladies' Auxiliary decided to move
the service indoors because some of the first war
veterans are getting on in years and can't stand the
cold. Lorraine Lumby sang "In Flanders Fields" —
she took over after her brother Fergus joined up,
but her voice isn't as powerful. When she reached:
"To you, from failing hands we throw the torch,"
she broke down. I don't know if I mentioned it
before, but Fergus is missing in action.

Then Vera Day, who was playing the organ,
slammed her foot down on the loud pedal and
roared out with all her strength: "Be yours to hold
it high!" And we all chimed in at the tops of our
lungs. After we finished there was kind of a solemn
hush and sobs could be heard all over the room.

Suddenly a little boy burst in the back door
and yelled: "Daisy Day has her tongue stuck on
the railing!" Vera leaped to her feet and grabbed
a cup of tea, and carried it outside and poured it
over Daisy's tongue. Between the frost and the
scalding tea, the poor little thing had to go around
with her tongue stuck out for the rest of the day!

It helps to have the children around to make us
laugh. Otherwise I think this war would be unbearable. Everyone believes if we could get conscription
passed it would be over soon. It's ridiculous that

Canada is the only country in the world without the draft, when our forces are so short of men. Seventy thousand zombies are refusing to go overseas, and not all of them from Quebec. The Bothwell boys disappeared last spring. Nobody has seen hide nor hair of them, but rumour has it they are running a trapline up north. If they come home too soon they may wish they had faced the Huns after all.

I will send your Christmas parcel next week, my darling. It will be number thirty-nine. I hope it gets there on time, as the mail has been so backed up lately. We pray that this is the last Christmas you will spend away from home.

All our love, Mother

⁂

Rockcliffe, Ontario
November 24, 1944
Dear Posy,

I've got sixpence, jolly, jolly sixpence.... Can you guess where I'm going? When I came out of head-quarters with my marching orders, I found two people sitting on the curb, blubbering away like babies — the woman because she wasn't going overseas, and the man because he was!

I can't tell you where I'm posted, but I know what I'll be doing — sorting mail! I can only con-clude that being a postal clerk is my lot in life. There's an unbelievable backlog of mail building up, millions of Christmas letters and parcels, and the big push is on to get them to the boys and girls in time.

Longing to see you, Prune

35

As I came down the steps of the railway platform in York two days before Christmas, a cold draft whistled around my legs. The train disgorged its load of uniforms. Kitbags, hats, and helmets bobbed past — and then I saw her.

"Prune!" I screamed. We fell into each other's arms, knocking our blue caps askew. The crowds jostled us as we embraced for a long moment. Then June bent to pick up my bag, putting her other arm through mine. "Let's find somewhere to sit down, old thing. We have a lot of catching up to do!"

We located a nearby teashop, settled ourselves at a round table with a snowy lace cloth, and spent the next few minutes studying each other with tremulous smiles. "Posy, you're so pale and elegant! And look at those stripes! Very impressive!"

"You've changed, too, Prune. You're not a little girl anymore." I knew why her pretty face looked older and sadder. I reached across the table and squeezed her hand. "I'm so terribly sorry about Sonny." I couldn't say anything more, since the ready tears began to fall.

June's blue eyes overflowed as well. "And Jack," she quavered. The bond of shared suffering ran between us like a river, and the years fell away. I had left June far behind, but now she had caught up with me — not only following me across the ocean, but closing the emotional distance as well.

She was the first to draw back and wipe her eyes. "We'd better talk about something else or we'll create a scene."

I pulled out my handkerchief and blew my nose. "Tell me about your new posting."

"What's there to say about Allerton Hall? You've seen the bloody place. No wonder everybody calls it Castle Dismal!"

The headquarters for Six Group was a baronial mansion that could have been occupied by Dracula: a gigantic pile of stone plunked down in the bleak wilderness west of York, massive towers rising eerily out of the mist.

"Can't you picture Emily Brontë, sitting out there on the moors, writing *Wuthering Heights*?" I asked.

"They do wuther, too," she said darkly. "I've heard them."

"Do you work with some nice people?"

"Oh, yeah, we have a ball. I wish you could come to our Christmas concert! Nine of the postal clerks have gotten up a beer bottle band and we play 'Good King Wenceslas' by blowing over the tops of the bottles!" Her face changed. "It's my first Christmas away from home, but at least Mum and Dad won't be alone. They have Daisy, and of course Mum's never one to sit around moping. She'll have a whole houseful of aircrew for dinner."

A red-faced Yorkshire lass came over to take our order and we asked for scones with our tea. When they arrived, huge and fluffy, June reached into her gas mask container and pulled out a jar of homemade strawberry jam. "Here, try some of this!"

"Heavenly!" I slathered my scone and took a bite. "Wild strawberries from that patch down by the river! Do you know how much you could make on the black market?"

"Probably a tidy fortune. Mum's loaded me down with supplies. You'd think I was going off to the front myself."

I didn't realize how much I had missed her. The old June emerged, chattering away about home and friends. "Say, do you ever see Charlie Stewart? He's stationed up here, isn't he?"

"He's at Middleton St. George. I haven't seen him since August, when I was on leave after my accident." I spoke in my best casual voice. "He looks so different — you would hardly recognize him."

"Better or worse?"

"Oh, better, definitely." I pushed back my chair. "Well, we've emptied the teapot twice. Let's go and see the sights."

We left our bags at the women's hostel and set off on a walking tour. Almost everything in York was built from the same pale stone, from mansions to cottages to the streets beneath our feet.

"The Romans founded this city eighteen hundred years ago," I said. We were silent as we struggled to imagine the sheer age of our surroundings. Back home a sixty-year-old house was considered practically historic.

"Well, we'd better not miss York Minster," June said. "It seems every Canadian and his dog visits that place. I must have a dozen postcards already."

By now I was accustomed to large churches, but this one was staggering. "You could tuck St. John's into one corner and not even notice it," June said in a hushed voice, referring to our little Anglican church in Touchwood.

We wandered through the immense stone structure, gingerly tiptoeing over tombs set into the floor, admiring the marble memorials to the fallen soldiers of other wars, and gazing up at the magnificent stained-glass window with its red heart glowing in the centre.

"Shall we light a candle?" June whispered. We each put a penny in the box and lit a candle, silently voicing our own prayer before setting it among hundreds of flickering tallows, bright with hope and promise against the cold stone wall.

With a slight feeling of relief at having done our duty, we escaped into the late afternoon sunshine to seek out Betty's Bar, the pub frequented by Canadian flyers. It was a couple of hundred yards away, along a narrow, cobblestoned street and down a flight of steps into the basement.

A group of aircrew was seated together at a large table; on the far side of the room two soldiers and two civilians were having a spirited game of darts. A large mirror over the bar featured the names of Canadian aircrew, etched with a diamond-tipped pen. We sat down at a table near the fireplace.

"I can really use this leave," June said, as we took off our caps. "I've been sorting Christmas parcels every day for two weeks. We finally have the mountain whittled down to a hill, but I start again tomorrow at seventeen hundred hours."

"How did the post office fall so far behind?"

"Since the RCAF formed the MailCan squadron last year, more mail is getting through. Each aircraft brings seven thousand pounds of mail from Ottawa to Scotland. It comes down to Yorkshire by train, and we sort it for everyone in Six Group, plus thousands of Canadians serving with the RAF." She laughed. "I used to think I had it bad in Touchwood. Last week I went up to Thirsk with the mail truck and watched the train being unloaded. They kept throwing off the mailbags until the pile on the platform was higher than the train! I climbed up to the top of the stack and stood there with my hand shading my eyes like a mountain climber squinting into the distance, and the driver took a picture to send home to Dad."

"Surely it isn't all Christmas parcels?"

"Rose, you should see the things people send! Clothes and food and even booze — last week a whole mailbag full of letters was soaked with gin from a broken bottle. We have hundreds of bundles of hometown newspapers and thousands of cartons of cigarettes. Unfortunately, some of them never get delivered."

"Why not?"

"We check the casualty list every morning to find out which men have been killed overnight. If there's a return address, we send his mail back home. If not, it goes to the Red Cross. Honestly, sometimes I wonder if it's worth the effort."

"Excuse me, ma'am." The voice came from a nearby table, where a Canadian soldier was sitting alone. "I couldn't help overhearing. Do you work for the postal service?"

"Yes, I do."

"I want to thank you. The mail means a lot to us, more than you can ever imagine." He had an open, likeable face with twinkling eyes. His unruly brown hair stood up at the back of his head as if he hadn't combed it for a week.

"Thanks, that's very nice."

"May I buy the two of you a drink?" He leaned toward us. "It's wonderful to hear a Canadian girl, it just brings back memories of home."

We exchanged glances. I could see that June was smiling, so I nodded. "Sure, why not?"

He grinned so broadly that his eyes scrunched up into slits. Reaching under the table, he drew out a pair of crutches. When he stood up, we saw the empty leg of his uniform pinned under his left knee. He manoeuvered his way awkwardly to our table, arranged his crutches, and sat down. "The name's Peter Knight, but my friends call me Shorty."

We shook hands. The bartender stepped up to the table and plunked down three mugs of beer. "On the house, sir. No charge for a wounded serviceman."

"Thanks, old man! Cheers — King and Country!" We hoisted our foaming mugs and drank. Then we settled down to get acquainted. Shorty's manner was so unaffected that I couldn't help liking him. Even better, it turned out he was a prairie boy from Winnipeg. I remembered the saying: spade calls to spade.

As evening fell, the room began to feel quite intimate. The fire blazed on the hearth and the faded Christmas ornaments strung around the ceiling made the pub almost festive. I finished my beer and sank farther into the comfortable red plush chair while June and Shorty chatted.

"So what happened to your leg?" June asked. "Or would you rather not talk about it?"

"Oh, I don't mind. I lost it in Italy last spring. I've been in the hospital ever since, just got out yesterday."

"Are you on your way home?" June asked. I thought she sounded a little anxious.

"Not yet. I'll be in York for a couple of months while the doctors do some more patchwork on me. Then I'll be mustered out back to Winnipeg."

Shorty took another drink, leaned forward, and looked into June's eyes as if he were telling the story to her alone. "We were a few miles out of Monte Cassino, dug in solid. What a crummy place! Nothing to look forward to except the mail. Somebody would go down to the dispersal point every morning and pick up the mail pouch and bring it back across no man's land. That's a strip of mud between our front line and theirs.

"One day a guy from my regiment was on his way back and he got nailed by a sniper. He crawled back to our lines but the poor guy passed out before he could say a word, and was taken away on a stretcher. Unfortunately he'd dropped the pouch along the way."

Shorty paused. "It's probably hard for you girls to understand, but out there, the mail is a matter of life and death. When a guy gets a letter from home, he'll read it until he has it memorized. He'll read it until it falls to pieces. Just to touch that piece of paper that's come all the way from home — it makes you want to live a little longer, if you can. It boosts morale like nothing on earth, and I do mean nothing."

He took another long drink. "Well, that mail bag was good and lost. Every one of us sat there and pictured his precious letters from home sinking into the mud. So we divided the area into sections, and one by one, the guys slithered out there on their bellies and felt around with their hands. The rest of us sat in our slit trenches and waited.

"Finally it was my turn and while I was wallowing around in the mud like a big old hog I set off a mine. I heard the bang and looked down, and whaddya know — my foot was gone! It didn't even hurt then, although it hurt plenty later. I took my field dressing out of my vest and made a tourniquet above the stump, and then I started back to my side.

"To make a long story short, I crawled right over that mail pouch, so I slung the strap around my neck and kept going. The boys sure made a big fuss over me. I never saved anybody's life — but that was the closest I'll ever come to feeling like a hero."

By the time Shorty had finished his story, my eyes were filled with tears and June's chin was trembling.

"Hey, I didn't mean to make you girls all weepy!" Shorty sounded stricken. "Luckily, the sawbones left my knee, so I can get an artificial leg fitted, easy. Bartender! Can we have another round, please?"

‹▼›

The next morning we slept late, enjoying the luxury of not being wakened by a bugle. We had stayed in the pub until closing time, while Shorty entertained us with funny stories. He and June had barely taken their eyes off each other. They had made plans to meet in York on her next leave.

I lay quietly in the big double bed while the sunshine crept across the wall and June slept peacefully beside me. I was happy for her — happy she had met someone, happy he was disabled.

That sounds so cruel, I thought. Yet I meant it. I prayed for her sake that she would never fall in love with a man on active duty. I hadn't told her yet about my own feelings for Charlie. If I put them into words, then I would be forced to admit that I cared.

June stirred and opened her eyes. "Morning, Posy. I'm starving." We dressed and ate a leisurely breakfast, including fruitcake from June's bottomless gas mask container, before setting out for the bus station.

"Let's go into this little shop," I said. "I need a newspaper to read on the bus."

We pushed open the door and a bell tinkled. This shop was one of the shabbier ones — mostly canned goods, with a few pathetic vegetables tricked out on a bed of green tissue paper.

"Afternoon, ladies," said the thin-faced young woman behind the battered wooden counter.

"Good afternoon," I said. "The *Times*, please."

As the woman turned to reach for the newspaper, a dirty little face with solemn brown eyes rose up from behind the counter. I studied him with interest. I had seen so few children since I left home that they seemed like foreign creatures.

"Hullo," said the boy. He stared at us without smiling.

"Hello, there. What's your name?" I asked.

"Arfur."

June reached into her shoulder bag and pulled out an orange. "Here, Arthur, would you like this?"

He stared at the orange without expression. His mother turned back to us and gasped. "Oh, my stars, miss, a real orange! He's never seen an orange before, except in picture books! He's only five years old, see, born since the blockade."

June handed it to the mother, who accepted it reverently as if it were a piece of rare crystal. She lifted it to her nose and inhaled, closing her eyes with a rapturous expression.

"Here, Arfur, love, smell this!"

Arthur took it in his hands, rolled it around like a ball, smelled it, and then opened his mouth and sank his pearly teeth into the skin. His face took on a horrible expression as the bitter taste filled his mouth. All three of us burst out laughing.

"No, Arfur, Mother has to take the skin off first." She was chuckling as she took the orange away. She sounded as if she didn't laugh very often. "You'll like what's inside, I promise! Tell the kind lady thank you ever so much."

"Fank you ever so much, kind lady."

June reached into her bag again. "Look, my mother's sent me a dozen oranges from Canada. I was going to share them with my friend, but I'm sure she won't mind. I'll keep two for us and you can have the rest."

"Oh, that's smashing." The young woman's voice broke. "I'll give one to my grandmother and one to each of the kids — oh, we'll have a happy Christmas this year, thanks to you, miss. God bless you! And God bless Canada!"

36

The sixth wartime Christmas approached. Still the Germans refused to surrender.

Saturation bombing reached new intensity as we dropped thousands of bombs on German cities, night after night. The theory that German civilians wouldn't display the same magnificent courage as the British had proven utterly false. Berlin alone had been bombed hundreds of times.

The flying bombs over London finally petered out as the Allies surged through France and captured the launching sites. Then, as Londoners crept back to their homes from the countryside once again, the first jet-propelled rocket in history was launched from far behind enemy lines.

More deadly than the flying bomb, the rocket carried no warning — just a blinding streak of light followed by a tremendous explosion. Shooting down the rocket was impossible since it travelled five times faster than the speed of sound. There was no time for air raid sirens. From launch to landing, the rocket's hundred-mile trip took five minutes. If German scientists had invented their revenge weapons earlier in the war, the Allies would certainly have gone down to defeat.

All hope now dulled to one desire: that the war would not drag on for another year. "Our losses are terrible and the new boys coming out so green," I wrote to Sally. "They're usually gone before we know their names."

I had always hated bomb damage assessment, and now I did little else. The entire continent looked like a sandcastle destroyed by a giant madman. The wreckage of thousands of crashed aircraft littered the routes across Germany. Allied aircraft bombed everything in front of our advancing troops, levelling the landscape to the bare ground. Every day I saw streets filled with heaps of furniture from the smoking ruins of bombed-out homes, flooded with water from useless fire hoses.

And the bombs were getting even bigger: four-ton bouncing bombs, five-ton Tallboys, and the granddaddy of all bombs, the ten-ton Grand Slam. They buried themselves before detonating, setting off small earthquakes that left craters in the ground. When filled with rainwater, they formed small lakes.

One day I saw photographs of a convoy of German trucks, winding along a country road. Strafing from an Allied fighter had struck the first truck, starting an explosive chain reaction. Black smoke billowed from every truck, the last one bursting into flames just as the camera took the final shot.

I groaned aloud. "Why, oh, why won't they give up?"

◂▾▸

One December afternoon I was studying photos taken during a day-light raid against a munitions factory in a French village. Dummy houses sat on the roof, surrounded by painted roads and gardens, but the camouflage wasn't good enough.

Photos taken moments after the raid showed the factory, now smashed and burning, surrounded by craters. The dummy houses were toppled on their sides. Bombs were visible falling away from the open bomb bay into the wreckage below.

Next I examined the fields around the village. About a mile away was a large stone building on the brow of a hill, one of the lovely French châteaus that sprinkled the valley. Two vehicles were parked in the curved driveway leading up to the door. A cluster of black dots was scattered around the entrance.

I studied the next photograph in the sequence, but the shutter had clicked just as the bomb bay doors on the aircraft began to close. The château had been cut off. I checked, but it didn't appear on another photograph.

I studied the dots but couldn't make them out. I put down my tools and hurried over to the darkroom through the ghastly Yorkshire combination of fog and rain called clag, and requested enlargements of the château.

An hour later, I sat down again. This time I identified the black dots as people. Clearly, they were standing outside the château watching the raid — one man's arms were raised as if holding a pair of binoculars. Two men had their feet up on the bumper of a military Jeep parked outside the front door. Several others stood on the lawn with their heads thrown back at an angle, probably watching the bomber as it passed overhead.

They were German, not French. I knew this by the distinctive grey shade of their uniforms.

Back to the darkroom I went. This time I requested ten copies of the same photograph, each with a different exposure. I tucked them under my rain cape and returned to the briefing hut.

Jenkins was seated at the table, shuffling through the batch of photographs. "There you are, Section Officer. I thought you were supposed to be on shift."

"I was over at the lab, following up on something."

"Another one of your visions, no doubt." He gave his usual nasty laugh.

"No doubt." I wouldn't give him the satisfaction of an explanation.

I sat down with my back to him and spread the ten photographs before me, ranging from lowest to highest exposure.

The lightest was unreadable — the shapes were nearly white. The darkest wasn't any use, either: even the men's faces were black. I took up my magnifying glass again.

A few minutes later, I gave a cry. "Jenkins!" I forgot that I was annoyed with him. He pushed back his chair with maddening slowness and strolled over, hands in his pockets. "Look at this shot! Do you see anything significant?"

Jenkins glanced at it. "This doesn't look like a bombed factory to me. It's just a bunch of Huns standing around in a courtyard."

"Yes, but look at their trousers!"

Jenkins leered. "Surely you aren't so desperate that you have to study men's trousers with a magnifying glass, Section Officer."

"Don't be ridiculous. Just look at their uniforms. Isn't it true that German generals have a red stripe running down their pant legs?"

This time I got his attention. He snatched up the print and examined it closely. "It does look like there's a lighter line, doesn't it? It isn't a scratch on the negative?"

"No — you can see it on three or four prints, but it shows quite clearly in the one you're holding. You can see the stripe on this man, and the one beside him, and both men who have their feet up on the bumper, and at least four others in this group. That's eight generals, maybe more!"

Jenkins lowered the glass and we stared at each other in disbelief. The generals were the military planners, the logistics experts who scheduled the movement of troops and weapons on a global scale. Without them the armed forces would be like an aircraft without a pilot, a chicken with its head cut off.

"Eight generals!" Jenkins repeated. "That's a bloody nest! Why the hell are they standing around as if they were at a picnic when there are a dozen bombers right over their heads?"

"They aren't worried at all, are they? They either don't know that we're taking photographs, or else they don't care."

I stared at the prints again, trying to come up with an explanation. "You don't suppose they're acting as some kind of human decoy?"

For once Jenkins seemed to have forgotten his antipathy. "Get on the blower and ask for Tilbury. If the brass are staying in that château, he'd better knock it out!"

It didn't take long to convince the commander. Unlike many officers, he trusted our conclusions without scrutinizing the photos himself. And Jenkins — somewhat grudgingly — backed me up. "They definitely have striped pant legs, sir," he said. "You can make of that whatever you like."

After we were dismissed, I went off duty to the henhouse and brewed myself a cup of good strong Yorkshire tea. While waiting for the kettle to boil, I heard the sound of engines and went to the window to see three bombers disappear into the mist.

After mess that evening, Tilbury called me into his office. "We knew from an intelligence report that fourteen high-ranking generals were summoned to a joint chiefs of staff meeting in northern France, but we didn't know where. That photograph was a tremendous break. Rather, your discovery of that photograph."

"Excuse me, sir, but why were they being so careless?" I knew I shouldn't ask, but I couldn't help being curious.

"We can make an educated guess. Hitler is transferring his generals from the Russian front back to France. As you know, we've never done reconnaissance on the Eastern Front. The generals who have spent the entire war in Russia don't know how much we've accomplished — probably don't even know what reconnaissance is. They had absolutely no bloody idea that they were being spied on from the sky. They were sitting ducks."

"Yes, sir." I didn't care for that expression.

"This afternoon that château was wiped off the face of the map, and with it, fourteen of Hitler's top-ranked officers, possibly more. They probably never even knew what hit them. Excellent work, Section Officer. Dismissed."

◄▾►

It was four months since I had seen Charlie at Sunny Banks. Twice he had suggested meeting, but our leaves hadn't coincided. I was almost thankful. The absence of his physical presence might be a good thing. In fact, I wasn't sure if I wanted to see him again until after the war.

But on Christmas Day I received a greeting card with a picture of a pretty stone church. Inside was a message in his familiar neat handwriting: "I'm off duty New Year's Eve. Any chance of getting together in York to welcome 1945? As always, Charlie."

I hesitated for a split second before my good intentions collapsed. I went straight to Tilbury and begged for special leave. Because it was Christmas and because I was in his good books, he said yes.

As the week wore on, I found myself increasingly agitated. Sometimes my heart soared at the thought of seeing Charlie again. Then I would remember having to say goodbye and my veins would be flooded with dread as if black ink was pouring through them.

I read his letters over and over, trying to decide whether there was anything intimate in them. No, they were decidedly impersonal. Perhaps he was just looking for an old friend from Touchwood to spend the holiday with. I would gather up the letters and jam them into my foot locker. The next morning I would pull them out and read them again.

The morning of December 31 dawned overcast and grey, as usual. I choked down my Spam and powdered eggs. After an icy bath, I dressed nervously, cold fingers fumbling my buttons into the holes. I donned my dark blue greatcoat and pulled on the ugly galoshes that we jokingly called glamour boots. As I was pinning my cap on my hair, a junior officer stuck her head in the door. "Telephone for you, Section Officer."

I dashed into the hallway and took down the receiver. Personal telephone calls were discouraged. Pinned to the wall above the telephone was a sign: *I am on War Work. If you must use me, be brief.*

"Hello, Rose!" Charlie's voice was faint down the crackling line.

"Hello, Charlie." I knew at once why he must be calling and my heart sank down to my glamour boots.

"I'm really sorry, but our station's been shut down."

"Oh, Charlie." I bit my lip. "I was looking forward to this."

"Me too."

There was silence on the line, sagging with disappointment on both ends. I swallowed hard and concentrated on sounding chipper. "Well, not your fault, Charlie. We'll try again another time, shall we?"

"Of course we will. Write and tell me when you get your next leave. Happy new year, Rose!"

"Happy new year, Charlie." There was a silence. I didn't want to be the first to break the connection, and neither did he. At last I heard the *pip-pip-pip* sound that meant the pay telephone had run out of money, and I put down the receiver.

I turned away from the telephone and left the building. I walked across the wet grass to the henhouse and collapsed into an armchair.

I knew perfectly well why I was so miserable. It wasn't Charlie's cancelled leave — war had hardened me to these minor frustrations. It was the reason for the cancellation. Before a raid, the station was shut down without notice so the men could rest and prepare. Obviously he was going to fly tonight.

I was finally brought face to face with what I had been avoiding for months. As long as I didn't know when or where a raid was taking place, I didn't have to worry. When I pictured him, which was frequently, I always conjured up the same mental images: Charlie with his boots off, lying on a metal bunk, writing a letter to me in his familiar bold, square handwriting. Or Charlie fast asleep on the chesterfield at Sunny Banks, one arm thrown over his face. Or Charlie as a boy, hockey stick in hand, skating across the slough at home while Jack chased him for the puck.

Now all at once the image of a cockpit came into my mind: the darkness, the roar of the engines, the sound of bursting flak, the shuddering of the aircraft as it was hit, the flames leaping and spreading across the wing, the aircraft plunging into a death spiral, the final explosion.

And then Charlie's eyes, smiling into mine before they faded into blackness.

I moaned aloud.

A fellow officer on the other side of the room looked up from the desk where she was writing a letter and said something.

I didn't hear her. My heart was pounding like a galloping horse and I was sweating inside the woollen overcoat, sickened by the force of my own fear. How many more missions did Charlie have to fly? I had never asked him. It seemed simpler not to know, to go on pretending that all was well.

Now I realized that I might never see those smiling eyes again, might never hear his voice. Charlie might not even live to see 1945.

That was a bad day. Hating my own weakness, I went down to the control room and tried unsuccessfully to find out where the raid from Charlie's station was taking place. I sat there until just before midnight. I must have looked awful, because three people asked me if I was ill. Before the clock struck twelve, I pleaded a headache, stumbled back to my room, threw myself on my bed with my face to the wall, and wept.

The following morning the sun was shining weakly against my tiny window when another knock came on my door. "Section Officer! Telephone!"

I didn't answer. I had a sudden fierce memory of my younger self running down the stairs at home, snatching up the receiver to hear Jimbo's voice. Suddenly I never wanted to take another telephone call in my life.

Another knock, a little louder. "Are you there?"

I struggled to my feet. "Coming."

I forced myself to walk down the hall and pick up the receiver. The muscles in my abdomen were as tight as the spines of an umbrella. Finally, I managed to whisper hello.

"Hello again! I'm calling to wish you Happy New Year!"

My knees gave way and I sank into a nearby chair. "Oh, Charlie." I couldn't say anything else.

"We got back an hour ago. I'm just on my way to bed. Did you drink my health last night?"

"No, I — I wasn't feeling very well. I went to bed early."

"That's too bad. Well, there's always next year, eh? With any luck we'll be back in Touchwood by then."

"Yes." I struggled to bring my voice under control. I wouldn't ask, I wouldn't — but I did.

"Charlie, how many more operations do you have to fly?"

"Fourteen."

"What will you do when your second tour is over?"

Charlie's answer was abrupt. "Give it up. I've had enough."

There was a pause. I knew we were both wondering whether he would be around to make that choice.

"Look, you don't have to worry about me, Rose. I've survived thirty-six missions and I guess I know enough to make it through another fourteen. As soon as I've done my last raid, I'll ring you. Until then, no news is good news. All right?"

"Yes, please." My voice was faint but I couldn't find the strength to speak louder. "I want to know when you're finished. I hope you don't mind." I tried to laugh, but it sounded forced. "I guess I have a case of the jitters today."

His voice was like a caress. "I promise I'll be careful, Rose. I'm a lot less reckless than I was in the beginning. I have more reason to live now."

We left it at that. Charlie rang off and I went to breakfast, sleepless and exhausted, but a little comforted nevertheless. When I reached the intelligence room, I took a pencil and a piece of paper, and tried to work it out: when would Charlie be finished?

I soon gave up. Weather, faulty aircraft, illness — anything could affect the outcome. There was no way to tell. I gritted my teeth and prepared to soldier on.

37

I threw down my magnifying glass and rubbed my eyes. "There's absolutely no way to distinguish between red and green and yellow flares," I told Jenkins. "I've tried to decipher the different shades of grey, but I've compared hundreds of photos and nothing makes any sense."

He looked up from his desk. "You could be wasting your time, Section Officer. Next week they're going to fit up one of the bombers with that colour film called Kodachrome."

"I can't imagine seeing photographs in colour."

We had read about the new film, but it was prohibitively expensive. I fell into a reverie, contemplating what it would mean to see the greens and browns of grass, earth, trees, and buildings. "You know, this could revolutionize our jobs."

"Well, it will change my job, that's for sure." Jenkins sounded even more bitter than usual.

"What do you mean?"

"I'm colour blind. That's why I washed out as a pilot."

"Really? Yet you became an interpreter?"

"It makes no difference whatsoever, in the case of black-and-white prints. But I'm not going to function if there's colour film, that's for damned sure." He pulled out a cheroot and lit it, blowing smoke out of his nostrils.

I took pity on the wretched man. "Don't be too discouraged. When I was at Medmenham, I heard about a colour-blind American soldier who was an absolute demon at ferreting out camouflaged rifle pits in Guam. No one could explain it. He didn't know the difference between the colours, but he could distinguish them perfectly. Maybe you'll be a real whiz."

His face twisted into a smile. "Thanks. Decent of you to tell me that story." He hesitated, then said in a strangled voice: "You're quite a magician yourself, Section Officer."

❧

The following week every bomber on the base took part in a raid against Dresden. It was a good raid — not a single aircraft was lost. But in the briefing hut the men didn't laugh and joke as they usually did after a successful mission. Instead they were quiet and subdued, their faces sombre.

On the tarmac, darkroom technicians removed the new colour film magazines from the bombers and rushed them into the darkroom. While we waited, Jenkins paced back and forth, chain-smoking. Finally the prints were brought in.

When I picked up the first set, I couldn't help uttering an exclamation. I hadn't felt like a bird for a long time, but now I experienced the lift beneath my wings and I was carried up, up, and above the world below.

The images showed an upside-down waterfall of ruby, emerald, sapphire, and gold. It was light flak, chasing upwards toward the bombers from the ground. All these years I had seen anti-aircraft fire without knowing how lovely it was.

The next set of prints was even more striking. The yellow smoke from the target flares streamed and fluttered along the ground like a handful of yellow ribbons. Glittering against the deep purple of the sky were the incendiary bombs, thousands of pinpoints of light like sequins scattered across purple velvet.

But my mood quickly changed when I picked up the next set of prints, taken moments later. Dresden was already one great conflagration of crimson and gold, a giant blood-red ball of flame. The firestorm had not spread so much as erupted.

There was little to interpret. The other photographs showed nothing but masses of swirling flames. Hamburg's fire had been four square miles; a few quick measurements found this one was at least fifteen. From a distance the city looked like the setting sun, a red glow on the horizon with columns of inky smoke pouring from its heart.

I studied the photographs with growing revulsion. The colours of blood and bone and burning flesh made the scene more real, more loathsome than anything I had ever seen.

I knew that Dresden had no strategic value whatsoever. Called the Jewel Box of Germany, it was famous only for its beautiful domed cathedral and the splendid architecture that had miraculously survived centuries of conflict — until now.

What made it worse was the knowledge that the city had recently doubled in size and housed more than one million people. Hundreds of thousands of refugees fleeing from the advancing Russians had poured in from the east, filling every hotel and home and stable in the city.

And Dresden, because it was never considered a military target, was without bomb shelters, without defences of any kind.

I forced myself to concentrate on my written report. Then I signed off duty, pulled on my greatcoat and galoshes, and walked briskly away from the station, almost running in my desire to escape into the open moors.

The buildings behind me were quickly swallowed up in the low mist called haw that hung over the winter landscape. Fog was piled against the low stone fences that wandered drunkenly across the fields. I pressed through the mist, my breath emerging in clouds as I hurried along in an effort to put distance between the bombing station and myself.

Never before had I been so close to a complete rejection of the war. The role I had once yearned for — to support the men who flew thousands of miles every night to drop bombs on innocent people toward whom they harboured no personal ill will — now seemed nothing short of lunatic.

I remembered those first early raids on London, when everyone had been outraged at the deaths of several hundred civilians. Now, four short years later, fifty thousand had died in a single night. *Next it will be millions,* I thought wildly. *What madness, what mass destruction lies ahead?*

I wasn't aware that I was crying until I felt warm tears on my cold cheeks, like droplets of mist.

I walked for miles, not knowing or caring where I was. The brisk, clean wind whipped my hair and stung my face. As the hours passed, I drew strength from the low, sweeping hills, so similar to the landscape around Touchwood.

As I climbed a rocky crag, the fog lifted briefly and I saw below me a broad valley. I stopped, panting for breath. A flock of sheep tumbled over the crest of the nearby hill and began to make their way down to the stream that ran along the foot of the crag. The ragged white animals were followed by an old shepherd with a beard, long brown coat flapping around his ankles, tweed cap pulled low over his forehead, a crooked staff in his hand.

But it wasn't the shepherd that caught my attention. It was his dog, the Border Collie herding the sheep, dodging back and forth, nipping their heels, wearing the same familiar expression of keen doggie enjoyment that I had often seen on Laddy's face. I felt a rush of desire to kneel down and hug the dog's warm, furry body.

"I want to go home." I cried aloud, my words carried away by the keening wind. "Oh, God, please let me go home!"

⁂

RCAF Allerton Hall
February 20, 1945
Dear Rose,

You must get leave on March 2 so you can walk up the aisle with me. Yes, darling Posy, we're taking the plunge! I desperately want you there as my bridesmaid. Ring me up and let me know if you can make it.
Best love, Prune

⁂

"I can't wait to be a married woman," June said as we undressed for bed. It was the night before her wedding, and we were sharing a double room in the York women's hostel.

Her happiness had restored some of her old vivacity, although I couldn't help thinking she would never be the same carefree girl again. "Why did you decide to get married now, anyway? Why not wait until you're home?"

"Do you think I'm going to let Shorty go back to his old girlfriends in Winnipeg, all wounded and heroic, without a ring on his finger?" She laughed. "No, of course that isn't the reason. Rumour has it that they will demobilize married women first — and believe me, I plan to be on the first boat. It's funny that Shorty will get home before me, but he's already been mustered out and we want to spend some time together before he sails, if you know what I mean."

It wasn't necessary to answer, since June hadn't stopped chattering.

"Anyway, I know I'm one of the lucky ones. We plan to start a family on our wedding night, if we can. Right now every married woman in the world wants a baby, not knowing if her husband is coming back. Or whether he'll be able to father children even if he does come back."

"Don't your parents want you to get married at home?"

"They don't mind. They're arranging a reception for us so everyone can pay their respects to the blushing bride."

"And what about your lifelong desire to wear your mother's wedding dress?"

"Don't you know there's a war on, Rose? I'll wear my uniform and like it. Even if servicewomen did get clothing coupons, there's nothing in the shops here anyway." She sighed, and I knew she was secretly yearning for orange blossoms.

"That reminds me, I haven't given you my gift yet." I went to my kitbag and pulled out a brown paper parcel. June untied the string and lifted out the white silk nightgown.

"Oh, oh, oh! Where did you find this?" Her pretty face lit up with delight as she held it against her shoulders. It really was a lovely thing, and it went so well with June's golden hair.

"For your wedding night, perhaps?"

"Wedding night, hell! I'm going to be married in it! Posy, do you know how much I hated the idea of that bloody uniform?"

"You know it's a nightgown."

"I don't care what it is. It's gorgeous!" She was tearing off her tie and unbuttoning her shirt. "Now do tell — where did you beg, borrow, or steal this?"

"My lips are sealed, but I promise it's never been worn. It can be your 'something new.'"

When June slipped the gown over her head, I saw that it could indeed pass for a wedding dress. June looked virginal yet seductive — probably the way Fowler had once thought of me.

"I'll have to turn up the hem and the sleeves. Good thing I brought my sewing kit. I'll wear my pearl necklace and my white slippers. Oh, Rose, it's the wedding dress of my dreams!"

June's eyes were shining. She put her arms around me and we exchanged a long hug. "Well, one thing will be the same as when we played wedding with Mum's lace curtains — and that is my bridesmaid," June said, sniffling.

"Mind you, I always imagined the groom as tall, dark, and handsome — isn't that ironic? Shorty is only two inches taller than me. He told me that he used to be short on both sides, but now he's even shorter on the left! Isn't that a scream? But he doesn't care about his height. He says he loves to see my legs in high heels. I'm just crazy about him, Rose."

·▾·

RCAF East Moor
March 2, 1945
Dear Mother and Dad,

June's wedding was so lovely. It took place in an ancient stone church with a path winding up to the front door and ivy clinging to the walls. The only thing missing was the bells, which of course haven't rung since the war started.

Shorty's landlord, Bruce Wallace, gave the bride away. He and his wife have been billeting Shorty for months and they've become good friends. Shorty was very solemn, not like his usual self at all, and when June said: "For better or for worse," he just looked at her in a way that gave me a lump in my throat.

It was a small wedding and almost everyone was in uniform, so we formed an honour guard — men on one side and women on the other — when they came out of the church. June looked radiant in a long gown of white silk, and a fingertip-length lace veil borrowed from Mrs. Wallace. She carried an armful of pink roses from the garden, and I had a bouquet of blue bachelor's buttons to match my uniform.

After the ceremony we went next door to the parish hall and had a scrumptious tea, by wartime standards. The guests had scrounged ration cards and sent them to Mrs. Wallace a week earlier, and she made the most of them. We ate tinned apricots, pickles, bread with real butter, and even two dozen devilled eggs, courtesy of her sister who lives on a farm.

Standing on the head table was a fancy three-layer cake with white icing, surrounded by pink roses. Shorty and June posed for their pictures holding a knife, and then Mrs. Wallace said: "Go ahead! Cut it!" Were we ever surprised when it turned out to be real! Usually they just fix up a cardboard dummy and paint it white for the photographs. We gobbled up every crumb.

As you can imagine, there were lots of jokes about June Day turning into June Knight. When the happy couple was leaving for their hotel, June threw her bouquet from the back of the car straight into my arms so I couldn't possibly miss it! The others went off to a pub, but I decided to come home and write to you instead. I was the only guest there from Touchwood and I was a bit lonesome after the bride left.

I guess you will meet Shorty before you see me again. June's father promised him a job in the post office. Mr. Day says he's sick of working with women and it will be a treat to have a man around the place! So as soon as Shorty visits his

family in Winnipeg, he'll be off to Touchwood.
He's looking forward to working in the post office.
He has a soft spot for the mail since that's what
brought him and June together.
Love and kisses, Rose XXOO

38

It was the Ides of March and the heather had been blooming for weeks. Still, the day was overcast and I was shivering in my new lightweight summer uniform — a khaki skirt and short-sleeved shirt with red albatrosses on the shoulders. I hurried out of the chilly air and into the henhouse, where I sat down to finish my weekly letter to Mother.

I wondered how many more letters I would write bearing that impressive red-inked stamp: "On His Majesty's Service." The war was being measured in terms of weeks now. The life was being slowly, inexorably squeezed out of the enemy, yet the fighting was still fierce.

As the German defences weakened, the losses on the station had dropped from an average 5 percent to 1 percent. That didn't make anyone breathe more easily — just the opposite. Now that the end was in sight, the tension was greater than ever before, with everyone praying to survive just a little longer.

"Mail call!" The young clerk handed me a tattered brown paper parcel. I turned it over, examining the stamps and labels.

It had made the rounds — from Medmenham, to RAF headquarters in London, then the hospital, then RCAF headquarters, and now Yorkshire.

I cut the string with my letter opener and undid the paper. A set of tiny wings fell into my hands. Jack's personal effects, missing for the past nine months, had been found at last.

I fingered the gold embroidered wings while I waited for the surge of pain to subside. I hadn't been angry when Jack's things hadn't turned up. At my own station alone, some sixty sets of personal things were collected after every raid and sent home to their stricken families. It was likely that a few precious packages would go astray.

I pulled open the brown paper and picked up each item, holding it between my palms as I pictured my dear brother's hands touching these very things.

Here was the familiar blue hardcover pilot's logbook, with the handsome golden RCAF crest stamped on the cover. Here were his razor, the ivory-handled pocket knife he had carried since he was a boy, and his fountain pen.

A few underclothes, a blue pullover in which I recognized Mother's cableknit stitch. A family photograph — Jack had a copy of the same one I had brought with me, the four of us standing with Laddy on the front steps of the farmhouse.

Here was a snapshot of a pretty blond woman sitting on a bench beside the sea. And quite a large bundle of letters. I saw my own handwriting, then Mother's, then Dad's. There were at least two dozen letters in the same feminine, rather childish hand that I didn't recognize.

Then I spotted a sealed, unstamped envelope bearing my own name, addressed in Jack's usual scrawl. With a painful sense of apprehension, I knew I was about to read his last letter.

RAF Tangmere
June 5, 1944
Dear Rose,

The big show is set for tomorrow and I'm writing this letter in case I don't make it back.

I don't know how else to put it, so I'll come straight out and tell you. I'm married. Her name is Esme Lorimer and she lives in Chichester. She's a great girl. I can't wait for you to meet her.

We met two days after I arrived in England. We hit it off right away and unfortunately we were both too green to know what we were doing, so Esme got in the family way. When we found out, we went straight to the registry office and got married, but she took it into her head that my family would look down on her because of the baby coming, and she point blank refused to let me write to anyone. I wanted to tell you that night at Covent Garden but it didn't seem like the right time.

It's been real hard on her, Rose. She's a year younger than me, only nineteen, and her parents were killed in the Blitz. She had to quit her job with the land army and my pay isn't much, but she really knows how to manage money, and she fixed up a room in Chichester and I go down to see her whenever I can.

Our son was born on April 10, named Jack Junior. I've been wanting like heck to ring you but I decided to wait until you had leave and you could come down to Chichester and meet Esme and see for yourself what a swell girl she is. I was kind of hoping you would break it to Mother and Dad, though I know they'll be real good about it.

Anyway, I started thinking if I get the chop nobody will know about Esme and the baby, so I decided to write this letter. I hope you never see it, but if you do, I know you'll be good to my wife and my son. He's the smartest little baby you ever saw. We're planning to go back to the farm, since this country is no place to raise a child, especially not now, and I'm sure looking forward to seeing him grow up in a place where every single gopher hole is loved the way we love it.

Love from your brother Jack

⁘

I leaped to my feet and my chair went over backwards with a crash. My little brother with a wife and baby! But where were they now? I smoothed the crumpled letter and read it again, my eyes darting down the lines. It was dated June 5, 1944 — the day before he died. This was March 15, 1945. Almost a year since the baby was born!

I felt a surge of sympathy for poor Esme, a young widow with a child. I must find them immediately. I snatched up my hat and rushed from the room.

I was on the next train to London. Tilbury had been surprised at my request for emergency leave, but very kind. "So you're an aunt!" he said jovially, and I gave a start of surprise. I was an aunt! Mother and Dad were grandparents!

I thought briefly of writing to them, but then checked myself. First I must find Esme. For all I knew, she might have left Chichester. My active mind sifted through every possibility before the train reached London and I changed to the southern connection.

It was late afternoon when the train pulled into the pleasant seaside town on the south coast, not far from RAF Tangmere. I hailed a taxi and went straight to the town's registry office. Jack and Esme must have given an address when they married.

An old man behind the counter, old like everyone not in uniform these days, obligingly checked the record book, a large volume with green cardboard covers and ornate gold script on the front that read *Record of Births, Marriages, and Deaths*. He turned the pages with deliberation.

"Esme Jane Lorimer. Here it is. Wed John Thomas Jolliffe on November the 7th, 1943."

"Is there an address?"

"Yes." He followed the writing with his finger while I fidgeted.

"Is she a relative?" he asked, glancing over his spectacles.

"She's my sister-in-law, but I've never met her."

"Dear me." The old man shook his head. "I'm sorry to tell you, but Esme Lorimer is dead. There's an asterisk beside her name. That means deceased. Just wait a moment."

He consulted the book again. "Here it is. On the opposite page, it says she died on June 9, 1944."

Esme dead just three days after Jack! But what had happened to the poor baby?

"Is there any record of their son?" I asked in a trembling voice.

The old man turned the pages again, then ran his finger up and down the lines. "Here it is — John Thomas Jolliffe, born April 10, 1944, and christened here at the local church on May 15, 1944."

I gripped the edge of the counter. "Is there an asterisk by his name, too?"

He consulted the book with maddening slowness. "No."

"What should I do now? How can I find him? Where can he be?" With each question, my voice rose higher.

"First of all, you should come around the counter and sit down while I make a cup of tea. You look done in." The ubiquitous cup of tea! I felt like screaming, but I checked myself. The old man lifted up the heavy plank in the countertop and I went through to the other side.

"Now, you sit here while I have a think." He led me to a battered armchair, filled the kettle, and put it on the gas flame. "Since they were married here, there would be witnesses." He returned to the book. "Martha Snapper. She gives the same address as the bride. Must have been her landlady. Martha's lived here all her life. If anyone knows where this baby is, she will." He poured boiling water into the teapot and covered it with a knitted cosy. "I'll give Martha a dingle."

Another long wait while he disappeared into another room, and then came shuffling back into the front office. "She's on her way."

Before I finished my tea, a red-faced woman appeared on the other side of the counter, huffing and fanning her cheeks with a rolled-up magazine. I put my cup and saucer down so quickly the tea slopped over the edge.

"You the young lady who's asking after Esme Lorimer?" The woman frowned at me.

"Yes." I was on my feet, leaning over the counter. "Do you know anything about the baby? I'm his aunt."

"And I'm Esme's landlady, or was. You took your own sweet time getting here, I must say."

"I'm so sorry, but I didn't even know he existed until this morning."

"I wondered why nobody came looking for her," said the landlady, somewhat mollified. "The poor thing was half out of her mind when she got word about her husband. I says to her, you must find his sister and tell her about the baby. So she telephoned the number Jack give her, and somebody there said you'd gone down to London on leave. I told her to wait until you returned to your quarters, but she said no, she had the address in London where you were staying, and she dressed the baby in his best bib and tucker, and off she went on the afternoon train. I didn't like the way she was acting, like she was a bit off her head, poor girl.

"The next thing I know, somebody rang me up from a London hospital and said she'd been killed by one of them doodlebugs. I told them the father was dead, too. The authorities fetched the baby and put him into a home for war orphans in Devonshire."

The old man shoved a chair up to the back of my knees. "Here, don't you go fainting on me. Sit down and put your head on your lap. That's the girl."

I bowed my head until the black stars dancing in front of my eyes faded. Then I looked pleadingly into the landlady's red face. "Do you have the address in London, the one where she was going?"

The landlady reached into her tapestry bag and pulled out a folded piece of paper.

"Seventeen Harlington Mews."

◄▼►

Was there something familiar about the baby who had reached out to me? Mother would call it fate, but I knew my level-headed father would see it more scientifically. I could almost hear his voice. "She was in London, looking for you, so naturally she was on the spot when the buzz bomb fell that knocked you flying. There's nothing uncanny about it, my girl."

I didn't have time to wonder at saving my own nephew's life. Or had he saved mine? I was back on the train again, on my way to Devonshire. I had to keep swallowing, as my throat felt constricted. The poor infant, losing both father and mother in the space of a week! I kept remembering the baby's bright blue eyes — Jack's eyes, of course. And the way he had stretched his little arms toward me as if he, too, recognized a familiar face. If only I had been able to save Esme as well!

As the train rushed into the growing darkness, I tried to collect my thoughts. I had no way of making arrangements for a baby in Yorkshire. My leaves were so rare that I couldn't even guarantee regular visits.

My nephew was living in the Lord Alfred March Home for War Orphans. I remembered meeting the lord himself at Medmenham, but the very word 'orphanage' conjured up visions of Oliver Twist begging for more porridge. I'll give the place a real going-over, I decided, and if it isn't up to scratch, I'll take him away on the spot and find somewhere else for him.

By the time I arrived in Tiverton, it was too late to continue the search. I found a women's hostel, and, after a sleepless night, woke early the next morning and asked directions to the orphanage.

When I hastened up the long gravel driveway leading to the stately mansion, I was pleasantly impressed. The lawns were trimmed and several prams were parked outside on the terrace, filled with sleeping babies. I found the tiny grey-haired matron seated in her office. She looked like a motherly soul.

"They all have a sad story behind them, the poor wee bairns," the matron said in a soft Scottish accent. "Every once in a while a relative turns up, like you did. Just think! So his father was a Canadian. I had no idea," she said wonderingly, if something about the baby should have given away his parentage.

"Is he all right?" was my first question.

"Oh, yes, he's healthy enough. Would you believe he took his first step at seven months? We were ever so surprised. That's the earliest walker we've had."

"His father walked at seven months," I said in a choked voice.

"Ach, that'll be the reason." The matron looked at me closely. "There is one thing, though, dear."

I stiffened. "What's that?"

"He doesn't laugh, doesn't even smile. He *coo-coos* along with the rest of them, so we know there isn't anything wrong with his voice. And he's quite clever at piling up blocks and things. But he hasn't gotten around to favouring us with a smile yet. I asked the doctor, and he said the wee baby had quite a shock when his mother was killed. Perhaps he hasn't quite gotten over it."

We left the office and walked down a long hall, painted bright yellow. "This used to be the library. We've turned it into a playroom, because it's so pleasant and sunny. I want the children to get lots of light." She opened the door, and I followed her.

In a room filled with toddlers, I saw him instantly. He was sitting in a patch of sunshine, his head gleaming with a shock of fine golden hair. When he heard the door open he fastened his bright blue eyes on me.

I went up to him on unsteady legs, trying not to cry.

"Hello, old fellow." The baby stared at me without blinking.

"I'm your Auntie Rose." I sank to my knees on the carpet and reached out. "Will you come to me?" Without a word, Jack stood and walked a few unsteady steps into my arms. I buried my face in his shoulder. How sweet he smelled. I leaned back and looked into his face. Jack stared at me solemnly. Surely there had never been such an adorable baby.

I set him down on the floor and sat down beside him, tossing the rubber ball he had been playing with. Jack toddled after it and threw it back to me. We played for about an hour, and although he squealed a few times, he didn't crack a smile.

At tea time, Matron allowed me to feed him. I spooned mashed potatoes and peas into his mouth and he ate steadily, fixing me with his blue gaze.

At last it was time to catch the night train to London. I hugged him again, and felt his sturdy little arms go around my neck. I had to tear myself away.

"Now don't you worry about a thing!" the matron called from the front steps. "We'll take good care of him until this dreadful war is over!" She crossed herself and then waved until my vision dissolved in a blur of tears.

⁂

Touchwood
April 6, 1945
My dearest Rose,

Waiting for the war to end is more nerve-wracking than anything we've been through in the past six years. Every day we hear fresh reports of victories, yet two more Touchwood boys have died in the last month, and four taken prisoner. Every woman here is writing to her menfolk: "Keep your head down and don't try to win a medal!"

Yesterday Mrs. Ronald's neighbour saw the telegraph boy leaving, so she ran across the street to find the poor woman in a dead faint with a telegram clutched in her hand. It said: "Finished my last tour. No more worries." It was from her son Freddie. I feel like giving him a piece of my mind. How did he think his mother would react when she saw the telegram?

At Red Cross the other day Jane Sullivan was complaining about not seeing her girls for so long — two are in the Wrens, and two working in Vancouver — and Vera Day said very quietly: "At least your children are coming home again." Families without sons are blessed, I sometimes think.

We have made our official farewell to the RAF. The station sponsored a community dance, and many tears were shed. The commander has spent four years here, and said he regards it as his home. He and his wife plan to move here after the war.

It's strange to see the planes sitting idle on the runways, covered with dust and thistles. There's no word on what the government plans to do with them. I've enclosed a newspaper clipping that says our country trained one hundred and thirty thousand aircrew, more than half of them Canadian. Six years ago we would never have thought such a thing possible.

Our thoughts and prayers are with you, as always. You said that you were planning to visit Jack's grave. I believe his spirit is here with us, no matter where his body lies, but it would be a comfort to know that his grave is properly looked after.
Your loving Mother and Dad XXOO
P.S. Parcel forty-three left today.

39

I was seated in the breakfast room at the orphanage, surrounded by children of various ages and sizes, trying to force oatmeal between Jack's reluctant lips. His blue eyes stared at me calmly as he spat the cereal onto the table.

"Jack, you little beast!" I couldn't help laughing. As I wiped his mouth for the umpteenth time, the door flew open and banged against the wall. The matron stood in the entrance, her face pale, her mouth opening and shutting. Fearing some new tragedy, I took several steps toward her.

"The war is over!" She gasped out the words. "The Germans have surrendered. I just heard it on the BBC!"

Bedlam broke out in the breakfast room. One of the nurse-maids flung her apron over her eyes and howled. Several of the babies began to bawl in sympathy. I swept Jack out of his chair and danced him down the aisle between the tables.

"It's over! Jack, my precious, it's over!"

The room was too small to contain my overflowing heart.

Holding the baby in my arms, I ran down the long hall and through the front door into the sunshine. Such immense news had to be absorbed outside. I stopped on the wide lawn and twirled in a circle, looking upwards into the blue sky. Jack began to struggle and I set him down on the grass. He immediately pulled up a handful and shoved it in his mouth. I sank to my knees on the lawn and bowed my head.

The waiting is over. Charlie is safe.

For a few moments I knelt, motionless in the summer sunshine. It was uncannily quiet. The leaves were still, and even the thrushes had stopped singing. I found myself straining my ears. At first I wasn't sure what I was listening for — but then I knew. It was the sound of peace. The cannons, the anti-aircraft guns, the tanks, the ships, the aircraft, every weapon from the largest bomb to the smallest revolver — all were silent. Not another mother's son would die.

I spent my quiet hour of thankfulness with Jack. Then I took him inside and hugged him goodbye with such enthusiasm that he squealed. "It won't be long now, my lad!" I waved from the long driveway and hurried toward the station.

Breathlessly I threw myself onto the London train just before it pulled out. All the passengers were laughing and talking. Strangers shouted their congratulations, shook hands, and slapped each other on the back. "We'll be going home now," said an army officer with Australia flashes seated across from me. Home! I hadn't even thought that far ahead.

When the train pulled into London, I stepped off to make my connection to the northern line. The platforms were surging with people and I was caught up in a large crowd that swept me off the platform and up the steps. Outside, the streets were crammed with a joyful mob moving in a single direction.

"Where's everyone heading?" I shouted at the man next to me.

"Buckingham Palace!"

I was going to miss my train, but there was no turning back now. "Who cares?" I said aloud. "The war's over!"

I said it again, in an even louder voice. "It's over!" No one was listening. "It's over! It's over! The war is finished!" I wanted to hear the words ringing in my ears again and again.

I should have been frightened at being swept along in this helpless way, but I wasn't. It felt as if I were swimming strongly along with the current. When the crowd reached the square outside the palace, I strained my eyes toward the balcony.

At last the royal family appeared — King George and Queen Elizabeth, flanked by the young Princesses Margaret and Lillibet, trim in her khaki Auxiliary Territorial Service uniform. The crowd roared.

Then a squat figure stepped forward into the centre of the balcony, cigar in mouth. It was Winston Churchill. A solid wall of sound rushed up from the crowd, running down the side streets and echoing back from thousands of people too far away to see what was happening.

Churchill took the cigar out of his mouth. The sound stopped suddenly, and there was a hush as the crowd leaned forward expectantly.

I heard just four words: "This is *your* victory …" before the tidal wave of sound rushed back. All around me, mouths were wide open in a howl of triumph.

The next few hours saw a blizzard of images. People tearing down the blackout curtains and throwing them into the streets, setting fire to them. Thousands of bits of paper fluttering from above as office workers inside tore up every scrap they could find and flung them out the windows. An effigy of Hitler hanging from a lamppost, twisting in the wind. Union Jacks everywhere, draped from windows and waving over the heads of the crowd. Everyone wearing red, white, and blue scraps — pinned to their lapels, tying up their hair, even lacing their shoes.

People blowing on combs covered with paper, beating pots and pans with spoons. "There'll Always Be an England" and "God Save the King" sung over and over again. Scottish soldiers in kilts playing the bagpipes. Bonfires flaring, firecrackers spluttering in the darkness, sending up coloured showers. Couples kissing, soldiers climbing lampposts, sailors dancing the hornpipe. A group of Canadian airwomen in their blue uniforms sitting astride the black stone lions in Trafalgar Square, screaming and laughing and taking photos of each other.

A few lucky civilians carrying dusty bottles of champagne, hoarded against this day, uncorking them and spraying the crowds. Handshakes and hugs from dozens of people, including an old lady in a flowered hat who looked too fragile to be out in such a crush, telling me: "If it hadn't been for the likes of you and the other Canadians, we'd likely never have won the bloody thing!"

Finally I drifted away from the maelstrom. In the light from the distant bonfires, the spire of a church loomed. I slipped through the heavy oak doors. Here the mood was more subdued. Several figures were seated in the pews, heads bent in prayer, or quietly weeping. Above the font the stained-glass window showing the ascension of Christ glowed in the dimness.

The wooden bench creaked as I sat, then slipped to my knees onto the blue and gold embroidered cushion. I bowed my head over my clasped hands. If only Jack could have lived to see this day. And Max, and all the others.

Suddenly the silence was broken by the thunderous sound of church bells. They were pealing for the first time in six years, shouting the song of victory. I went outside to listen. The sound of the bells came from all directions, as every church struck up its own melody. I recognized them from my childhood nursery rhyme. "Oranges and lemons, said the bells of St. Clemens. Shall we be rich, called the bells of Shoreditch. When will you pay me, boomed the bells of Old Bailey." They pealed forth in a song of triumph, filling the night with their sonorous music.

As I stood on the pavement, the darkness was shattered by a torrent of light like the sun rising. The powerful searchlights that had for many years sought the invading bombers now illuminated the city's most famous buildings — the Houses of Parliament, Nelson's Column, Buckingham Palace, the face of Big Ben, the dome of St. Paul's Cathedral. Hundreds of lighted rectangles began to leap out of the darkness as people in flats and office buildings tore down their blackouts and threw on their electric light switches.

I had never seen London at night. I had never seen any city at night. I slowly revolved in place while my eyes adjusted to the sight of windows, doorways, rooftops, chimneys, and streets bathed in golden radiance.

Someone began to sing, and dozens of voices joined in. "When the lights go on again, all over the world …" I had no voice for singing. I stood rapt in the darkness, my heart overflowing with mingled sorrow and joy.

❖

I dressed my nephew in his new blue woollen sweater and tied the bonnet I had knit for him under his chin. "Wave bye-bye to nursie!" Jack obediently opened and shut his tiny hand as I bore him down the driveway.

It was a long train journey for a toddler, but Jack proved to be an excellent traveller, pointing out with gusto every sheep and cow that the train passed. When we reached our station we transferred into a red double-decker bus that dropped us at our destination. I hitched Jack onto my hip and pushed open the iron gates with one hand.

I was glad, for Mother's sake, that the graveyard was such a peaceful spot. The fourteenth-century stone church was situated on the crest of a hill, and the surrounding jade lawns swept to the edge of the cliff. Beyond them the blue sea glittered with whitecaps. The flat blue expanse of the ocean was not unlike the sweep of the prairies.

From where I was standing the beach defences — rolls of barbed wire and concrete blocks — weren't visible. Far out to sea a scarlet fishing boat bobbed on the waves, its owner no longer afraid of German submarines.

The graveyard was jammed with headstones, some upright, others tilted. Their tops and sides were covered with green lichen and moss, the carved inscriptions almost unreadable. Beside them the simple white stone that marked Jack's grave was pristine.

The branches of an elm tree dappled the snowy headstone with shadows. I knelt beside it and traced the words with my fingers: JOHN THOMAS JOLLIFFE, MARCH 10, 1924 TO JUNE 6, 1944.

He had so little time to be a man. Childhood, adolescence, then just a glimpse into manhood before death, the ripening grain still green when it bowed to the blade. Jack would always be a boy, one of the countless legions of boys who had left us as quickly as bubbles bursting in the bright summer air.

They shall not grow old, as we who are left grow old.

Carved into the surface of the white stone was the RCAF crest and motto: *Per Ardua Ad Astra.* Through Adversity to the Stars. A bouquet of pansies was lying on the grave, tied with a piece of ribbon. I was thankful for the care someone had shown, thankful that he had a grave. Many men were listed as missing in action. For their families it would be a long and weary wait before they finally relinquished their last hope.

I set the baby down on the grass, and he discovered the graveyard with its slanting tombstones was an ideal place to play peek-a-boo. While I sat beside Jack's grave, he toddled among them, his bright little face appearing over the top of one stone, then around the side of another.

There had been no funeral for Jack. The airmen no longer had ceremonial funerals — there were so many that it was too demoralizing for the other men. But I wanted to honour him in my own way. I opened my bag and took out the blue and white coffee tin I had carried through the years. I twisted off the lid and sprinkled the rich, black earth from Touchwood over Jack's grave. His son appeared beside me, picked up a handful, and crammed it into his mouth.

"Jack, no!" I smiled through my tears. I took out my box camera and photographed the baby sitting on his father's grave, a memento for my parents, and for baby Jack himself.

Then I unfolded a piece of paper I had found among Jack's possessions. It was a poem called "High Flight," written by Pilot Officer John Gillespie Magee, an American teenager who had joined the RCAF and been killed in December 1941.

I took a shuddering breath, and read aloud:

Oh! I have slipped the surly bonds of Earth
And danced the skies on laughter-silvered wings;
Sunward I've climbed, and joined the tumbling
mirth
Of sun-split clouds, — and done a hundred things
You have not dreamed of — wheeled and scored
and swung
High in the sunlit silence. Hov'ring there,
I've chased the shouting wind along, and flung
My eager craft through footless halls of air....

Up, up the long, delirious, burning blue
I've topped the wind-swept heights with easy grace.
Where never lark, or even eagle flew —
And, while with silent, lifting mind I've trod
The huge unsurpassed sanctity of space,
— Put out my hand and touched the face of God.

40

Summer sunshine flooded the office where I was filling out forms. War's end had brought a tidal wave of paperwork. Millions of aerial photographs were classified, to be placed in storage for the next fifty years. The work was irrelevant, and every few minutes I fell into a daydream of home.

I hadn't heard from Charlie since the war had ended ten days earlier, but I wasn't worried. The telephone was in constant use and the mailboxes stuffed with letters. For now it was enough to know that he was safe. I still woke each morning with a drenching wave of relief.

Through the open door I heard voices exchanging greetings outside on the tarmac, an erk whistling as he strolled past the window, a couple of sparrows chirping from their nest under the eaves. A footstep sounded outside, and the room darkened as a pair of shoulders filled the doorway.

"Anybody here from Touchwood?" asked a familiar voice.

My pencil went skittering across the floor as I leaped to my feet. It was Charlie, leather jacket hanging open and chestnut hair tousled, grinning the old grin.

"Charlie!" I practically yelled. I ran toward him, then stopped abruptly, blushing and embarrassed. I had almost flung myself against his chest. "What are you doing here?"

"Come to take you for a ride, if you want. I've already squared it with your wingco."

"Where to?" I asked, thinking of the local village.

"France." Charlie's eyes were smiling. "I've been ordered to fly over there this morning to bring back some English prisoners of war. I asked your commander if you could come along. I don't suppose you've ever been up, have you?"

"No," I gasped. I had never flown, never thought I'd have the chance, although I knew several of the ground crew had been taken for joyrides since the war ended.

Without another word I snatched my cap off the desk and followed Charlie into the bright sunlight. Our feet stuck slightly to the hot asphalt as we walked down the runway toward Charlie's aircraft. The original *Prairie Rose* was long gone, but this Lancaster called *Prairie Rose Two* had seen Charlie and his crew safely through the remainder of the war.

I climbed the short ladder that led into the open hatch. Inside the aircraft I crawled on my hands and knees under the mid-upper gun turret. Conscious of Charlie behind me, I was glad I was wearing my khaki trousers rather than my skirt.

We emerged behind the cockpit. There was no co-pilot's seat in the Lancaster. Instead a passage led down into the nose of the aircraft to accommodate the front gunner. Charlie folded down the flight engineer's seat, on the wall just behind the pilot and to his right. I sat down and he buckled my shoulder harness.

"Are you ready?"

I nodded speechlessly.

Charlie climbed into the pilot's seat and checked his instruments before starting the engines. They came to life with a deafening roar, sounding much louder in here than they did from the outside. There was a strong smell of oil and gasoline.

The propeller blades began to turn slowly and then faster, blurring into invisibility. Charlie opened the four throttles until the Lancaster was straining against its brakes. The sense of thundering power made me feel very small.

The engines were revving at full bore now and the aircraft began to shudder slightly. I looked down. We were high off the ground, yet we hadn't even taken off. The crewman pulled the chocks away from the wheels, and the airplane surged forward.

I clung to my seat with both hands as we bounced along, picking up speed. It was much rougher than I had imagined when I watched the bombers soaring smoothly into the night sky. But suddenly, we were lifting, and I felt my heart fly upwards while my stomach seemed to lag behind, and then catch up.

The Lancaster rose, and the fields and trees fell away beneath me. It was so much like the feeling I had when I was pretending to be a bird, and yet so infinitely much better that I laughed aloud with joy, and saw that Charlie was looking back at me and laughing, too.

The soaring sensation, the sun shining through the windscreen, the sight of a tiny child riding a tiny bicycle down a tiny country lane far below — these things filled me with a kind of glee, so that I went on laughing with delight. I wanted to see everything — the village on the horizon as it drew closer, the farmhouse changing shape as we passed overhead, the pond flashing silver in the reflected light.

For a while my busy eyes darted everywhere and then I laughed again, because we were already over the Channel, and I saw millions of white wavelets below and miniature fishing boats bobbing up and down. A few wind currents caught us over the water and the plane swayed back and forth. Charlie glanced back to see how I was taking it, and I nodded reassuringly and lifted both thumbs in the air.

It was a lovely feeling, as if my body had left its burden of care behind on the ground and was gliding weightlessly along on the wings of a zephyr. I saw the clouds drift lazily past the window and wondered why they seemed to move so slowly when we were travelling so fast.

Charlie pointed ahead, and I was surprised to see the French coastline already coming into view. I had forgotten that the strip of water between the two countries was so slender, how close the enemy had been to England's shores. As we drew near, I saw steep, rocky cliffs defended by barbed wire and concrete barricades. The shore was filled with shell holes and littered with burned-out tanks and Jeeps, but there was a fleet of Allied ships anchored along the coast, and convoys of trucks moving inland.

As we passed over France, I began to recognize landmarks I had seen so many times in photographs. Although I knew Charlie couldn't hear me, I shouted, my voice lost in the din of the engines.

"That's the Seine!" I screamed, and then, "Paris!" Charlie pushed the throttle forward and the Lancaster began to lose altitude. I cried out again as the big bomber circled the Eiffel Tower once, dipped its wings, and turned toward the southeast.

The fields and farms went tearing past too quickly, and I caught Charlie's eye and pointed down. He nodded and nudged the throttle forward again. The Lancaster dropped to a lower altitude and he throttled back so that the farmland began to move under us more slowly.

I gazed in fascination at the farms and villages with their red tiles and brown thatched roofs, the hay and grain crops so clearly visible from this vantage point, the horses in the field shaped like elongated pears. The surrounding landscape was pitted with bomb craters, and every village was marred by crumbled and broken buildings, piles of rubble and dirt.

I wasn't shocked by the extent of the damage. I had seen it all before, hundreds of times. But what surprised me were the signs of renewal. Nature was working overtime to restore the beauty of the countryside. A wash of green covered the fields, and even the most recent tank tracks were fading. I remembered the way the prairie looked in spring, after we burned the dead grass. The green came rushing in like water, covering the blackened earth as if ashamed of its nakedness.

We flew over a country village, where piles of stone were stacked neatly in one corner of the village square. Already new foundations had been laid. Several tiny figures were working on a rooftop, and one waved his hat to the aircraft as it flew overhead. Although I knew we couldn't be seen, I waved back.

Charlie pointed down, and I spotted a grass airstrip ahead. I watched his big hands as he deftly adjusted the instruments, then the aircraft was circling the field and dropping gently. I was alarmed when I saw the bomb-pitted runway, but Charlie landed so carefully I wasn't even sure when the wheels touched the grass. There was a series of gentle bumps and the aircraft drew to a halt. The propellers became a visible smear as they slowed, then broke apart and separated into individual blades again.

Charlie looked over at me. "Like it?" he shouted, and I laughed again and nodded enthusiastically. He unbuckled his shoulder harness and climbed past me, reappearing a moment later on the ground, talking to an officer who had come out of the shed on the runway's edge. They exchanged bundles of paper. The officer turned toward the shed and beckoned.

A group of twenty men straggled toward the waiting aircraft, looking more like refugees than soldiers. Some wore army tunics, others wore ragged civilian clothes. One man clutched a Red Cross blanket around his shoulders. All were thin and haggard. They went around to the side of the aircraft and prepared to clamber into the belly of the plane. After an interval, while they settled themselves, Charlie crawled past me once again, buckled himself into his seat and motioned to the ground crew that he was ready for take-off.

I was better prepared this time for the long, fast ride toward the end of the runway and the sailing sensation in my stomach, but it still made me laugh. I was looking down at the opposite side now, seeing different farms and fields and villages. In a short while the sparkling sea loomed up again and we flew on toward England. A thin white line appeared on the horizon and I recognized the famous white cliffs of Dover.

Charlie turned his head and looked straight into my eyes. This time he wasn't smiling. Without saying a word, I knew what he wanted to share with me: what it felt like to leave enemy territory behind and reach the safety of England's shores.

He beckoned to me to come forward. I unbuckled my harness and bent over his right shoulder. His warm lips touched my ear as he shouted: "Tell them to come up, three at a time!"

I scrambled clumsily into the belly of the plane, clinging to various bits of metal. The men were crouched uncomfortably in the darkness on their duffle bags. I bent my head and screamed into the closest ear, then crawled back to my seat.

When I finished buckling up and lifted my eyes again, I saw the white cliffs of Dover directly below. They were snow white, sparkling white, as if they had been scrubbed clean to welcome home their returning sons, and the water washing up against their base was dark, navy blue.

Three heads appeared behind me and I saw the nearest face. His eyes lit up at the moment of recognition and his lined face crumpled with sobs. Embarrassed, I averted my eyes and watched the coastline below as the three men clung to each other and wept, gripping each other's shoulders while the tears rolled down their unshaven cheeks.

Another three took their place, with the same reaction. One man's knees buckled and he had to be helped back inside by his two friends. Another crossed himself and kissed the crucifix that hung around his scrawny neck. Charlie slowed the aircraft and took a long sweep north along the coastline and then south again, allowing each man his own personal homecoming.

I found myself sobbing in sympathy. Home. The word had such a magical quality that I felt its impact even second-hand. It was as if my homesickness, smothered and damped for all these years, had burst into a blaze. How I wished that we could keep flying, across the vast ocean and the forests and the rocks and the prairies, and come down in Touchwood.

By the time I found a handkerchief and wiped my eyes, the aircraft was preparing to land. I saw the familiar green rooftops of the camouflaged airbase, the long runway ahead, and then we were down. Charlie taxied to a stop and switched off the engines. It was suddenly very quiet. I felt the impact of the hatch door as it swung open, and the movements of the men climbing out. As they streamed raggedly across the tarmac, one man fell to his knees and kissed it.

"Come on." Charlie helped me out of my seat and led the way to the hatch. He lowered himself first, then held out his arms so I could jump into them. Without saying a word, he gripped my hand and pulled me into the shadow of the huge wing.

Charlie took me in his big arms and kissed me. The kiss went on for a very long time. I wanted it never to end. A mechanic came around the tail, gave a snort of laughter, and retreated. Charlie ignored him. He was busy making love to my mouth with his own mouth, and I wasn't aware of anything except the smell of his leather jacket and the hot rubber tire pressing into my shoulder blades, and the powerful waves of pleasure running up and down my arms and legs.

Finally he lifted his head and his smiling eyes smiled into mine. "In case you haven't heard, the war's over," he said. "Now will you marry me?"

◂▸

June 25, 1945
To: Tom and Anne Jolliffe, Touchwood
Sailing Empress of India July 2 Stop Arriving
Touchwood July 12 Stop Love Rose

41

It was a happy voyage. No more blackouts or drills, and everyone's hearts sang the same song as the frothing wake unrolled behind us: "Going home! Going home! Going home!"

The excitement built as our ship steamed ahead. On the fourth day, someone started a pool: what hour would Canada's shores loom into view? We threw in English pence and shillings because nobody had Canadian money.

On the sixth day I lined the rail with hundreds of others, straining my eyes.

"There it is!" The cry went up and a cheer broke out. "Hip, hip, hooray!" I snatched Jack up from his deck chair and pointed at the distant shore. "That's Canada!" I whispered in his little ear. "That's home!" He stared unblinkingly at the horizon.

When the ship docked in Halifax, my eager eyes examined the crowd below. Everyone had an air of wealth and health, with glossy hair and shining teeth, so different from the war-weary English. And their clothes were so colourful and new. My eyes fell on a blond woman wearing a scarlet suit and chip hat with a black feather sweeping down over one eye. Was her outfit in fashion? I looked down at my wrinkled uniform. I had no idea whether skirts were long or short or narrow or full.

But I soon forgot about clothes in the excitement of boarding the troop train that carried us through Nova Scotia and New Brunswick, people cheering and waving flags at every station. I held Jack up to the window and he waved back.

In Toronto, we transferred to the train that would carry us home. Wherever it stopped, welcome parties were waiting, bands playing "Sentimental Journey" while servicemen rushed toward their loved ones.

Across the mighty Canadian Shield, past the enormous lakes, through the dense forests, and then, as dawn was breaking in the eastern sky, the train emerged onto the prairies.

I could feel my heart swelling in my chest, pushing apart my ribs. The light, the beautiful scarlet light turning to gold. I watched the sun rise into the sky, windows open to smell the growing grain.

"Where are you headed?" A young soldier sat down across from us and stared at Jack.

"Touchwood. How about you?"

"I'm getting off at the next stop." He didn't take his eyes off the baby. "I have a child myself, a daughter. She was only the size of this one when I left. She's five years old." He wrung his hands in his lap. "She'll be talking by now. I won't know what to say to her."

"You won't need to say anything." As the train pulled into the station, the young man threw his kitbag over his shoulder.

"Good luck! God bless!" I watched as a pretty young woman ran toward him, a little girl clutching her skirt.

The train ticked off the miles. It wasn't until Touchwood was three stops away that I started to feel nervous. Before leaving England, I had written to tell my parents about Jack, fearing the shock might be too great if I showed up with a strange baby in my arms, but there hadn't been time for a reply.

Two stops away I put on Jack's blue sweater. One stop away, I washed his face and combed his blond hair. The train crossed the trestle over the Mistatim River, and I looked down into the water, feeling the river's strong current pulling me home.

Five more minutes. I began to tremble from head to foot. Even my teeth were chattering. The train gave the familiar whistle as it went over the crossing at the edge of town: one long sad note, two short happy ones, then another long sad one. The brakes squealed, and the train slowed.

I saw them on the platform standing close together, arms entwined like tree branches. I clutched Jack so tightly that he let out a squeal, and hurtled down the steps. Mother and Dad rushed toward me and squeezed us both in a four-armed bear hug.

Then they turned as one to look at the baby. Mother's eyes widened and the colour drained from her face. "Dear God in heaven, it's Jack to the life," she said. She held out her arms, and the baby — who had been making strange with everyone else on the trip — went to her without a peep.

Still clinging to each other, we made our way to the old blue Ford truck. We drove down Main Street, and while Mother cooed at the baby, I swivelled my head to see everything — the red-brick post office, the Queen's Hotel, the *Times*, its front window now washed and sparkling, the high school and then the gravel road leading toward home.

When we crested the east hill, I saw the farm laid out below me, the most welcome sight in the world. "How the trees have grown!" I exclaimed as the truck turned into the long driveway.

As I jumped down from the cab, a black-and-white blur came around the corner of the barn and streaked toward us. "Laddy!" The old dog, his muzzle now mostly grey, leaped up on me, grovelled on his stomach, jumped three feet into the air, spun around, and jumped on me again. He was making queer whining sounds in his throat.

"Down, boy!" I was half-crying, half-laughing, but Laddy paid no attention. He put his muddy paws on my shoulders just as Mother emerged from the truck, holding the baby in her arms.

Before I could stop him, the dog opened his mouth and made an enormous swipe with his lolling tongue from the baby's jaw to his forehead, covering his whole face with saliva.

"Laddy!" I cried again. Jack sputtered and ground one fist into his eye. Then he opened his mouth and laughed — the biggest, heartiest laugh that ever came from a baby's throat.

⋆⋆⋆

I awoke the next morning in my own bed, Pansy at my feet. The sun cast a wash of dappled light through the poplar leaves outside the window, still whispering their secrets. I stretched luxuriously and lay still, my eyes travelling around the room to feast on all that was familiar.

The bevelled glass mirror hanging over the chest of drawers reflected the slanted ceilings and yellow flowered wallpaper as if the small room were filled with smoke. On the dressing table sat my few treasures: the clamshell dug from the sandy shore of the Mistatim River, a flint arrowhead found in the pasture, a snapshot of myself seated on Buckshot.

I sprang out of bed and went to my closet. My clothes were still hanging in the same places. I found my favourite old blue cotton sundress and pulled it over my head.

Through the open door to my brother's room across the hall, I saw the baby, sitting in the battered crib that had been brought down from the attic. He was murmuring to himself and inspecting his toes in a shaft of sunlight.

We had stayed up late the night before, with so much to talk about. I showed my parents Jack's last letter to me and told them over and over again the story of saving Jack's child. As I had predicted, Dad found it perfectly understandable that we would be in the same place at the same time, while Mother considered it nothing short of a heavenly miracle.

I also asked them, a little diffidently, if they felt young enough to tackle the prospect of raising another child.

Both of them spoke at once. "Of course we are!" Dad said, while Mother added: "I'm only forty-five, Rose! I'm not exactly in my dotage! That child will be nothing but a blessing for the rest of our lives!"

They certainly seemed prepared. In the short time since they had learned about the baby, Dad had unearthed Jack's favourite toy wagon and given it a new coat of red paint, and Mother had knit him two sweaters.

Secretly I reflected that if they needed any help, I would be living right across the road. And with any luck, my own children wouldn't be much younger than their cousin.

I was smiling as I ran down the broad staircase and into the kitchen. After years of being on the verge of tears, now I couldn't wipe the grin off my face.

Mother turned away from the counter and we flew into each other's arms without a word. After a long embrace, she wiped her eyes on her apron. "Sit down and let me cook breakfast for you. What would you like?"

"Fried eggs from our own chickens, three of them!"

"When is Charlie getting home?" Mother asked while she cracked the brown speckled eggs into the cast-iron frying pan.

"He's booked to arrive on August 2. He wants to get married the following Saturday." I blushed. "He says we've wasted enough time already."

"That's certainly true," Mother said dryly. "We had almost despaired of you two getting together. Well, it was meant to be. Do you want a big wedding?"

"I didn't think so, but now that I'm home I've changed my mind. I want to get married in St. John's and invite everyone in Touchwood! Maybe we can have a barn dance. What do you think?"

As I dipped my toast fingers into the beautiful golden yolks, Mother and I planned the wedding. I would wear her pink silk wedding dress, the colour of wild roses. Naturally June would be my matron of honour, since she and Shorty had arrived home three weeks earlier.

What I didn't tell Mother was that Charlie and I had already had our honeymoon, four glorious days in Sunny <u>Banks before I</u> caught the ship in Liverpool. There was no question of waiting until we arrived home. We had waited long enough.

The nights in our big featherbed, the days lying on a blanket beside the pond, had been so passionate that they had made up for all the years of sorrow. To my joy, Charlie's every touch was like a match to a bonfire. In fact, I could feel my face burning now, as I remembered the things we had done together.

Quickly I changed the subject and we discussed the endless fascinations of baby Jack. I described what little I knew about him — his early walking, his reluctance to laugh, and, what seemed to me, his remarkably precocious ways. "Mother, you should see him clap his hands in time to music! I'm sure he's a born musician!"

As if on cue we heard a squawk from the crib, and Mother practically dropped the teapot in her eagerness to fetch him. I carried my plate over to the sink. "I must run over and see Mr. Stewart," I called up the stairs. "He'll be anxious to hear about Charlie."

I walked down the road to the Stewart place with a song in my heart louder and sweeter than that of the meadowlark on the fence post. The air was so clear that I could see the post-office tower from the top of the east hill as if it were across the road. Grasshoppers whirred out at me from the ditches and bees buzzed in the bright yellow clover.

As I approached the front door, I saw that it hadn't been used for some time. The lilacs and honeysuckle had grown across the veranda and smothered the front steps. I went around the corner of the house to the back door. As I raised my hand to knock, I heard a shout and turned to see George Stewart coming across the yard, grinning just like Charlie.

"Rose! Home at last, safe and sound." Shyly he shook my hand. "After Charlie left, I moved back into the old house. Come on over. I just put on a fresh pot of coffee."

I followed George past the wooden granaries that lined the yard and through a patch of poplars to the old house, a two-room shack where George and his wife lived before building the new house in 1925.

We entered a small room with a wooden table, covered with tools and oily bits of machinery, surrounding a space for George's plate and cup. A big, soft armchair was pulled up beside the cook stove, with a greasy patch where George rested his head. Beside the chair was a stack of newspapers and magazines. A photograph of Charlie in uniform stood on the kitchen shelf. Through an open door, I could see George's bed, neatly made with a striped woollen Hudson's Bay blanket.

"This suits me fine," he said, as if reading my thoughts. "I didn't like to rattle around in the new house by myself after Charlie left. It was his mother's house, anyway. Now it will be yours. You and the boy need your privacy, and so do I."

I thanked him, and accepted a cup of strong, dark coffee from a battered tin coffeepot. I took a sip and rolled it around in my mouth, savouring the taste.

"Have you and Charlie talked about buying more land?"

"We haven't had time to plan anything, but we might be interested. We have our veteran's benefits, both of us." Like any farmer, I knew it was important to own as much land as you could reasonably farm.

"The Department of National Defence is selling that quarter-section next to us, the one used as a satellite airfield. It's going cheap. The buildings are included. They're selling off the planes, too."

I paused in the act of raising my mug to my lips. The seed of an idea planted in the back of my mind sprang into full bloom.

I thought of all the farmers in Western Canada who would love to own aerial photographs of their farms, neat and pretty from the air. I thought of Charlie, yearning to fly. I thought of the large, well-built hangar with the concrete floor. I thought of the windowless radio shack, easily converted into a darkroom.

I could hardly wait to ponder my idea in private. There wasn't any point in writing to Charlie now; he would be home soon. But in the meantime it wouldn't hurt to make some enquiries with the government.

"Drop in and take a look at the new house," George said, as I made my farewells. "You'll probably want to fix it up."

I entered the new house through the unlocked back door. The kitchen was large and sunny, with blue-and-white patterned linoleum on the floor, the nicest farm kitchen I had ever seen. On the wall hung a calendar from the Massey-Harris dealership in town, dated November 1939 — the month Charlie had left home.

I strolled across the hardwood floor in the dining room and through the arched doorway into the living room. The stained-glass window shed bits of coloured light onto the walls. I climbed the stairs and went into the front bedroom that had been designed especially for Mrs. Stewart. It had a large bank of windows facing south, so that she could see the entire farm and the blue hills of the river on the horizon.

I sat down on the wrought-iron bed, neatly covered with a double wedding ring quilt. I traced the overlapping circles with my fingertip, smiling as I imagined myself here with Charlie. I rose and went into the hall, peeping through the other doorways. There were four bedrooms. The Stewarts had planned to have a large family. "Just you wait," I whispered to the empty house.

I left through the back door, pulling it shut behind me. I walked down the east hill, hitched up my skirt, and climbed expertly through the barbed wire fence into our own pasture.

At the edge of the wheat field, I stopped. From here I could see the horizon in every direction. I stood exactly half-way between my old home and my new home. My body was lighter, the atmosphere so thin and transparent that I felt as if my feet would leave the ground.

I flung myself down on the scratchy prairie wool and lay on my back, eyes drowning in the blueness of the sky. The smell of grain, still green with moisture yet ripe with the swelling kernels inside the husks, filled my nostrils. I rolled over onto my stomach and flung my arms wide, pressing myself into the earth's surface. I embraced the ground, feeling the earth's heart beating beneath my own.

The wind made a harsh, scratching sound as it swept across the short grass, then changed to a soft, swishing sound as it rolled over the surface of the grain. One of my outflung palms lay on the edge of the field, where the virgin wool gave way to the tilled earth. I dug my fingertips into the ground and felt the coolness of the black earth under the warmth of the surface.

Stretching out my hand, I broke off a morsel of rich, dark topsoil and carried it to my mouth.

Acknowledgements

My heartfelt thanks to all veterans, both men and women, who defended our democracy and guaranteed me the freedom to write this book.

Special thanks to the individuals who told me their stories: RCAF veterans Leo Richer, Ed Kluczny, Duncan McIntosh, and Art Wilks; RCAF Women's Division veterans Nancy Lee Tegart and Lou Marr; WAAF veteran Eileen Scott; and RAF veterans Arthur Bradford and Russ Jeffs.

My thanks to the subject matter experts: Dave Birrell of the Bomber Command Museum in Nanton, Alberta; Doug Sample of the Allied Air Forces Memorial in Yorkshire; Peter Singleton of the Air Historical Branch (RAF) in London, England; Canadian postal historian Kenneth V. Ellison; and Dr. John Willis of the Canadian Museum of Civilization.

While gathering historical details, I read dozens of books. One of them in particular was most helpful: *Evidence in Camera*, by Constance Babington Smith of the Women's Auxiliary Air Force, who discovered the first flying bomb on an aerial photograph while serving at RAF Medmenham.

I appreciate the contribution of my capable editors Sylvia McConnell and Jennifer McKnight of Dundurn Press.

My very best thanks to my father Douglas Florence, who served in the RCAF, for his ongoing encouragement and his uniquely Canadian perspective.

And my deepest gratitude, as always, to my husband Heinz Drews for his unfailing love and support.